FOR THE SUMMER

Camille Harte

For D & K, 1978, the greatest love story I've ever known.

CONTENTS

1983 - THAT FIRST SUMMER

Ronald Reagan serves his third year as
President of the United States.

Star Wars Episode VI: Return of the Jedi is
released in theaters May 25th.

Karen Carpenter dies of complications due
to anorexia nervosa at age 32.

* * *

F ish are so disgusting. Look at the way they flop all over each other, just a pile of fat, scaly bodies inhaling the stale hot dog bun I'm tossing into the water. Their eyes bulge and their mouths gulp in desperation. It is the grossest, most coolest thing I've ever seen.

"Hey you! Girl! I wanna try," I hear this kid say, and I look around, wondering who he's talking to. The sun is glaring in my eyes and I squint as I try to make out the shadowed boy before me. He shifts, his head blocking out the sun, and his face comes into view.

He glows. The golden halo behind his head causes his white blond hair to blaze like fire. He's my age, I think, and sticky syrup collects in the corners of his mouth, like he just finished a popsicle. His green eyes shimmer from the reflection of the water, and he has the longest eyelashes I've ever seen. I wonder if they're as soft as they look.

He's a Paycheck. It's obvious in his pale skin. His thin legs are interrupted by knobby knees sticking out from under his blue swim trunks, and there's a little alligator stitched into his white polo shirt. On his feet are brand new leather deck shoes,

1

ones I could only dream of affording. I look down at my old sandals. I always have to stop walking to shake out sharp rocks.

"I have a name," I say, annoyed with his tone.

"Well, how am I supposed to know your name? I only just met you," he says, placing his hands on his hips.

"We haven't really met. Technically, I'm not even supposed to be talking to you," I say as I stand up. I'm taller than him and I suddenly feel very confident. I smirk down at the pretty pale boy, and throw him the bag of bread. "Here, you can have it. I'm done here anyway. Make sure you throw the bag in the trash can when you're through."

I turn to walk back to the office, but the boy grabs my swimsuit strap and the elastic snaps against my back with a sting. I spin around ready to knock him out, but he just stands there grinning. And then he winks. My mouth drops open, his stupid smile making me furious. What a jerk!

My normal response would be to punch his lights out. That's what I learned from my older brother, if anyone touches you, you punch them. Jay made sure I knew how to throw a decent punch, and this kid is scrawny. I could take him.

Something about his smile makes me freeze up though. I can't think of anything to say and I feel like an idiot.

Just then, a magnificently beautiful lady calls out and we both turn and look at her. Her skin is like silk and her golden hair is perfectly feathered. She wears a very skimpy black bikini and little red running shorts with white trim that stands out against her slender legs. I'm a little embarrassed at how I stare at her perfect body, but then she opens her mouth and her magnificence quickly fades.

"Willy! Get your fucking ass over here! I told you not to go running off, you little shit!"

It's not really her words that are offensive, I hear language worse than that out of my own father's mouth, but her voice is so full of hate. The boy's smile fades and he runs back to her with his head hanging. She looks really young, but I guess she's his mom because she pulls his hair and jerks him around and he stumbles onto a houseboat tied to the dock.

I march straight to my dad's office. Tears burn in my eyes thinking of how I was ready to knock that kid out. No wonder he's so rude, his mother is horrible!

My dad, Red, owns this marina. Red Rock Cove is located about 10 miles south of Hoover Dam on the Arizona side of the Colorado River. It's already packed with the first vacationers of the season. Families are boarding the houseboats they've rented, or they're launching their pontoons and speed boats and jet skis. They putt around the no wake zone and swarm the floating gas station.

I have to force open the door to my dad's office. It sticks sometimes. The office is attached to the twelve room motel that's part of the marina. He inherited the resort from his father who started the marina with just a campground and a gravel launch. Now, the resort includes the motel, with a pool and spa, a cafe and general store, lots of spots for trailers and motorhomes and tents, sixteen modular homes for those families that stay the whole summer, over a hundred boat slips at the dock, and a recreational area with volleyball, horseshoes, a swing set and a dozen fire pits along the small private beach. Plus, all the paddleboats, kayaks, tubes and stuff. My dad's really good at business.

"Hey, Kit Cat, look at that scowl! It's too early for you to be wearing a face like that," Dad chuckles as I storm into the small room. It's not much cooler in here than it is outside, but at least there's a large fan blowing near the window. "What's got your feathers ruffled?"

"Nothing," I mutter, the encounter with the green-eyed boy too humiliating to retell. I plop down in one of the vinyl chairs in front of his desk. He scribbles something in his book, before looking up at me with wrinkly eyes. His thick mustache twitches over his thin lips. He knows I'm not being truthful; his mustache always twitches like that when he's trying to figure stuff out.

"Aw, see? Now, I don't believe that for a second. You've got anger written all over that pretty face of yours," Dad says softly. I shake my foot to free a rock stuck between my toes.

"I hate the beginning of the summer. All these people think they're so special with their big boats and their fancy clothes," I say, thinking about the boy's new leather shoes and the way he winked at me.

I pull at the uncomfortable elastic of my swimsuit. The lycra of the one-piece suit will become my uniform this summer, but right now it's digging into my shoulders and riding up my butt. I need a new suit but Dad can't afford it, not for another couple of weeks. My dad tries to ration the money we make during the summer so it lasts all year, but things like new swimsuits are rare. The one I'm wearing I've had for at least two seasons. I remember when Dad had to tie the straps together in the back and I had to wear shorts over it because it sagged in the rear. Now it's starting to get thin and I'm stuck wearing my shorts over it again.

"Those big boats and fancy clothes put a roof over your head, missy. And an ice cream in your hand." Dad holds out a couple of shiny coins, and I know he's right. We're luckier than most folks.

"I know, Dad," I say, slightly ashamed I even bothered him. He gets up and places the coins in my hand before kissing me on the head. That's my cue to leave, and I pocket the money before walking back out into the smothering heat. This is going to be a scorching summer, I can tell.

I skip to the general store, the coins jingling in my pocket, and I see a familiar face standing by the door. His black hair curls around his shoulders and his dark brown eyes look like pebbles. I've known him for as long as I can remember. Steven Young has lots of brothers that look just like him. There's six of them altogether and every year the teacher always says how there's another Young in the class. His dad runs the only boat storage place in town.

"Catty the Fatty," Steven yells as two of his older brothers march out of the store. Dad says Steven makes fun of me because he thinks I'm pretty. I think he's just trying to make himself feel better because he has such a big nose. There were some mean kids here last year who kept calling Steven 'snout'. He didn't like it very much.

I walk past him but stop when I open the door to the store. "No one calls me Catty anymore, Steven. It's just Cat now. You might want to try Fat Cat? Or Cat the Brat?" I say with my fakest smile. Making fun of myself always sucks the sting right out of his insults.

"Close the door, Cat. You're letting all the hot air in," Josie barks at me from inside.

"Later, Stupid Steve," I smirk and Steven scowls at me from behind the glass door. I'm surprised he didn't flip me off. He thinks he's so cool, and always acts especially rude in front of his brothers. They'd tease him terribly if they knew he cried when we saw that rattler on the hiking trail last week.

"Hey Josie," I say and pull the coins from my pocket. My dad hired her to run the shop this summer. She's sixteen and has short wavy black hair and eyes the exact color of the dark clouds during the storm season. She's going steady with Steven's oldest brother, Ricky. He works with his dad at the boat storage place. He'll take over when their father retires, just like Jay will eventually take over the marina.

"One IT'S-IT please," I say and place the coins on the counter.

"Don't know why Red bothers giving you money, he owns the store," Josie remarks and pulls the chocolate covered ice cream sandwich from the freezer behind her.

"I like to buy them myself," I say indignantly.

I've been asking him to give me a job all year but he keeps saying I'm just a kid and should be out doing kid stuff, but I feel like a useless slug. My brother easily charms the customers with his dimpled grin. He fills up their tanks with gas, mentioning all the amenities our marina has to offer, and thanks them for their patronage like Dad taught him. Jay is a natural salesman and the customers always fall for his pitch. I think it's because he's tall for his age. He's only fourteen, but everyone thinks he's a grown up. He has the same dark brown hair and hazel eyes that I do, and the same tanned skin, but everyone calls him a "looker". I don't see it. His ears are way too big. He's way smarter than your normal fourteen year old, though. I think he could be president someday. I mean, if a movie star can do the job, surely my smart-alecky brother can.

Sometimes, Jay will take me out on the boat to ski or he'll pull me on the inner tube. That only happens towards the end of the summer, in late August when the Paychecks fire up their motorhomes and hitch up their trailers and drive away from Red Rock Cove, sunburned and waterlogged, and back to the comfort of their real lives.

For them, this is just a vacation. For us, this is real life.

❋ ❋ ❋

I sit between my father and my brother in my dad's old pickup truck as the radio blares. The cramped cab fills with the songs of The Carpenters, The Eagles, and Fleetwood Mac, and Dad sings along with the lyrics. The windows are rolled down all the way and the wind is blowing my hair all over the place.

"Jesus, Cat, tie that shit back or something," Jay cusses, and Dad reaches around me to smack him in the back of the head.

"Jay, I'm warning you. You'd better watch your mouth in front of your mother. If I hear one complaint about you swearing, you can say goodbye to the rest of the summer. I'll put you on dump detail," Dad warns, a cigarette balanced between his calloused fingers.

"Yes, sir," my brother says, but then mutters, "Asshole" under his breath. I glance at my dad out of the corner of my eye. If he heard Jay cuss, he's not letting it show.

We drive over Hoover Dam and across the state line into Nevada. I lean over my brother, trying to get a good look.

"It's still there," Jay rolls his eyes.

"I know." I like the big curved wall of the dam and the concrete cylinders sticking out of the water. I sit back in my seat and try to find something to look at for the next forty-five minutes. I wish I hadn't left my Nancy Drew mystery in my backpack in the bed of the truck.

I also wish my mom lived closer, but when my parents got divorced she said she wanted to live her dreams. I don't know what that means, but Vegas does seem pretty dreamy. She works at The Tropicana. It has a big pool, and sometimes she lets us swim there. I pretend I'm a rich lounge singer relaxing before my big show.

"Wanna play slug-bug? Outta-state license plate? I spy?" Jay asks. I guess he's bored too.

"Outta-state license plate," I choose, noticing the car in front of us. "OUTTA-STATE LICENSE PLATE, ARIZONA!" I shout at him and grin.

"All right, you got one," Jay laughs. We continue to play until we reach the 15 freeway and take the familiar exit to the Tropicana. My dad always drops us off at the hotel. He says he doesn't want to drive any further than he has to, but I think he just doesn't want to see where Mom lives. She has a pretty little house about fifteen minutes from the hotel. She never liked living at the marina. I was eight when she left. They decided we would be better off living with my dad since my mom has to work at night all the time.

My dad parks in the lot and I can see my mom standing outside waiting to meet us. She flicks her cigarette to the ground and jogs over to us as we get out of the truck, her fake blond helmet of hair bouncing oddly as she runs.

"Hi there, my babies!" my mom screeches and pulls me into her chest, the tiny glittering disks of her vest scratching against my face.

"How's my Catherine the Great?" Mom whispers to me and kisses my temple. "You know you have a queen's name, don't you?"

"Yeah, Mom, you've only told me a million times," I respond

shyly.

"Have I?" she grins and I smile back at her. My mom is silly sometimes.

"Can I drive?" Jay asks, and Mom turns her attention to my brother.

"Have you aged two years in the last month?" she asks him, and I can see his dimples appear.

"Yep. Alien abduction," Jay shrugs and she laughs and musses his hair.

My mom spends the rest of the week spoiling us with goodies. Good food, new clothes, she even takes us to the theater to see the new Star Wars movie.

The night before we leave, my mom braids my hair and lets me sleep in her silk pajamas. I lay in her bed while she paints her toenails. She glances up at me and smiles as she dips the brush back into the bottle, her eyes inspecting my face before she tightens the cap on the polish.

"How's Steven been treating you?" she asks. She knows all about how he teases me.

"He still calls me names. I did what you told me to. I was nice and tried to show him his comments didn't mean anything to me, but he just doesn't give up," I say, collapsing into her pillow.

"Oh, honey. I know this doesn't make any sense now, but you'll understand in a few years. Who knows? You might even want to be his friend." I stare at her. Surely, she's joking. Why would I want to be his friend?

She chuckles at my facial expression and smoothes her hand over my head and cheek before kissing my forehead. "I know, life is weird. You just remember that you only get one crack at this thing, so do it right, baby."

I quickly fall asleep next to her, my legs slippery in the silky pajamas, and her pillow smelling like the Laundromat back at the marina.

✻ ✻ ✻

Before I know it, we're back in Red Rock Cove and I'm kissing my mother goodbye. She drops us off in town because she refuses to drive on the uneven pavement back to the marina in her new car. She hugs me for what seems like an eternity before she stands by her car and wipes the tears from her eyes. I hop into my dad's old beat-up truck, my brother sliding in beside me. It seems a little dirtier, a little older, and smells musty after riding around the city in Mom's new convertible.

It's business as usual when we get home. I wash the dishes my dad left in the sink, then me and Jay sort the laundry. We fill a couple of canvas bags with dirty clothes and toss them into the back of the utility cart. Jay drives us to the Laundromat down by the motel and we take turns sitting with the laundry while the sun sinks behind the hills that surround our little cove.

When it's Jay's turn to watch, I walk down to the general store and sneak a pack of Pixy Stix from the candy aisle. Josie doesn't say anything, just rolls her eyes, and I take them down to the little private beach. I stick my sandaled toes in the warm water and rip the paper from the stick, pouring the sour powder onto my tongue and swishing it around my mouth. The gentle waves lap against the sand and it's still hot outside even though it's well past nine o'clock at night.

I look up. The sky is dark and spotted with millions of little stars that I can't see in Vegas. The moon is high in the sky and I stumble, a little dizzy from craning my neck.

The metal chain of the swing set squeaks behind me and I spin around nervously. I immediately recognize his white hair. His head is slumped forward, gazing at his shoes digging into the dirt beneath the set. I can't see his face, but his pale arms and legs glow in the moonlight. He's upset, maybe even crying, and I try to sneak away but my stupid sandals catch in the sand and I fall flat on my face. I immediately look up to see if he noticed. He's staring at me now. He wipes his nose on his sleeve and continues to stare at me so I get up off the ground and dust myself off.

"Are you okay?" the boy asks in a broken voice, and I soften a little.

"I'm fine. I just tripped," I answer and walk over to where he's swaying on the swing. "Do you want a Pixy Stix?" I hold out the crumbled sticks and I'm a little embarrassed by their appearance.

"Okay," he mumbles and takes one from my hand. I sit down on the swing next to him and tear the paper from the candy, the sour sugar forcing a pucker on my face.

"Were you crying?" I ask him, and he looks at his feet again.

"So?" he responds in a sharp voice.

"Is it because of your mom?" I speak without thinking and then realize maybe my question was a little rude.

"She's not my mom. My mom's dead. She had cancer." He twists in the swing, winding up the chain and letting it go. I watch him spin, spin, spinning around.

"My mom lives in Las Vegas. She works at the Tropicana Hotel and Casino. She lets us swim there sometimes and I pretend I'm famous," I ramble, because I don't know what else to say. His mom is dead? I don't really know what cancer is but I think of my own Mom and how I'd feel if she were replaced by a beautiful wicked witch. "That other lady's not very nice."

"Kimmy? She's my stepmom. I hate her. She's a monster," he says quietly.

"We should expose her! Like a Nancy Drew Mystery!" I say excitedly before I can think about how stupid I sound. He's going to think I'm a weirdo.

"She hardly ever eats. I bet she's a witch and drinks the blood of her husbands and their children. We need to warn my dad!" His lips are smiling now and he no longer looks upset, so I smile back at him. We're quiet for a long time before he speaks again.

"We went on a houseboat. Now we're staying in our motorhome," he says. "My dad brought us here for the summer so he can finish his book. He's a doctor and he does lots of tests and experiments and then writes books about it."

"Where are you from?" I ask him. I'm always interested to see where the Paychecks come from. The people that come to vacation here are mostly from California or Nevada, but last year there was a family from New Jersey. I liked listening to them talk.

"The Bay Area," he says but I'm not sure where that is so I shake my head. "San Francisco? It's in California. It took us a whole day to drive here. Where do you live?"

"I live here," I say proudly. Sometimes kids are impressed by this, and I'd be lying if I said I wasn't trying to impress this boy. It's strange how he makes me feel, all fluttery in my belly, and the words that come out of my mouth sound silly.

"You live here? Cool! You get to live here all year long?"

I like this reaction and I nod my head. "Yeah. I can drive our boat too," I add.

"No way! Can we go for a ride in your boat tomorrow?" he asks, but I think before I answer. Jay will have to go with us. I'm not allowed to drive the boat by myself.

"Maybe. I have to ask my dad," I say, disappointed I can't tell him yes right away.

"Yeah, me too," he says, and I'm relieved. "Do you want to do something else tomorrow?"

"We can go for a hike. Sometimes we see snakes and scorpions and wild donkeys. Or we can go swimming at the pool or the beach, or we can take out the paddle boats. There's lots of stuff to do at the marina," I tell him. I remember how my brother uses his smile to charm customers, so I smile and try to be charming too.

"Scorpions! Cool!" He kicks at the dirt underneath his feet. "What's your name?"

"Cat. Short for Catherine," I say quietly. "And you're Willy."

"Just Will. Short for William," he corrects me with a scowl. "I hate the name Willy. Only the vampire witch monster calls me Willy."

"How old are you, Will?" I ask.

"I just turned twelve. My birthday's in June," he says, his chest puffing out a little.

"Me too!" I say. "Well, I'm not twelve yet. My birthday's in September, but we're still the same age."

"Well, not really the same. I'm older because I'm twelve before you," he says smugly and I frown, partly because he's arguing with me but mostly because he's right.

"You know what I mean," I mutter. I kick my feet off the ground and he does the same. We swing higher and higher until the legs of the swing set start to shake.

"Cat! It's your turn to watch the laundry!" I hear Jay yell from the Laundromat. I drag my feet in the sand until I'm going slow enough to jump from the seat. I land on my feet and a sharp pain shoots up my leg, but I pretend I feel nothing.

"That's my brother, I gotta go," I say to Will and he drags his feet too.

"You have to do your own laundry?" he asks, and I sigh.

"Yeah, my dad says it builds character," I explain, but I can see this means nothing to Will. He's a rich kid. They probably pay someone to do their laundry.

"I'll come with you," he says and hops off the swing.

"Okay." I'm a little hesitant as he follows me up the sidewalk. Jay's sitting on one of the folding tables and he jumps down when he sees me walk through the door. The already hot room is sweltering now from the heat of the dryer.

"What took you so long," Jay grumbles before he notices Will's behind me. He frowns and straightens his back to stand a little taller.

"Will, this is my brother, Jay." Will gives a slight nod of his head but Jay doesn't flinch. "Will's from California."

"North or South?" Jay asks like it's a very important factor in his acceptance of him.

"North," Will responds, his eyes confused and hesitant.

"Huh," my brother scoffs. "I gotta piss. I'll be back in a few." He glares at Will as he walks slowly out the door.

"Your brother's scary," Will says once Jay's gone.

"He's actually a big baby. He's ticklish too. If he ever gets you in a headlock, dig into his armpit and he'll let you go. Works every time," I tell him as the dryer buzzes. I open the door to let the clothes cool before pulling the bundle of whites from the machine. I almost choke when a pair of my undies fall to the floor, and suddenly, folding clothes in front of Will is a really, really bad idea.

"I don't have any brothers or sisters. I'm a lonely child," Will mumbles as he fiddles with the knobs on the washing machine. I quickly pick up my underwear from the floor and shove them with the rest of the laundry into one of the canvas bags. Jay's going to be pissed at me for not folding, but I'll just have to do it back at the house.

"You mean, an only child." I toss the clothes from the washer into the dryer. I turn the dial and push the start button and the machine begins to tumble.

"No I don't," Will says quietly, and again my stomach feels all strange and mushy. I know how he feels. Sure, I have Jay, but he spends a lot of his time with the Young brothers. I'm alone a lot.

"There's this kid that lives in town, Steven. He makes fun of me all the time. He calls me names," I say, wanting to tell Will something now, because he shared something with me.

"What does he call you?" he asks, but I don't want to say. I don't want to look foolish in front of him. Then I remember that he was crying on the swings and so I tell him.

"Catty the Fatty," I mutter without looking at him.

"Well, that's dumb. It's not even true," he says as his fingers pick at the chipped countertop. "No offense, but you're just normal."

"Steven's not exactly the sharpest tool in the shed," I say with a grin, and the little dig gives me some satisfaction.

"Next time he's mean to you, you should tell him everyone can see his epidermis," Will grins at me but I have no idea what that means. I guess it's obvious I'm clueless, because he explains.

"Your epidermis is your skin. It's always showing, only Steven will think it means something embarrassing. That's the joke," Will laughs, and I grin because it's the perfect comeback for Steven's insults, much better than the "kill him with kindness" crap my mom always tells me to say.

"You know a lot of big words," I remark and Will shrugs.

"Only because of my dad. He wants me to be a doctor too. Do you know what he's doing right now?" I shake my head, not even bothering to mention how it's impossible for me to know what his dad is doing right now since I'm here with him.

"He sitting in the motorhome, writing his stupid book. He spent the whole time on the houseboat, writing. We didn't go fishing or hiking or do any of the things he said we were going to do." Will kicks at the linoleum floor. His new leather shoes are dusty and scuffed from the dirt and gravel.

"Well, that stupid book puts a roof over your head," I quote my dad, but Will doesn't seem to like my response. He gives me a dirty look and I feel a little bad for acting so snotty when he obviously feels sad about it.

"I just mean that he works hard so you can have nice things and do fun stuff. Things cost money, that's just the way it is." Dad talks about money all the time. He sees every opportunity as a chance for Jay and I to learn something.

"Yeah, I guess," Will mumbles, and uses his shirt to wipe the sweat from his forehead.

Will tells me a little about San Francisco and his friends back home and I tell him about the river and Hoover Dam and we talk until the dryer buzzes. I pull the last of the laundry from the machine just as Jay walks up the sidewalk. His hair is wet so he must have gone for a night swim.

"You didn't fold it," Jay accuses, eyeing Will, and I shrug my shoulders.

"I'll fold it all when we get back to the house, okay?" I beg, and thankfully he shuts up about it and hauls the large bags out to the utility cart.

"Well, I gotta go now," I tell Will when we step out onto the sidewalk.

"Okay. I'll see you tomorrow, right?" Will asks, and I nod my head.

"I get up with the sun so be ready early. You might want to put on a lot of sunblock. You're really pale," I remark without thinking. Again.

"Yeah, well, your eyes are weird," he smirks back. "They're like two different colors, like a reindeer or something."

I narrow my eyes at him and he laughs even harder. I can feel my face getting hot and I'm sure I'm as red as a tomato.

"Take a chill pill, I was only joking. Your eyes are pretty," Will says as he shrugs. I can feel the blood burning in my face and I'm embarrassed that he knows his comment bothered me. So I do the only thing I can think of to do.

I punch him in the gut.

I don't hit him hard, but he isn't expecting it so he stumbles backward and falls on his butt. I didn't mean to hurt him, I just didn't know what to do. But now I'm afraid he's going to rat me out to his parents and that could mean a lot of trouble for my dad. Rule number one, take care of the customer. And that's what Will is, a customer.

"Are you okay?" I ask him hesitantly.

"Yeah," he answers defensively.

"Are you going to tell?" I ask as Will gets himself up off the ground.

"It depends. Are you going to tell anyone I was crying?" he asks, and I shake my head no.

"Pinky promise?" He licks his thumb and holds out his pinky and I do the same. We hook our pinkies and shake.

"Seal it." I stare into his eyes, and we press our spit-covered thumbs together. The bond is made. He will not speak of it and neither will I.

"Cat! I'm gonna tell Dad you skipped out on chores!" my brother yells, and I drop Will's hand and take off running towards the cart.

"I'll see you tomorrow, Cat!" Will shouts after me, and I wave back, grateful to have at least one friend, even if it's just for the summer.

* * *

I hang around with Will all month. Sometimes, Jay comes along and we go hiking, or he drives us around in the utility cart. We try to camp out in a tent one night but Will gets scared when I tell him about the mountain lions and coyotes that live in the hills, and he begs to go back to his motorhome. We go swimming in the river and float on inner tubes that we tie to rocks with long rope. I show him how to use the gel from the Aloe Vera we have in our rock garden when he gets sunburned and every day we eat ice cream from the general store. He always gets a rainbow sherbet Push-Up and I get an IT'S-IT and we sit on the swings and jump in the water when we get too hot. We plot ways to destroy his wicked witch monster stepmom and think of funny names I can call Stupid Steve at school this year, and I laugh so hard I almost pee my pants.

The night before Will leaves, we have ice cream on the swings again. I know he's leaving because his campground is clear. All the towels and shoes are all packed up, and the awning is rolled back and hooked into place. Only the motorhome sits in the spot now. We silently sway on the swings, and the air smells different. It's August, storm season, and the sky is dotted with high clouds that billow and bow.

"I'll get him to come back next year," he says eventually. "I'll make him." He speaks in a confident tone and I feel hopeful for an instant, but then I remember that a year is a really long time. Things change. People do too.

"Maybe we can go to Laughlin for the Fourth of July," I say half heartedly.

"I made you a birthday present," Will says, and I look up at his face now. His cheeks are pink from the sun and the skin on his nose is peeling. "I know it's not until next month, but I wanted to give you something. So you can remember me."

My heart feels big in my chest, like it takes up too much space, and my eyes start to burn, but I can't cry in front of Will. Instead, I look down at the shell in his hand. It's small and white and ridged, and he holds it out to me, flat in his palm.

I recognize this shell. He found it while we were hiking and he wondered why a seashell would be found so high up on the hill. He had said it must be special and shoved it into his pocket with the black glassy rock and the piece of wood that's shaped like an eye. Will likes to collect interesting things.

I carefully take it from his hand and turn it over in my fingers. On the inside, where the surface is smooth, printed in tiny neat writing are the words: *Will & Cat 1983*. I close my hand over the shell so I can't see the black letters anymore because if I look at them again, I will cry.

The next morning, Jay and I watch Dr. Henderson unhook his motorhome from the site. He eats a popsicle beside me while mine melts in my hand, the sticky liquid dripping onto the dirt. My insides feel like they're sloshing around in my belly.

Once they have everything sealed inside, I start to panic, worrying that I'll never see him again. I can see him in the back window of the motorhome as they pull away. He's waving, so I wave back and the tears slip down my cheeks. I quickly wipe them away before Jay can see, but it's too late.

"Get used to it, Sis," Jay says quietly. "Summer friends don't mean shit."

1984 - THAT TIME I LEFT FIRST

The cost of one gallon of gas is $1.10.

*Queen releases their eleventh studio album
"The Works" in February.*

*The Summer Olympics are held in Los Angeles,
California, United States.*

* * *

C at! Wake up! Do you know what day it is?" Jay jumps on the end of my bed and my head bounces around on my pillow.

"Is it murder your brother day?" I mumble as he yanks the sheet off my small bed.

"Yeah, that's exactly why I'm waking you up, because I'd like to meet my death at the hands of my lame-ass sister." I can practically hear the rolling of his eyes. "Dad said you have to get up. You're going to help me pump gas this year."

I check the alarm clock by my bed as Jay disappears down the hall. Four-thirty. Ouch. Dad has always been an early riser. I can already smell coffee brewing.

I wiggle into my swimsuit, the pink and purple stripes stretching awkwardly over my body. I look at myself sideways in the bathroom mirror and frown at the stupid bumps on my chest. Boobs. How am I supposed to do anything with these? I can't even wear my new suit without a t-shirt anymore because I'm afraid people will notice. My mom noticed. She had a big discussion with me about it. She told me my body would change soon and that I'd start my period. I'm terrified. I already learned about this stuff last year in health class, but then Josie told me about tampons. I told my mom I don't want a period if it means I have to use tampons, and she laughed at me. Laughed! I don't care, I will never use those, ever.

So far all I have is boobs. My mom bought me a bra and a pack of maxi pads, just in case, but I hope to God this whole bleeding from the crotch thing holds off for at least another year or two.

I throw on a tank top and tie a knot in the front like I've seen Josie do, only she lets her belly show and I'm not that brave. I pull my hair into a tight French braid and slather on sunblock.

Jay is already gone and he's taken the utility cart, so I walk the quarter mile past the campground to the docks. The marina is buzzing with activity already, and I wonder if Will and his family are here. I look for their motorhome but I can't find it. I've thought about him often, hoping he'd show up this summer, but I've had the same hopes before. A year is a long time. Plans change and people do too, so I try not to have too many expectations. But I still remember Will every time I look at our shell.

I stop in at my dad's office to say good morning, and he gives me a kiss on the cheek. He hands me some money so I can get breakfast, but I'm not really hungry yet. I purchase a muffin and juice from Josie, and nibble on the dry bread which makes the back of my throat itch. I stop on the bridge to watch the fat fish swim. The greedy little things wait for me to toss them my leftovers, so I crumble the rest of my muffin over the water and watch them gulp it up.

"Cat!" I follow the sound to see white blond hair and a pale face. Will runs down the sidewalk by the hotel. I'm still taller than him but he doesn't seem as scrawny. His hair is shorter and combed neatly back and to the side. He's wearing khaki shorts and a polo shirt and he looks out of place. I beam at him and wipe my hands on my shorts. I'm so happy he's here! I want to hug him. That might be weird though, and my new boobs would have to touch him, so I wave instead.

"Hey!" he says as he stops in front of me, slightly out of

breath. "I knew it was you because of your big huge braid."

"Well, I could tell it was you because of your fancy clothes. Going golfing later?" I laugh and he looks confused, like what he's wearing is completely normal for the river.

"No, we're going out on my dad's new boat. My dad bought a boat! And the wicked witch is gone, Cat. They got a divorce. It's just me and my dad this year. We got here last night. I told you I'd get him to come back," he rambles. The wicked witch is gone? I wonder what happened. And his dad bought a boat! This means they might become regulars! We have a few families that vacation here every year. They pay in advance to reserve their spots and they keep their boats in Big Jimmy Young's boat storage.

"Does your dad even know how to drive a boat?" I ask warily. There are a lot of rules about boating, sort of a mutual respect for each other and for the river itself. It can be really dangerous out there on the water and stupid people have gotten killed because they weren't following the rules.

"He drove a houseboat last year," Will says pointedly.

"So? There's a lot more to it than just steering," I respond, and Will frowns.

"Well, he took a class. And he bought me a life jacket," he adds hopefully. I can't tell if he's serious. Will's lips slip into a sly grin and I'm just so happy he's here.

"I have to help my brother at the gas station right now, but let me know when your dad wants to launch the boat. We'll come help," I offer as I start walking towards the station. I can see my brother looking for me and I know that as soon as he sees us, he's going to yell across the dock, and it will probably be something embarrassing.

"Okay! We're staying at the motel this year because we had to tow the boat. But I'll come find you soon." Will walks backwards as he speaks. He's watching me and smiling like he knows I'm happy to see him, and I roll my eyes, fighting the grin that's taunting my lips.

Jay and I work all morning, ushering the customers through

the small gas station. We only have four pumps and ordinarily we don't have anyone working the station, but during these first weekends of summer, we're like traffic cops, directing the long line of boats dying to fill up so they can burn out.

By afternoon the line has dwindled and I ride back home with Jay in the utility cart. We make peanut butter and jelly sandwiches for lunch and sit in front of the large circular fan to eat, letting the breeze cool our bodies. I can already feel my skin tight on my shoulders and my face stings when I wrinkle my nose. After lunch, I rub fresh sunblock onto my face and shoulders. I'm searching my dad's collection for a hat to wear, when I hear a knock on the door. I run down the hall to get to the door before Jay does. It might be Will.

I fling open the door, with Jay right on my heels, to find Steven standing on the porch, his hair hanging in his eyes and sweat beading on the bridge of his nose. I try not to let the disappointment show as I let him inside.

"Hey, Ricky's gonna drive us all into Laughlin for the Fourth. You guys wanna go?" Steven grins and wiggles his eyebrows in a way that makes me want to barf. Oh, ew!

Laughlin is a big river town in Nevada, south of here, with hotels and casinos and shops. They have a lot of special activities for the Fourth of July. Jay and I have always wanted to go, but Dad's always too busy or too tired to drive the two hour trek.

Usually we go to Home Cove. The bank is sandy, surrounded with low trees and shrubs, and it's protected from the wind. We call it Home Cove because it's the cove we visited most often when we were little kids; our second home. We bring an ice chest full of drinks and food, and barbecue right on the beach. We swim and eat and hike until it gets dark. Sometimes Dad takes us on a night ride up the river and he stops the boat in the middle of the deep, deep water so we can jump out and swim. Jay always tries to scare me with stories of alien abductions and hundred-foot-long catfish that eat people, but I don't fall for it. Well, not anymore anyway.

"Depends. Who's all going?" Jay asks. I think he's hoping Josie's cousin, Heather, will tag along. Heather just moved here from Flagstaff. She has long, soft hair that she curls every day, and she wears short shorts and shaves her legs. She's only fifteen but she has a boyfriend back in Flagstaff. Sometimes, Heather helps Josie in the store and I hang out with them when I'm bored, which is often. They talk about French kissing and getting to third base, and while I have no idea what this means, I'm pretty sure it has something to do with boobs.

Jay's been eyeing her all year long but she won't give him the time of day. And I like her times infinity for it. Jay grew four full inches this year and thinks he's so cool, which means he can't hang out with me anymore. It makes me sad. My brother used to take me along on his crazy adventures.

"Everyone. It's going to be totally bitchin'," Steven says. He taps my cheek with his outstretched fingers and I flinch away. I knock his hand away from my face and he smacks my head in retaliation, so I shove him into the wall.

"Look, Steven, you know I can beat you up, so you better stop while you're ahead," I warn him, but he just grins. The smile on Steven's face makes me uneasy, like he does all this on purpose just to get a rise out of me.

"That won't always be the case, Kitty Cat. I'm going to be bigger than you one day. You'd better watch your back," Steven taunts.

I laugh incredulously and raise my eyebrows at his remark. "Is that a threat? What, you're gonna beat up a girl? Real classy, Ace."

"Oh Cat, you're not a girl. Last time I checked, girls were pretty, and had tits," Steven says with a sneer, and my arms instinctively cross in front of my chest. My face flushes red and tears start to collect in my eyes. I bolt from the house and slam the door behind me, the windows shaking in their ill-fitting frames. I hate him so much!

I'm storming off towards the general store, looking for relief in the form of a frozen treat, when I see Will walking towards me, and my heart starts to pound in a completely different way. My anger fizzles into excitement and I wipe the tears from my eyes.

He's wearing his swim trunks and a white cotton t-shirt with green sleeves. A baseball cap hides his eyes, but I can see his lips pulled into a wide smile as he waves.

"Hey!" I shout cheerfully as he approaches, and I notice a large red scrape on his palm as he waves. "What happened to your hand?"

He looks at his palm and shrugs. "I don't know. I've just been sitting around all day waiting for my dad."

I grab his hand and hold his palm very close to my face to inspect the wound. I get scrapes like this every summer.

"It's from the dock," I state. He kicks a rock and the dirt rises in gentle clouds around our feet. He pushes his hat up so he can wipe the sweat from his forehead.

"Maybe," he says, and I glance at him out of the corner of my eye.

"What do you mean maybe? I know it's from the dock. What did you do?" It sounds all wrong. The tone of my voice is wrong, the words are wrong, and I don't sound concerned at all.

"Alright, yeah, I ate shit on the dock," he says, and glances at me to see if I heard his curse. Yeah, I heard it but it's not really a big deal. Everyone curses around here.

"I just wanted to make sure you were okay," I say and nudge him with my shoulder.

"Oh, I know. I just think it's hilarious that you can't even ask if I'm okay without a snotty attitude." He nudges me back.

"I do not have a snotty attitude!" I declare fiercely, my hands flying to my hips. Will is clearly amused, and he smiles at my silly tantrum.

"Alright, maybe I'm a little snotty," I respond, and drop my hands. "I can't help it if I'm snotty. You would be too if you had to put up with goons harassing you all day."

"Goons? Who, Stupid Steve?" Will asks, but I think it's fairly obvious who the goons are.

"He's so annoying. All he does is make fun of me. I hate him so much." Steven's remark about my chest comes flooding back to me and I'm mad all over again. My development is completely normal, my mom said so.

"He's mean to you because he likes you," Will responds, and I frown. I don't want him to like me. I want him to leave me alone.

"You're not mean to me, and you like me," I observe, and Will stares at the ground.

"No, I mean he like *likes* you. Like, he wants to be your boyfriend," he explains quietly, his eyes watching the cloud of dirt collect around his feet, and I stop dead in my tracks.

"What? Why would he want to be my boyfriend? Trust me, Steven does not like me," I chuckle, the thought so absurd I have to laugh.

"Maybe he just doesn't know how to act around you. You're a little scary. I mean, the first time I met you, you punched me. Maybe he's afraid you'll punch him," Will says, his lips curling into a grin.

"I've punched Steven lots of times," I argue. "I'm not scary. Snotty, maybe. But not scary. I'm a nice person."

"Yeah, you are." Will's eyes are barely visible under his baseball cap.

"I am what? Snotty or scary or nice?" I ask him, and he laughs.

"All of the above?" He shrugs and I give him a playful shove.

"Jerk," I mutter under my breath, which only causes Will to laugh more. Unable to fight it, I turn my head and sneak a smile. I can't help it, Will's laughter makes me want to laugh too.

"Where are we going?" Will asks as we continue down the sidewalk to the marina.

"I was following you. I thought we were going to launch your dad's boat," I reply.

"He doesn't want to go out on the water today. He's supposed to be writing a new book for medical students or something," Will explains as we make our way across the main parking lot between the campsites and the motel.

"Do you want to get an ice cream?" I ask him, and he nods, so we head over to the general store.

Josie and Heather are at the counter when we walk into the store. Heather's leaning against the counter, reading a Teen Beat magazine. Josie is refilling the displays on the counter: gum, lighters, batteries, little tubes of sunblock. The wall behind the counter is covered with pictures of people who have caught big fish out of our marina, and a couple of pictures of famous people who stayed here back when my grandfather ran the place.

"Hey Cat, who's your friend?" Heather asks when we approach the counter. She's wearing her bikini top and shorts that are so short I wonder why she even bothers. Her boobs fill out the top nicely, and I'm suddenly thinking of Steven's comment again. The memory stings and makes my face burn red all over again.

I'm not the only one who notices her boobs. Will is trying to avoid staring, but every time he looks somewhere else his eyes drift back to Heather's chest, and I want to punch him for being so obvious.

"This is Will. He's from the Bay Area. It's in California." I introduce him, but I don't want Will to know Heather. Will is my friend, and I want to keep him to myself.

"Nice to meet you, Will from the Bay Area. How old are you, Will?" Heather asks, her eyes twinkling.

"I just turned thirteen," Will says quietly, his pale face burning red, and I can't help but roll my eyes at how easily he's smitten with a pretty girl. Josie roll her eyes, too, and this makes me feel better. At least I'm not imagining this.

"Do you play baseball, Will? I like your cap," Heather flirts. She leans back to rest her elbows on the counter behind her, sticking out her perfect boobs on purpose. Oh, gag me.

"Yeah, I play shortstop. But I'm not really that good. I'm

better at basketball. I've got a mean jump shot," Will smiles an odd smile, a smile I haven't seen before, and I frown. I had no idea he played sports.

"Can we get two Push-Ups please?" I ask Josie so we can get out of here. I don't like the way Will watches Heather, like he can't tear his eyes away from her perfect figure, and I feel very insignificant in my twelve-year-old body. Heather waves when we leave and Will practically trips over his tongue walking out the door.

We walk to the swings in silence. The plastic seats are steaming and I pull my shorts down a little so I won't burn the backs of my legs when I sit down. The lower part of the chain is guarded with a plastic covering, but it's still hot on my hands. We swing and silently eat our Push-ups. Once in a while, a boat drives by or putts through the marina, drowning out the pop music blaring from a large group of teenagers lounging on the private beach. My gut still feels twisted from the way Will acted around Heather, and I don't know why. I can't even thoroughly enjoy my ice cream.

"I hate this song," Will says suddenly, and I try to focus on the music. "I mean, who wears sunglasses at night? And then writes a song about it? So lame."

I smile, the comment loosening the knot taking up space in my belly. "When this song first came out my brother insisted on wearing his fake Wayfarers every minute of every day, even inside our house and especially at night."

"You're kidding? I'm totally going to rip on him for that next time I see him," Will chuckles, and my ice cream tastes a little sweeter.

"I do like that new album by Queen, though," I proclaim, sucking the last of the sherbet from the cardboard carton.

"Of course you do, and that, my friend, is why you are totally awesome," Will replies, and my face burns. The sun is seeping into the skin of my shoulders and I have sweat on the back of my neck.

"Do you want to go swimming?" I suggest and Will shrugs.

He flings off his shirt and cap. It seems as though someone stretched him out. He's still skinny but his shoulders and arms are shadowed and lined, and I can see thin muscles on his chest and stomach.

"What?" Will asks, and I realize he's caught me staring. *Nice one, Cat!* Why was I even staring at him to begin with? I spent all last summer with him. I've seen him without a shirt before.

"Are you wearing sunblock?" I deflect with the only excuse I can think of. "That pale skin of yours is going to fry to a crisp out here. How can you live in California and be so pale?"

"It's cloudy, like, ninety percent of the time in San Francisco, and what kind of fool do you take me for? Don't you worry about my pale skin," he says with a smug grin. I self-consciously remove my shorts, and hesitate in taking off my shirt. I had formerly decided I would wear my tank top over my suit as long as I had boobs, which I guess will be forever, but now I can't stand the thought of wearing this shirt in the water. And besides, it's just Will. *Stop being such a dorkus!* I pull the tank top over my head and toss it onto the swing.

Will looks at me and his eyes are neon in the sun, interrupted only by his lashes blinking quickly over the green. His lips pull into a sideways smile, but whatever he's thinking, he keeps to himself. He takes off running towards the shoreline, shouting while he runs.

"Last one in the water is a rotten egg!"

* * *

My dad doesn't let me go to Laughlin for the Fourth. He says it's too crowded and I'm too young, but Jay gets to go with Steven and his brothers. Josie and Heather go, too, and at first I sulk, but then Dad takes Will and I out on the boat for a night ride and lets us swim in the deep water. Dr. Henderson even takes a break from his writing to ride along and it's kinda funny how much a doctor from California and a fisherman from Arizona have in common. I know that Dad only sees the opportunity to rope in a steady Paycheck, though. This is what he's good at, making the guests feel special, and giving them extra attention so they'll come back.

Will and I tread water by the gently rocking boat. My dad's big spotlight shines out over the water, a signal to other boaters that we're out here. It's still hot as the temperature hovers around ninety, but the water seems warmer than it was during the day. We float on our backs, submerged in the underwater silence, but we can feel the percussion of the fireworks being set off all across the desert. Once in a while, Will's foot bumps against my leg or I feel the graze of his arm slip through my swirling hair, and I know I'm not alone. It's comfortable and I wish I could fall asleep out here, under the stars, floating weightlessly with my favorite friend.

I haven't felt Will's presence in a while and I look around to find him gone. I listen for him on the boat, but all I hear is my dad and Dr. Henderson talking politics. He's nowhere in sight. I'm completely alone in the water. Jay's stories of huge people-eating catfish and alien abductions start to creep into my mind, and my heart jumps into my throat. The boat has drifted a little ways from me now and I start to feel the panic rise. I swim quickly back to it, desperate to get out of the water.

I'm almost there when I feel a sharp sting on the back of my thigh. I scream and my voice echoes off the rocks around us. I kick my legs frantically, trying to make contact with whatever bit me. My foot collides with something hard, and I turn to see Will's blond head floating before he surfaces. His face is covered in blood and he's holding his nose as he treads water.

"Jesus Cat! You kicked me in the face!" Will says. Water drips into his eyes and he pinches his nostrils shut.

"Oh, God, I'm sorry!" I cry. I grab his arm and lead him over to the stepladder that hangs off the back of the boat. Will climbs up the ladder and sits on the back of the seats.

"A fish nipped me and I got scared," I try to explain as I follow him into the boat.

Dr. Henderson pinches and prods at Will's face. He sets him down in one of the front bucket seats and leans him forward while Will pinches his nose with a towel.

"I don't think that was a fish that got you, Catherine," Dr. Henderson smirks. "Maybe a ninety pound pincher with blond hair and a sunburn."

Will grins sheepishly from behind the bloody towel. I narrow my eyes at him and try to look upset, but it's kinda hard to be mad at a guy grinning through a bloody nose.

"I guess we're even then," I say sternly, and Will just laughs, along with my dad and Dr. Henderson.

Will and I sit facing each other along the back bench on the way back. Our legs stretch out side by side as we let the warm spray and wind hit our faces. I almost fall asleep from the rise and fall of the boat. It's midnight by the time we pull the boat into the slip.

We say goodnight to Will and Dr. Henderson at the motel and dad puts his arm around my waist so he can support my sleepy body as we walk back to the house. My brother's not home yet, but when I crawl into bed I can still feel the movement of the water. I fall asleep quickly, pretending I'm still floating in the water, watching the wide expanse of the dark universe.

❋ ❋ ❋

I told you, we weren't in Laughlin all night!" Jay shouts. It's early morning and he's fighting with my dad. From what I can gather, he just got home. I crack open my door and listen to their argument.

"Then where the hell were you?" my dad shouts back, his thudding feet pacing the kitchen floor.

"Around. We were just hanging out. It's really not a big deal, Dad," my brother says defensively.

"Hanging out where? And who was with you? I wasn't born

yesterday. I know what kids your age think hanging out is," my dad retorts. I can visualize him standing there with his hands on his hips, his mustache twitching like it does when he knows we're lying.

"Look, we got back kinda late and the girls wanted to go swimming, so we went swimming. No big deal." I hear a cabinet door slam shut, the sharp sound causing the windows to rattle.

"Which girls? Josie and that cousin of hers?" Dad asks sharply.

"Her name is Heather," my brother snaps.

"I know what her name is. She spends every day loitering around my store, and drinking my diet cokes. You seeing this girl?"

"Of course I see her. Doesn't everybody? She's not invisible, Pops," Jay says sarcastically and I hear my dad's feet thunder across the linoleum floor.

"You listen to me, kid. I don't have too many rules. You pull your own weight around here and I don't hassle you when you want to play. But if you ever do that to me again, it'll be your ass. You hear me?" My dad's voice is the epitome of authority, commanding obedience in every word.

"Yeah," Jay says quietly.

"What was that?" Dad asks just as quietly.

"I said, yes, Sir." Jay draws out the last syllable just a bit longer than he should, a little twist in his tone that allows him to save face, even if it's only for himself. I'm sure my dad catches it, but the battle is over, the resolution swift. You really don't win when you argue with my dad.

"And you're on restriction. You don't leave the marina," Dad adds before opening the front door.

"Like you'd even notice if I did," my brother mutters. I walk into the hall now because I know Jay has gone too far. Dad turns slowly and moves to stand overbearingly close to Jay. They're eye to eye, but my brother slightly slouches in comparison to my dad's straight, strong posture.

"I notice everything in my marina. You don't make a move that I don't know about. You remember that. And you'd better be out there on that dock today. This is one of the busiest weekends of the year and you have a job to do." Dad shoves a finger in Jay's chest, a sharp point right to the heart, and turns and storms out the door. It shakes the whole house when he slams it.

Jay sticks up his middle finger at the slammed door and mutters something I can't hear under his breath, but I'm pretty sure he's cursing.

My brother quickly wipes his face, the tears trailing clean lines on his filthy face. He won't meet my eyes so I make a pot of coffee. He's going to need it if he's been up all night. He sits down at the kitchen table and rests his head on his arms.

"You can sleep an hour. I'll wake you up," I say to him.

He sits up and rubs at his eyes. "No, that'll just make it worse," he mumbles. I set a hot cup of black coffee in front of him. He looks at the cup and drinks, his face grimacing as he sips the bitter liquid.

"God, I hope I'm not like him when I grow up," Jay says. I think about how well my brother charms the customers, how he wears expressions that match my father's, and how right now, sipping a cup of black coffee, his curly dark brown hair sticking to his sweat-stained face, he reminds me so much of Dad already.

✳ ✳ ✳

Will stands in the center of the cement edge at the deep end of the pool. I don't really like swimming in the pool, the chlorine makes my skin itchy and the water's too warm, but for this game we need boundaries. I've played Sharks and Minnows in the river before and it just gets too confusing because people around here are cheaters.

The rest of us are treading water against the side of the pool.

We finally sorted out all the rules. Steven thinks he knows everything and argues with everything I say. I say the shark is supposed to be in the water and Steven says no, the shark stands on the edge. Heather says in Flagstaff, the shark has to call the minnows across the pool, but I explain that we don't play that way here. Jay sticks up for her, of course, and says that we should give it a try, and now we've formed some kind of morphed hybrid game with exceptions to rules and special circumstances, and I've already argued with Steven half a dozen times.

The "minnows" are Jay, Heather, Steven and I. We're supposed to swim from one side of the deep end to the other, without disturbing Will, the "shark". At any time the shark can jump into the water, and if he tags someone before they get to the wall, that person becomes the new shark. We've been playing for about an hour and I haven't been caught once.

"Come on! You guys have to cross," Will says from his place on the decking.

"Stop peeking so we can cross," I argue back. Will turns his back to us, and I silently slip beneath the water while he's not paying attention.

I frantically kick my legs as fast as I can. The blurry wall is inches from my fingers but before I can reach out to touch the tile I hear a splash behind me and my heart jumps. Will's in the water! I kick wildly, stretching to the surface, and my hand clutches the top of the wall just as Will's fingers wrap around my ankle and pull me back.

"I got you!" he cries when we surface, our heads bobbing along the water. I'm out of breath and a little bitter I got caught.

"I touched the wall before you tagged me," I argue, his face close to mine. His nose has started to peel, and the skin peeking through is splotchy and freckled. Technically, it happened at exactly the same time, but I'm not going to tell Will that. Everyone could clearly see my hand clutch the lip of the deck before he pulled me back.

"No you didn't. I pulled you away from the wall," Will says matter-of-factly, like this makes it so.

"Yeah, but not before I touched the wall," I contend. "You guys saw me touch the wall before he grabbed my leg, right?"

Heather and Jay aren't paying attention, they're too busy playing mercy. Their hands are interlaced and they push back and forth, the whole point of the game being to hurt the other person enough to make them cry mercy, but Jay's not even really trying. Heather squeals and yelps like Miss Piggy so it's obvious they saw nothing. Steven shrugs his shoulders, his lips pulled into a sly grin, and I know he saw me touch that wall, but he's not going to say anything.

"Fine. I'll be the shark, but I got to the wall first," I mumble. I climb out of the pool just as my dad walks down the sidewalk to the poolside.

"Jay, Cat, out of the pool. We're leaving for your mom's in fifteen," he says, the bill of his hat pulled down over his eyes.

I grab my towel and wrap it around my chest, and slip on my thongs, dreading how my feet will get caked with dirt walking back to the house. Will hops out of the pool and stands before me dripping wet, his eyebrows creased.

"You're leaving?" he asks, and I nod.

"I have to go to my mom's," I reply. I'm a little sad I have to leave, but I miss my mom. Her work schedule changed and I haven't seen her in two months.

"Why didn't you tell me? When will you get back?" Will demands, and I am shocked at his tone of voice. He's angry.

"Why do you care?" I respond defensively.

"I *don't* care," he says angrily. My shirt and shorts are tangled with his and they fall to the wet concrete when he yanks his stuff from the pile on the chair.

"Hey!" I bend to pick up my wet clothes from the ground. "What is your problem? You're acting like a real jerk."

"I'm acting like a jerk? You...you're the jerk," Will yells. His voice cracks and his face is beet red, and I can't tell if he's sunburned or just angry. Why is he so mad at me? I feel tears start to mix with the chlorinated water still on my face, so I wipe at my eyes with my towel, trying to hide the fact that William Henderson is making me cry.

"Are you crying, dude?" I hear Steven laugh, and I look up at Will. His eyes are red and watery, the same as all of ours from spending the last hour swimming. But he's upset, and it's my fault.

"Fuck you, Steven!" Will shouts, startling me. I've never heard that word out of Will's mouth and it sounds harsh and foreign and ugly. I watch him march back to his motel room, his back stiff and his walk rigid.

Frustration, confusion, anger, defensiveness, it's all forcing its way from my belly to my head, the emotions climbing on top of each other like the fat fish that swim by the dock.

"It's alright, Cat. You're not a jerk. It's not your fault we have to go," Jay says as he throws his arm around my shoulders. "And you'll see him again next summer. Dad said Dr. Henderson already reserved his spot."

I spend my time in Vegas sulking and irritable. I just want to go home to the marina and try to make things better with Will. But when I get back, he's gone.

My dad brings me a package, a tiny white envelope that has my name written on the front in Will's neat and precise printing.

"Will left this at the front desk." My dad sits on the edge of my bed waiting for me to open it, but I feel like it should be done in private so I shove it under my pillow. "You know, Kit Cat, Will's a really good friend for the summer. But he lives far away, that's just how it is."

As soon as he's gone, I tear open the envelope and shake the braided thread from the paper. It's a friendship bracelet, a rainbow of colors woven in a flat pattern about half an inch thick and decorated with little silver beads. It's my birthday present. I tie it around my wrist and vow to wear it until Will comes back.

1985 - THAT TIME AUNT FLOW CAME TO VISIT

The Goonies is released in theaters June 7th.

Michael Jordan is named NBA Rookie of the Year.

Pat Benetar is nominated for two Grammy's for best Pop and Rock Performances.

✼ ✼ ✼

Fourth of July. I snap a few pictures with my camera, a birthday present from my father last year. I like to take pictures of the red sun-stained mountains. They reflect off the rippling water and look like they're on fire. The sun is beginning to set, finally some relief from the blazing heat, and the sky is streaked with color.

There's still no Will. I'm beginning to get anxious. The last time I saw him, we argued by the pool. I called him a jerk and he left me a birthday present. I've thought about him every day, regretting how I hadn't said goodbye, and now I can't wait until he gets here so I can say I'm sorry. Dr. Henderson reserved his spot last year, space 207. I know because I've asked my dad three times this week.

"It's already paid for, Cat. I'm sure they'll be here soon. Maybe something came up. Plans change, honey." I know. People do too. My dad is trying to help but this makes me feel worse, because now I'm thinking of all the bad things that could have happened. Why hasn't he shown up yet?

I'm working the gas pump again this year. Activity has died down a bit and I'm sitting on the dock with my feet dangling over the edge when Jay runs out to get me. Dad's training him to take over the books, reservations and stuff like that. Dr. Henderson is checking in.

I waste no time jogging to the site. I walk right up to the motorhome, sweaty and out of breath, but before I can knock, the side door opens and a girl steps out into the sun. I freeze, confused. Do I have the wrong spot? I look at the wooden post beside the motorhome and there it's etched, plain as day, the number 207.

She shields her eyes with her hand, her lips pursed. Her face is round and pretty and she has big blue eyes and a sharp pointy nose. Her hair is cut in a short shag and it's jet black, like the moonless night sky at midnight. She's wearing a torn red t-shirt over a tight yellow tank top, and black stretchy leggings tucked into black boots that are going to get hotter than Hades in a couple of minutes. And the makeup, oh holy Pat Benetar the makeup! Her lids are lined dark and her already large eyes look like they're popping right out of her head. I've never worn makeup. My mom gave me lip gloss and nail polish, stuff like that, but it's pointless when you have to keep jumping in the water to cool off.

There's another girl behind her in the door frame; she's older and serious. Her honey colored hair is clipped out of her face, showing off the same pointy nose and round eyes. She's completely plain, wearing a pair of long khaki shorts and a beige blouse with a collar that buttons down the middle. She stretches her arms over her head, a large novel in her hand, and yawns, pushing small wire-rimmed glasses up off the bridge of her nose. They look alike, they might be sisters, but they are opposite ends of the spectrum. The dark and the light. The small and the tall. The primped and the prude.

"Hey, you're Cat!" the small one says, and I nod. The tall one looks in my direction. Her lips are full and bright pink and the sun glints off her braces as she speaks.

"I'm Lauren, and this is my sister, Margot. We're Will's stepsisters," she says in a matter-of-fact voice, like being associated with Will is a life sentence.

"He talked about you the whole way here," the small one chimes, her voice jeweled and crisp. Just as my mouth is dropping open, Will pushes his way out the door, his Vans hitting the gravely dirt with a thud, and a cloud of dust rises around his legs.

He looks up, his hair hanging in his eyes. It's long and messy, and less blond. He's taller than me for sure now. He's wearing new swim trunks and he still looks like Will, but I feel like I don't know him at all.

"Is it always this hot here?" Margot asks, moving between the motorhomes to find shade. Shade doesn't really help when it's a hundred and twenty degrees. Lauren flops down at the picnic table and crosses her legs, holding the book up to block her face. I get the impression she doesn't really want to be here.

"Sometimes hotter," I murmur and Will flashes me a big silly grin. His eyes squint as he walks over to me and I feel my stomach drop as he approaches. I can't smile back, I'm too weirded out by what's going on, but I'm relieved that he's finally here and that I can be close to him. Close, like in the same proximity, not like *with* him, like *touching* or anything. I don't like him like that.

At least, I don't think I do.

He slides his hand through his hair, his aquamarine eyes antagonizing in the intense sun, and his nose is covered in faint freckles. My heart thumps in my ears and I have to make an effort to inhale deeply just to breathe. What is happening to me?

"Hi Cat," his voice cracks. This little imperfection lets me relax. I was going to apologize for how I acted last summer, but it's not needed. He's forgotten, I guess, because he's not angry now. His lips are pulled into a cocky grin and I have to look up at him now to meet his eyes.

"What took you so long?" I ask with my hands on my hips.

"My dad got married again. His wife, Rachel, had to work. She's a teacher," Will says quietly, and his voice puckers with

37

bitterness. "I wanted to come down early and have the girls meet us down here, but Dad shit on that idea real quick. I've been dying to get down here."

Will smiles and looks down at me through his hair again, and my stomach flips.

"Stop doing that," I tell him.

"Stop doing what?" he asks defensively, his face moving closer to mine as his fingers run through his hair again, and I wrinkle my nose.

"Stop looking at me." I playfully push him, and he stumbles backward a little too dramatically.

"You want me to stop looking at you?" he snorts. "What am I supposed to do, close my eyes all summer?"

"No, I don't want you to stop looking at me," I try to clarify, my face flushing because now it sounds like I *want* him to look at me. "Stop looking through your hair at me. It's weird. And kinda creepy."

Will's about to argue when he stops and sighs. His eyes are fixed on something behind me and I turn to find Jay walking up the path with Dr. Henderson and who I can only assume is his new wife. She walks beside him, her arm linked in his, her yellow sundress welcoming as it curves around her legs. Her hair is the same honey color as the tall girl, Lauren, but I can see a few faint streaks of peppery gray running their course. My mom doesn't have gray hair because she gets her hair colored every month.

"That's her," Will mutters into my ear, his breath hot on my neck. Tiny goosebumps spread over my arms and legs and tingle on my scalp.

My brother is already working his charm on the new Mrs. Henderson. He's going to be seventeen in November. He wants to enroll at the University of Las Vegas after graduation, but both Mom and Dad have told him it's a no-go unless he can find financial aid. He's pretty insistent on going, though, and wants to major in finance or something so he can take over the business. Dad keeps claiming college isn't necessary; he already has the business, all he has to do is teach Jay how to run it.

I think Jay just wants out of here. He's always fighting with Dad. I think if Jay got the chance to leave, he'd never come back.

"Girls! Come meet this kid, he's hilarious!" Mrs. Henderson shouts from across the campsite. The tall one rolls her eyes, but the small one fluffs her hair and quickly hurries to meet my brother. "See girls, I told you this was going to be fun."

"Fun for a bunch of mouth-breathers maybe," I hear Lauren mutter under her breath.

Dr. Henderson walks over to us and gently puts his hand on my shoulder with a smile. "Hi there, Catherine. You're shooting up like a weed, aren't you?" he remarks, and Will glances at me apologetically.

"I guess so," I reply with a shrug. I guess I did get a little taller, but not really anything noticeable, unless he knows. Oh my God, can he tell? He is a doctor, but I didn't think that was something you could tell just by looking at a person.

Oh no, can Will tell? Is that why he keeps looking at me through his hair like that? Oh God, I'm going to be sick!

This past October, just after my thirteenth birthday, one of my ovaries released an egg into my fallopian tube for the first time and I shed my uterine lining. That is exactly how my mom explained it to me. I gagged a little. The words are so weird, uterus, fallopian, vulva, it all sounds like plant matter from an alien planet. All I could visualize was that part in Alien when the pod opens up and the face hugger jumps out all slimy and attaches itself to the guy's face. Now once a month I get a pain in my gut and I feel like I've been kicked in the crotch and I bleed for days. Josie calls it Aunt Flow. I'm so glad Josie works in the store. She doesn't glare at me or laugh when I need maxi-pads. She just puts them in a paper bag and smiles sympathetically.

No, they can't tell. There's no way. Someone would have told me. Josie or Heather, or my mom would have told me something like that.

"She's not a weed, Dad," Will snaps. Dr. Henderson chuckles, shaking my shoulder with his buoyant laugh. He sure seems happy, and I'm glad. Maybe this Mrs. Henderson can be a good mother for Will.

"Rachel, honey, come meet Catherine, Jay's sister." Dr. Henderson calls his wife over and she greets me by extending her small hand, her delicate wrist draped with a sparkling diamond bracelet. I clasp her hand in mine, Will's friendship bracelet still tied to my wrist.

"Nice to meet you, Catherine," Mrs. Henderson says in a calm, gentle voice. "Did you meet my girls? They're about your age." I nod, and she drops my hand to put her arm around Will's shoulder. He's obviously uncomfortable by the contact.

"This is going to be a great summer!" Mrs. Henderson squeals cheerfully. I smile, partially at her words but mostly at the uncomfortable look on Will's face as he rolls his eyes and I have to agree.

This is going to be a great summer.

❊ ❊ ❊

G od, will you just shut up!" Steven barks at Margot who is seated in front of him, and I turn around to sneakily grin at Will behind me. I know Steven only insisted on riding in Margot's kayak because he likes her hot pink bikini. I bet a million dollars Steven is hoping her top falls off. He didn't consider the fact that Margot talks. A lot. She hasn't stopped asking questions since we set out in the kayaks this morning.

"What? I'm curious, I thought you knew everything there is to know about this place." Margot refuses to paddle while Steven's verbally attacking her.

"Watch the wake!" Jay yells from his kayak beside us, and I dig my paddle into the wave made by a speedboat that just zoomed past. Jay shares a kayak with Lauren. He uses the paddle to steady the rocking while she clutches the sides of the small slender boat. Her face is almost as red as her polka dot swimsuit.

"You do know what you're doing, correct?" Lauren yelps, but Jay just laughs. Jay knows how to handle a boat better than anyone I know.

"He laughs, we're about to capsize and he laughs," Lauren says. The water isn't even that rough.

It's early August, the hottest time of the year. The temperatures reach high into the 120's and there isn't a breath of wind to save your life. In about two weeks everything will change; the clouds will roll in and the water will get rough. The storms will come, signaling the end of the season. And Will and his family will leave.

But for now, they're here and I spend every day I can with Will and his stepsisters. They aren't so bad, Margot and Lauren. Lauren is quiet mostly, save for a sarcastic quip once in a while. Margot doesn't shut up. She gets along fabulously with Heather, and the girls spend their summer lounging by the pool or on the sand of the private beach, talking about makeup and fashion, stuff that really doesn't interest me much. Instead, I take pictures with my camera. I click photos of the marina and boats on the launch. I snap shots of the fish under the bridge and the Arizona lupines that grow in front of the motel. Will's skin goes from fair to red to brown, and when his nose begins to peel, I know the end is getting close. His shoulders are freckled with color now, and he wears his shirt even in the water to protect against the sun.

We paddle along the south side of the river, the side that borders Arizona. If you cross the river you're in Nevada and there's another little marina about twenty miles downstream. Further south, there's Katherine's Landing, Davis Dam, and then Laughlin below the dam. Along the sixty mile stretch of river, there are arms and coves that spiral back into the red rocks and dirt-covered hills. We're searching for a specific cove as we maneuver downstream, the tall rocks rising out of the water in multicolored layers.

"Where is this cove? What did you guys call it?" Will leans forward to speak lowly into my ear. I turn slightly, his face disturbingly close to mine as he breaks from paddling now that the rough water is behind us.

"Donkey Cove," I say quickly. "There's a little outlet and herds of donkeys come down the hill to drink from the river. They're really tame because people always feed them hotdogs and chips and stuff. But don't stand behind them. They'll kick you right in the sack."

"Oh damn, warning received," Will cringes. "Maybe we can get Steven to stand behind one and then pull its ear or something so it'll kick him in the nuts. Then I won't have to."

"There!" Jay points to a sudden offshoot of the main river. The water is quiet and smooth like glass and our kayaks cut across the surface easily. We paddle around the bend towards the shore of the wide semicircle beach. You wouldn't even know this beach was back here unless you knew where to look.

"Whoa," Will mutters, and I smile, glad I could show him something cool.

Jay jumps into the water and pulls his boat ashore, helping Lauren out before wading over to grab our kayak. Will jumps out to help but it's a little too soon and the water is too deep. He sinks to the bottom and surfaces with a splash, a big grin on his face, and laughing at his mistake.

"Watch your step there, newbie," I say before jumping from the boat myself. I land in the shallow water and it's a relief from the overbearing sun. I help pull the kayak to the shore and grab our bags. I need my hat, the top of my head is sunburned between my two French braids.

"You're a Bulls fan?" Will asks as I pull the baseball cap over my head.

"It's my dad's hat," I shrug. "Who are the Bulls?"

"The Chicago Bulls. They drafted Michael Jordan, he was Rookie of the Year. He's going to revolutionize basketball, you just watch," Will says excitedly. I recognize the player's name. I think my dad's mentioned him once or twice. "You should give me that hat. You really can't appreciate it."

"No way! Get your own hat," I tease. I pull my sunblock from the bag and slather it on my arms before covering up with my shirt. I toss the sunblock to Will and he gives me a dirty look, but it's really important to take care of your skin out here. It's one of the first things I learned as a kid, cover up and drink lots of water.

He peels off his wet shirt and shakes out his wet hair, slicking it back with his fingers, and I can't stop staring. My knees feel gooey and my heart's trapped in my ribcage. I must be dehydrated.

"Got a thing for pasty white boys, Kitty Cat?" Steven remarks as he pulls his kayak up to the shore with ease. Margot hops out with a knowing grin, and I want to sock Steven in the face for his comment, especially because of the way Margot is looking at me.

The water gently laps at the shore and the girls lay out their towels. Lauren lies on her back, her eyes closed and her knees bent. Jay sits down on Margot's towel. She laughs at all his jokes and asks him a dozen questions and everything he says is the most interesting thing she's ever heard.

"Why do they call this Donkey Cove again?" Margot asks. She leans back on her elbows and crosses her legs, her bathing suit clinging for dear life. I don't think my dad would let me wear a bathing suit like that, and Margot is only a year older than I am.

"Well, there's these animals, they have four legs. Almost like a horse, but a little smaller. They're called Donkeys, and they live around here," Jay says with a dimpled grin, and Margot cackles and smacks his bare shoulder. I hear Lauren scoff before she rolls over onto her stomach and burrows her face in her crossed arms.

"So where'd you learn to paddle a kayak?" Margot asks him, and I can't take it anymore.

"Let's go for a hike," I say to Will, and he nods and grabs his Vans. I slip on my shoes, my feet gritty, and Will pulls his shirt back over his head.

"I'm in," Steven says. "These guys are boring as hell." I want to tell him no, but he's already marching up the hill, his shirt tucked into the back pocket of his denim shorts, the brown skin of his back and shoulders tinted red. Steven would be okay to look at if he'd just keep his stupid mouth shut.

"So do you like him now or whatever?" Will asks quietly beside me, and my face burns pink. Oh, God, he saw me staring at Steven. My mouth gapes open and I turn to look at him in horror.

"No...ugh, barf! The opposite, actually." I shake my head, embarrassed that Will thinks I like Steven. I would never in a million years like him.

"Do you like anyone else?" Will asks, and I shrug my shoulders.

"I like lots of people." I climb the rock-ridden path, the gravel making the climb a little slippery and unstable. I've climbed this hill so many times, I know exactly where to place my feet. Steven's already at the top looking down on us with a sneer.

"Come on, losers! I'm gonna sweat to death by the time you get up here!" he yells.

"That's the plan," Will mutters under his breath, and I laugh, my voice echoing off the side of the mountain.

"What? What's the joke?" Steven demands as we reach the large flat span of rocks and shrubbery. There's nothing but desert up here, hot, dry, dusty desert.

"Do you really want me to answer that?" Will asks him as he pushes his way to lead.

"You sure you don't want me to go first? This place is crawling with rattlers," Steven taunts

"They're rattlesnakes. Can't you hear them rattling?" Will crouches to inspect a black pitted rock.

"You'd be surprised," Steven replies, chucking a rock toward Will's feet. Will quickly stands up and looks around, and I try to hide a giggle.

"Rattlesnakes aren't out right now, it's way too hot even for the cold-blooded," I say and Steven wanders off. Will pulls a hand through his hair. It hangs in his eyes constantly.

"Hey guys! I found a dead donkey!" Steven yells back at us. Will's eyes flash with excitement, but I feel my stomach twist. I hate it when they find dead animals. They always smell and the boys poke at them. I wish they would just let them be.

Will trots off to see Steven's find and I trudge over to where they're standing. Sure enough, there's the picked over carcass of a donkey among the rocks. It's lying on its side, the wide broad skull complete with big square teeth, hooves still attached to the legs, a small amount of skin stuck to the skeleton, and my stomach gurgles. I can't get any closer.

"Whoa! Look at its teeth," Will remarks, crouching close to the skull.

"Don't touch it!" I shout, and Will looks over at me with concern. "You could get a disease or something."

He bends down and Steven kicks it with his foot. The smell of dried skin and dirt fills the air and I feel like I'm going to be sick.

"Stop it, Steven! Please!" I beg, my voice quavering now. "Just leave it alone!" Steven reaches down as if he is going to pick up one of the bones and I scream frantically. "Stop!"

"Knock it off, man!" Will pushes Steven away from the skeleton.

"What? It's just bones. There's not even that much flesh left on them," Steven says with a sly smile.

"You're such an ass!" I turn around to walk back down the hill, away from the poor dead donkey.

"No, this is an ass," Steven laughs behind my back, and I feel my neck and cheeks flame.

"Hey, wait up." Will jogs over to me, but I keep walking. "Cat, wait!"

He catches up to me and I'm too embarrassed to look at him. I don't want him to know how much this bothers me. I hate it when people know what bothers me. Then they can use it against me, like Steven does.

"I just don't like dead things," I blurt out, and we carefully start the climb down the hill. "And I feel like a dork. Because I screamed like a girl." Will follows me, his feet stepping in my old footsteps as I slightly bounce down the hill.

"You are a girl," he says as he slides slightly then catches his balance. "Well, kind of."

"Shut up. You know what I mean," I mutter. "Steven knows how to make me look like an idiot and he does it on purpose. He knows where my goat's tied."

"You have a goat?" Will asks. I stop and turn to see if he's serious. He smirks down at me, his hair falling in his eyes, and I throw him a dirty look before heading back down the path.

"He knows where your donkey's tied too," Will smirks as he gently tugs one of my braids. I'm about to spin around and sock him in the gut but he missteps and falls on his butt. He slides into my legs, but I'm leaning up the hill and able to steady myself.

I help him up, trying not to fall while he untangles his legs from mine. He knocks the dirt off his shorts and inspects his hands, a dozen little scrapes all along his palms.

"See? The universe doesn't like it when you're mean to me." I can't help but rub it in, and he laughs.

"Then why is it so much fun?" Will retorts, and I stick my tongue out at him and start back down the hill. He snags the baseball cap off my head and puts it on backwards. His eyes are mischievous as he darts past me and bounds down the path, leaving a trail of dust behind him. I follow, determined to get my hat back. Will runs straight past the girls and Jay, still lounging on the beach, and into the water, shoes and all. He laughs thinking he's won.

Well, he should know better. I never give up that easy.

I follow him into the water and his face changes as he backs into deeper water. I narrow my eyes and lunge, grabbing him by his arm and trying to grab my cap off his head. He's slippery from the sunblock and he wiggles away, grabbing my leg and pulling me into the deep water where I can't reach the bottom, but he can.

I kick and thrash trying to break free but he's still smiling, a fact that makes me want to pinch his pretty little face.

I dunk below the water and adjust my position. I surface behind him, climbing on his back and throwing my arms around his neck. He loses his grip on my leg but dips underwater, hat and all, in an attempt to shake me free. I hang on, holding my breath and closing my eyes as he turns and twists before surfacing.

As soon as I can breathe, I grab my hat and swim as fast as I can when I feel a sharp pinch on the back of my thigh. I scream, kicking my legs as I turn around to swim on my back, and Will surfaces, laughing hysterically. I try to kick him but the water makes the blow ineffective. Will grabs my wrists and I struggle but he can stand in this depth and as much as I hate to admit it, he's stronger than me. Jay and Margot are laughing on the shore and it pisses me off even more that they've seen Will get the better of me.

"Whoa! Are you seriously mad? I'm only playing around with you," Will says, panting. "Stop trying to kick me."

"Don't mess with me and I won't try to kick you," I retort, trying to catch my breath and letting my body relax before realizing that Will's face is very close to mine. I can see water drip from his eyelashes. He must realize it too because he drops my wrists. I turn and swim to shore, putting the hat back on my head and sitting on the sand with the others. Will swims further out into the deep water and I feel uneasy, like I've hurt his feelings or something with my overreaction.

"Hey, Polka Dots," Jay says as he gently nudges Lauren with his hand. "You'd better turn over. Your back's getting a little pink."

"Oh shit." She cranes her neck to look at her back, pulling the strap away from her shoulder. Sure enough, her back is splotched and red, a distinct line of white where her strap was. She's more than a little pink, she's sunburned.

"You're gonna feel that later tonight. Take a real hot shower when you get back to your motorhome. It'll take the sting out,"

Jay says. Lauren pulls her shirt over her head and cringes. "We should probably get you out of the sun for today. We don't want anyone hallucinating from heat stroke."

"Hallucinating? Are you serious?" Lauren asks. Steven still hasn't come back down the mountain, so I walk to the edge of the path and yell his name. Jay gets the girls back in their kayaks and is ready to leave when Steven comes jumping down the hill.

"Jay, did they tell you? We found a dead donkey. I'm gonna come back with my brothers and get the skull. So bitchin' man!" Steven says, and he climbs into the kayak with Margot as she gags dramatically.

"A skull? Ew gross!" Margot shrieks, but Steven just laughs.

"Cat especially loved it," he says with a nod in my direction and I flip him off. Jay helps me push our kayak into the water. Will's still swimming in the deep water and I paddle out to where he's floating.

"Hey!" Will opens his eyes and swims over to the boat. "We gotta leave. Lauren got sunburned and needs to get out of the sun."

"Really? Well, that blows," Will says as he tries to hoist himself into the boat. He struggles so I reach over the side and grab his arm, an attempt to help him in without tipping us both over. He throws his leg over the edge of the rocking boat, his soggy blue and white slip-on shoes still on his feet. He climbs into the kayak, purposefully falling against my leg and dripping water all over me. He settles into his spot with a smirk, and I give him a little shove. I turn around and place my paddle in the water. Will snags my baseball cap and I spin around to see him grinning from ear to ear, dripping wet and wearing my cap, and I don't have the heart to fight him for it again.

Besides, he looks kind of adorable in my hat.

❊ ❊ ❊

O h crap," I stare at the smear of blood in my underwear. Aunt Flow. I sigh, frustrated because now I won't be able to swim for the next week. The Hendersons are leaving tomorrow and we had plans to snorkel the shoreline that stretches south of the marina today. Now I won't be able to go. And I have to quickly come up with an excuse because I refuse to tell everyone that I can't go because I got my period. This whole period thing sucks balls.

I won't be needing my swimsuit today, so I change into my denim cutoffs and tank top, cursing my reproductive system the whole time. I really just want to go back to bed, but I know Will will be pounding on my door in five minutes, so I pull my hair back into a braid and brush my teeth.

Soon enough, Will is on my porch, mask and snorkel already on his face, and I laugh at how ridiculous he looks. It also makes it incredibly worse that I have to cancel.

"Where are the girls?" I ask.

"Lauren isn't coming. She's going on the boat with my dad and Rachel. And Margot is hanging out with your brother," Will says suggestively, and I gag. Gross.

"Do you want to go out on the boat with your Dad? I mean, he's finally taking the time to go out on the water. Don't you want to go too?" I ask, trying to seem curious.

"I don't care. I'll be spending ten hours in a Winnebago with him tomorrow. I just want to do whatever you want to do," Will says sheepishly, and the knot in my tummy tightens.

"I don't think we should snorkel today. The water's all choppy and it'll be too cloudy," I offer, which isn't a lie. "Let's go on the boat instead. Oh! We could drive up to the dam!"

"That'd be cool! I'll go tell my dad and meet you on the boat. Get your suit on," Will says as he walks out the door. I cringe. This is going to be bad.

"Hi Catherine!" Mrs. Henderson waves cheerfully when I get to the dock. Dr. Henderson gives me a nod, and Lauren looks up from her book for a second of acknowledgment. Will looks at me confused. He's noticed I don't have my suit on. *Please don't*

49

ask, please don't ask, please don't ask, I chant to myself, trying to Jedi mind trick him into minding his own beeswax.

"Hi," I say quietly with a wave. "I'll push you guys out, if you want," I say to Dr. Henderson.

"That'd be great, Catherine. Thanks! We've got a bunch of newbies here," he says, motioning to his wife and Lauren. I wait until he's seated behind the wheel and he starts up the engine before I push the boat away from the slip. Will hops aboard as Dr. Henderson backs out of the slip, and I jump onto the bow before it gets too far away. I sit in one of the bucket seats across from Will on the bench and he looks at me thoughtfully. I usually sit on the bench with him, but I don't want to answer his questions. So I just smile and cross my outstretched legs and watch the water as Dr. Henderson speeds off towards the dam.

The wind drowns out any chance for conversation, but when we get to the huge concrete wall, everyone is hot from the ride and wants to cool off in the water. Dr. Henderson pulls out his red flag and affixes it to the windshield before jumping into the water. Mrs. Henderson follows, surprising me when she gets her hair wet. My mom never gets her hair wet. She doesn't like to mess up her makeup and she thinks she looks like a rat with wet hair. Even Lauren sheds her frock and jumps into the water with a yelp.

"Why is the water so cold?" she asks me as she treads water.

"This water is from the bottom of Lake Mead, above the dam," I say and glance out of the corner of my eye at Will. He's staring at me. Ugh, I'm going to have to tell him about my uterus.

I smile at him warily and sit on the bow, my butt getting a little wet as I let my feet hang off the front of the boat.

"Where's your swimsuit?" Will asks, climbing onto the bow and sitting next to me. I sigh.

"In my bedroom," I respond without looking at him.

"Well, duh. Why aren't you wearing it?" he presses.

"Why is it such a big deal? Lots of people don't swim," I say, grateful the boat has drifted from the others and they can't hear our conversation.

"Cat, I have never in my life seen you without your swimsuit on. Excuse me if it's a little weird," Will says quietly. "Are you mad or something?"

"No," I say, my voice a little too snotty. "I just don't feel like swimming today, alright?"

"Okay, fine. Sorry." Will watches the deep water and I've upset him again.

"Look, I...um...Aunt Flow came this morning," I say, scrunching my face as I peek over at him.

"You mean your period?" Will smirks, and I narrow my eyes, irritated at the volume of his voice. "Why didn't you say so? I live with three girls. I probably know more about periods than you do."

"It's embarrassing, you goon," I say with a scowl.

"No it's not. Getting caught whacking off by your new stepmom, that's embarrassing," Will says. My eyes bulge and my face is hot and blushing. I can't believe he told me that!

"You do that?" I whisper. I know what it is. I mean, hello, Jay Rossi is my brother.

"Yeah. Don't you?" he asks, and my mouth drops open. I have never done that.

Well, not really. I heard Josie and Heather talking about orgasms and masturbating and stuff. They were reading an article in Cosmo and I stole the magazine from the store. I read the article locked in the bathroom and I admit it, I tried to do what the article said, but I just got squirmy and messy and then frustrated.

"It's perfectly normal, my dad said so. And he's a doctor. He said everyone does it," Will says knowingly.

"Alright, fine. Once. But I didn't...you know, finish," I mutter, my cheeks burning.

"I kissed a girl. Back in San Francisco. She let me touch her boobs, too," Will confesses, and I quickly turn my head to glare at him.

"You...you kissed somebody?" I ask, forcing the feelings of betrayal from my voice.

I have no reason to be jealous, no reason to think Will wouldn't have girlfriends. He's very nice and cute and of course girls would like him. But this makes us uneven again.

"Have you kissed anybody?" Will asks me quietly, and I shake my head. I wish I could tell him yes, so that I wouldn't feel so bad right now.

"I could kiss you," Will offers, and I turn my head to look at him, his green eyes dark in the shade of the tall rocks and concrete dam. My heart pounds in my chest. My hands are shaking and I can't catch my breath. My stomach is fluttering and my head is foggy and I really, really want to kiss William Henderson.

And it scares the crap out of me.

So I do what I always do when I'm scared. I shove him. Hard. So hard, he falls off the bow of the boat and into the cold water below. I stare over the edge to make sure he's okay and all I see are bubbles and foam. Oh God, what if I hurt him? I'm about to call over Dr. Henderson when Will surfaces and looks up at me hanging over the edge.

"What the hell, Cat?" Will asks, and I really do feel bad. I just didn't know what to do!

"I'm sorry!" I yell down to him. Lauren climbs the ladder hanging off the back of the boat. She grabs a towel and wraps it around her body before sitting back in her chair, and she's followed by Dr. and Mrs. Henderson. Will climbs in last and plops down on the bench, not bothering with a towel, and pulls a pair of Wayfarers from a cubby on the side of the boat. He hides behind them and looks out over the water, even though we're in the shade of the rocks. I feel horrible for pushing him into the water.

I move to sit beside Will on the wet bench when Dr. Henderson starts the engine back up. Scooting back into the corner, I stretch my legs out on the seat and he looks over at me like I'm irritating him. I flash him an apologetic smile, forcing all my emotions into this one grin. *Yes, I want you to kiss me. Yes, I'm a big scaredy-cat. And I'm sorry.*

He shifts to face me, and puts his legs up on the seat beside mine, his wet thigh against my calf, his toe digging into my hip. All is forgiven as we ride back to the marina, but the heaviness remains. When we get back we will have to say goodbye and tomorrow the Hendersons will leave, their big motorhome heading back to San Francisco. Will will go back to his girlfriend, who lets him kiss her and touch her boobs, and I will be forgotten.

The next morning their campsite is clear, the motorhome pulled into the dumping station as Dr. Henderson takes care of the unpleasantries of camping, and I feel like total crap. I see Will in the gravel road, walking towards me on the swings, and I meet him on the sidewalk, a small bag in his hand. I smile. It's my birthday present.

"We're leaving in a few minutes, but I wanted to give you this," he says, handing me the package. I open the small brown baggie and pull out a silver ring with a large oblong stone.

"It's a mood ring. It reminded me of your weird eyes," he says as I slip the ring onto my finger. It immediately starts changing color from green to violet.

"What does purple mean?" I ask him. I gaze at the swirling ring. Now it's the color of the deep water when we go for night rides, and I feel my chest expand and my eyes burn.

"I don't know. There's a paper in the bag, I think," he smirks, but I don't bother looking it up. I'm sure it means horribly awful, because that's how I feel.

"My dad bought one of those houses, the ones like yours," Will says, and I look up at him with wide eyes. Steady Paychecks. The Hendersons are officially Steady Paychecks.

"You'll be back next year for sure?" I ask, beaming.

"Yeah, I'll be back. *I'll be back*," he says in a robotic voice, and I laugh at his horrible impression. His smile is shy and soft and I feel my face flush. "Hey! Maybe we can do fireworks next year!"

"For sure," I say, unable to stop the corners of my mouth

from twitching.

"Okay, I have to go," Will turns to leave and my belly twists, my forehead creases. I really don't want him to leave. "I'll see you next year, Cat."

I can't say anything because I'm afraid I'll cry. I miss him already as I watch him walk up the path. I see Dr. Henderson wave so I wave back with a lump in my throat. I look down at my ring and run my finger across the glass and I wish I would have hugged him or said something. I didn't even say thank you. I didn't even say goodbye.

I take off running in his direction and shout his name, my voice cracking as I try to hold back my tears. Will stops and turns, his face confused, and I throw my arms around his neck and squeeze him tight, holding him to my body and wishing like hell I didn't have to let him go. His arms wrap around my waist and he squeezes too, and I know he feels the same.

"Thank you," I say, and press my lips to his cheek, and with one last squeeze, I let him go.

1986 – THAT TIME WE JUMPED OFF A CLIFF

The A-Team airs its fifth and final season.

Sammy Hagar performs his first concert as lead singer of Van Halen.

Space Shuttle Challenger disintegrates after launch, killing everyone on board.

* * *

S o what's up with you and Steven?" Will asks, his lips stained from the rainbow sherbet Push-Up he's eating as he sways on the swing beside me. The Hendersons arrived last night, crammed into a big black Mercedes-Benz. I can see the front porch of the modular home Dr. Henderson purchased last year from my bedroom window and I've been watching for signs of life for weeks.

I finished my first year of high school and am now known by everyone as Jay's little sister. They call me Kit Cat just like he does. Every time I hear it, I want to smash their faces in. Heather let me eat lunch with her a couple times, but I high-tailed it out of there when one of her boyfriends asked me if I was a virgin.

Steven hangs around his brothers and their stoner friends, who hang around Jay and his clan of gear heads who occasionally hang at the tables with Heather and her popular friends. I don't fit into any of these groups. And I don't really have friends.

"Nothing's up with me and Steven. There is no me and

Steven. There's me and there's Steven and occasionally, we have to be in the same room. Other than that, I avoid him like broccoli," I explain before taking a bite of my IT'S-IT.

"Just wondering. A lot can happen in a year," Will says and I look at his face, the statement more true than he realizes.

"Yep, things change. People do too," I mutter. Will's changed. His hair is darker and very short, his jaw is sharp, his cheeks less full and he has muscles, long lean curves in his arms and shoulders. He's a full head taller than me now, his feet are too big for his body and there's a faint shadow of prickly hair along his upper lip. He looks like the boys at my school.

"I made the basketball team this year," Will says.

"You're a jock?" I laugh, surprised because Will tripped over his own feet twice between the store and the swings.

"Yeah, I guess. I won first place in the academic decathlon too, so maybe nerdy jock? Do you still take pictures?" Will asks me and I nod, my camera sometimes my only companion.

"I'm not anything. I don't participate in the whole socializing thing," I say quietly, licking the chocolate from my fingers.

"That's not true. You're something," Will says and I narrow my eyes because I'm sure his next comment is going to be a joke at my expense. "I'm serious! You're artsy, with your photography thing, and you're abstract the way you observe and dissect. And you are freakishly strong."

"You're just incredibly weak," I counter and Will shrugs his shoulders.

"Maybe I am, but maybe, you're part ant and that's why you can lift fifty times your body weight," Will remarks and I smile. He's still just Will, my best friend who doesn't think I'm weird because he's weird too.

"You're probably Mr. Popular now, huh?" I say in a dreamy voice and Will knocks his swing into mine.

"I don't know. I'm not *un*popular. I don't really pay attention to it. Mostly I just hang out with the team," Will says.

"What about you? You got a group of artsy fartsy friends?

Maybe a mopey boyfriend and the two of you talk about The Cure and how nobody understands your love?" Will grabs the chain of my swing, knocking his legs into mine.

"If I did, I wouldn't be wasting the day here with you." I kick my feet off his leg, propelling my swing diagonally across the dirt. Will catches my chain when I cross in front of him, the momentum causing my seat to twist and jerk.

"Yeah, you would," Will says confidently. His hand still grips the plastic covered chain to my swing and he stares at me for a long time before pushing me away. I don't like that he's right, and I don't like that he knows it.

"Hey, Dad wants to go to a cove for the Fourth. Do you think we could go back to that one we went to last year, the donkey one?" Will asks and I shake my head no. I know which cove I want to take the Hendersons to. It's on the west side of the river, south of the marina and closer to the warmer water. It's a small inlet in the middle of which is a sandy, brush covered island surrounded by rocky cliffs. Jay and I nicknamed the island Australia when we were little.

"No? You won't take us to Donkey Cove?" Will stops his swing. "Why not?"

"Because we're going to Australia."

* * *

H it it!" I yell, my knees pulled up to my chest as I lean back into the spongy vest strapped around my body. I bob in the water, two wooden planks strapped to my feet and a rope between my knees. Jay hits the gas and I tighten my grip on the plastic handles. I lurch forward, straightening my legs and leaning back to create more tension in the rope. Jay's going too slow. I'm going to eat it if he doesn't speed up.

I signal with a repetitive thumbs-up, pulling back on the rope as my skis glide across the top of the water. Every muscle in my body is tense as I fight to keep my balance, but as soon as Jay speeds up, I relax, easing into the ride as the boat snakes across the wide, glassy water. We got out here extra early so we'd have a clean ride. Choppy water is the worst for teaching first time skiers.

After a few turns, I let go of the rope and sink into the water so the others can have a turn. I pull my feet out of the rubber bindings, hold the skis under my arms, and wait for Jay to circle back.

I still can't believe Dad let us take the boat on the Fourth of July. I think it's a bribe. Jay will graduate soon, and I think my dad realizes that Jay can choose to hightail it out of here when he turns eighteen. They had a real bad fight right before the start of the season, and Jay went to live with my mom for a couple of weeks. They've been tiptoeing around each other ever since, like two alpha males trying to avoid confrontation. Jay agreed to take classes at the community college instead of the University and Dad agreed to pay for it if Jay helped run the marina. They worked things out and, hopefully, that was the worst of it but I'm not getting too comfortable with their truce just yet.

The boat approaches slowly and Steven holds the red flag in the air from his seat next to my brother. Will stands in the back, grinning down at me. Lauren appears beside him, her lips pulled into a smirk. Her teeth are white and gleaming now, braces gone, but she still wears her wire rimmed glasses, even on the boat. She keeps covered constantly, the fear of sunburn etched in her brain. Margot sits sideways on the bench, leaning back and closing her eyes, absorbing the morning sun. She opts for a bright red bikini this year, the straps tied around her neck, her dark hair choppy around her face.

"Who's next?" I call up to them and Lauren takes off her glasses.

"Me. I'll go," she says.

"Throw us the vest," Jay says and I unlatch the straps across my chest. He leans over the side of the boat and grabs it from me, shaking it over the edge to remove the extra water before

Lauren has to put it on. I hold onto the ladder with one hand and wait to help her into the skis.

Lauren pulls her long shirt over her head, revealing a royal blue bikini and man, does she fill it out. Lauren has developed over the year and by developed, I mean she's got boobs and hips and she looks like she could be in a rock band music video. My brother gapes at her like a freaking groupie at a Van Halen concert and I'm absolutely positive some crude commentary is running through his head.

She snatches the life vest from his hand but he doesn't release it, forcing her to meet his eyes and then he turns on the charm. I've seen it dozens of times. Jay knows all he has to do is smile his schmoozy dimpled grin and she'll be a pile of giddy mush. It's quite nauseating to witness.

The moment Jay's lips curl, Lauren clenches her jaw, and yanks on the vest. She doesn't crack a smile or giggle or anything. Jay gives in to her, his features transforming from coy to confused in seconds. He watches as she struggles to snap the latches across her generous bust, shamelessly staring at her monumental cleavage. *Oh, you transparent fool.*

"Relax, mouth breather, they're just boobs, nothing but fat and mammary glands," Lauren says and my brother stutters, running his hand over his short curls. Lauren hoists herself over the side of the boat and gracefully slides into the water, and for the first time ever, I think I see Jay blush. She swims over to me and I smile at her with glowing appreciation.

Lauren pulls the rubber bindings over her feet, and I show her the proper placement for her legs and arms.

"Stay in a ball until you're out of the water and then stand up. Don't fight the movement, let it pull you. If you want to go faster, give a thumbs-up and to slow down, thumbs-down. If you want to stop, just let go of the rope. Yell "Hit It" when you're ready and Jay will punch the gas." Lauren nods and I swim over to the ladder. Will hands me a towel as I climb into the boat. I take a seat next to Margot, and Will wiggles his way between the two of us. His thigh presses against mine, his hip against my hip and I'm very aware of Will's body next to mine. He stretches his arms to rest on the back of the bench and I pull the towel tight around my body, the parched sun already drying my shoulders.

My brother idles the boat to straighten out the rope. I notice the flag in Steven's lap and my anger flares at his negligence. That flag is a signal to other boats that there is a skier in the water and to take extra caution. Steven knows how important this is.

"Steven! Flag!" I shout in disbelief as Steven lazily raises the flag in the air. "Dude! What the hell? If you're gonna slack off, give it up. She could get killed!"

"Oh Cat, calm down. There's no one even out here yet," Steven replies. "Besides, I'm sure they'd see your ugly face and avoid the area at all costs."

"Dude, don't be such a dick!" Will shouts before I can respond.

"Can't speak for yourself anymore, Cat? Gonna let this Paycheck do it for you?" Steven spits and I want to sock him. Steven towers over me now. He hit a growth spurt or something and much to my dismay, I can't take him in a fight anymore.

"That's what I thought," Steven says when I refuse to respond and I can't look at him.

"Hit it!" I hear Lauren yell and Jay hits the gas, the roaring engine drowning out the argument. We watch Lauren disappear behind a froth of white water before popping up suddenly out of the wake. She maintains her balance for a long length of water but then Jay turns. She hits the wake at an unsuspecting angle and face plants. Still, it's a pretty good run for a beginner.

Jay circles around, positioning the boat in front of Lauren and Will gets up to snatch the flag from Steven's worthless hand. He resumes his seat next to me and holds the signal in the air before flashing me a goofy grin.

"Pretty impressive, Lauren," I say over the side of the boat to her. "You going again?" Lauren nods and Jay turns so the rope will drift towards her. She repeats her performance, followed by Margot, who only stumbles once before popping right up. Steven takes a turn, riding one ski, the 'log' we call it. Steven is an expert on skis and even more impressive on one. He puts on a performance, turns and tricks and by the time he's done, Margot and even Lauren squeal with delight.

Will's leg bounces, his thigh rubbing against mine in agitation and I give him a nudge to get him to stop. He bolts up, his eyes blazing, his fists clenched.

"My turn," he says and hands me the flag. He grabs the other vest, the larger one my brother wears and strips off his shirt. God, I hope he put on sunblock. He straps the vest across his chest and clumsily jumps off the side of the boat. I glide the other ski over to him and he catches it, holding it under his arm as he swims over to Steven. I can see them exchanging words, then Steven heads back to the boat, leaving Will to struggle into the skis on his own.

Steven climbs into the boat and sits next to me on the bench, his heavy wet arm flung across my shoulders and I squirm away from him.

"Steven! What the hell? You're getting me all wet!" I say and Steven laughs.

"I bet," Steven winks and Margot laughs, a high-pitched giggle.

"Oh, gross. You're a pig, you know that?" I say before jumping into the empty seat across from the bench.

"Try to hide it all you want, but you love it, Kitty Cat," he says but before I can argue, Will yells hit it from the water and my brother punches the gas.

I'm still seething at Steven's arrogance but Will on skis provides a distraction. He pulls up out of the water no problem but he's all limbs. His arms flail and he grips the rope handles for dear life. His legs are wobbly and his balance is off. He keeps pitching forward and pulling back, and I think he's going down at least a half a dozen times. His eyes are wide and terrified,

61

his lips pulled into a grimace as he struggles to stay up on the skis. I don't want to laugh, but it's the most hilarious thing I've ever seen. I pull my camera from the cubby in the side of the boat and snap a couple pictures, hoping to capture an awkward shot.

"Oh shit, he looks like Goofy out there! You know, the cartoon, where Goofy learns to ski? All he needs is a green hat," Steven shouts over the roar of the engine. Margot is cackling, holding her stomach, her mouth gaping and wide. Lauren snorts behind me, smacking Jay on the shoulder and telling him to sneak a peek and then Jay is laughing too. Will continues to struggle and I fight the muscles pulling in my cheeks because I know exactly which cartoon Steven is talking about and the resemblance is spot on.

Finally, Will loses his battle with gravity and tumbles forward, his feet flying out of the skis, a ball of arms and legs flailing into the water. There's a collective roar of laughter on the boat as Will falls and I frown. Steven's going to have a field day when Will gets back on the boat. I put my camera away and hold the flag in the air as Jay circles around to pick him up. His face burns red with frustration as he swims over to the ladder and I pass the flag to Margot. I lean over the side of the boat and Will hands me the skis one at a time.

"You going again, man?" Steven yells down at him, a smirk on his lips. "Because I haven't laughed that hard in years."

"Yeah, laugh it up, jackass. Glad I could entertain you all." Will's eyes focus on mine and I feel bad for laughing.

"Are you okay?" I ask him as he climbs in the boat, shedding the vest and plopping down in the chair behind Jay.

"Yeah, are you okay, Willy?" Steven leers. Will's eyes darken at the nickname and looks at me with irritation, like it's my fault he's Goofy on skis.

"What?" I ask, my tone harsh. "It was funny! I'm sorry, but it was hilarious."

"I'm just fine, so you can quit pretending like you give a shit," he says and I'm shocked. I expected him to laugh it off, like he normally does but instead he's fuming and I don't like that he's lashed out at me in front of everyone.

"Oh come on! If it was anyone else, you'd be laughing your ass off," I contest and Will ignores me. Steven's grinning like a mad fool and I get why Will's so angry. I've sided with the enemy.

"Anyone else want to ski?" Jay asks, attempting to break the tension.

"I'm good," Steven smirks and I glance over at Will. He refuses to look at me and I feel my stomach twist, regretting that I even opened my big fat mouth. Jay starts up the engine and steers the boat back to the cove. Dr. Henderson's boat floats languidly on the calm water and we can see him and Mrs. Henderson lounging in chairs beneath a blue canopy on the beach when Jay curves the boat around the small island.

Jay pulls up the outdrive so the propeller won't catch in the sand and hands me the anchor and ropes. Steven jumps off the side of the boat as it idles up to the beach and I follow. We anchor the boat so it won't drift, and Jay, Lauren, and Margot jump into knee deep water, but Will remains on the boat. I can't decide if I should go to him or let him be a big baby. I guess it's partially my fault he's upset so I climb back into the boat and plop down on the bench. Will looks up at me, his eyes dejected, and I feel my chest swell.

"I'm sorry I laughed at you," I say, sitting in the chair beside him. He sighs and runs his fingers over his short cut, the sun making the blond stand out. His chest is still bare and starting to pink and I want to tell him to put on a shirt or something but I don't want to piss him off further.

"You're right, though. If it would have been anyone else, I would have laughed too. Steven just gets under my skin. He's so damn cocky and after his little phenomenon on skis, I really wanted to show him he's not as cool as he thinks he is. Guess I failed miserably, huh?" Will's lips pull into a soft sad smile, his eyes vibrant in the sun. He really is beautiful. Boys can be beautiful, right?

"Steven's a fool and he knows he's shit. That's why he spends so much time making others feel bad, so he can make himself feel better. If anything I pity him," I say, explaining it to Will how my mom explained it to me. She didn't exactly say Steven was shit, she called him a bully but her message was clear.

"You pity him?" Will asks, a teasing smile playing on his lips and I nod. "And you think he's a fool?"

"Yeah?"

"So, one could say you pity the fool?" Will smiles expectantly and I'm confused. Is he making fun of me?

"Oh, come on, Cat! *I pity the fool*?" he says in a deep, throaty voice and I slightly recognize the turn of phrase.

"Are you serious? Mr. T? You're killing me here, Rossi!" Will teases and I shrug, letting him have a laugh at my expense because it makes us equal again.

"Come on, fool. Let's get some breakfast." I stand up. "And you need to cover up. You're already pink."

"Yes, sir," Will mocks with a salute. We climb over the bench and off the back of the boat. The water feels refreshing against my legs in the early heat and my toes sink into the silty sand.

Will kicks the water behind me, obnoxiously splashing me from behind, but I smile, because it means he's no longer upset. I'll take obnoxious Will over sulking Will any day.

We lounge in the hot sun, and swim when we need relief. Jay and Steven take the girls on another ski ride and Dr. and Mrs. Henderson go this time. Will and I hang back to watch our stuff. I lay on my towel on my stomach in the shade to read my book. Will puts his towel beside me and scribbles in a notepad. I try to see what he's writing but he keeps his thoughts to himself. The heat makes my eyelids heavy and I let them close, the water lapping at the shore providing a soft lullaby. The sand is soft beneath my body and sweat starts to roll down my spine and I am perfectly content.

"Hey lovebirds!" my brother shouts and I startle out of a deep sleep. My hair is matted and sweaty on my face, my body stiff and achy. I lift my head to find Will's cheek against my shoulder, his arm and torso pressed against the length of my body. His breath is warm on my skin and my belly tingles. His lips are so close, I could kiss him if I wanted to. I feel my cheeks get hot and I try not to think about how much I like Will's skin touching mine and quickly slide away from him before he can wake up.

Jay's the first on the shore with Margot and Lauren right behind him. Margot grins widely, her blue eyes twinkling, and I assume she thinks we've been cuddling. *Were* we cuddling? I mean, it would seem that way, but it wasn't on purpose. It was a sleep-induced accidental cuddle.

Mrs. Henderson is still wading through the water and Steven is showing Dr. Henderson a better way to anchor off the boat and I'm grateful as all hell they weren't the ones to witness the cuddle confusion. Steven would never let me live that one down.

It's late afternoon now, the sun sinking below the hills and casting a shadow across the cove. I'm burning up, though, so I jump into the water and decide to swim to the island.

"Cat, wait!" Margot yells. She smiles when she catches up to me and we turn to swim to the shore. She doesn't waste any time, starting right in on the cuddle heard round the world as if it's the most scandalous thing she's ever seen.

"Oh my God, how cute was that? You guys are such a cute couple," she blabs and I'm momentarily impressed by her ability to talk while swimming.

"We're not a couple, Margot," I gasp, trying not to swallow water in the process.

"Oh please, he's totally in love with you. He talks about you all the time. He even wrote you a poem for your birthday," Margot says and I stop swimming, my head going under as I choke on the water in my throat.

"What? Is that my present this year?" I cough, suddenly very interested in the conversation. "A poem?"

Margot nods as we reach the shore. She adjusts her top as she wades onto the beach with me right on her heels. I collapse onto the sand and she sits next to me. I'm a bit stunned at this disclosure. A poem is so intimate, so personal, something you would give a *girlfriend*.

But I'm not Will's girlfriend. Will's girlfriend will be from San Francisco, California, a girl who's like him, who has lots of money and wears nice clothes and makeup and fits with him. I'm just a river girl, his summer friend. Nothing more.

"Will doesn't love me, Margot. Doesn't he have a girlfriend in San Francisco?" I fish for information.

"Will has lots of girlfriends in San Francisco. He's very popular. But he doesn't look at them the way he looks at you. He loves you, Cat, whether you want to admit it or not," Margot says, leaning back on her elbows.

"Well, being in love and being a couple are two very different things," I mutter. Maybe Will loves me, but that doesn't mean he wants to be with me. That doesn't mean he wants to kiss me and hold my hand or anything.

"That's true. It'd be hard to date someone who lives so far away. But that doesn't mean it goes away, you know. Those feelings don't just disappear," Margot says after a long silence. She looks over at me and smiles. I frown, thinking about how I miss Will all year long, how I can't wait for him to show up. Margot is right, it never goes away.

Margot laughs at my expression. "Relax Cat, it's not a death sentence, you know. Love is a splendid thing." She closes her eyes and sighs, the very thought of it making her swoon. I don't see the appeal. Love is scary and stressful and confusing. I mean, I'm only fourteen. I wouldn't know love if it bit me in the ass.

"Are you in love with anyone?" I ask Margot and she grins, the chance to talk about herself too enticing to pass up. She launches into a story about a boy she knows at school who's dating her friend and how she knows they'd be perfect together.

"And then, Amber, my friend, was out of town last winter and he invited me to go to the roller rink but he also invited

Will and all these other people. What does that mean? Did he want to go out with me but knew he couldn't without causing a big fight? Or was he just bored and felt obligated to invite me because he's friends with Will? I don't know what to do." Margot stops talking to take a breath.

"Maybe you should let nature run its course. And if it's meant to be, then it will happen," I say, my extensive knowledge of the topic left to trite clichés.

"Leave it to fate?" Margot snorts. "Oh Cat, there's no such thing as 'meant to be'. If you want something, you have to make it happen. I'm not going to leave my future up to something as arbitrary as fate."

"So you don't believe in soulmates?" I ask, confused.

"As in, 'one person that is meant for you?' Not possible. I mean my mom thought my dad was her soulmate and he's gay," Margot says with a shake of her head.

"Your dad's gay?" I ask. I don't know anyone who's gay. At least I don't think I do.

"Yep!" she says proudly. "He's an awesome dad, and him and my mom get along fine. He's just not as into chicks as he initially thought."

"But then she found Dr. Henderson and they seem pretty happy together," I point out.

"So both her soulmates happened to live in San Francisco? It just isn't logical. No, love isn't about meant to be. Love is a connection, a spark. I can't explain it, but you'll just know. And you won't be able to stay away, no matter how many miles are between you." Margot winks at me and again, I frown because this love thing is way more complicated than I thought. I think of my parents and how they used to love each other. I'm sure my mom thought they were soulmates at one point and now they can hardly be in the same room together.

There's a faint smell of smoke in the air and I can see the orange glow of the campfire at the cove. The sun is starting to set and Margot and I decide to head back. We cover the distance in silence, the sound of voices getting louder as we swim closer to the shore. They're all seated under the canopy, even though the sun has fallen behind the hills. Dr. Henderson is busy cooking hot dogs on the barbeque while Mrs. Henderson pulls the condiments and potato salad from the ice chest. Margot pulls a towel from one of the chairs, wrapping it around her body and plopping into the woven polyester.

"You know people have been abducted by aliens from this river, right?" Jay starts and I roll my eyes. Jay's been telling this story for as long as I can remember. At this point, I don't know if he really believes it or if he just gets off on scaring people.

"That's highly unlikely," Lauren argues from her lounge chair, her glasses poised on her prim nose.

"No, I'm serious. You know that rundown mansion off the main road? You can't miss it, it's the only house on the road between here and town. The Bennetts used to live there. They were last seen at the docks, going out for a night ride. Their boat was found five miles downriver the next morning, crashed into the shore. No bodies, no trace anywhere but there were reports of a glowing orb hovering over the very spot the boat was found," Jay explains. I sit on my towel next to Will. He's awake and sitting cross-legged, digging a hole in the sand with a stick.

"No, you don't understand. I'm not arguing the probability of alien life forms in our universe. There's actually a formula that mathematically suggests there has to be life in other solar systems. Whether or not they're evolved enough to develop the technology needed to bend space and time in order to travel here is highly unlikely," Lauren contests and Jay gapes. I'm pretty sure he has no idea what she's talking about.

"You mean like on Back to the Future?" Jay grins, relying on his charm to outweigh his ignorance.

"Yeah, like Back to the Future. God, don't get me started on the scientific inaccuracies of that piece of crap," Lauren responds sarcastically.

"Piece of crap? That movie is a work of art, pure perfection, everything I've ever dreamed of in a cinematic masterpiece,"

Jay says in disbelief.

"They've been arguing nonstop since I woke up," Will murmurs into my ear, his warm breath tickling my ear.

"I hope Lauren is disagreeing with him on purpose, just so she can dominate him in the debate," I respond and Will chuckles.

"Alright troops, doctor your buns, these dogs are ready," Dr. Henderson says as Mrs. Henderson passes us each a paper plate. We eat, quietly submersed in conversation, and ignoring the occasional argument between Jay and Lauren. Steven wants to hike up the backside of the cliff but Mrs. Henderson vetoes the idea, claiming it's too dark and too dangerous and not even Steven can argue with her. Instead, we use the canopy to cover the folded chairs, placing rocks along the edge to prevent it from getting swept away during the night. It's our reservation, a sign to other boaters that this cove has been claimed. We ride back to the marina, the two boats side by side, warm air breathing in my ears and across my neck. Will sits across from me on our bench, his thigh against my calf, and the sky burns with fireworks we can't see.

* * *

My dad makes me work at the general store four days a week helping Josie and the rest of my time I can spend with Will. We race utility carts down the rutted dirt road and snorkel along the shoreline. Jay takes us out on the boat and Will does much better on the skis the more he practices. The sky is patched with great cotton clouds, billowing like cream against the bright blue sky, a forewarning of the storms that pummel this desert with the change of season. The summer is almost over, and the Hendersons will be gone in a week.

This morning, Steven mentioned the large cliffs behind Australia and of course, Will's intrigued. We get Jay to drive us all out to the cove with the plan to jump from the small ledges. It's only about a twelve foot drop from the smallest cliffs, and the girls and Will handle the jump nicely. Lauren and Margot jump together, flinging themselves off the rock cliff simultaneously and plummeting into the calm, deep water below. They surface, laughing at the thrill and surprised at their own bravery. Will swan dives off the ledge with a graceful fall head first and I hold my breath, unable to look as he enters the water and surfaces quickly. We all cheer and yelp at his form, even my brother seems impressed. This pisses Steven off, and now he's trying to goad Will into jumping from the highest cliff, something I've only ever done once and was terrified the whole way down.

"Oh come on, Will, don't be such a pansy-ass," Steven taunts.

"I already told you I'll do it," Will mutters. He walks in front of me up the hill to the ledge and I can see the sweat on his sundrenched skin. His back is splotched and freckled, his shoulders peeling. I quicken my step to walk beside him.

"You don't have to do this. Steven's just trying to get a rise out of you. It's not worth getting killed over," I whisper to him and he looks at me with wide eyes.

"You think I'm going to get killed?" he asks, startled. Maybe I'm being a little overdramatic, but I'm uneasy about this whole thing.

"No, not really. I'm just...I don't want you to end up an after-school special," I say and Will laughs loudly, throwing his arm around my shoulders and messing with my hair. I shove him away, feeling like a fool for being worried. Or at least for letting him know that I'm worried.

"I can handle this, trust me." Will nudges me with his shoulder, letting his arm linger on mine. I don't think he knows what he's getting himself into.

"Don't you think we should head back, Jay?" I shout up ahead at the crowd in front of us and Jay stops. "I mean, those clouds mean a storm's coming, right? Shouldn't we get off the water?"

"She's just looking out for her little boyfriend," Steven scoffs. "Did he ask you to find a way out of this for him? Because he's too chicken shit to do it himself?"

Will scowls at me and I shake my head. "Steven, you stupid idiot. You know we shouldn't be doing this. It's not safe. We need to get back to the marina."

"Is this really dangerous?" Lauren asks Jay and he glances up at the sky.

"Naw, those clouds won't turn dark for at least a couple hours or so," Jay says and I shove past him, irritated he chooses Steven's side over mine.

"Fine. Then I'm jumping too," I say and march up the hill, the others follow behind in silence and I'm so furious at their blatant stupidity I can hardly see straight.

We reach the top of the cliff and I peer over the edge. It's a thirty foot drop, the water licking the side of the cliff far below. My stomach turns and a wave of vertigo causes my head to spin. I can't back out now, not after my little temper tantrum, but I'm seriously starting to freak out a little at what I'm about to do.

"We'll jump together," Will murmurs in my ear and I close my eyes and nod my head, my heart pounding in my throat.

"Alright man, pony up. Unless you want to back out," Steven taunts.

"Nope, I'm good. You good, Cat?" Will grabs my hand firmly and I nod unable to speak. "She's good. I'm good. We're all good." I hear Will swallow and I look over at him. "Good to go."

He's stalling, his eyes telling me I can back out, that I don't have to jump but I grip his hand and narrow my eyes. I can do this.

"Ready?" I ask him and he nods.

"Are you ready?" he asks and I roll my eyes. Jesus, now I just want this to be over. I'm hot and irritated and tired of dealing with this whole ordeal. I drop his hand and take a couple steps back.

"On the count of three?" I ask and he shakes his head.

"No, that gives me three seconds to chicken out," he says, his voice shaking.

"Now!" he shouts and in a split second I'm running off the cliff, my sneakers still on my feet and everything. I scream the whole way down, my stomach in my shoes, my heart in my throat, the wind whipping my hair and then it's over.

The impact stings my legs as I plunge into the water, kicking myself to the top and breathing in great big gasps when I surface. I laugh, treading water and looking around for Will but I don't see his face anywhere. I start to panic, looking up to find the others have disappeared and I imagine the worse. Will's at the bottom of the river, and that it's my fault for letting him jump. I duck under the surface and open my eyes, searching for his bright blue swim trunks but I can't see anything through the cloudy muck. I resurface only to find it empty once again.

Oh God, please don't let him be hurt! Where is he? Where the hell is he?

"Will!" I yell, my voice quivering and tears start to roll down my cheeks. "Will?"

Suddenly, I feel a sharp pinch on the back of my leg and I scream. Will surfaces and he's laughing his ass off.

"You asshole!" I yell, trying to hit him with my fists. His face changes as he blocks my blows. "I thought you were dead! How could you do that to me? I hate you!"

"Whoa! Cat, stop!" He tries to grab my arms but I push him away, turning my back to him as I swim to shore. I can't believe he did that to me! Of all the horrible, awful things he could do, that was just the worst.

"Hey, come back! It was a joke!" Will shouts behind me but I ignore him. He grabs my foot and I try to kick free. "Are you crying?"

"No!" I lie and he lets me go. I swim to the shore and stalk back into the hills, taking a different path than the one the others will soon be traipsing down. The last thing I want is an audience right now.

I hear a slip of gravel behind me. "Wait, Catherine Rossi, wait just a goddamn second."

I stop and turn, giving Will a glaring look and cross my arms over my chest. I'll wait and I'll listen and then I'll tell him off real good and I won't speak to him for the rest of the day.

Will stops in front of me, his face dejected and worried and I can't look at his green eyes because I'll go soft. There's no excuse for what he did, faking his own death just so he can pinch me. It's not even remotely entertaining.

"Did you really think I was dead?" he asks and I nod, wiping the fresh tears from my cheeks and pissed as all hell that I'm letting him see me cry.

"Do you really hate me?" Will asks and I glance up. His face is soft, his eyes pleading and he looks destroyed. My words hurt him, and I feel awful that I said them.

"No," I say quietly as I shake my head.

"Good," Will sighs and he takes another few steps towards me. I back up instinctively and he steps towards me again until his nose is practically touching mine. I'm trembling, my chest heaving up and down when Will takes my hand.

And then I feel it, a crackling hum, an electrical impulse, a spark. Whatever it is that Margot was talking about, I feel it. He's so close I can feel his breath on my face. His hand slides around my back and he pulls me even closer. Our bodies touch, my wet tank top against his bare chest and I relax against his lanky frame.

Will leans forward and my heart begins to race. Before I can even stress about what's happening, he presses his lips to mine. I don't know what to do. My eyes watch his face, admiring the long lashes of his closed lids. His mouth is warm and gentle and he pulls away. He opens his eyes and smiles and I smile awkwardly back. It wasn't such a big deal, the kiss, nothing earth shattering or anything and I scrunch up my nose. Maybe I didn't do it right?

"I've never done that before," I say and Will grins.

"It was okay for your first time," Will reassures and I laugh because I know he's lying. He's touched boobs, for crying out loud.

"Yeah right, it was awful," I say, frowning a little as Will leans back.

"It wasn't awful," Will says. "You're supposed to move your mouth a little, kind of relax your lips."

"Can we try again?" I ask and that damn blush creeps into my cheeks. I don't want Will thinking I'm a terrible kisser because of a technicality.

"We can practice all week, if you want."

1987 – THAT TIME YOU SNUCK
IN THROUGH MY WINDOW

The average price for a new car is around $10,000.

Madonna releases her second feature film, "Who's That Girl" and files for divorce from husband Sean Penn.

Debbie Gibson becomes the youngest artist ever to write, produce, and perform a # 1 hit single with her song "Foolish Beat."

* * *

The sun burns with magnificent heat.
The water ripples in soft waves.
The hills bend and curve,
holding the river in a tight embrace.
She is my summer.
My heat, my waves, my tight embrace.

Happy Birthday, Cat. I'll see you next summer.
Love,
Will

Earth to Cat? Hello? Is anyone home?" Josie snaps her fingers and I open my eyes. "I said, can you restock the snacks? We're selling out of s'more stuff like crazy."

"Yeah," I mutter as I lean the broom up against the counter.

"Are you on drugs?" she asks, surveying my features intently.

"No, I'm not on drugs," I respond exasperated. Heather, Steven and his brothers sneak off behind the bleachers at school to smoke pot and they're always trying to get me to go with them, but my brother would kill me if he found out I was getting high. I know this because he told me. He said, "Cat, I will kill you if I find out you're getting high." He graduated a couple weeks ago. Dad got him a new jeep for graduation. It's a bribe. Dad's hoping it will make him stay at the marina. I think it's working.

"Right." She doesn't believe me. "Well, I have plans tonight, so get a move on it. Just because you refuse to have a life, doesn't mean I have to."

It's late June and Will's family should be here soon. They always show up after Will's birthday and I assume it's so he can have a big party with all his real friends back home. He's sixteen now and I wonder if he drives, if he still plays basketball, if he's kissed anyone else this year, if he still wants to kiss me. I think about him a lot, especially the kissing.

I walk into the stockroom and load up on marshmallows and chocolate bars when I hear the bell on the front door chime. Will!

I hurry out, my arms full of the provisions, to find Steven standing at the counter.

"We're closed, Steven," I say, dumping the cargo onto the counter. Steven runs his hand through his thick black hair. He's shirtless, like most people around here during the summer but it bugs me. He's been working out and he likes to show it off.

"I have to give Josie a message from Ricky," Steven replies.

"Why didn't he call the store?" Josie asks.

"He has to work late, start of the season and everything," Steven shrugs. "He can't go out on the water tonight."

"So he sent you instead? He can't take a minute to pick up the phone?" Josie says, her voice heated, her hands upon her hips.

"Hey! I'm just the messenger," Steven responds. "I was driving down anyway and he asked me to give you the message."

"Why would you be driving down to the marina at this hour?" Josie presses. She and Ricky have been fighting a lot lately. He's always working and she's in a perpetual state of irritation. She plays The Smiths constantly, the tormented lyrics and haunting melodies pouring from the small cassette player under the counter.

"I have my reasons," Steven says with a coy grin, his shiny brown eyes peering into mine. His stare makes me uncomfortable, like he can see right through me. I turn and hurry back to the stockroom to hide from his dark eyes.

I take my time, staring at the boxes of graham crackers, hoping he'll leave when I hear a small rap on the door. It's probably my dad here to close up the register so I stalk out of the stockroom, expecting to see my father.

I'm met with feathered fizzy green staring back at me instead. Will's face is a portrait of anticipation, and his lips pull into a nervous grin when he sees me. He puts his hand on the glass of the door, giving a slight wave and I beam, exuberance creeping into every inch of my body.

"It's open!" I yell and Will tries the door but it doesn't budge and he shakes his head. What the hell? I look over at Steven and he hides his face in a magazine but I can see in his eyes that he's smiling.

"Oh, grow up, Steven," I mutter. I set the crackers on the counter and quickly unlock the door.

"Hey!" Will says, stepping inside. "We just got here. I just wanted to say hi." His eyes dance across my face. He's wearing one of his polo shirts, the royal blue collar pulled up. In these clothes he's San Francisco Will, not river Will, not my Will.

"Hi," I say with a shy smile.

"Hi," he responds, his hands in his pockets.

"Hi," Steven barks from the counter and I turn to glare at him for interrupting.

"Hey, Steven! It's so great to see you," Will says through tight lips. "Hey Josie!" She mumbles a greeting and slips into the stockroom, her whole attitude shifting since hearing Ricky's message.

"Sorry about locking you out. Never can be too careful, there could be creeps trying to get in," Steven says, his voice dripping with sarcasm.

"Do you need a shirt, or something? I can loan you one, if you want," Will shrugs and Steven slams down the magazine. I sense a diversion is needed.

"Um, I have to finish closing up and then I can meet you on the swings," I say to Will, trying to change the subject.

"I'll just wait here, if it's okay," Will says. He walks over to the counter and grabs the boxes of crackers and starts putting away the snacks with a smile.

"We're planning a game of Capture the Flag for Thursday. There'll be no moon that night so it'll be extra dark out. You guys in?" Steven asks me and I look at Will.

"By no moon, you mean a new moon, right?" Will asks sarcastically. "There's no such thing as no moon. You know the moon is always there, right?"

"Is your collar supposed to be popped up like that, or are you hiding a deformity?" Steven responds and I roll my eyes.

"Oh my God, enough. We're in. We can get the girls to play, too. But you can't be on my team," I say to Will, a devious smile tugging on my lips. "You glow in the dark. You're a liability."

"Ha. Ha," Will says dryly. "But I'm super fast and agile, like a gazelle."

"Well, prove it. On the battlefield," Steven grumbles.

"The battlefield?" Will snorts. "O-kay."

"Thursday, asshole, you're going down," Steven says with a sneer before thundering out of the store.

"Is he for real?" Will asks incredulously.

"The Youngs are very serious about Capture the Flag. I'm talking war paint, fatigues, this isn't a game," I respond, gathering the empty boxes. I'm only partially exaggerating. Steven and his brothers are very competitive. Once, Michael and Steven got into a full on fist fight during a game of Risk.

"Well, he may have brawn, but I have brains," Will winks. "Big, huge brains."

* * *

My heart pounds in my chest as I glance behind me, sweat dripping into my eyes. I whip my head back around and stumble to a crouch behind a trailer to catch my breath. Margot was right behind me a minute ago. Luckily, this year she's obsessed with Madonna and I heard her bracelets jingling before she got close. She almost snagged my sash though, her finger grazing the strip of torn fabric tucked into the waistband of my cutoff jean shorts. The rule states the sash must be apprehended so I'm still in the game.

The rules to Capture the Flag are simple. Two flags in the form of old white t-shirts are set at opposite sides of the campground. The first team to get the other team's flag wins. We scribbled our names on slips of paper and Josie pulled the teams. I'm grouped with Lauren, Jay, Steven, and Steven's brother, Henry. He graduated with my brother last month and dates Heather sometimes. Heather dates lots of people. She claims she's too much of a free spirit to be tied down to one person.

Will, Heather, Margot, and two more of Steven's brothers, Michael and Little Jimmy, make up the other team. Ricky and Josie were supposed to play too, but Ricky didn't show, so Josie said she'd referee instead. I'm a little uneasy Heather and Will are on the same team. It's really dark out here, people could get hurt. Or accidentally fall into each other's arms, or boobs...

Stop it Cat! You don't own him.

Will's not mine, not by a long shot. If he wants to kiss Heather, he's perfectly at liberty to do so. It's not my business.

This fact doesn't stop the burning jealousy in my stomach. It doesn't stop the frantic need to get the stupid flag and end this game before something can happen between them. I've seen Heather in action. Will doesn't stand a chance.

I can see the other team's flag unattended, the white cotton draped across the branches of a low sagebrush and I'm about to run behind the brick building that serves as the public restroom when I hear my brother whistle. It's a warning.

It's a good strategy to have someone hide in the shadows and protect the flag and I try to rationalize who they picked for this position. I rule out Michael or Little Jimmy, they're too aggressive to play defense. That leaves Heather, Margot or Will and since Margot was behind me just minutes ago, I know it can't be her.

Will or Heather.

Will and Heather?

Will and Heather making out behind the bushes and that's why the flag is unattended...

Ugh! What is wrong with me? I shake my head and try to concentrate. Taking into account Jay's warning, I decide to sneak around the edge of the brush instead of cutting across the gravel path. I double back and dart across the path into the bushes, maneuvering through the brush as silently as possible though thorny branches snag at my skin. I can see the white flag. Just a few more feet and I'll make the dash.

"Stop." I hear Will's low voice warn but I can't see him. I drop to the ground, looking for his pearly skin or sandy hair and I can't find him anywhere. Will's the guard. He's hiding and he's close. And worst of all, he can see me.

I weigh my options. In three to five seconds, he will rush me and snag my sash. I'm actually not sure why he hasn't yet, but I can only deduce that he heard Jay's warning whistle too. He knows I'm not alone.

Jay! I'll create a distraction, Will will come after me, leaving the flag free for Jay to take.

I spring up and run, a mad dash to the flag, just as Jay comes barreling out from behind the restrooms. Shit! We had the same plan, and now we're both exposed and out in the open.

Margot appears out of nowhere, and snatches Jay's sash. She yelps with triumph and Jay curses, falling to his knees on the gravel in depraved defeat. Double shit!

I put my head down and run until my heart feels like it's exploding and my legs are wobbly. I'm almost there, when Will pops out from behind the sagebrush. I quickly put on the brakes and he stares me down. There's an antagonizing glint in his eye and a smug grin on his lips, like he knows he has me beat.

Determination flares in my lungs, burns in my face and I want that flag in my hand more than I've ever wanted anything in my life. I narrow my eyes and dart to the left just as Lauren jets around the building to snag Margot's sash.

Yes! Now's the chance! While he's distracted, I change direction and sprint to the right, heaving myself at the sagebrush. Will lunges for my sash, his hand catching my arm but I yank it away and regain my balance. He reaches for me again and clips the hem of my shirt. My foot slips in the gravel and I fall hard to my knee. God, it hurts, a warm trickle of blood oozing from the gash but I grit my teeth and am back on my feet in an instant. I can hear Jay yelling at Lauren to get the flag. No! It's mine. This game is mine.

I reach my hand out to grab the flag, elation bubbling in my chest when two strong arms latch around my waist. Will pulls me back, falling to the ground and bringing me down on top of him. His chest moves beneath me, my own haggard gasps escaping my mouth as I lay there stunned.

Lauren gets to the brush a millisecond after I was supposed to and snags the shirt, holding it up in her hand and cheering. Jay picks her up, swinging her around like an old time movie. I roll off of Will, collapsing on the gravel beside him and neither one of us moves. I'm exhausted, deflated and hurt, and I'm furious. I can't believe Will took me down like that!

I hear the crunching of gravel and I see my brother's big hand in my face, offering to help me up. His proud grin hovers over me and I can't even celebrate our success because I didn't really win. I let Will get the better of me. Just like always.

I clutch Jay's hand and he pulls me up, a wave of dizziness pummeling my head and I fall against his big body.

"Whoa there, Kit Cat," Jay says when I sit back down on the gravel. Will pops up, his eyes filled with fear.

He crawls over to me, concern on his sweat-stained face. He notices my bloody knee and I hear him curse under his breath. "Oh shit, are you hurt?"

I shake my head and close my eyes, willing the dizziness to go away when I feel a hand on my thigh. My eyes pop open to find Will's hot, dirt-smudged hands gently inspecting my knee and I'm dizzy now for a whole new reason. His thumb presses into my thigh, sending shivers right up my legs to my belly. My heart thumps against my ribs and I can't breathe. And I don't want him to stop.

Will looks up at me, the wide green circles burning with care and all my previous fury is dissolved.

"What did you do, asshole?" Steven storms towards us and I roll my eyes. Oh, for Pete's sake!

"He didn't do anything," I explain. "I fell."

"My dad has a first aid kit," Will says and moves to help me to my feet. His arm wraps around my waist and he lifts me from the ground.

"Little Jimmy has a first aid kit in his truck." Steven grabs my arm and I feel Will's arm tighten around me.

"My dad's a doctor, I think he knows a little bit more about first aid than Little Jimmy," Will snaps.

"Enough! Both of you just shut up!" Their eyes are glued to me, shocked at my tone. "I want to go home."

"You heard the lady," my brother says as he takes Will's place beside me. "You can walk, right?"

I nod, clenching my jaw as pain radiates in my kneecap. Blood streams down my leg and Lauren hands me the t-shirt turned flag to press to the cut. Oh man, it hurts! It hurts like a son-of-a-bitch, but I pretend it doesn't.

Will kneels before me. He takes the shirt from my hand and wraps it around my knee, knotting the cotton tightly. He looks up at me with apologetic eyes and I want to blurt out every thought spinning through my head right now. How I like the way it feels when he touches my thigh. How I want him to sweep me off my feet and kiss me passionately, like Richard Gere in *An Officer and a Gentleman*. Instead, I hobble back to our house, leaning heavily on my brother.

My knee is the size of a grapefruit when my dad greets us at the door. He helps me inside while Jay rushes to get the first aid kit from the closet.

"See, it's not so bad," my dad says as he pats my leg dry, a thick bandage covering my wound. "There you go, all fixed up."

He kisses me on the forehead and cleans up the wrappers and swabs. I have to stay out of the water until my knee is good and scabbed over. And I ruined a perfectly good pair of sneakers.

Later, there's a light rap on my bedroom window, three soft knocks. I hobble over to open my blinds and find Will's face smiling back at me. I slide open the pane and he holds up an IT'S-IT. I smile so big, my cheeks hurt and I pop the corner of the screen out so he can hand me the ice cream.

"How did you get this? The store's closed," I whisper and Will flashes me a mischievous grin.

"I forgot to tell you, I have superpowers. I can walk through walls," Will teases.

"Then why did you waste your time knocking on my window?" I retort.

"In case you were naked or something," he shrugs and I feel my face burn. There's an awkward silence, he shifts his feet and I can't look him in the eyes.

"So, are you okay?" Will asks finally, his hand running through his hair.

"Yeah, I'm fine," I respond.

"Can I come in?" Will's voice is quiet.

"What, like through my window?" I ask and Will nods.

"I ...I don't know," I respond, surprised at the request. I doubt my dad would approve of Will in my room.

At night.

With the door shut.

"It's okay, I understand if you're mad at me. I'm really sorry Cat. I just got caught up in the game, you know? And I couldn't stand the thought of Steven winning," Will rambles. "I feel really bad I hurt you."

"You didn't hurt me," I say defensively and the minute the words leave my mouth, I realize I sound like a snot. Will twists his fingers and I sigh, popping the screen out completely and leaning it against the side of the house. I sit on my bed, open the ice cream wrapper and take a bite of the ice cream sandwich. It's soft and chewy and dripping so I lick around the edge.

Will stares at me for a minute, unsure if he's invited in, I guess. I nod my head, motioning for him to hurry up. He climbs in clumsily and closes the window behind him before plopping himself down on my bed.

"Shhh!" I say and I reach over to my cassette player to put on some music to muffle our voices.

"What the hell are you listening to?" Will asks. I take another bite of my ice cream before answering.

"Debbie Gibson, I think," I respond.

"Oh no, Cat. How can you subject yourself to such torture?" Will's laughing now and I can't help but grin too.

"I don't know, Heather gave it to me," I shrug. Will inspects my glass bottle collection. They're lined up along the back of my dresser in all different shapes and sizes, curved, angular, tall, skinny, short and fat. Some are filled with shells or used as flower vases or to burn incense. Some are just pretty, the multicolored glass bubbled and warped and causing the light to refract in odd ways.

"Hey! You still have this?" Will picks up the small white shell, the one with our names on it. If he takes another look at the bottles, he'll see the friendship bracelet tied around one of the necks. I wore it until the thread snapped. The mood ring's there too, slipped over a few sticks of lavender incense and the poem is hidden in the small jewelry box just inches from his fingers. I wonder if he remembers what he wrote last summer. A lot can change in a year.

"I have all of them," I say softly, unable to look at his face. "I have to wash my hands. I'll be right back."

I shut the door behind me and limp to the bathroom, my knee pulsing with every step. I take one look at myself in the mirror and almost shit a brick. I scrub my hands and arms and splash water on my face and armpits, practically giving myself a sponge bath before slathering on a bunch of deodorant, just to be safe. I pull my hair out of the braid, my scalp sighing in relief. I let it fall loose around my shoulders, and stare at myself in the mirror.

What am I doing? This isn't a date. This is Will. He's seen me waterlogged and sunburned after a day on the river. He's seen me muddy and sweaty after a long hike. He's seen me pee in the bushes, for Christ's sake.

My house is quiet, except for the low hum of my cassette player drifting down the hall. I limp back into my room, thankful I'm at the opposite end of the hall from my dad and Jay. Will's sitting in my bean bag chair in the corner, playing this ring toss water game that was sitting on my bookshelf. He pushes the button, sending the tiny rings swirling through the water and trying to get them to fall on the plastic posts.

"I beat this game twice while you were gone," Will says without looking up. I sit down on my bed, propping my injured leg up on the mattress and lean back into the pillows lined along the white iron Daybed frame. A slow, melodic plinking of piano behind a soprano croon now plays on my cassette player, but I don't have this album.

"Did you change the music?" I ask and Will shrugs.

"Maybe," Will grins mischievously, his eyes still on the stupid game. "That pop shit was wearing on my nerves."

"Fair enough," I say, listening to the lyrics. "Is this Styx?"

"Maybe," Will says again, still refusing to look at me, so I stop the music and pull the tape from the player. Written on the rectangular label in neat, tiny letters there's a message.

Songs to Remind Cat of her Super Awesome Friend Will. Happy

Birthday.

"You made me a mixtape?" I ask, incredulous. I can't wait to see what other songs he chose for me.

"Well, your taste in music obviously needs help," Will says, taking the tape from my hand and putting it back in the player. He hits play and sinks into the opposite side of my bed, by my outstretched leg, and squeezes my big toe. I instinctively jerk away, pulling my knee and wincing at the sharp sting.

"Sorry!" Will apologizes.

"I'm just ticklish and having a brother who likes to torment me makes me leery of anyone near my weaknesses," I explain. Will smiles his devious grin and I'm immediately sorry I told him.

"Oh relax, Cat. I won't tell anyone you have a weakness. Your secret's safe with me," Will says.

"Pinky promise?" I ask doubtfully and his eyes glimmer in my softly lit room.

"You don't trust me?" His hand slides over the top of my ankle, causing my skin to ripple with goosebumps. I'm trapped, caught between wishing he'd touch me more and plotting my escape. It's not like I can make a quick getaway with my bum knee, but I might be able to deliver a swift kick to the head with my other foot if tickling ensues.

"I'm not going to tickle you," Will soothes, his eyes boring into mine. His voice is low and rich, like I imagine hot chocolate would sound like. You know, if hot chocolate could talk, of course.

He hovers his hand up my shin. Again with the stinking goosebumps, and when his hand slips around to lightly grasp the back of my knee, I almost pass out.

Breathe, Cat, damn it!

He carefully peels the bandage away from my skin and I don't even flinch, even though I feel the sting. He inspects the wound, his face close to my leg, his breath on my skin, his eyes fixated on the bruising and swelling surrounding the large gash and series of shallow cuts before affixing the tape back in place. He smiles at me, and I can't help but grin shyly back as his hand trails back down my leg.

"Ouch!" Will says suddenly, yanking his hand away from my leg. He eyes his hand and I'm completely confused when a coy smile tugs at his lips.

"What?" I ask warily.

"Oh, just your leg stubble. It's like a million little daggers clawing at my skin," Will says overdramatically. "Cat! Are you the real Teen Wolf?"

"This is why I don't trust you. This is why I need pinky promises, because you trick me into liking you and then you say something mean like that." I swing my bad leg away from him as he chuckles. I started shaving my legs last summer because Steven made the same exact smart-ass comment, called me Teen Wolf and everything.

"Alright, alright," Will scoots over until his leg is touching mine. He licks his thumb and holds out his pinky. "Cat, I promise you, I will never, ever tell anyone about your ticklish feet."

I hold Will's gaze for what seems like an eternity, his face very close to mine, before I do the same and hook my finger to his.

"Seal it," I dare, and my voice is barely audible. Will flashes me a sly grin and I'm filled with a mixture of excitement and nervousness and dread.

He presses his lips to mine and I sigh against his soft, full mouth. I try to remember what Will taught me last year and what I've heard Josie and Heather talking about at the store. It's all forgotten though, as soon as Will licks at my bottom lip with his tongue.

A hundred little explosions go off under my skin and I freeze. Oh crap, he wants to French kiss. I feel it again, a soft pull of lush warmth across my lip. I inhale sharply and then, Will's tongue is in my mouth. And he tastes like heaven, like rainbow sherbet, sweet and smooth and melting on my tongue.

The kiss is messy and wet, and I feel like one of those gaping fish under the dock. I'm not doing it right. Will's hands move to my cheeks. He tilts my head slightly and the space between us disappears. We're sealed now, connected. Will leans in closer pushing me back against the pillows and I gasp a little when his body presses into mine. His hand slides over my stomach and hip and then up my spine and my whole body aches to get closer to him. I push my hips up into his, and rub my legs together and I feel like my thighs are going to explode. Will is everywhere, his hand circuiting my back, his breath hot in my mouth, his hip bone grinding into my thigh.

Or is that his hip bone grinding into my stomach?

Wait, is that his...

Holy erection! Will has a boner. My heart practically flatlines when I figure this out. Maybe this is too much, maybe we should stop, maybe I'm not ready for this.

Maybe I am.

Will pulls away, his eyes searching my face. His palm rests against my cheek and I like this tender touch.

"What's wrong? Are you okay? Is this okay?" Will asks in a hurry and I can't help the smile that's stretching across my face. It's kind of funny, this whole making out thing. I mean, touching tongues and boners and exploding thighs.

"What?" he asks and I shake my head, my face burning red. "You have to tell me, you know. I'll tickle you if you don't."

"I can feel it," I blurt out, covering my face with my hands. I can't believe I'm telling him this.

"It?" Will wonders.

"*It*," I say emphatically and push my hips up against him so he gets my drift.

He groans, shifting away from me and I feel lonely.

"It's a perfectly normal reaction in an aroused male," Will says and I peek through my fingers to see him shove his hand down his pants and adjust the goods and I watch. Good God, I can't tear my eyes away from his crotch.

"I'm not making fun, I promise. But the whole thing is kinda funny," I argue, wishing I would have just kept kissing him.

"Funny? You think kissing me is funny?" Will asks defensively. "Weren't you turned on too? I mean, you seemed to enjoy it, especially the way you were dry humping my leg."

"I was not dry humping your leg!" I say indignantly, my arms crossing across my chest. Will stares down at his hands, hands that were just rubbing all over my back and stomach and I feel like a total ass.

"I was turned on too," I spill before hiding my face with my hands again. Oh God, this is so embarrassing. "I mean, I liked it. Making out with you is nice."

Will's quiet for a full minute and I'm afraid to look. His fingers gently wrap around my wrists and he tugs at my hands.

"Cat, come on, look at me," Will says quietly, and I allow him to pull my hands away from my face. "It's okay, you know. To be turned on. And you can trust me. I don't want you to ever feel weird around me. I won't ever make you do anything you don't want to do."

"It's not that I don't want to. I've never…done this. I've never felt these things before," I try to explain.

"Never? You've never been turned on?" Will asks and I frown, embarrassment just won't leave me alone today. Oh well, since we're spilling secrets.

"Top Gun," I say quickly and Will grins. "That part when they kiss and then there's the licking and yeah, that was pretty hot. I had to watch it sitting next to my brother and my mom. I couldn't even enjoy it properly."

"I really like you, Cat," Will says with a soft sincerity that makes my chest swell.

"I like you too," I respond. "You're my best friend."

"Friend?" Will asks, those green circles boring into mine. I want him to be more. So much more.

I know this is just his vacation, but for two months, maybe Will can be more than just my friend. For two months, maybe Will can be mine.

* * *

W hat do you mean, we're growing apart?" Josie whispers into the phone. I try not to eavesdrop as I flip through a magazine, the faces of teen heartthrobs glossy on the pages. I'm not really looking at the pictures, I just don't want Josie to know I'm listening.

"I know, just don't leave me, Ricky," Josie says. "Please! I can't believe you're giving up on us."

It's so strange to see strong, confident Josie begging someone for anything. I don't like it. It's not like her. I want to hug her or something and try to make things better, but she'd probably bite my head off so I pretend to read my magazine instead.

My stupid job at the general store sucks up all my time and I hate it. I've been here since noon, taking a break to meet my dad and brother at the café for dinner but I still have three hours to go before I can leave.

Will hangs out with me when I'm working but I feel like he's wasting his summer. Sometimes the girls hang out too and when there's a lull in customers, we play cards or dominoes, and the days pass quickly when they keep me company.

Today, however, the Hendersons took a boat ride down to the dam so it's just me and Josie, and I feel like I'm stuck in *The Neverending Story*.

"Is there someone else?" Josie says frantically and I can hear it in her voice. She's going to cry again. "Don't hang up! I'm sorry, just - Ricky?"

"Motherfucker," she says through clenched teeth and slams down the phone.

"Josie, I can close up. Why don't you just go home?" I say quietly and Josie wipes at her face, her eyes tired and worn.

"It's fine. Everything's fine," Josie says and before I can second guess myself, I wrap my arms around her. She's stiff a minute before collapsing into my shoulder. Josie's the closest thing I have to a sister. I can't stand to see her hurting.

"Go home and eat some ice cream. It will help, I promise," I say and Josie chuckles, wiping at her face with her shirt.

"Are you sure you'll be okay?" Josie asks and I nod.

"My dad's in his office if I need anything," I say and Josie grabs her things and jets, leaving me in the empty store.

My dad comes by to lock up most of the cash from the register. When he asks me where Josie is, I tell him she's sick and went home early and he believes me. He always believes me and I feel really horrible stretching the truth when I know he trusts me so much.

It's just past eight when Will comes bounding into the store, his nose and cheeks are pink and his hair is freshly wet. And he's shirtless.

"I fell off the dock," he laughs and I can't help but laugh with him.

"Damn, and I missed it?" I say. Man, I hate this job!

"Dad pulled me on skis. First time he tried to tow a skier. He did pretty good too. Rachel tried to ski but she couldn't get up. It was hilarious, better than Goofy on skis," Will laughs and I think of last Fourth of July on the cove. This year we barbecued and played volleyball here in the marina. Maybe we'll get to see the fireworks next year.

Who knows how he'll feel when he comes back next year. What if he meets someone he likes kissing more than me? What if he doesn't come back at all?

"Your nose is peeling," I choke out, and he reaches for my hand.

"Come on, let's get out of here," he says and pulls me towards the door.

"I can't. Josie went home early, I have to close up the store," I say.

Will stops and turns, his face close to mine and I'm hypnotized. "Then close up the store."

No one will know. I'll leave the lights on and my dad will

think I'm in the back or something. I can come back later and shut the lights off. Probably won't have any customers anyway.

I lock the door and wrap the stretchy cord that holds the key around my wrist. Will grins as we walk to the docks. I'm not sure what Will has planned but I'm just so glad to be free of the store. Even the sweltering, muggy heat can't weigh me down.

He leads me to his family's boat anchored in the slip and we climb on board. The ice chest is perched on the bench, still full of soda and beer and juice boxes. Will pulls a beer from the chest and hands it to me before taking one for himself.

"You drink beer?" I ask him.

"No, do you?" he responds and I shake my head. "Do you want to try it?"

I shrug. Beer's not such a big deal, my dad and Jay drink beer when they watch sports games or on holidays.

"We'll try it together," I say. Will grins excitedly and I'm a little excited too.

We sit on the floor of the boat, and crack open our cans. We stare at each other for a minute before Will raises his can and I do the same. I drink, a big gulp like I'm drinking water and I almost throw up. It's bitter and tastes like soggy bread that's been marinating in pee. Or that's what I imagine it tastes like. I've never actually had soggy pee bread.

"Ugh! It's horrible! Why would anyone drink this on purpose?" I remark. Will shrugs, taking another drink before squishing his face up.

"It's not that bad," Will says and I snort.

"Is that why you make that face when you drink it?" I tease and Will rolls his eyes, downing the can in a matter of seconds.

"Your turn," Will challenges and I don't think I can drink the whole thing. I seriously might gag. *Oh, buck up Cat. If Will can do it, you can*, I tell myself and choke down the rest of the beer.

"I don't feel any different," I say as Will spreads out on the carpeted floor beneath us, the boat gently swaying as the water laps at the side of the dock.

"Me neither," Will frowns. "Beer's a bust."

"Maybe we need more?" I suggest and lay down beside him but he isn't quick to drink another. I look up at the wide expanse above, the millions of stars like pinpoints against the black backdrop. I love the night sky out here.

Will turns towards me, his hand tentatively sliding across my belly. He nuzzles my neck and I forget everything. I forget Will's not really mine and that he's leaving soon. If I turn my head, I will surely be making out with him in the next two seconds.

He inches closer, his bare skin against my arm and I turn to face him. In his eyes I see sadness reflected. He pulls me closer, his arm squeezing beneath me to twine around my waist, my chest pressed against his, our legs twisted and he kisses me. His mouth moves slowly, like honey poured from a stubborn spout, and I want him to use his tongue again.

Maybe it's the beer, but I feel brave so I ask for it.

I part my lips and lick at his, and he's quick to respond. His tongue rolls with mine, his free hand grips my hip and then slides to the small of my back. Sparks shoot up my spine everywhere he touches so I touch him too.

Trailing my hand down his side, he gasps when I touch the smooth muscles of his stomach, and he pulls me closer. His hand travels up my side and over my stomach and then between my boobs, his touch specifically avoiding those places I want it most.

Just then we hear the dock creak, the sound of thudded footsteps and we freeze. Then there are voices, familiar voices. Voices that are going to be very close to the boat in two and half seconds. We quickly untangle and roll onto our backs, looking like two panting star gazers now, instead of the heap of hormones we were a moment ago.

I look at Will, his eyes smiling as he takes deep breaths. I cover my mouth because I want to laugh at how loud I'm breathing.

"I'm not saying it's impossible, I'm just saying that if Lochness really existed, they'd have found some kind of remains by now. It only makes sense that-" Lauren's voice stops and she stares down at us from the dock. "What are you doing?"

"Star gazing," Will and I say at the same time and Lauren narrows her eyes. She's suspicious and smart, a terrifying combination. I sit up to find Jay standing behind her, his hand quickly dropping hers the moment he sees my face.

"You're supposed to be at the store," Jay says but I ignore him.

"Why are you holding hands?" I ask, standing up. Lauren suddenly finds her feet fascinating. Jay and Lauren. Lauren? But they have nothing in common. And they argue all the time and she's completely not his type.

And that's exactly why he likes her.

I wait, Jay glaring at me, a sibling standoff as he decides what to do. He could rat me out, but not unless he wants to come clean too.

"I won't tell if you won't," Jay offers.

"Deal," I say quickly before he can second-guess his decision. Jay won't tell. He doesn't want to deal with my dad anymore than I do.

Lauren climbs into the boat and pulls the remaining cans of beer from the ice chest, handing them to Jay.

"You'd better get home, Cat. Dad's gonna know something's up if you don't get home on time," Jay orders and I roll my eyes. Yeah, yeah, I know.

❋ ❋ ❋

I'm going to miss you so much," Will whispers into my ear, his arms crushing me to his chest. He wrote down his phone number on a piece of paper and told me to call, that we could talk over the phone and it would almost be the same. I already know I can't call him. There's no way my dad will let me call Will long distance. Besides, long distance relationships never work. It's better this way. No obligations, no expectations, no long distance bullshit.

"I feel like I'm losing a limb," I mumble into the collar of his polo shirt, the emotion welling in my chest.

"I'll be back before you know it," he says and then he's gone. Again.

I trudge my way back to the store, the hot sun burning on my back when I hear Josie's voice boom out over the marina. She's irate and screaming and I run to the store to see what's going on.

They're all on the sidewalk in front of the store. Steven's holding Josie's arms, holding her back from something and my eyes shift to Ricky, his arms wrapped around Heather, restricting her arms.

No, he's not holding her back. He holds her like he's comforting her, gentle and protective.

Like he loves her.

"How could you do this?" Josie shouts, her eyes wide and furious.

"Josie, please," Heather begs, tears and snot pouring from her face.

"I knew something was going on, I fucking knew it!" Josie shouts. "You both disgust me!"

"She's pregnant, Josie," Ricky says quietly. Josie blinks, shrinking back from the confrontation.

Holy Days of our Lives! Heather's pregnant? With Ricky's baby? I thought she was dating Henry.

"I'm so sorry, we never meant for any of this to happen," Heather sobs and Josie laughs, a maniacal tremor from her lips.

"Oh, it was an accident? The months of sexual intercourse was an accident?" Josie asks incredulously.

"We love each other," Ricky says.

"Fuck you, you bastard!" Josie screams, clawing at Steven's arm. She's going to kill him! I run over to help Steven push her inside the store where she crumbles to the floor. He's destroyed her. She put her whole life into that boy and he betrayed her.

I'm already too attached to Will. He's the only friend I have, the only part of the whole damn year that I look forward to. I don't think he would ever hurt me on purpose, but I have to get myself in check or I'm going to end up like Josie, betrayed by a boy I never really had.

It's for the best, the only solution that makes any sense. I put up a wall and wrap my heart in a tiny cocoon.

I detach.

1988 – THAT TIME WE ALMOST
GOT ARRESTED

A US Postage stamp costs 24 cents.

*Columbia records releases Journey's greatest hits album,
which remains the band's best-selling record.*

*George H. W. Bush becomes the first serving Vice President
to be elected President of the US since 1836.*

* * *

S o Jay said you have a boyfriend?" my mom asks. I slam
on the brakes and come to a screeching halt on the corner
of Tropicana and Las Vegas Blvd.

"When did you talk to Jay?" I ask her. Jay and I drive into
Vegas one or two weekends a month to see my mom. She
bought me a car for my sixteenth birthday, a white VW Rabbit.
It's not new but it has air conditioning. We've never had a car
with air conditioning before. The only problem is it's a stick.
Jay tried to teach me how to drive it, but I'm still a little jumpy
off the clutch.

"He drove up after his finals last week." Jay took a few
finance classes at the Community College last semester.

I adjust the radio, trying to find a song I don't despise but
all I can find is stupid pop bullshit. Why can't one band on the
radio write a decent fricking song?

"It's a green light, Kit Cat," my mom says. I punch the gas and
ease off the clutch and the wheels spin on the hot pavement.
She inhales sharply and digs her manicured nails into the
dashboard. I make a quick left and pull into the parking lot of

the Tropicana. I park by the door but my mom refuses to leave the car.

"I'm not leaving until you tell me about this boyfriend." She pulls a cigarette from her purse and places it between her painted lips. She lights up, rolls down the window and looks at me expectantly.

"It was one date. Josie's brother, Jake. We went bowling. Not my boyfriend. Not a big deal." I don't tell her how he kissed me afterward and then told everyone at school I was his girlfriend. I had to set him straight and now Josie's acting like I've committed crimes against humanity or something.

"And what about Steven? Is he still trying to woo you?" my mom teases, flicking the ash from her cigarette out the window.

I've been trying really hard not to think about Will this year. I went on a couple dates, just guys from school, but every time I think about Will, I think about how I'll never be able to do the silly high school stuff with him. He'll never ditch school with me to go get a soft serve at the Dairy Burger. He'll never take me on a date or to a Friday football game. And he'll never take me to prom.

So when Steven asked me to Junior prom, I said yes. I had heard Journey's *Don't Stop Believin'* on the radio that morning, track number seven on my *Songs That Remind Cat of her Super Awesome Friend Will* mixtape and I was missing him so much I couldn't breathe. I was mad at him for having this power over me and mad at myself for letting him. I don't know why I said yes. Maybe it was spite or to prove to myself that Will doesn't control my life. Whatever the reason, I said yes to Steven Young.

My mom bought me a dress with lace and satin and pleats. I curled and teased my hair, just like it said to do in Cosmo. Steven wore a tuxedo and bought me a corsage. I brought my Polaroid and snapped pictures of the crepe papered extravaganza. Steven smoked pot with his friends behind the gymnasium and drank whiskey from a flask he carried in his pocket. And we danced.

Everything was fine and then that song came on. That fricking Styx song, number one on my mixtape, *Lady*. I wanted it to be Will so bad that I wrapped my arms around Steven's neck and I buried my face in his shoulder and I pretended. I imagined it was Will's shoulder my face was pressed against, his hair I was running my fingers through, his hands sliding over the small of my back.

And then Steven kissed me, a sloppy, wet kiss with tongue. This shocked me back into reality, and then all I could feel were Steven's big clumsy hands groping my ass and his hot breath on my ear while he slurred the lyrics. I was disgusted with myself. I spent the next half hour crying in the bathroom before asking my photography teacher to call my brother. Luckily, Steven had gone out to toke up again and didn't even notice I was gone.

"Steven can't take a hint," I mumble, collapsing onto the steering wheel. "I don't know what to do, Mom."

"Just be honest, honey. Steven likes you because you're a wonderful person. It's nice that he cares so much." My mom runs her fingers through my hair and I want to argue with her. I don't want it to be nice. I don't want Steven to like me because I can never return the gesture. I can never be what he wants me to be.

Because deep down, blooming within the cocoon, no matter how much I try to deny it, I know in my heart I already belong to someone else. Someone who is waiting for me at the marina right now.

As much as I'm dying to see him, I am determined not to let Will seduce me. We're friends and that's it. That's enough. No kissing of any kind. It's better this way, detached and guarded. No obligations, no expectations, no pain.

I speed back to the marina, slowing to an unbearable 25 mph through town before zipping along the uneven pavement. The cops in town are real sticklers for speed limits.

I don't even bother going home first. I park my car beside

the big black Mercedes-Benz and hurry up the steps to the front door. Three swift raps later, Will's standing before me, his strong jaw covered in stubble, his hair scruffy around his ears and neck and he smiles. I feel my heart soften and I frown. This is going to be more difficult than I thought.

Will slips his feet into a pair of Vans by the front door and I start walking to the swings, to our spot where maybe things will feel better and I'll know what to say.

The minute Will slides his hand into mine, I realize my whole plan is screwed. His hand is warm and gentle as our fingers twine. It's just holding hands. Friends can hold hands, right?

I let him lead. He doesn't say a word, just throws me sly glances over his shoulder every so often. He pulls me into the Laundromat, and then his mouth is on mine and I drink him in eagerly, a sweet relief to the nagging ache that's been plaguing me all year. His fingers slide beneath the hem of my tank top and I melt, my whole body exhaling as he wraps his arms around my waist. For one moment, everything makes sense.

And then I remember my wall and I pull away. That was not a friend kiss. I hop onto the counter to put some space between us. Okay, so, holding hands is off limits. Besides, he's not going to want to touch me after I tell him about Jake and Steven. Especially Steven.

Will stares at the floor, his hand running through his hair, the fluorescent lights making it glow like a halo. I focus on the tiny scatter of freckles across his nose, his eyelashes feathered on his cheekbones and it takes every ounce of strength I possess to not call him over to me.

I need to say something, the silence like thick cream in the hot room, curdled and stinking to high heaven.

"I went on a date with Josie's brother and I kissed him," I blurt out. Will peers up at me and folds his arms across his chest before shifting his eyes back to the floor. "And I went to prom with Steven. And I kissed him too."

Will doesn't move. He's quiet for a long time and I wait.

"I know," Will says finally and I look at him, confused.

"Jay. He writes Lauren letters, calls her on the phone sometimes," he says quietly and I'm completely taken aback. And furious. I do not like my brother gossiping about my love life.

"What?" I ask, dumbfound.

This also means that Will could have called me, could have written me letters, but he didn't. The rejection stings.

"Wait, what?" I ask again and a smile spreads across Will's face. Betrayed by my own brother. I'm going to kill him!

"It's okay, Cat. I'm not mad or anything," Will says and I snort.

"Good, because you shouldn't be," I say, my voice snotty as all hell and I don't care. I feel so stupid, thinking Will would be upset, thinking what we have is anything more than just a fling.

"I just meant that I don't expect anything. I don't want you to feel restricted by me. You're allowed to be with other people. And so am I," he adds quietly.

"Oh, well, I'm glad I have your permission," I say sarcastically, still irritated that Will knows everything and I know nothing.

"I slept with a girl I go to school with," Will says suddenly. I blink, my mind completely numb.

"By slept with, you mean..." I trail off, confused. Will's eyes burn into mine, smoldering and oozing exactly what he means. *Sex.*

"Oh," I gasp, the wind knocked right out of me. My pulse races and I grip the counter. Oh God, I'm going to pass out.

"It was awful," Will continues. "I was completely blitzed out of my mind and it was a total mistake."

"It's okay, I'm not mad or anything," I lie. I lie like a son-of-a-bitch.

"I wanted it to be you," he whispers. I inhale sharply as he walks towards me, conflicting emotions raging through my body. I want to yell at him, tell him that it never will be, not now, not ever but I can't find my voice.

"I still want it to be you." Will's voice is smooth and low and my wall crumbles, a pile of dust his declaration tramples and kicks into the air.

His hands move to my waist, his hips slide between my knees and he closes the space between us. And I let him.

Just for the summer, just for the summer, just for the summer, I chant in my head as his mouth closes over mine and pulls from me the last ounce of willpower I have left.

* * *

O h shit, you're a Republican?" Jay says, exasperated as he leans back in his folding chair on the sandy cove. My dad's hunched over the small portable gas grill, poking at the meat patties sizzling over the flame. Like always, he insists on getting a cove for the Fourth of July. No fireworks again. I swear, one of these fricking days I'm going to see some damn fireworks. I point my second-hand Polaroid camera at my brother and he sticks his tongue out at me when I snap the picture. The camera buzzes and spits out the soggy gray picture, the chemical smell I now equate with anticipation as I wait for the photo to appear. A couple minutes later, there he is, my brother against the backdrop of brush, his smart-ass face forever captured on the small rectangle of paper.

"No, I said I'd vote for Bush. I don't believe in political parties. A politician is a politician. They're all puppets, their strings being pulled by the more substantial powers at hand," Lauren says, pushing her glasses up off the tip of her nose. Margot rolls her eyes and turns over on her towel beside me.

"Oh no, I guess the wedding's off," Will whispers in my ear and I stifle a giggle.

"And who might these substantial powers at hand be?" Jay asks skeptically.

"Those who control the majority of the wealth," Lauren

answers as if it's completely obvious.

"So, you mean the Republicans," Jay quips. "Face it, babe, you're sucked into their bipartisan brainwash just as much as the rest of us. Frankly, I don't trust the government."

"Jay!" my dad scolds, pulling the cigarette from between his lips. "Don't say shit like that. It's Fourth of July, God damn it. It's unpatriotic."

"Actually, one could argue that at its root, his statement is very patriotic. I mean, isn't that what our founding fathers did over two hundred years ago? Questioned their government?" Lauren challenges.

My dad squints at Lauren lounging in her chair, her wide brimmed hat shading her face from the hot July sun. Lauren is some sort of stunning. Besides being wicked smart, she's got the body of a supermodel. She's just so confident, lounging in her green halter one-piece swimsuit and challenging my dad on politics of all things. I can totally see why Jay likes her.

"Yeah, Jay's a regular Thomas Jefferson," my dad replies and motions to the ice chest. "Hey, hand me one of them beers there, Kit Cat."

I dig around in the chest, looking for the red and white can, and take the Budweiser to him. I wipe the sweat from the back of my neck and forehead. Man, I am melting out here. The heat rolls off my body, my face and shoulders tight and itchy and it's time for a swim.

I wade out into the bay and dunk my head, the water meandering through my hair bringing sweet relief to my overheated scalp. I swim until I'm nestled between the walls of sediment and rock, the layers of reds and oranges and browns exposed from eons of erosion. This all started as a stream, a slow, persistent trickle of water forcing the hard, packed earth to crumble and soften into the silt beneath my toes.

"Beautiful." Will's voice makes me jump. Water beads on the bridge of his nose, his wet hair dripping in his eyes and I'm overwhelmed by how handsome he is.

"I know. Look at those rocks. You see that, the layers? Can

you believe you are looking at something that has been here for literally millions of years?" I float on my back, the bright sun forcing me to close my eyes. A shadow hovers above me and I lift my lids to find Will's dancing eyes, his lips pulled into an astonished smile.

"Not the rocks, you goon," he laughs. "You. You're beautiful."

Beautiful. Full of beauty. Not just a physical appeal, but he thinks I'm full of beauty. It is the greatest compliment anyone has ever given me.

Will reaches through the water to wrap around my wrist. He pulls me into the deep water behind my father's boat. Weaving his arm around my waist, he pulls my body to his and kisses me gently. Will's hands crawl across my back and I wrap my legs around his waist. His eyes widen, his lips still but I don't care. He can't call me beautiful and kiss me and expect me to behave myself.

"What? Is this not okay?" I ask, my heart pounding in my chest, my arms wrapped around his neck.

"It's okay. Shocking, a little, but it's definitely okay," he grins. I run my hands through his damp hair and my lips press into the wet skin of his jaw, his neck, his shoulder. I don't like the way I need him. This is precisely why I had the no touching rule, and now it's all gone straight to hell.

My brain won't shut up. I wonder if he thinks that girl he slept with is beautiful. I wonder if he kissed her like he kisses me. I wonder what it's like to have sex with Will. I'm jealous someone else was close to him, closer than I've ever been. I want to be that close to him.

I kiss Will, hungry and determined, and I let my hands roam over his chest. His mouth moves to my chin and then to my neck, his lips nibbling on my earlobe and I squeeze my thighs tight around his waist. Will's mouth moves to my shoulder and then to my collarbone. His hand slides tentatively up my side, and I thank God I didn't get the suit with the padding. He stares into my eyes, his finger playing with the strap of my bathing suit and I press my forehead to his and try to focus on breathing.

"Is this okay?" he asks.

"It's shocking," I say, mimicking his words. "But definitely okay."

Will's finger traces the bathing suit over the swell of my chest and I'm panting. *Please, please, please put your hand on my boob.* I never thought I would want a boy to put his hand on my boob.

But this isn't just a boy, it's Will. And he's everything.

"Can I touch you?" Will murmurs against my neck, his lips smoothing over my skin. I nod, finding his lips and pulling him into my mouth. I'm already gasping when his hand slides over my breast and I pull myself tighter to him, like I can't get close enough.

"Your heart is pounding," Will whispers and I try to catch my breath.

I slide my hands over the long lean muscles of his stomach. Will's hand pauses for a millisecond, his eyes close and whispered profanities slip from his beautiful mouth against mine. My fingers glide just under his waistband and they're met with silky flesh, and I gasp. Holy shit, I just touched him. I just touched *it* and it's soft and smooth and so warm.

"Cat!" he gasps, his eyes wide and I'm about to kiss him again when we hear the buzz of a boat engine turn towards our cove. We instantly separate just before Dr. and Mrs. Henderson idle up to the shore. We swim over to catch the boat, pretending we weren't just rounding second base under the protective blanket of the water. Will gives me a sly grin, and I roll my eyes but I've never felt so powerful in all my life.

I make Will feel good, I make him breathe my name. Even if it's just for the summer.

C at! Stop groping your boyfriend and get back to work!" I hear Josie yell from the front of the store and I freeze, trying to ignore Will's lips on my neck. He grins into my shoulder and I push him away.

"You're destroying my productivity," I say, grabbing a box of chip bags.

"Screw your productivity, you shouldn't even be here. You should be out on the water with me," Will says and takes the box from my arms. I sigh and grab two more boxes, before heading back out into the store.

Josie is perched behind the counter on a stool, a large novel in her hand, her leg bouncing while she reads.

"He's not my boyfriend," I mumble as I set the boxes on the floor next to her and she snorts, the beginning of a loud laugh that she exaggerates on purpose.

"What's it like?" Josie asks.

"What do you mean?" I ask hesitantly. I'm almost positive this is a set-up, but my curiosity overrides my common sense.

"Living in denial. Is it really as blissful as they say?" Josie smirks.

"Get bent, Josie," I say in a hushed voice. I glance over my shoulder to see Will haphazardly restocking the chips in the snack aisle, his focus on us instead. He quickly looks away and accidentally drops a bag of chips when I catch him eavesdropping. I bite my lip, suppressing a grin.

I look back at Josie and her face is stone, her gray eyes chilling as she stares at me. She doesn't say another word, just pulls a pack of cigarettes off the shelf behind the counter. She steps outside, pulling the wrapped tobacco from the carton and a lighter from her pocket and soon she's engulfed in haze. Her arms are crossed in front of her chest, her eyes focused on the sky as she smokes.

Heather had her baby in March, a little girl she named Claire. She's working reception at the Young's storage place. Yesterday, Ricky proposed. He's going to buy a mobile home in town and move Heather and the baby in as soon as possible.

Josie's not taking it too well.

Will's arms weave around my waist from behind and fold around my stomach as his lips press into my neck. "What were you arguing about?" he murmurs, his breath tickling my skin.

"Nothing, it's not important," I sigh and we watch Josie quickly light another cigarette.

"Hey! Jay said something about checking out the Bennett place tonight?" Will says just as I see my dad walking up the sidewalk and instantly his arms disappear from around my waist.

"Chicken shit," I laugh and he shrugs and leans against the counter. My dad pats Josie on the shoulder before walking into the store. His mustache twitches as he glances between the two of us.

"Hi Dad," I say as inconspicuously as possible. My dad's not an idiot. I'm pretty sure he knows there's something going on between us, but I think it's better if he thinks Will and I are just friends. Really, really good friends.

We're not dating, we're not boyfriend and girlfriend, we're not "seeing" each other. We just are. And that's really hard to explain to my old-fashioned dad.

"Hey kids, how's it goin'?" my dad mutters as he walks over to the cash register. He punches a couple buttons, checks the tape and pulls the bills from the tray, zipping them up in a black vinyl bag.

"Will, why don't you go take a swim," my dad says.

"I don't mind staying," Will says confidently.

"Get out of here, kid. Go enjoy your vacation," my dad says in a cool voice and Will hesitantly moves toward the door.

"I'll see you later, Cat," he mumbles before stepping outside and taking off down the sidewalk.

"What the hell, Dad?" I ask, exasperated.

"He doesn't need to be hanging around here all the time. This is a business, and you are my employee. You don't need any distractions." My dad's voice is matter-of-fact and cold, and this pisses me off to no end.

"I am not business," I argue. "I'm your daughter and Will's practically family."

"Will is a *Paycheck*, Cat. I know you've sort of adopted him and he's a nice kid, but he is not your family. Your family is here, at the marina." I start to argue but my dad doesn't give me the chance.

"I don't want Will hanging around at the store while you're working anymore." His tone of voice tells me this topic is not up for debate.

"But Dad, that's comp-" I try but he cuts me off.

"This discussion is closed," he says definitively. "Look, I'm sorry honey, but it's for the best."

It's so unfair! I hate this job. I hate that my dad thinks he knows what's best for me and most of all, I hate that he called Will a Paycheck. Tears stir beneath my lashes as I stare into his cold, hard gaze. *Do not cry, Cat. Don't you fucking dare.*

I spend the next hour breaking down boxes in the stockroom, visualizing my dad's face as I punch the boxes with my fist. I gather up the shreds of cardboard and haul them to the dumpster outside, tossing them into the bin with gusto.

"Hey." I spin around and see Will grinning by the back door. "So I take it things didn't go well."

"You can't hang around the store anymore." I kick the side of the dumpster, my toe stinging a little at the impact.

"I figured. We can still hang out after and on days you don't have to work, right?" Will asks and I nod. "Then it's okay."

"No it's not," I say bitterly. Will ambles over to me and kisses my cheek.

"Let's go do something," he says in a smooth voice and my heart flips in my chest. "Tell Josie you're sick. Meet me back here and we'll bail, like hay." Will's eyes sparkle a deep, devious green.

"But my dad-"

"Won't be coming back to the store. And he won't expect you home for another two hours." It's true, my dad never comes back to the store once he's cleaned out the register. It's all the persuading I need.

I stumble into the store, holding my gut as I use the counter for support. Josie eyes me suspiciously and I cringe, pretending I don't see her watching.

"What's the matter with you?" she asks.

"Nothing, I'm fine," I sigh, turning away from her.

"Cramps?" Josie asks and I freeze. Why didn't I think of that? It's the perfect cover! My dad isn't going to ask me about lady plumbing problems, even if he does come back.

"Yes. I just started. I feel like I'm being ripped in half." I clutch at my stomach again, probably a little too overdramatic but Josie just shrugs.

"Just go home," she orders me and I want to cheer, but I force myself to look crampy.

"I think I will," I say in a pitiful voice and Josie goes back to her cleaning. I slip out the door and meet Will out back by the dumpster.

"We have to get a cart. I don't want to risk going home to get my car and it's too far to walk. We can use one from the marina." I shake my wrist, the keys dangling from the cord and Will smiles, sly mischief spreading across his face.

"You're quite the rebel tonight, Miss Rossi," Will remarks. "Ditching work, and stealing a cart."

"It's not stealing if I have the keys. It's borrowing without consent," I clarify. The lights in my dad's office are out so I know my dad's already left. I unplug the cart and roll up the cord before turning the key. Will gets in beside me and I put the electric cart in reverse, the wheels spinning in the gravel as I back away from the building.

"Are you sure you know what you're doing?" Will asks, clutching the roof of the cart.

"Relax, this cart only goes about twenty miles per hour. If you fall out, just tuck and roll," I respond and Will laughs as we drive off to find my brother.

We drive along the dark, vacant road in silence, only a sliver of moon to light our way. It's eerily quiet, the air thick with moisture and it smells like a storm is coming.

The deserted Victorian mansion is big and white with terraces and gables out in the middle of nowhere. Some kids at school say the Bennetts were serial killers and that there's an underground secret passageway that leads to the river, in case they had to get the hell out of dodge.

The front is a junk yard, old tires and rusty shells of cars littering the lot. I can see the other cart parked on the side and I sigh in relief, feeling more confident now that I know my brother's here.

Will and I walk up to the front door. It's cracked open, a quiet murmur of voices inside and I motion to Will to be quiet. He catches on and we sneak in through the door. The house smells of mildew mixed with the remnants of parties past, the alcohol and cigarette smoke soaked into the walls. Will slides his hand along my back and over my hip, trying to find my hand in the pitch black room and my heart races at his touch.

We inch towards the whispering voices, a skunky smell drifting through the house. They're smoking weed. It won't take much to freak them out. I see a beam of light flash in our direction and their voices silence. They've heard something.

I slowly drag my nails against the wall. No doubt Jay's theatrics have gotten the girls good and antsy. I hear a panicked voice, probably Margot and then another. I can feel Will laughing, his face falling into the back of my shoulder. I do it again, and this time Will's hand thuds and drags against the hollow plaster.

"Let's get out of here, this isn't fun anymore," Margot says, her voice increasing in volume as she approaches the hallway where we're hiding.

"Margot, wait," I hear Lauren now, her footsteps getting louder as well, followed by the heavy thudding of my brother, I'm sure.

"Oh, let her go." Steven? Shit, what is Steven doing here?

Suddenly, a massive form grabs me from behind and I scream at the top of my lungs, my heart pounding with panic.

I clutch to Will as he curses and tries to pull me away from whatever is trying to abduct me. I'm still screaming, my eyes clenched tightly when I realize someone is calling my name.

"Cat! Cat, open your eyes!"

"Maybe you should slap her."

"Fuck off, Lauren."

It's Will's voice that pulls me from hysterics and I open one eye to find my brother gripping my shoulders and grinning at me like an idiot.

"Of all the stupid, asshole, shithead things you could do," I say bitterly as I smack at him with each insult. "How did you know it was us?"

"We heard you walking across the gravel," Jay laughs and I try to hit him again but he grabs my wrist to block the blow. He's been drinking too, I can smell the beer on his breath. "Come on, Cat! That was classic."

"You're still an asshole," I mutter, irritated he made me scream like a banshee.

"You're still a wuss," Jay remarks.

"So, what were you guys doing before you decided to try to kill me with bloodcurdling panic?" I ask, yanking my arm away from him and trying to change the subject.

"Summoning the dead," Margot says and I raise my eyebrows.

"What?" I ask her.

"She," Lauren points accusingly at Margot, "brought a Ouija Board."

"It's just for fun," Margot defends, her hands on her hips. She must have seen *Dirty Dancing* this past year because she's dressed like Baby in jean cut-offs and a white shirt knotted in the front. She's even wearing white Keds.

"Of course it is, it's a toy. It's made by Parker Brothers for Christ's sake," Will remarks sarcastically.

"Where is it?" I ask, looking around and Margot grabs my hand and pulls me through the low doorway into the other room. There's a large stone fireplace on one of the walls and the light from the sliver of moon can barely get through the grimy windows. The board is on the floor next to an unopened six pack of beer. Margot sits on the floor by the board and I do the same. She hands me one of the unopened beers and I pop it open, but my brother snags it from my hand.

"I don't think so, Sis," Jay says, before taking a big swig. "You're underage."

"We're all underage," I contend but Jay shakes his head and chugs the rest of my beer, crushing the can and tossing it in the corner with the others.

"Okay, everyone touch the pointer thing," Margot instructs and Lauren is the first to comply, then Steven and even Jay sits down and folds his long legs. I look up at Will, expecting him to play but he just stares out the window.

"No thanks," he scowls. Geez, what's got his feathers ruffled?

"Okay, then we ask it a question, and see where it goes. Don't put any pressure on your fingers," Margot explains. "Alright, ask it a question."

"Will I get laid this weekend?" Steven asks obnoxiously and I abandon the game.

"What? It's a legitimate question," Steven scoffs at me for leaving.

"Yeah, one we already know the answer to," I respond coolly.

"I know, how about, will Cat's dad find out she ditched work to fool around with a boy?" Steven sneers and I want to wring his stupid neck. Dammit! How the hell does he know that?

"You ditched the store?" Jay asks and I shrug.

"Kill the lights. It's the 5-O!" Will interrupts frantically. "They look like they're slowing down in front of the house."

I peek out the window to see Officer Warren's police car slowly creeping past the house. We have to get out of here. He's going to turn around and come back and my father is going to kill me!

"It's Warren," I panic. "Get out! Go out the back!"

We scatter, stumbling around in the dark, and once we're outside we split up. Will stays with me and we creep along the side of the house. We're looking for a hiding place, when we hear the crunch of gravel under tires in the front drive. Shit, shit, son-of-a-bitch!

Will motions to an old, rusty truck. I hear the slam of a car door, then feet marching through gravel. We sneak towards the truck just as he opens the door and walks inside the house.

My heart races as I quickly climb into the back of the truck. I lay flat in the small space and Will climbs in behind me. The bed is covered in a filthy tarp and my shirt saturates with warm mud. I hope to high heaven I won't need a tetanus shot after this.

With any luck, Warren will see that no one is here and book it before any of us are found. Then I think of the empty beer cans and the house reeking of weed and I begin to panic, my chest heaving with frenzied gasps. Will's hand smoothes over my stomach and comes to rest right over my heart.

"Shhhh," he whispers into my ear, his lips on my lobe and then my neck and I feel a surge of warmth seep through my body. Oh God, what a distraction. I turn my head to catch his mouth, trying to remain as silent as possible as we kiss.

"Well, what do we have here?" A bright light blinds us and I squint to see the uniformed silhouette, a MAG light held high overhead as he grins, the white gleam of his teeth causing my stomach to roll.

"Fuck," Will mutters beside me.

Yep, my sentiments exactly.

✻ ✻ ✻

Dad paces as I sit on the couch, my thumb trying to erase a smudge of grease on my palm. He hasn't said anything since Officer Warren left. Warren didn't arrest us, thank God, and he didn't find any of the others. He assumed Will and I were the only ones out there. He also assumed we were responsible for all the empty beer cans. But Officer Warren knows my dad so instead of taking us to the station, he dropped us off at the marina. He made Will sit in the cruiser while he explained to my dad how he found us trespassing and now I am in trouble for so many reasons, I don't even know which one to explain first.

"Dad, I swear, we weren't drinking," I plead, hoping I sound convincing.

"Do not lie to me, little girl. I know everything that goes on at my marina. Everything. I know you skipped out early from work. You stole a cart to do God-only-knows-what with that boy, and you broke into an abandoned house to get drunk." My dad is furious and hot angry tears start to build behind my lids.

"That boy is my best friend," I say defensively. "And I left work early because I had been there all day and I was sick of it."

"It's work, of course you were sick of it. What the hell are you doing, Cat? I did not raise you to behave this way." My dad points his finger at me and I grit my teeth, the gesture so condescending I can hardly stand it.

"You raised me to do whatever you want," I yell but my dad blows me off. No trial, no presenting my case, he goes straight to the sentencing.

"No more Will. You're on restriction and you're not to leave the marina," my dad lays down the law.

"What? Does that include the water, for ski rides and stuff?" I ask, flabbergasted.

"You don't leave the marina," my dad barks and I want to scream.

"For how long?" I'm going to freak out, like I want to break something.

"For as long as it takes," Dad says, again the stupid finger taunting me as he jabs the air.

"This is such shit!" I shout.

"You watch your language, young lady!" my dad growls.

"Oh what, Jay can cuss but I can't? Jay can do whatever the hell he wants around here and you just ignore it. I hate living here!" I storm to my room and slam the door, looking for something to break. My eyes fall on my glass bottles and for a minute, I visualize myself heaving them at the wall and watching them shatter.

Instead I crumble onto my bed, hiding my head in my pillow and letting my tears soak my sheets, gasping into the soft cotton that smells like my mom.

Jay knocks on my door a little after midnight. I tell him what happened and he tries to make me feel better by offering to do all the laundry next week, but it's no use. I'm not allowed to see Will and I'm devastated. By the time I'm free again, Will will be gone and the summer will be over.

Will visits me at the store in the morning, buying some gum so he can defend his stance as a customer. He didn't get into trouble at all. His dad gave him a lecture about alcohol consumption and what it does to the body and that was it.

When I tell him I'm not allowed to see him, he's furious and wants to march down to my dad's office and confront him but I tell him not to. It'll just make things worse. My dad doesn't back down, ever.

Will doesn't back down either. That night, he's at my window. Even though I know I shouldn't, I pop out my screen and let him in. We play Uno and Will solves my Rubik's cube, and then does it three more times when I accuse him of cheating.

Will climbs in my window every night for the rest of the summer. Sometimes, he brings me ice cream or Pixy Stix. I tell him about my photography classes and he tells me about basketball and how he plays the piano. We argue and laugh and discuss the stupidest shit, whispering under the hum of INXS and Bon Jovi and the rest of the bands on my mixtape with my shoe shoved under the door in case my dad decides to barge in without knocking.

We do other stuff, too. The first time Will gives me an orgasm, I laugh uncontrollably. I read in Cosmo it's supposed to feel like an explosion and so I always pictured fireworks shooting out of my who-ha. Cosmo didn't mention it would cause my whole body to seize like one of those flopping fish under the dock. So when Will touches me, all the embarrassing things my body is doing combined with the image of crotch fireworks gives me a bad case of the giggles. Will acts all mopey at first but I crawl into his lap and I explain and he laughs too.

I like fooling around with Will. The way he touches me is just really special, like he's handling something he wants to take care of. It's always slow and lingering and passionate and I can't ever remember feeling this important.

This scares the shit out of me.

Will comes over the night before he's supposed to leave. He's wearing his river clothes, jean shorts and a t-shirt, and his hair is hidden under a Chicago Bulls cap. He's quiet and somber when he climbs in my window and I can tell this isn't going to be a night filled with ice cream and kissing.

He sits on my bed, a small gift bag in his hands and stares at the pale pink tissue paper. I smile because pink is so not my color. It's far too soft, and that's just not me. I am harsh and bold, red and orange, like the sky at dusk or the layers of sediment that cradle the river.

Will doesn't say anything, just picks at the paper in his lap. I do not want to spend our last night together all pissy.

"Are you mad at me or something?" I ask, my tone sharp and accusing and not how I want to sound at all.

"Why didn't you call?" Will asks and I look over at him, confused. "Last year, when I gave you my phone number, why didn't you call?"

"It's long distance," I mutter, keeping why I have to tuck him away in a neat little box to myself.

"Jay called, and he wrote letters. Letters are practically free." Will's brow creases, forming two thin dents of frustration. "I really miss you when I'm at home. When you didn't call, I thought maybe...you didn't want to be friends anymore."

"Friends?" I ask. I glance over at Will to find him staring at me, his green familiar eyes holding a familiar pain.

"You know it's more than that."

"Cat, I-" Will starts and I don't want to hear him say it. If I hear him say it, it'll make everything so much worse when he leaves tomorrow, and he will leave. That is a certainty.

"No!" I shout, clenching my eyes shut like a five year old throwing a fit. "Don't say it. It'll make it unbearable."

"Unbearable?" His face crumbles and it all comes pouring out.

"When you leave, it's unbearable. And if you say what I think you're going to say, it's going to make things so much harder. I love our summers. It's all I can think about, it's all I live for, but it's not reality," I try to explain.

"Why is this so hard? Back home, when I like a girl, I ask her out and boom, it's done. But with you, it's so different. Everything is so difficult," Will says. My chest throbs and I bring my hand up to stop the swell, like I'm trying to hold my heart inside my body.

"You're right. This isn't like at home. And being together like this, it would be so difficult," I whisper, tears welling in my eyes. I turn to face him. His head leans against the frame of my bed, his eyes stuck to the ceiling as his lashes blink furiously.

I smooth my thumb across the bridge of his nose, the little flakes of peeling skin rolling under my fingertip. He closes his eyes, his face turning into my touch, another tiny tear slipping from his lids.

"I don't know what all this stuff between us means. I don't know what to do or how to feel about you. All I know is that I like it when I'm with you. I like the way you make me feel. And I'll always be your friend. No matter what, okay? We'll be friends." Will stares at me and I don't know what he's thinking.

He doesn't say a word just hands me the present. I remove the tissue paper and pull out a bottle. It's tall with a thick neck and a capped lip, the white lettering splashed against the glass. It's filled with sand and chunks of gold rock, a twig of green pine, and a handful of fish hooks settled in murky water.

"It's San Francisco. There's a twig and a rock from Golden Gate Park, sand and water from Baker Beach, some fish hooks from Fisherman's Wharf, and fake gold nuggets, because well, everyone thinks San Francisco is paved with gold. It's my home in a bottle," Will explains and I am speechless.

"Will, I...I love it," I whisper, the thoughtfulness of the gift heavy in my chest.

"I thought maybe you could put it with your collection," he says and I immediately settle it next to my jewelry box. I choke back a sob that's burning in my chest and hide my face from him. *Do not cry, Cat. Do not cry.*

"I'm sorry Cat. I'm sorry I live so far away. I'm sorry I can't take you to prom or on dates. I'm sorry you're sad. I'm just really sorry," Will says. I don't want Will to feel sorry for me. The thought makes me sick, Will in San Francisco, surrounded by his girlfriends and his jock friends and feeling bad about the poor small town girl he fooled around with at the river.

"Don't be sorry," I say proudly. "I'm fine, Will. Don't feel sorry for me."

"That's not what I meant," Will mutters. "Why does it feel like we're breaking up or something?"

"We're not breaking up. We were never together. You can't lose something you never had." I sit down on my bed and let my shoulder lean against him.

"You're still my friend, though, right? You promise we'll always be friends?" Will whispers and I can't suppress the tears any more. I lick my thumb, tears silently rolling down my cheeks and hold out my trembling pinky.

"Pinky promise."

1989 – THAT TIME YOU BROUGHT YOUR FRIENDS

*Massive protests in Germany bring about
the collapse of the Berlin Wall.*

*Nirvana releases their first album, Bleach, for
the independent record label Sub Pop.*

*Drew Barrymore and Corey Feldman have a brief
affair after meeting on the set of the CBS after
school special "15 and Getting Straight."*

* * *

A dull red light illuminates the trays of chemicals. I can hear the gentle murmur of other students in my class. They're dicking around because no one really does work on the last day of high school. Well, no one except losers, like me.

I gently plunge the paper into the developer, agitating the tray to slosh the solution back and forth. Streaks of dark and light slowly appear on the page. Carefully handling my photo with a pair of tongs, I shake the solution from the page before placing it into the stop bath. Again, I swirl the chemical over the page. I repeat the process, the solution in the third tray fixing the image in place, and then hold it up to expect my work. There in varying grays, is the bend of the river. I wash the chemicals from the photo and hang it up on the wire line next to the developing station of my school's darkroom, when I hear a muffled cough behind me.

"That's really unique," a low, husky voice murmurs. I wipe my hands on my apron and glance over my shoulder. Scott

Merrit is inspecting my photo. "I like how you overexposed the film, gives it a sun-bleached effect."

"Thanks," I smile shyly, but inside I'm ecstatic. That's exactly what I wanted it to look like!

"You could make this your career and shit." Scott moves closer and he smells like cigarettes and developing solution. He's tall and thin, one of those mopey, artsy-fartsy types, with long, shaggy brown hair and his wallet chained to his pants. We did a project together this year, a collage urging support for the destruction of the Berlin Wall. It was picked to showcase at city hall in Boulder City.

"Yeah, right. I can totally see my dad letting me set up a darkroom at the marina," I mutter sarcastically. I slip my next photo into the developer, and watch the image appear. This time it's my dad, his cap pulled over his eyes, a cigarette between his lips and he's fiddling with the outdrive of our boat. I want this one a little darker so I leave it in the solution a little bit longer.

"What about UNLV?" Scott persists.

"Why do you care so much?" I ask him, slightly annoyed by his persistence.

"I just hate to see talent go to waste. We can't allow ourselves to be limited by the capitalistic mockery our government uses to hide the blatant oppression of its people." Scott is right behind me now while I hang my father's photo to dry.

"Doesn't your dad work for the city? He's a lawyer, right?" I ask with a smirk.

"Yeah, but that doesn't mean I accept his ideals. I'm like you, Cat," Scott's fingers graze over the top of my arm and I freeze.

"What do you mean, like me? Poor?" I say sharply.

"No, shit, I guess that didn't come out right. I meant, real. You don't stand for all the superficial bullshit. You're just you and you're pretty cool," Scott grins sheepishly. "Look, I'm just trying to tell you that I like you. I've been dying to ask you out all year."

"I don't date," I sigh.

"I know. I thought we connected." Scott brushes his hair out of his face and I consider him for a minute. He's cute and easy to work with. And he's passionate about things, goes on and on for hours about government conspiracies. I could like him, maybe.

But there's only one person on this planet I'm connected to.

"Scott, you're a good friend," I start but I can't finish when his eyes drop to the floor.

"It's okay. I just couldn't graduate without at least giving it a shot," Scott mumbles and I feel awful. I'm so stupid! I should go out with him. He's nice and he likes me.

And he's here.

"I guess we could get a soft serve at the Dairy Burger after school," I say and Scott's eyes dart up to mine.

"Really?" he asks hopefully, and I cringe. Oh, geez. He really likes me.

"Yeah, really," I mumble, placing another photo into the developing solution. Before the lines even connect completely, I know whose picture this is. His taunting smirk, his cap hiding his hair and his eyes burning right off the paper.

I hate that I can't forget him. I hate that I still want him. I hate that I dream of kissing him and that I've scribbled Cat Henderson in my journal dozens of times in varying scripts and arrangements. Catherine Henderson. Catherine Pricilla Henderson. Cat Rossi Henderson. Catherine Pricilla Rossi Henderson. God, I make myself sick.

I hate how every boy pales in comparison. I hate that he's not here and that he's not mine and that he never will be. I just hate.

I stare at his handsome face on the page and I forget to agitate the solution. I leave him submerged, drowning him out and letting the image fade to black.

* * *

T he Hendersons arrive two weeks after I graduate from high school. I don't have a party or participate in any of my school's celebratory events. I have dinner with my mom at the Tropicana. She gives me a necklace, a silver horseshoe embedded with real diamonds and she says it's for good luck.

Scott and I go out a couple of times, mostly for sundaes at Dairy Burger or bowling in Boulder City and we make out sometimes. He has a lot of interesting theories on life and the universe. I like him, just not enough.

I don't know what to expect when Will gets here. I hope we can go back to being friends, and how things were when we were kids. Ice cream and silly jokes and just spend time together, as friends. Without touching.

I watch from my porch as the black Mercedes-Benz parks at the Henderson's unit, followed by a brand new red Saab. Lauren and Margot step out of the Mercedes, along with Mrs. Henderson and then Dr. Henderson and I see my brother cross the campground towards them.

Will slides out of the driver's seat of the Saab, a graduation present I assume, and a flood of very pretty, perfect people exit the car. They look like a fricking shampoo commercial, the two girls shaking out their long tresses and smoothing their pleated shorts, the two boys stretching and eyeing their surroundings and I want to puke, right there on my porch.

What the hell is going on here?

My brother jogs over to Lauren and pulls her into a big hug, holding her for a good minute before shaking Dr. Henderson's hand. He hugs Margot and Mrs. Henderson and waves over to Will. Will saunters over to my brother, punching him in the arm, looking around, and then he stops. His eyes sear into mine, even across the distance and my stomach churns.

Why would he bring them here? This is our place, our summer and now I have to share it with his San Francisco friends. I'm so pissed I'm shaking and then one of the girls, a tall blond, jumps on Will's back. He laughs sheepishly, and gently sets her down. He looks at me again, but I'm too disgusted to continue to watch and I storm inside my house.

I try to think rationally as I pace. I wanted this. I told him it was okay. It's for the best. He doesn't belong to me. He's not mine. This is what I wanted.

There's a rap on my door and I almost want to hide. It has to be him. I quickly wipe my face and smooth my cotton tank over my jean shorts, feeling a hundred percent insecure in my old, ratty river clothes. *Cat, get over yourself. Just open the door.*

"Oh my God, Cat! He's here!" Margot barges into my living room and I close the door behind her.

"Who's here?" I ask her. My mind immediately skirts to Will and I kind of want to smack myself in the face.

"Andy! I know I told you about him. He's here. Will invited him to come and he's here!" Margot looks like she might explode from anxiety. I remember the discussion a couple years ago. Margot told me Will was in love with me that summer.

"Well, that's a good thing, right?" I try to control the tremble in my voice. Margot shakes her head no and shakes her hands. "No, it's not a good thing?"

"No, it's not! He's going to see me without makeup and first thing in the morning when I have crusties in my eyes and oh, my God, Cat, what if I snore? What if I talk in my sleep?" Margot is on the verge of tears now.

"Margot, relax!" I grab her hand and pull her to sit on the couch. "It'll be fine. If he doesn't like you with crusties, what's the point? You can't hide that stuff forever."

"I know, I'm just really nervous. I like him a lot. I don't want to mess it up," Margot sighs.

"Just don't freak out like that again and you'll be fine. Chicken-shit Margot is not cute," I tease and Margot's lips spread into a grin.

"So, who are all those people?" I ask hesitantly.

"Will's friends. They're only staying a couple weeks," Margot says.

"By they, you mean..." I trail off.

"Well, the dark haired guy wearing the hat and white t-shirt, looking like a cross between River Phoenix and Dean Martin, that's Andy. He's wearing suspenders, Cat! Isn't that adorable?" Margot gushes.

"He's wearing suspenders? Here?" I snort and Margot keeps talking.

"The other guy is Drew, he plays basketball with Will. The girl with the curly hair, that's Jess, Drew's girlfriend." Margot pulls her ear, the diamond stud twinkling under the fluorescent lights.

"And the other girl?" I choke out. It doesn't take a genius to figure this out.

"I think her name is Amanda. She's Jess's friend." Margot won't look at me.

Yeah, Jess's friend my ass.

"Margot, it's fine. I'm not jealous." *Liar! Liar! Liar!* "Will and I are just friends."

"Cat, I don't think you and Will have ever been just friends," Margot says sadly and I hate the tone of her voice. It's all there, in her big sad blue eyes and in the crease in her forehead. Pity. She thinks I'm pathetic.

"Well, we are," I snap, this whole situation grating on my nerves. "Besides, I'm kinda seeing someone. Kinda."

"Are you? Dish, Cat. What's his name? Wait, is it Steven?" Margot asks with squinting eyes and I scowl. Why does everyone always think I like Steven?

"No, it's so not Steven. His name's Scott. He was in my photography class," I tell her.

"Do you have a picture? What's he like? Preppy? Jock? Oh wait, photography class, he's Punk or Gothic or something, huh? Oh hot, Cat!" Margot squeals.

"He's more like, Unabomber chic," I mutter. "I've only been out with him a couple of times. It's not really anything."

"It's enough," Margot says, a mischievous twinkle in her eye.

"Enough for what?" I ask confused.

"A spark," Margot says knowingly with a wink and I roll my

eyes. "Come on. Come say hi. I know Will wants to see you."

I hesitate because while I really want to see Will, I don't actually want to see Will. Things have obviously changed. People change too. What if he's rude to me? What if he kisses her in front of me? What if I have to punch her in the face?

This is what you wanted, Cat.

"Sure, okay. Let's go say hi." I force a smile and take a deep breath.

Margot leads me to her family's unit. They've dispersed, and the group is no longer congregating in front of the prefabricated home. Margot walks inside and I hesitate on the porch, my heart beating in my throat when I finally step through the door.

"Catherine!" Mrs. Henderson wraps her arms around me, her floral perfume reminding me of the department stores in Vegas. Dr. Henderson is setting up his typewriter at the table, and he pauses a moment to give me a small wave and a big smile.

"Where'd everyone go?" Margot asks, her hands on her hips.

"I think they were heading down to the docks, to get an ice cream or something," Mrs. Henderson says. She gathers up a few bags by the front door and walks them into the kitchen.

"Okay, we're going to go find them," Margot says, linking her arm through mine as I swallow the massive lump in my throat.

"Okay girls! Have fun!" Mrs. Henderson remarks absentmindedly from the other room.

"So, how's school?" I ask Margot as we walk, desperate for a distraction.

"It's school. I don't know, I'm not really cut out for the college scene. Lauren is the brain, not me. I'm more of a people person, you know?" Margot pushes her bangs out of her face. Her hair's cut in a sharp angular bob with bangs that cut straight across her forehead. "You know what I want to do? I want to go backpacking across Europe. Wouldn't that be so awesome?"

"Yeah," I answer half-heartedly.

"I got a job at a coffee place downtown," Margot babbles. "I really love it. I get to talk to people and it's locally owned. I don't know, maybe I'll own my own coffee shop."

I can't help but feel envious of Margot. She can, literally, do whatever she wants. Not once does it occur to her to worry about money or family obligation or even logistics. Every opportunity is right at her fingertips and she just has to decide which one to grab.

As we get closer to the docks, I can see the group hanging out by the swings and my stomach is in knots. I have no right to be jealous. Lots of people use these swings. Lots of people eat ice cream, but I can't ignore the bowling ball of dread rolling around in my gut as we get closer.

The girls are sitting on the swings. One of the guys, Drew, I guess, is pushing them both, grabbing their swings and jerking them around, and they're laughing and shrieking. Andy sticks out like a sore thumb, in his black, tapered pants and loafers. Yep, and suspenders pulled over a white button-up shirt. And then there's Will, sucking sherbet from a cardboard carton.

He looks up when we approach, his intense eyes contradicting the innocence of the red syrup trapped in the corner of his mouth and I can't fight the smile spreading across my face. Oh God, he's the same as always. He's still beautiful. His hair is longer, messy and hanging in his face but shorter around his ears and neck. He's wearing his river clothes now, jean shorts and a blue tank top and I want to run and tackle him but I can't. I can't and it kills me.

"Hey guys!" Margot greets them cheerfully and the girls slow their swings. The dark haired one smiles. This one is Jess, according to Margot's descriptions. She's petite and pretty, her bangs poofy and sprayed into place. Her white pleated shorts are crisp, and her pink top clings to her curvy shape and I feel a little sick at the thought of her perfect figure in a bikini. I can't look at the other girl, Amanda. I don't want to look at her. I don't want to see her. I hate her and I don't even know her.

Grow up, Cat! It's not her fault. She might be really nice.

"Is this that little river friend you were talking about, Will?" My cheeks flush and I finally look at her. Amanda is tall and blond, her hair teased and curled in long poufs. She looks just like Jess. I mean, she's blond and freckled, but she looks just the same. Same pleated shorts, only in brown. Same top, only in lavender. They're paper dolls.

How could Will like me and also like this girl? She's the anti-Cat. She's blond and busty and just, so trendy. And I'm just not.

"This is Cat. She's my best friend," Will says with a soft smile.

"Hi Cat! Like, oh my God, you are hella pretty. Like, isn't she so pretty, Amanda? Seriously, your eyes are gorgeous. Are they brown or green?" Jess stands up and moves closer, to get a better look, I guess, and I feel ridiculous.

"Um, thanks. My driver's license says hazel?" I mutter, confused and feeling like a complete tool.

"Aw, you're adorable!" Amanda gushes and I feel like I've entered the Twilight Zone. "You totally have one of those body types where you can eat whatever you want and never get fat, huh?" I don't have many girlfriends but people don't really talk like this, right? I mean, this isn't normal, is it?

"Cat, that's your name? Like a pussy cat?" Drew speaks and I see Will's head drop as he laughs. He thinks this is funny.

"It's Catherine actually. Like the queen." Will grins at me with a wink and I feel Margot's arm twitch.

"Well, we're going to get an ice cream," Margot says cheerfully. "See you later."

"Later," Will remarks through his muffled laugh and I'm disappointed. I have to remind myself as we walk to the general store that I'm fine. Every step I take away from him I internally chant, *I'm fine, I'm fine, I'm fine.*

Liar.

Josie's at the cash register and I can see she's curious about Will's little gang of country club protégés.

"Hey Cat, Margot." She watches me the whole time, her eyebrows creased, her lips pursed.

"Hi Josie! Nice to see you," Margot says politely. "Can I get

127

a Strawberry Shortcake please? What do you want, Cat? I'm buying you an ice cream. You deserve it."

"What do you mean by that?" I ask her as Josie turns around to dig in the freezer behind the counter. I'm a little bit sick of the patronizing bullshit. I'm fine.

"This has to be hard for you. I know about your relationship with Will. I *know*," she says pointedly and my mouth drops open.

"Will told you?" I whisper and Margot shakes her head no.

"No, I saw you guys making out last year. And his hand was up your shirt," Margot says matter-of-factly. Josie snorts and I want to die, my face flushing with embarrassment.

"Jesus, Margot, will you keep your voice down?" I whisper and Josie laughs out loud now.

"Oh, come on Cat, everyone knows you were boning," Josie says and my eyes pop out of my head.

"We never...we didn't." I close my eyes and try to pretend I'm invisible. This is right out of my nightmare. Just then the bell on the front door rings and Will peeks his head into the store. Margot giggles, prompting me to sock her in the arm.

"Ow," Margot scowls and rubs her arm.

"Hey! Cat, can I talk to you for a sec?" Will walks into the store and I shrug, trying to be cool. I head towards the stockroom and he follows, Josie chuckling behind us

"What's up?" I ask him, my voice cool. Be cool, Cat. Just relax.

"What's with Margot?" Will asks suspiciously. He pulls his hand through his hair, his eyes peering down at mine. God, he's really tall. He must have grown like six inches or something.

"Why are you so tall?" I blurt out and he laughs.

"I don't know, genetics? My grandpa was like six five or something," Will shrugs. He steps closer and my breath stops in my chest. He smells so good, like soap and sunblock and I can still see the little bit of sticky syrup caught in the corner of his lips and I want to kiss him. I lick at my lips absent-mindedly. *Box it up, Cat!*

"Um, what did you need to talk to me about?" I ask as I take a step back. Will looks at me, the expression on his face is something I can't place. Like when you're searching for the perfect word to describe what you're thinking and you can't remember it. It's right there and you just can't grasp it.

"I missed you," he says quietly and I look down at the floor. "I know this is weird, with Amanda and everyone but-" Will starts and I can't stand the patronizing one minute longer.

"Will, I'm fine. It's okay, I'm completely fine. Everything is...fine." God damn adjectives, don't fail me now! Will smiles and I know he can see right through me.

"Good. I'm glad everything's so fine." He winks at me and without thinking, I playfully shove him.

"Hey!" he laughs. "What was that for?"

"You're such an ass," I roll my eyes, which prompts another chuckle.

"So, I have a favor. Do you know a good cove for camping? We want to sleep out on the river for the Fourth, like in tents and I kind of hoped you'd help us find a good spot," he asks.

"Oh. Um, yeah, I know a spot," I mutter, a little dejected.

"You guys can come too. You and Jay and whoever, everyone's invited," Will says quickly. Now I'm just lumped in with whoever.

"Sure, sounds great. I'll let Jay and whoever know." I can't even look at him.

"Cool. Well, I'll see you around," Will says quietly. But he doesn't move. I glance up slightly to find him staring at me. I inhale sharply, my eyes connect with his and I can't look away.

For one second, one tiny little moment of weakness, I let myself remember. I can see him remembering too. He smiles slowly, his hair falling into his face and the distraction breaks the connection. *Stop looking at him. You can't have him. You're fine.*

"I'm fine," I whisper.

"You certainly look...fine," Will whispers back.

"You should probably get back to your friends," I mumble

and he nods. He walks out the back door and I can finally breathe.

I am *so* not fine.

* * *

"Why do you insist on inviting him everywhere?" I hiss at my brother as we grab the last bags of camping supplies from the boat.

"What? Just because you're holding on to some grade school rivalry doesn't mean I have to. Steven's dope," my brother says. Yep, Steven is indeed a dope.

"If he tries anything, I'm going to hold you personally responsible." I hold the chairs overhead, my sandaled feet sloshing through the water.

"Steven's so over you, Cat. He's moved on. Don't be so conceited," Jay scolds as he floats the ice chest to the shore.

"Is it going to be hot like this all night?" Jess and Amanda are wearing matching two-toned pink bikinis. They went shopping together.

"Get used to it, sweetheart," Steven smirks and removes his t-shirt. "Make sure you lotion up, we wouldn't want that delicate skin of yours to get sunburned."

Oh God, Steven makes my skin crawl. I don't care what my brother says, he sounds like a creep.

I set the folded up chairs on the shore. This cove is pretty large, big enough for three tents and all our chairs and a bonfire pit. Lauren is filling one of the tents with food as Jay, Drew and Margot put up the canopy. I glance over to see Will and Andy digging a hole for the fire. Andy finally changed, he's wearing a pair of black swim trunks with his collared, button-up shirt. At least he ditched the suspenders.

Will's crouching down, lining the pit with rocks and he's shirtless. The long muscles of his back are carved and defined, his shoulders freckled and already browning. I fixate on the two little dents on either side of his lower spine, his shorts slung low and revealing the top of his butt crack, the pale white skin of his behind striking against the brown of his back.

Another form steps into my line of sight. Amanda. She reaches down, her perfect ass now blocking my view, and pulls up Will's shorts. He spins around, practically falling over, and his eyes lock with mine. I quickly look away, disgusted with myself for staring, and even angrier for getting caught.

Andy and Drew break out the beer early and they spend the rest of the day in a drunken haze. Amanda and Jess lounge in the sun, sipping wine coolers and reliving their senior year of high school and all the amazing shit they did.

I stalk their conversation for clues about Will. Will and Amanda went to prom together and he was valedictorian. He was captain of his basketball team and he throws the most "bomb-ass" parties. It makes me question what I know about Will. I don't know him like these people know him. And if I don't even really know him, how can I trust what I feel for him?

"So, Queen Cat, do you have a boyfriend?" Jess asks me, a coy smile on her lips.

"Um...no. I don't really date," I mutter, hoping this excuse will quell their curiosity.

"Yes, you do. What about Unabomber guy?" Margot asks, as she props herself up on her elbows and I want to strangle her. I glare at her and she just mouths the word "spark" to me.

"He's just a friend," I say without thinking and I hear Will snort. All our eyes turn to him, and he scribbles in his notebook before he looks up.

"Oh, sorry, I just remembered something funny," he says sarcastically and I stare at him in contempt. At least I hope it's contempt, because I'm feeling a little contemptuous.

"What like a 'friends with benefits' thing?" Amanda asks lazily and Will stares at me, waiting for my answer.

"He was in my photography class. We just go out for ice cream," I say. Will snorts again and I glare back. How dare he?

He can have sex and throw bomb ass parties and then bring all these people here, to our place, and I have to be completely cool. I can't even have ice cream with some dumb boy? This is exactly why we can't be more than friends.

"Like, oh my God, that's so romantic! How hot would it be to do it in a darkroom? Like so fucking hot, right? Right?" Jess gets sidetracked by sexual fantasies and I am so grateful the conversation is over. I try not to look at Will again, but I can feel his eyes on me still.

The boys throw around a football in the water for a while and Jay pulls everyone on inner tubes behind the boat. Will writes in his notebook, and Andy strums lazily on a guitar. Drew and Jess take off on various "nature hikes" and Amanda chomps her Bubblicious gum, blowing huge pink bubbles and then popping them loudly until I can't stand it anymore.

I hate the way I don't want Will to be happy with Amanda. If he likes her, he should be with her. This shouldn't be this complicated. I should be used to accepting things as they are. It's like what my dad says, there's always someone better off than you, and there's always someone who's got it worse. And this is not that bad. It's just how it has to be.

Jay builds a roaring fire, piling on wood and brush and we grill hot dogs speared on wire hangers. Things are better when it gets dark, when I don't have to really see Will's chest and stomach and remember the way it felt when I touched him. It's still fricking hot out, and we take frequent swims to cool off. I tie my hair up in a bun on top of my head to keep it off my back.

"Hey Cat, do you want a beer?" Andy asks me as I stare at the fire, the orange and red flames licking at the sides of the deep rock pit. I glance up, expecting my brother to tell him no, but Jay's making out with Lauren. Oh, barf-o-rama.

"Cat doesn't like beer," Will says. He takes the can from Andy's hand and cracks it open for himself. He polishes it off in a few massive gulps. This irritates me, like he knows all about me when I don't really know him.

"Yes, I do," I say indignantly and Andy grins, tossing me a

beer from the cooler. I pop the top, the fizzing foam spilling over the lip and onto my chest and lap and down my arm. "Shit!" I curse and lick my arm and hand.

A towel drops into my lap and I look up to find Will staring at me, the fire making his eyes dance. I mumble a quick thanks and clean myself up. He sits back down in his chair, and then Amanda's there at his feet, her back resting against his legs. This hurts, seeing them together like this. It hurts bad. I bring the can to my lips and I drink. I don't even let the liquid touch my taste buds, I just swallow until it's gone.

Andy cheers and throws me another can and I want to feel nothing. So I drink again, a little bit of the foam coming up my nose and this makes me laugh. Then Margot is beside me on my towel, a fuzzy navel in one hand and a joint in the other. Steven crashes into my other side, his hot, heavy arm falling across my shoulder.

She puts the paper to my lips and I inhale like I've seen Steven do so many times. The smoke burns in my lungs and I gag and choke and I cough. But I don't care because there's another beer in my hand and I can't see Will anymore.

Jay tells the story about the Bennetts again and how he thinks they were abducted by aliens. It's always his topic of choice when he's been drinking.

"Are there really aliens?" Jess's eyes are saucers as she gazes into the sky. "Can they see us?"

"I'm sure they can see everything. Their technology has to be incredibly advanced," Jay muses.

"And why would they come here, to our little Podunk shit town? To fish? Waterski? Why the hell would they come here, Jay?" I snort, my voice thick with sarcasm.

"We're just miles from where they test Nuclear Weapons. If you were an alien life form investigating a foreign planet, where would you go?" Jay asks persistently.

"Vegas. I'd go to fucking Vegas," I slur and Margot giggles.

A few more beers and I'm spinning. I pull the rolled weed to my lips like a pro now. The starry sky spins around me, even when I close my eyes, and I can't tell which way is up. I lay on my back, the dirt and rocks sticking to my sweaty skin. Steven hovers over me, the stars rotating around his head like a pinwheel. They look so close, like I can reach up and grab the white specks right out of the darkness. I lift my heavy hand and try to grab the stars, opening and closing my fist next to Steven's head.

"You are so high, Kitty Cat," he taunts. "What are you doing?"

"I just...I want to hold the stars." I'm laughing so hard now. My words are ridiculous even to myself. I roll onto my side, vaguely aware of Steven's head on my shoulder, his body shaking with laughter. I try to sit up. Margot is lying beside me, blowing smoke circles from her rosy mouth. Andy strums his guitar, a cigarette between his lips and Drew croons a mournful, self-loathing song I've never heard before. My brother has disappeared, probably off somewhere with his Lauren, basking in his part-time quasi-relationship. Jess is puking in the shrubs, Amanda holding her long curly hair out of her face and I giggle. And then I see Will.

He's still seated in his chair and he's glaring at me. I stop laughing, I stop breathing. I freeze and stare into his antagonizing eyes that smolder in the light of the fire. His teeth grind together, his whole face tense and he is glaring at me.

"Cat, let's go for a walk, Cat," Steven's lips are on my skin, his breath hot in my ear and I never thought I'd be nauseated at the sound of my own name. "Cat, has anyone ever kissed you under the stars?"

"Yes," I whisper, my eyes filling with tears as I stare into those fiery green eyes. Steven's lips are still on my neck and I feel like I'm going to crumble into dust right here in front of everyone and I can't do it. I have to get out of here.

"Stop, Steven, knock it off." I shrug away from his arm and he grabs my wrist, his fingers digging into my skin.

"Cat, come on. You were feeling it, don't tell me you weren't feeling that just now," Steven slurs and I look over at Will murderously tense on the edge of his chair.

"All I'm feeling is sick. I need to cool off." My voice wavers as I pull my wrist away from him and wade out into the water. Clumsily climbing into the boat, I pull one of the huge inner tubes over the side. I tether the tube to the front of the boat and climb in, my legs hanging over the edge. Floating away from the cove, I sit on the warm canvas cover as water floods the bottom of my little sanctuary and I sob. How did I get to this place, where some silly summer Paycheck can break me? Why do I let William Henderson have this effect on me?

"Cat?" I feel a warm, wet hand on my foot and I scramble to look over the edge.

"Can I sit in your tube?" Will asks, out of breath and treading water. His wet hair drips into his eyes as he looks up at me through his long eyelashes.

"No, go away," I mumble.

"Cat, just let me in the tube. I swam all the way out here. I'm going to pass out and drown if you don't let me in the tube. Do you want that on your conscience?" he teases, and I go back to hiding.

"Get your own tube," I reply stubbornly. I feel him grip the side before his foot pops up over the edge.

"I don't want my own tube. I want to share yours." His face appears, then his shoulder and then the rest of him as he rolls into the small space. His wet body presses against me and I give up the argument.

We face each other, hip to hip. His long legs slide under my arm and dangle over the side. My knees are bent, my feet tucked against the slick warm skin of his lower back. He traces the scar on my knee, his fingers tickling the damaged skin and I can't breathe.

"I'm not supposed to let you touch me," I mutter. "It was my rule. No touching."

"Well, that's a shitty rule," Will says, his fingers now running circles around my knee.

"Stop, Will. Just stop, please," I whisper, my eyes welling

with tears again.

"I don't want to stop," Will grumbles defiantly.

"Well, you have to," I say sharply and nudge his hand away with my foot. "Jesus, Will, your girlfriend is right over there."

"Amanda's not my girlfriend. She never was. It was just the one time... She's only here because Jess has a big mouth and invited her. There's nothing between us, Cat." Will rests his hand on my knee again, his words resonating in my head.

He's wrong, there's everything between us.

"Could have fooled me," I remark as I absentmindedly pull at the hair on his legs. "I wasn't supposed to get jealous either. That was my other rule. Don't be jealous."

"Are you jealous?" Will asks me.

"Well, duh," I roll my eyes and Will's hand traces my scar again, sending little shivers tingling in my legs.

"You don't hide it well," Will teases and I kick his hand off my knee again.

"I just hate it that your friends know this side of you that I don't. I mean, with me, what you see is what you get. I'm not anything more than what I show you, Will," I try to explain.

"What are you talking about? You are the most confusing person on this planet. I never know what I'm going to get from you. It annoys the shit out of me!" Will says, exasperated.

I look up at the dotted sky, trying to make sense of these feelings and trying to find the words to explain them. I don't even know what I want to explain.

"What do you want to be, Will, when you grow up?" I ask him instead, because it seems we're grown. We look like adults, but I really miss that little girl swimming in the pool of the Tropicana pretending to be a lounge singer.

"I'm going to be a doctor," he says quietly. "I'm starting my undergrad at Johns Hopkins in September and then I will go to medical school."

"Where is Johns Hopkins?"

"Maryland. It's just during the school year. I'll be home for the summer," he says and I sigh. Maryland? Fricking Maryland?

"I don't even know where Maryland is," I mutter and he squeezes my knee.

"It's on the East Coast, as far away from my dad as I could get," he says, triumphant. "I only applied to East Coast schools."

"Okay, well, pretend you're not moving to the other side of the country to become a doctor," I snark. I can't fight the snotty attitude. He could have applied anywhere, he could have applied *here,* and he chose to go to Maryland.

"I want to be a lounge singer in Vegas," I confess and he looks surprised. "Oh, is it really that hard to imagine?"

"Yeah, I can totally see you in a sequined dress, spread out on a grand piano," Will laughs and I dig into his ribs with my foot.

"Seriously, what do you really want for the future?" I press. Will doesn't say anything. He circles my knee again, his eyes focused on the patterns he's drawing into my skin.

"It doesn't matter. I can't have it," Will mutters and I roll my eyes.

"Yes, you can! You can have whatever you want. You don't have to worry about money or opportunity. You literally can do whatever you want," I argue.

"It's not that simple, Cat." Will looks at me through his hair, his eyes dark with intensity, his hand clenching my knee. "Not everything can be solved with a check."

"I know that, Will. But pretend. If you could do anything, what would you do?" He grins, mischief in his eyes as his grip on my knee eases into the delicate tracing again.

"I want to play the piano for your lounge act," he says and I inhale sharply.

I wasn't expecting this response. I can see it. Will would look really sharp in a black tuxedo and poised behind a grand piano, his long fingers flying over the white keys. I would wear a sapphire sequined dress, my hair curled around my shoulders in big soft rings. For one minute I forget about reality and I pretend it's real. It's ridiculous but I let my mind indulge in the fantasy for just a minute, one goddamn minute of pure relief before I snuff it out. We're quiet for a long time, and I wonder if he's imagining it too.

"I don't really want to be a doctor," Will says quietly. "That's the first time I've ever said that out loud."

"You don't have to be a doctor," I tell him. "Write or play the piano or play basketball, you can do anything."

Will snorts. "Tell that to my dad. He never once saw me play. I led my team in scoring in the State Championships and he never showed. He only let me play because it looks good on a college application."

"I'm going to be stuck here for the rest of my life," I murmur. "I already know everything I need to know about running the marina. Paying for college would be a waste."

"You could be a photographer, take pictures of the river and sell them. Turn your talent into something that can make you cash and then you won't need the marina."

"I don't need the marina, Will. The marina, my dad, my brother, they need me. I can't leave, I can't walk away from my family," I stress. Trust me, I could totally live without the marina.

"My mom made me take piano lessons when I was four. She wanted me to be well rounded, have extracurricular activities and shit." His fingers circle my knee again and I don't bother to stop him anymore. I listen, trying to hold on to every word.

"The first song I ever learned was Twinkle, Twinkle, Little Star. I played it for her before she died. I don't remember it. My dad told me. My dad said my mom was so proud of me that day and that's all I want to do. I want to make my mom proud. I want to be the man she wanted me to be. It's why I still play piano, because she wanted me to. She wanted me to be a doctor too and I can't stand the thought of letting her down."

I've never heard Will speak of his mother this way before. I've hardly heard him speak of her at all, to be honest. I don't know what to say. I don't know if there is anything I can say. Everything I think to say sounds perverse.

"I've never told anyone that either." Will runs his hand down my calf now, his arm wrapped tightly around my legs. He's hugging my legs. He just needs a hug. I can give him that. I shift in the small space and crawl into his lap and I hug him. I wrap my arms around his neck, my face pressed into his shoulder. His tense body relaxes, his arms wrap around my waist and he squeezes me tight. We don't move for a long time, just sit there wrapped together and floating on the calm, dark water.

* * *

Will leaves two weeks later with his friends, his red Saab driving away from the marina and it's only July. I'm frustrated and disappointed but the memory of what Will shared with me on the river slightly fills the void.

I work at the store and hang out with Margot when I have time. Lauren has abandoned her to spend every waking hour with my brother. I'm not sure exactly when Margot becomes my friend, but we have more in common than I initially thought. She feels displaced, stuck between Lauren the brainiac and Will the boy-wonder. And she's infatuated with a guy she can't have.

"He doesn't even know I exist, Cat," Margot groans as we sit on the swings. She's still talking about Andy. "I mean, if he wanted to be with me, he would have by now, right?"

"I don't know Margot, maybe he thinks you're out of his league. You're unattainable so why even try." I have no clue what I'm talking about.

"All that really means is he doesn't like me enough," Margot says. She leans back in the swing, letting her head fall back.

"That's not true, maybe he likes you too much and it scares him," I suggest.

"Nope, if he really liked me, then nothing would be able to stand in his way, not even himself," Margot counters, pulling herself upright to make her point. "Love involves risk and sacrifice of pride and ego. Love is saying here I am, you might reject me but I'd rather deal with the pain and find out than never know. If Andy isn't willing to take a risk, he doesn't really want me."

"You aren't exactly throwing yourself on the altar of self-sacrifice there, now are you?" I snort.

"Oh, Cat, sweet darling Catherine. He has to do the sacrificing. I am a prize, and Andy should have to do something to win me." Margot has been reading Cosmo again.

"Well, I don't want to be a prize. That makes me think of those shitty stuffed animals at the carnival. Shouldn't it go both ways? You know, like yin and yang, give and take, peanut butter and jelly?" I argue.

"Drew and Corey," Margot says wistfully.

"Who?" I ask her and she looks at me in disbelief.

"Are you kidding me? What, do you like, live in a vacuum or something?" Margot asks sarcastically.

"Pretty much," I mutter.

"Oh! I forgot! I have your birthday present back at the house," Margot says with a wink and I look at her in surprise. I just figured he'd forgotten this year.

"It's a book," Margot spills and I laugh. "I peeked after he left. Hey, do you have a CD player?"

"Nope, it's just trusty old cassettes for me," I say. My dad refuses to buy a CD player because then he'll have to replace all his cassettes with CD's and he thinks it's a waste. Maybe I can ask my mom to get me one for my birthday.

"Well, I'm going to leave you a tape then. There's this band I want you to listen to. They have a totally unique sound, like if the Sex Pistols and Black Sabbath had a baby. I think they're going to be big." Margot gets up off the swing and we head back to their unit.

"What are they called?" I ask her, my feet crunching through the gravel.

"Nirvana."

I follow Margot through the door of the unit, the inside spotless and clear of any evidence of its inhabitants. Everything is packed up and put away. The Hendersons are leaving in the morning.

Margot hands me a striped bag off the counter. I dig through the yellow tissue paper and pull out a large square book. It's bound in red leather and filled with thick black heavy parchment. The pages are blank and I look to Margot for answers.

"It's a portfolio. For your photographs." Margot beams and my eyes fill with tears. I don't even try to fight them. This present is exactly the breath of confidence I need right now.

"Oh no, what's wrong?" Margot asks and I wipe at my face with the back of my hand.

"It's perfect, Margot, really. Why does he do stuff like this?" I ask her and she pulls me into a tight hug.

"Because he loves you," she says into my shoulder.

"Maybe," I whisper.

But we both know love's not enough.

1990 – THAT TIME I WORE THE BIKINI

R.E.M. records their seventh album, "Out of Time."

*The animated sitcom "The Simpsons" is
aired on Fox for the first time.*

*Operation Desert Shield Begins as the United
States and UK send troops to Kuwait.*

* * *

I just feel like I can be myself around you. You know the real
me," Scott murmurs over the receiver.

"Uh-huh," I say into the phone pressed between my ear and
shoulder, the cord tethering me to the kitchen. I flip to the last
pages of the book I'm reading and skim the end to see what
happens. I can't stand reading through a whole book unless I'm
going to like the ending.

"I feel so connected to you. Like there's electricity between
us, something cosmic pulling us together," he says in a hushed
whisper and I roll my eyes. I sound like a sock stuck to the back
of his R.E.M. t-shirt. Maybe I should suggest dryer sheets.

"Cat? Are you there? Did you hear what I said?"

"Huh?" I ask, startling out of my Laundromat lament.

"I said, you should come over and we can drive out to the
point. And maybe get to a point ourselves, if you know what
I mean," he says in a low voice and I think he's trying to be
seductive.

I don't know what he means. Scott has never ever gotten me
to *that* point.

I guess I'm dating Scott. We go to the movies and out for ice
cream. We go for boat rides and I take pictures and Scott talks

about his classes. We fool around and have pretty much done everything aside from seal the deal. Bless his heart, but Scott can't get me off to save his life. Luckily, I have become quite skilled in the area of self-service, thank you very much Cosmo.

I don't see how this problem can be fixed with sex. I mean, really, why bother? Scott doesn't expect too much, and he doesn't smother me with attention. But I know this relationship isn't ever going to get to the point.

"Um, okay. I'll meet you in twenty minutes," I tell him and hang up. I put on my favorite white eyelet camisole and comb my hair. I even put on mascara and lip gloss before stepping out onto the porch, only to see the Henderson unit is all lit up. They're here.

I know it would be wrong to blow off Scott for Will. I know this. And yet all I want is to run down to the swings to see if he's there. I have about five minutes. I could take a peek and still make it to Scott's in time. If I run. And speed.

My sandaled feet slip a couple times in the graveled dirt as I jet down to the docks. I'm sure my face is beet red, and I wipe the sweat from my cheeks with the back of my hand. I can see him on the swings from the sidewalk. He's still in his San Francisco clothes, polo, shorts and loafers and he's eating a rainbow sherbet Push-Up.

He looks up mid-slurp and freezes when he sees me. His eyes very obviously roam and I look down, thinking I'm exposing something I shouldn't be.

"What are you looking at, creeper?" I ask and sit on the swing beside him. He hands me an IT'S-IT and I'm completely predictable.

"I almost thought you wouldn't come and I'd have to eat that myself," he says between slurps. "I was almost looking forward to it."

"The ice cream called to me," I say, ripping the plastic wrapper and taking a big bite of the chocolate covered cookie sandwich. "You look kind of shady out here on the swings peddling ice cream to young girls."

"What about you? All dressed up and soliciting young boys on the playground." Will gently crashes his swing into mine, his lips pink and syrup stained. "What's wrong with your eyes?"

"It's just mascara," I say defensively.

"I know, it's all smeared." His hand holds my face, his thumb wiping across my sweaty cheek and I try to pretend his fingers wiping mascara off my face is completely fine.

"Thanks," I mutter through another big bite and he chuckles. He finishes his ice cream and crumples the carton when a somewhat familiar face saunters out of the general store.

Sporting a t-shirt with long black pants tucked into big black boots, a flannel shirt tied around his waist and a string of tiny round shells around his neck is Andy.

"Hey, Catherine the Great," Andy says to me, his long wavy hair falling across his face and I blush. He unwraps a Blow Pop and puts the sucker in his mouth. "Man, that chick in there is one angry bitch."

"Josie's not a bitch. She just has a low tolerance for bullshit. Were you feeding her bullshit, Andy?" I ask, sarcastically.

"Of course not. I was a perfect gentleman." Andy's voice is low and smooth and I don't believe him for one second.

"So, Cat, where are you off to all dressed up?" Will asks, turning the carton over in his fingers.

"Nowhere important," I respond and lick the last of the chocolate from my fingers.

* * *

P lease Josie? Please? I'll work two weeks for you," I plead and Josie rolls her eyes. Dr. Henderson rented a houseboat and Jay and I were invited to spend the week with them. It's to celebrate Lauren's college graduation. She's going to be a lawyer, which means she's going back to school, but she completed her bachelor's degree.

My brother is now fully entrenched in running the marina. He's given up on college and over the winter, persuaded my dad to get rid of the paddle boats and kayaks and to get some WaveRunners we could rent out instead. Business has been kind of slow. The Youngs even dropped their prices, and Steven's been looking for another job. There just isn't enough work for all the boys, even with Michael away at college and Little Jimmy moving to Los Angeles. Anyway, my dad is stressing over the large purchase and is making Jay spend the summer pushing WaveRunner rentals to make up for the blunder. It isn't really his fault, how was he supposed to know the economy was going to take a nosedive?

At any rate, he persuaded Dr. Henderson to rent two of them along with the houseboat and plans on coming out to the cove for a couple days, but I want to stay on the houseboat the whole week. My dad said no at first. He told me I have to work, so I quit. Yep, I looked my dad in the face and said, "I quit then." And he laughed at me. After a couple hours of yelling and screaming in which I used the "I'm eighteen, I can leave if I want" card half a dozen times, my dad said I could go if I could get Josie to cover my schedule. He thinks this is impossible.

Josie looks at me and purses her lips.

"Alright, two weeks and," I sigh, because I really, really hate doing this. "I'll clean the restrooms for a month." It physically hurts to say the words.

"Deal," Josie grumbles and without thinking I throw my arms around her neck. "Now, get outta here, your cheerfulness is suffocating."

A week later, I'm lounging on the roof of the houseboat with Margot and Lauren while Dr. Henderson looks for a cove. Andy and Will circle us on the WaveRunners, speeding off ahead and then circling back. The boys wear these baggy canvas shorts in the water, forgoing the swim trunks this year. It must be a new style or something.

Margot is wearing one of her stunning bikinis, this year it's a lavender paisley print. Lauren brings a black halter two piece and I bought a new swimsuit a couple days ago for this trip. I went shopping with my mom in Vegas and under the influence of parental pressure, I did something I never thought I'd do. I tried on a bikini. Then, because I love putting myself in awkward situations, I bought it. I don't know what I was thinking.

Alright, I know exactly what I was thinking and none of it was good. I was thinking about last year and how all the girls looked fabulous in their two pieces and I looked like a complete frump. I was thinking about Amanda and how she was so confident in her skimpy bathing suit and it made me angry that I couldn't be confident too. I'm not saying I didn't have ulterior motives. I'm just saying I bought the damn thing.

The only problem is my stomach is so incredibly white. This skin has never before seen the light of day and I look ridiculous. My arms and legs are golden brown and my stomach shines like a beacon of pale.

"You'd better put on sunblock," Will said when he first saw me in the small suit, the beaded strings tied at my hips, neck and back. "You're gonna fry to a crisp out here."

That was it. That was the only reaction I got out of him. He didn't even look at my boobs, and I quickly hid under my tank-top, feeling like a fool for even thinking I could pull off a bikini.

Dr. Henderson finds a nice, large cove about twenty miles down river and anchors the houseboat. When I think about spending a whole week with Will, I remember last year when Margot was freaking out about Andy. I get it now. Sleeping in cramped quarters, seeing him first thing in the morning with stinky breath and yes, the crusties all makes me a little nervous. Not that it matters. Will and I are friends.

Will in pajamas is confusing. I don't know why. I've seen Will in far less clothing. I've touched Will in far less clothing but I notice everything about him in pajamas. Will in pajamas is comfort and relaxed and it affects me in a whole new way. Pajamas are everyday, no matter where he is. Pajamas are routine. Pajamas are almost real life.

Once in the bathroom, I slip off my bikini and inspect the damage. I poke at the skin of my stomach. It's a little bit tender, the pasty white just a tad pink and I'm glad I decided to wear my tank top. I take a quick shower, and slather on some aloe vera lotion after toweling off and pull on my undies and cotton shorts. I'm about to put on my sleep shirt when I realize I forgot my bra at home. Shit! I pull my shirt over my head and inspect. It's baggy enough, you can hardly tell. I can probably get a bra from Margot, but then I realize this is stupid. Who wears a bra to bed? *Don't be such a prude, Cat. They're just boobs.*

Andy's leaning against the wall and a slow grin spreads across his lips when I duck out of the bathroom.

"It's all yours," I mumble.

"Thanks," Andy says with a smirk. "Nice shirt, Wonder Woman. But you forgot your gold bracelets."

"Yeah." I guess I forgot a couple things.

"You know, you kind of look like her." His eyes don't leave my face.

"She's an Amazon," is the only thing I can think of to say. Andy's mouth forms a wide Cheshire Cat grin and I spin around and leave him in the hallway. That was weird, right? That was just a weird conversation.

I plop down on the couch next to Margot. She's sitting cross legged in these tiny little shorts and a tank top. She's not wearing a bra either. The plan is to watch the first two Godfather movies because apparently, they're making a third.

"Really, I don't know why they're even making a third one. It's redundant, like beating a dead horse," Will says. He looks up at me for an instant and then his eyes are gone. He must not think pajamas are a big deal. He's probably seen lots of girls in their pajamas.

"More like beating a dead horse's head?" I chuckle and Margot snorts.

Will walks over to the couch, the spot currently occupied by a bowl of popcorn, and motions for Margot to move the bowl. Margot stares at him, nudging her head in my direction and the meaning is obvious. He doesn't want to sit by me. I feel my stomach twist and I stare at him in disbelief. We're supposed to be friends, we pinky promised. Why doesn't he want to sit by me?

Andy comes out of the bathroom in his sweatpants and a Red Hot Chili Peppers t-shirt and plops down next to me, like it's no big deal. Margot and I are both glaring at Will now and he refuses to look at either of us. He pushes play on the VCR and sits on the floor next to Margot's feet and I feel like I want to kick him in the head.

"Do you want a soda, Cat?" Margot asks me as the mournful theme sounds.

"No thanks," I mutter but she nudges me and gives me a look.

"Um, I think I'll have a Fun Dip though," I say, catching on and I start to get up from my seat so Margot can move over.

Andy thwarts all our plans though, because he beats me off the couch. "I'll get it, I'm gonna get a soda anyway. Margot, do you want a Fun Dip?"

"You have no idea," Margot mutters under her breath and I try not to laugh. Andy looks at her, confused and she just shakes her head no.

Andy pours himself a soda and grabs two Fun Dips off the counter and Margot gives me a look again. I shrug, unsure as to what she wants me to do so I start to scoot over but she grabs my arm and shakes her head just as Andy turns off the living room light and settles back in. He grins at me, handing me the candy and I mutter thanks.

"Someday, I may call upon you to do a favor for me," Andy misquotes into my ear, his hot breath in the cool air conditioned room causing the hairs on the back of my neck to prick. He lets his arm rest against my body, and his leg is pressed against mine. Holy cannoli! Is Andy hitting on me?

I look at Margot out of the corner of my eye. Her eyes are set on the screen and I'm positive she heard him. She's upset, I can see it in the thin line of her pursed lips. It's the same face Josie makes whenever anyone mentions the Young's boat storage place. There's no way I'm sitting next to Andy, not after he breathed on my neck. I grab one of the blankets and pillows from the huge pile that is to become our bed later and curl up on the floor. I lay longways in front of the television with all three of them to my back.

Somewhere around Sonny getting shot, I fall asleep. When I wake up, the room is dark and Margot has crashed on the couch. The boys are gone and I don't see Lauren so I imagine she's still on the roof with my brother which makes me want to gag a little. It's very, very quiet in the dead night of the desert and I'm wide awake. I start to think about Will asleep in his room just a few feet from me. I could sneak into his room. I could climb into his bed. I could touch him and let him touch me and I would be happy.

And then he will leave at the end of the summer and I will be heartbroken. I feel the twist in my belly and I can't lay here anymore. I kick off my blanket and walk into the kitchen. Looking for confectionery comfort, I open the freezer, pull out the small tub of cookies and cream and grab a spoon. Jumping onto the counter, I drown my sorrows in the frozen treat.

A tall silhouette stumbles into the living room, and I freeze mid-bite. I slip the spoon from my mouth silently as Will scratches his head, his hair tangled and sticking up in odd places. He walks into the kitchen, opens the fridge and pulls out the orange juice, drinking straight from the carton. He's illuminated by the light of the fridge, a slim beam highlighting his chest and abdomen while his face remains shrouded in darkness. I can faintly make out the lines of his jaw and neck, his Adam's apple bobbing when he swallows and I accidentally let my brain remember what his skin tastes like. I crave it.

I stuff my face with ice cream, a big huge bite that almost makes me choke. Too much! Sharp pangs pound behind my eyes and I squeeze my temples. Brain freeze! Oh God, it hurts! I try not to cry out, and the spoon slips from my hand and clatters to the counter. Will startles, orange juice dribbling down his chin and spilling onto his shirt.

"Cat?" Will gasps. "You scared the shit out of me!"

"Balls!" I squeeze my eyes shut. The brain freeze still clenches my head, and a single syllable is all I can get out. Finally it passes and I'm able to function again.

"What are you doing?" Will asks as he wipes his mouth with the bottom of his shirt, exposing his sinewy stomach, his fricking hip bones highlighted by the small fluorescent light of the fridge.

"Ice cream?" I offer him the tub and he closes the fridge. Surrounded in darkness, he walks over to my knees and places his hands on my thighs. Goosebumps spread like wildfire across my legs, my heart beats out of my chest. He gently nudges my knees out of the way so he can get a spoon from the drawer and then his hands are gone. I can barely see him, and he's not touching me anymore but I can feel him. Warmth radiates off his body, his soapy smell slightly tinted with sweat from sleeping and the hum, God the hum of the thick energy between us vibrates.

If Will kisses me right now, I will not resist him. I will kiss him back, I will wrap my legs around his waist and I will never let go. If he kisses me right now.

He dips into the carton, his lips wrapping around the spoon and I'm practically drooling when he licks the back of the utensil. He grins at me, he knows what he's doing and I'm a fool for falling for it.

"Are you trying to be sexy? Because you're failing miserably," I try to save face and Will takes another bite. He licks the spoon grotesquely now, closing his eyes and crudely pulling his lips and tongue over the metal. I groan, and push him away with my foot.

"You're so gross," I laugh. Will chuckles and the easy comfort is back. He leans against the counter beside me, his side pressed against my leg, his arm resting on my thigh as we take spoonfuls of ice cream.

"How do you like college?" I ask him in between bites.

"It's okay," Will says, shrugging his shoulders. "Actually, I hate it."

"You hate it? I thought you liked school," I ask confused.

"I never liked school. I liked basketball, I liked partying, I liked my friends," Will mutters. I'm pretty sure by friends he means the girl ones too. "Luckily I still get to play ball, but college is work. I listen to some old dude talk, and then I take a test. I'm more of a physical learner, like hands-on, you know? I can't just sit and listen and then get it. Do you know what I mean?"

"College isn't for everyone. Jay dropped out," I respond.

"Yeah, but I'm not like Jay," Will says and I frown. "I don't have any other options. I have to do well in school. There's no other choice for me."

"Do you think my brother wants to work at the marina forever? Do you think this is what I want for my life? What are my options, Will? What choices do I have?" I ask him, trying to be quiet but I can't help the snotty tone of my voice.

"You have choices. You choose to ignore them," Will says sharply.

"It's more like my choices are ignoring me," I snap and Will turns his head to meet my eyes, his nose just inches from mine.

"Well, you're the one who wanted it this way," he says in a low voice. I'm trying to find a way he's wrong, but I can't.

The sliding door opens and Lauren creeps in silently. We hear the roar of my dad's boat and I know it's Jay heading back to the marina. Will turns his head, his arm leaves my leg and he puts his spoon in the sink. Lauren looks at us with dreamy eyes and I envy her.

If it were anyone else, I wouldn't mind being a part-time girlfriend. I don't want Will part-time. I want him always. Maybe Lauren and Jay don't feel this way. Maybe this is just a summer thing for them. Maybe I'm too immature for a relationship because right now I feel like a five year old, pouting because I can't have what I want.

Will and I don't discuss much for the next couple days and we don't meet for midnight snacks again either. We take the

WaveRunners back to the marina to gas up and then ride them all the way up to the dam. Margot rides with Andy, claiming there's no way in hell she's straddling her brother. Will lets me drive, his thighs pressed into my hips, his hands loosely gripping the sides of my vest, and his chin sometimes rests on my shoulder. Jay comes back every night. I bet my dad's just pitching a fit and I'm glad I'm not home to witness the debacle. He takes us on the boat for night rides a few times and he sneaks us wine coolers and beer from the marina. Every night we watch movies or play Super Mario Bros on Will's gaming system. We play cards and board games and Mrs. Henderson even makes us strawberry margaritas on the Fourth of July.

Andy's flirting makes me uncomfortable. I can't tell if he's just a friendly person or if he's really hitting on me. I try to assess the way he treats the other girls and it seems he steers clear of Lauren altogether. He's flirty with Margot. He teases her, kicks sand on her when she unties her bikini to tan. I guess he's just friendly, and I'm relieved. I don't want to have any bad feelings with Margot. She's a good friend, even if I only get to see her once a year.

I start to feel more relaxed in my bikini. The other girls aren't shy, even Mrs. Henderson wears a two piece this year and none of them feel the need to cover up. Sponging their confidence, I forgo the tank top and I have to admit, it's much more comfortable without the weighted wet shirt all the time. I'm paranoid about burning still and constantly apply lotion but despite my best efforts, by the fifth day on the water, I have a sunburn. And it's not even on my stomach. In all my haste to protect my tummy, I forget about my back, and the pale strip of skin right above my butt normally covered by my one-piece is now bright red and stings. I rub aloe vera lotion into the sensitive skin after my shower but it's going to blister and peel, I can tell.

Everyone is sitting in the living room when I'm finished in the bathroom. Jay and Lauren are cuddling on the couch and it bothers me that I can't see their hands at all times. Margot is seated next to them, cutting strips of paper into squares and Andy's stretched out on the carpet.

"We're playing the hat game." Will hands me a pen with a grin. I sit on the floor, my shirt annoyingly rubbing against my sunburned back. I can feel the heat pulsing and if I were at home, I'd put my swimsuit top back on and go shirtless. That's not going to happen here.

"What's the hat game?" I ask when Will sits down next to me on the floor, his long legs stretched out in front of him as he leans back on his elbows.

"We all get ten slips of paper. You write down ten famous things, it can be people, songs, movies, places, whatever. But they have to be well-known," Margot says as she looks up from her scissors. "You have to try to get your team to guess what's on the paper by using clues. The key is to guess as many as possible in one minute."

"But you can't say shit like, "rhymes with", or "sounds like". Like if the paper says "The Simpsons" you can't say rhymes with blimpsons," Will interjects and I look at him blankly.

"Who are The Simpsons?" I ask and he laughs, giving me a playful shove to the side. I wince, my sunburn throbbing at the contact, and he looks at me, confused.

"Sunburn," I say sheepishly. He pulls up the back of my shirt to look at the burn and I swat at his hands.

"Oh relax, it's not like I haven't seen your back before," he murmurs, his hands still pulling at my shirt. My face flushes with heat, and I hold the fabric tightly in place over my chest. "Nice one, Cat! It's already blistering. Did you put lotion on it?"

"Of course," I respond as he gently lays the shirt over the stinging skin. Margot hands us our slips of paper and for the next couple minutes the room is silenced by contemplative thought. I can't think of anything to write, my head still baffled by the unsolicited sunburn surveying. I glance over at Will, trying to see what he's writing but he hides his papers so I just scribble down the first names that come to my head. How do you spell *Labyrinth*?

"Okay, teams," Will says and we all jot our names on the slips. Andy gets up and collects the papers in his Frank Sinatra hat, his eyes electric as he grins.

Will pulls me, Andy and his own name from the hat. The other team will be Lauren, Jay and Margot and I'm slightly nervous I'm going to suck at this game.

"Wait! We need drinkage," Jay says and the boys go out to get the beer from the cooler on my dad's boat, setting the ice chest outside the slider on the deck. Margot grabs us some wine coolers and the boys start with the beer and I'm definitely thinking this is a bad idea. Beer and board games do not mix.

We ro-sham-bo to see which team goes first and Margot's scissors beats Will's paper. I'm glad because this means I can watch a round before actually having to participate. Margot goes first, standing in the middle of the living room, the hat perched on the television. Will uses the timer from the Pictionary box to keep time and the moment he flips the plastic timer, the room is chaos.

"Okay, she has a rock star alter ego, and she pushes the earring and there's Synergy and-"

"Jem!" Lauren shouts and Margot makes a motion with her hands indicating there's more.

"Full name," Margot says.

"Jem and the Holograms," Lauren spits out and Margot tosses the slip of paper, choosing another one from the hat.

"This is a guy who sings a stupid song-"

"Really, Margot? Could you be a bit more vague?" Jay says dryly.

"Let me finish! He stole the beat from Queen..." Margot adds.

"Vanilla Ice," Jay blurts. Margot squeals and chooses the next name.

"She's a dancer. Used to be a cheerleader for the Lakers," Margot rushes.

"I know this!" Will mumbles in my ear and I sigh. I have no idea who she's talking about.

Jay and Lauren look stumped and Margot grows more

frantic.

"She's small, um, shit! Oh! She has a video with a cartoon cat!" Margot jumps up and down as Will watches the time.

"Oh crap, what's her name?" Lauren says, hitting the couch with her hand and Jay just shrugs. "Um, Paula something..."

"Paula Abdul," I say. Will and Andy both glare at me and I clasp my hand over my mouth.

Margot smiles and throws down the paper, taking another from the hat.

"Okay, these are little blue creatures that-"

"Smurfs!" my brother shouts and Margot moves on to the next name. She reads the slip, frowning before looking at her team.

"Um, okay, this one's hard. Um, the second word is a shape," she says, shrugging her shoulders.

"Circle, triangle, square..." Jay rambles.

"Square! Okay, I think it's in India or Asia or somewhere?" She shakes her head clearly at a loss.

"Time!" Will shouts and holds up the timer. "Time's up."

"Who wrote Tiananmen Square?" Margot says, crumpling the paper and throwing it into the trash can in the kitchen.

"You should be ashamed of yourself for not knowing that one," Lauren gripes while Margot collects the papers from the floor.

"We got four."

"Okay, Cat. You're up," Andy says with a wink and I down the rest of my Pina Colada. Will hands the timer to Margot and I stand up.

"And...go," Margot says. I pull a paper from the hat and it's an easy one.

"Okay, um, slimer?"

"Ghostbusters!" Andy shouts and I'm stunned. He actually got it.

"Go, go, next, next," Will says and I frantically toss the paper to the ground and fumble around in the hat for the next name. *NKOTB*. Shit, what the hell is that?

"It's an acronym, I think."

"NKOTB!" Andy blurts out and again I stand there blinking. It's like he can read my mind or something.

"Next!" Will says, his voice irritated and I pick another slip of paper. Why is he so pissed? He's on our team!

"Okay, um, *thank you for being a friend*," I sing.

"Golden Girls," Andy and Will say at exactly the same time and they glare at each other. I hesitantly grab the next paper, my body suddenly tense as Andy and Will face off.

"Oh, I know this one! He's an alien and he eats cats," I say.

"Alf!" Will shouts with a fist pump. Margot must have muttered something inappropriate because both my brother and Lauren groan in disgust. I ignore them and pull another slip.

Legend of Zelda. Oh hell.

"I don't even know where to start. The first word is like an old tale that might be true."

"Legend of Zelda?" Andy guesses and I just laugh. How did he guess that?

"You guys are cheating!" Lauren accuses as soon as Margot calls time.

"We are not. Cat and I just think alike. We must have twin brains," Andy says, pulling me into a hug and kissing my cheek. My eyes instantly flash to Margot and she refuses to look at me.

I sit down on the floor next to Will and I can feel him fuming beside me. He chugs his beer, crushing the can and shooting it into the trash can by the counter. He misses.

"I need a drink," Margot mutters. She walks into the kitchen and grabs the tequila from the cabinet before pulling a tupperware of limes from the fridge. She pours a round of shots, six tumblers on the counter splashed with alcohol. "Come on, everyone's doing at least one."

"Margot, I'm not drinking tequila. You remember what happened last time," Will mutters, his eyes glancing at me a couple times. I instantly wonder what happened last time.

"Yes, you are. Everyone's fucking drinking tequila. Now!"

Margot says loudly.

"Keep it down! Our parents are going to hear you, dumbass," Will says and Margot rolls her eyes.

"Whatever," she mutters. She holds up the glass and Andy's the first to take one.

"I'm in," Andy shrugs and Margot's eyes are like daggers. Lauren and Jay mosey over to the counter and a reluctant Will joins them. Ugh peer pressure!

"Fine," I say, walking to the counter and picking up the glass. I have no idea what I'm doing. I watch Margot lick her wrist and shake the salt on her skin. She licks the salt, downs the tequila and bites into a lime wedge in one swift, fluid motion. I get the impression she's well acquainted with Mr. Cuervo.

The others follow suit. They all grimace and groan, their faces contorted as they gag and the last thing I want to do now is drink this shit. Will stares at me, his eyes sharp and narrow, and I'm pissed because I didn't even do anything wrong. He's mad at me and I didn't even do anything.

"What?" I snap.

"Man up, Cat," Will says sarcastically, his eyes glassy and red.

"Don't you mean woman up?" I ask him in my best snotty voice and he snorts. I don't know what this laugh means, but it's infuriating.

Will grabs my wrist and licks my palm, his eyes on mine the whole time and I gasp. Will just fricking licked me and I'm torn between the burning in my thighs and the clenching of my fist.

He covers my hand in salt and holds the palm to my face, still staring right through me. He's challenging me, he thinks I won't do it. Well, he should know better than to challenge me.

I lick the salt from my palm, and bring the cup to my lips, swallowing the tequila quickly and then Will's shoving a lime in my mouth, the citrus bringing relief to the burning in the back of my throat. My face squishes up in disgust, but I spit out the rind before sticking my tongue out at him in triumph.

"See? Easy as pie," he says. He drops my wrist and sits back down on the floor as the tequila seeps through my body.

"New rules," Margot says, throwing back another tumbler. "Losing team of each round takes a shot."

As the game progresses, the descriptions get more and more ridiculous. Since I'm already so clueless when it comes to pop culture, I rely on Andy's ability to read my mind. His hands get more and more liberal. He hugs me, he pushes and pinches and pokes and kisses my cheek half a dozen times. Margot drinks every round and now the tequila is gone and she's finishing off the wine coolers, but refuses to drink beer because it makes you fat. Lauren and Jay keep groping each other and Will fumes on the floor, his knees pulled up under his elbows and I can see right up the leg of his basketball shorts. He's not wearing any underwear.

It's our turn and I squint, trying to read the words blurred onto the paper. I giggle, trying to stand in one place, the room swaying as Margot turns the timer.

"Go fucker," she barks and I erupt into giggles.

"Oh! She's on my shirt!" I point to my chest and Will glares. God, what the hell is his problem?

"Wonder Woman," Andy says easily and I grab another slip, almost knocking the hat off the television set.

"Um, she's...she's like...a virgin," I giggle.

"Cat Rossi! It's you, right?" Jay chokes out and they all burst into laughter.

"No asshole, it's not me," I scowl at my brother.

"No it's not you, or no you're not like a virgin?" Will says. He's been silent this last round and we all turn to stare at him.

"Not your business, Mr. Grumble," I say and make an exaggerated sad face.

"Madonna! Give us a fucking challenge, people!" Andy replies and I pull the next slip.

"Oh! Will, you know this one. This is song number one on my *Songs that Remind Cat of her Super Awesome Friend Will* mixtape," I look at him expectantly and he just stares. "Come on, I know you know this."

"I don't know, Cat," Will says through clenched teeth and I've about had it with his crappy attitude. He's lying. I know he remembers. He remembers everything.

"Like ten seconds," Margot says.

"The name of the song is another word for woman," I grumble and Will's eyes don't soften.

"Lady!" Andy shouts before Margot calls time and I'm caught in Will's hard stare. I don't even realize it when Andy picks me up and spins me around. I don't even notice it when he grabs at my sunburned back. I don't even notice when he presses his lips to mine, giving me a full, hard, sloppy kiss that causes the room to freeze over.

"What the hell, Andy?" I say after I finally realize to push him away. I look for Will and he's gone, the back of his sandy hair disappearing down the hall. Stupid, stupid Andy!

"What? You've been coming on to me all week. I thought you liked me," Andy says and my gaze darts to Margot. Her eyes are on her lap and I feel awful.

"Margot! You should be kissing Margot," I struggle with the words as I try to turn his attention to her. The moment she looks at me, I know I've made a horrible mistake. I'm pretty sure if she could shoot laser beams out of her eyes, she would incinerate me right now. Instead she storms out of the room, locking herself in the bathroom.

"Margot? But I thought..." Andy trails off and he looks dejected. He looks down, turning away from me and walking out onto the deck. I sigh, and look at my brother and Lauren, who sit in stunned silence.

"Damn Cat, maybe you shouldn't drink," Jay says and I collapse on the couch. I feel horrible for what I've said. I totally outed Margot, made Andy look like a fool, and Will! I let his friend kiss me. I was snotty to him and I let his friend kiss me. I have to go to him. I have to apologize at least.

"Will?" I whisper into his dark room and he doesn't answer. I step inside and close the door behind me. It's totally black in the room and I grope to find some purchase.

"Will, where are you?" I say quietly and I hear him sigh. I

trip over a duffle bag, knocking my knee into the wooden bed frame.

"Shit!" I exclaim and rub my knee furiously. Will suppresses a quiet chuckle and I feel along the bottom bunk but it's empty. I try to run my hand along the top mattress but it's too high so I use the frame as a guide and find the ladder. I clumsily climb and feel along the bed, my hand running over the soft hair of his leg and the slinky material of his basketball shorts. I slide my thumb in between my pointer and middle finger and pinch his leg.

"Ow! Cat!" he cries out, exasperated.

"Move over." I climb over his legs and squeeze between his warm body and the cold wall.

"You're gonna push me off the bed," Will gripes and I feel the bed shift. I reach out in the darkness to feel his face, my fingers running over his cheek and lips, my thumb grazing the sharp stubble on his face. My hand slides down his neck and shoulder and along his chest. I just want to be close to him. I just want to feel him.

"Cat, don't," Will whispers and I ignore him.

"You can't tell me what to do," I whisper back.

"Oh, believe me, I wouldn't think of telling you what to do," he scoffs and I let my hand rest on his arm, pulling gently at the soft hair.

"I'm so sorry about Andy."

"It wasn't really your fault. Andy asked me about you on the ride here. I told him to go for it," Will says. "I knew he didn't stand a chance."

"You know Margot has been in love with him forever, right?"

"I thought she hated him. She's always so weird when he's around," he remarks. We're silent for a few minutes and I'm looking for a way to close the distance between us.

"Yes," I say.

"Yes what?" he asks.

"Yes, I'm like a virgin," I mumble. "I'm kind of seeing this guy Scott, although I'll be surprised if I ever hear from him again.

I blew off plans with him that night you guys got here. And I forgot to tell him I would be gone all week."

"That's really shitty, Cat."

"I know." I pull up my shirt and let my sunburned back press against the cold wall. Oh, sweet relief! "I've pretty much done all that I can do with him and I really don't want to sleep with him. But I think he's starting to expect it to happen soon."

"Why don't you want to sleep with him?" Will asks, his hand finally reaching out for me. I feel his fingers graze my stomach and I close my eyes, memorizing the way his fingers feel on my skin. Nothing feels as good as Will. Nothing.

"I don't know. He reads Tom Clancy novels," I giggle and I feel Will shift, his legs rubbing against mine. Oh, thank God I shaved.

"I've had sex a bunch of times and I barely remember it," he says, his breath warm on my face. He smells like beer and tequila and I wonder if he tastes the same. It's almost enough to distract me from the fact that there are multiple people out there now that know Will in a way that I don't.

Almost.

"Who were they?" I ask, because obviously I hate myself. "What were they like?"

"Um, well, you know Amanda," Will starts, his fingers tracing figure eights around my belly button. "And the others are just girls from school." Will moves closer, his chest pressed against mine now, his hand lightly resting on my hip. "They didn't mean anything to me. They just satisfied an itch."

"That doesn't sound very satisfying," I say, my lips now grazing his neck as I whisper.

"It wasn't," he whispers back, his lips moving against my forehead. His hand slides across the sunburned skin of my back and I cringe away from his hand. There isn't a shred of space between us and I can feel all of him, every inch flush against me.

"Sorry," he murmurs against my skin, his hand skimming up my spine beneath my shirt and settling in the middle of my back. I'm starting to get sleepy, the alcohol making my limbs heavy. I yawn, snuggling into Will's chest, and breathing him in.

It is very, very satisfying.

I wake up in the morning before he does, and I don't think we moved all night. This might be the most comfortable I've ever been, lying here with my sunburned back pressed against the air conditioned wall, Will's hot breath in my hair, and his arm draped across my middle.

The early morning light streams in through the window and everything seems different now. In the dark, I felt protected. It was easy to tell Will all that stuff about Scott, and it was easy to hear about those girls he screwed. It was easy to let him hold me but, now, in the light, everything's more complicated.

I want Will. I want him so bad it hurts to breathe when I think of him going back to school in Maryland and being with other people. What if I can have him part-time? Is part-time better than not at all? Even this cuddling is better than not at all. We could write to each other, we could maybe talk on the phone. It could almost be the same.

But then what? Can I really see a future where Will comes to live at the marina forever? I refuse to ask that of him.

I want to stay here forever, tangled with Will on the top bunk but I need to pee so I gently try to move his arm. He stirs, tightening his arm around me and I don't even try to fight him.

"No," he mumbles. "Too comfortable." I grin into his t-shirt, inhaling his soapy smell tinged with beer and tequila when everything that happened last night comes flooding back to me. I groan, a gnawing grumble in my belly.

"What?" Will asks lazily.

"Margot. She hates me. I kinda, maybe said something to Andy. About her. About how he should be kissing her. She's going to be mad at me, huh?" I ask into his shirt so as not to assault him with tequila morning breath.

"Probably. I'd be mad at you," Will says and I'm trying to wiggle out of his clutches, when I feel him hard against my leg.

"Do you have a boner?" I ask him, exasperated, and he laughs. "Jesus, Will!"

"What? I can't control it! What do you expect? That's like being mad at me for blinking," he chuckles, finally letting me loose.

"Oh God," I mumble and try to hide my smile as I crawl over his legs and down the ladder. Andy's bed is still empty. I step silently into the hall, creeping into the bathroom so I can pee and brush my teeth. Once finished, I walk into the living room and my brother and Lauren are asleep on the couch. Still no sign of Margot or Andy. I'm afraid of what I will find if I go looking so I start cleaning the kitchen because it looks like a liquor store exploded. I throw the empty bottles and cans in my brother's cooler, letting the trash float in the melted ice and quickly rinse all the glasses and wipe down the counters.

Will ventures into the living room, and his pajamas look especially nice after spending the night cuddled up to them. He helps me clean up, gathering up all the scattered slips of paper and dumping them in the trash. I wake up Jay because it's well past dawn and he's going to be in big trouble once he gets back to the marina. Plus, he needs to get that cooler out of here. He and Will carry the cooler of trash to my dad's boat while I finish cleaning the kitchen. I hear the boat roar to life and take off down the river when a stunned Will walks back in through the slider.

"You look like you've seen a ghost," I laugh and Will sits down at one of the barstools by the counter.

"Worse. I just saw Andy's naked white ass. On top of my sister," Will shudders. "I'm scarred for life."

"Maybe Margot won't be too angry with me after all," I grin.

Margot forgets to be mad at me. She's too busy sucking face and groping Andy to be angry. It's downright revolting. If this is what happens when you start having sex, I'm going to stay a virgin forever. Which won't be too hard, seeing as how Scott dumps me when I get home.

After working my two weeks straight for Josie and then

resuming my normal shift, I rarely get to see the Hendersons. Will comes into the store to buy an ice cream and we sit on the swings and talk during my breaks. We resume our normal friendship but I still wonder if Will would want to be my quasi-serious, part-time boyfriend.

When the storm season starts to roll in, the Hendersons start to pack up. I know they're leaving when Will shows up at the store with a brown paper bag. Josie takes her smoke break when she sees him come in.

Will hands me the bag and I pull out a thick gray sweatshirt, the word Hopkins across the front in blue lettering. My fingers graze over the embroidered letters.

"It's from my school," he says, scratching the peeling skin from his nose and I smile.

"There aren't a lot of opportunities for me to wear a sweatshirt around here," I murmur, putting the soft cotton against my face.

"Then you'll just have to fly out to Baltimore," Will says quietly. "Seriously, you should come visit me. You'd love it. The city is full of stuff you can take pictures of."

"I can't afford a plane ticket to Baltimore," I say instinctively.

"I know and your dad probably won't let you leave," he says.

"No, my dad won't let me leave," I repeat and the statement resonates.

"Well, in case anything ever changes, now you have something you can wear," Will says. He wraps his arms around me and I inhale, committing his smell, his touch, his voice to memory.

"Bye, Catherine the Great. I'll see you next summer."

1991 – THAT TIME YOU BROUGHT THE SKANK

Thelma and Louise, a movie about two women fleeing their caged lives, is released in May.

Perry Farrell organizes the first Lollapalooza as a farewell tour for his band Jane's Addiction.

The Chicago Bulls win the first of six NBA championships achieved during the 1990's.

❋ ❋ ❋

It seems to me that epiphanies always happen at the worst possible time. Like, how I didn't realize bikinis weren't for water skiing until I almost lost my bottoms. Or like at prom when I figured out that Steven liked me just seconds before he kissed me. Or like when I realize I'm in love with William Henderson.

I wear my sweatshirt all winter long, even when it's seventy degrees out. If I'm the least bit chilled, I pull that soft cotton reminder over my head and imagine what it feels like to be a college girl. I pretend I go to school with him and that I'm the girl he goes to parties with. I pretend I'm the one who satisfies his itch.

I want to tell him. I think about how I can earn money for a plane ticket and I count the days until the start of the season on the calendar twice. I'm going to call him. I want to hear his voice and it won't be weird because he asked me to call him. He wants me to call, he wants me to visit, even. I don't care if it's only for a second, I can call him.

I use the office phone so my dad won't notice the long

distance charges. It's after nine-thirty. I don't know the time difference exactly but I dial the number anyway. It's Friday night, for crying out loud, if he's in bed already, the least I can do is tease him about it a little.

Some dude answers the phone and he is completely faded. He sounds just like Steven does on the phone and Steven only calls me when he's stoned.

"You've reached the Head Foundation, would you like to make a donation?" he says deep and serious, the sound of dozens of voices laughing in the background.

"Can I speak with William Henderson, please?" I ask.

"Who?" Oh, pull it together man.

"Will, Will Henderson," I shout.

"Oh! Big Willy. Naw, he's not here, baby. Is this Anya?" he asks and I cringe away from the phone.

"No, can-"

"Robin?"

"No, just-"

"Wait, is this Angela?" I don't like the way he says this girl's name. His voice is almost reverent. I don't like this. I don't like this one fricking bit.

Without another word, I hang up the phone. Apparently Will's been awfully itchy this year. I sit in my dad's chair at his desk and I'm shaking. I close my eyes and try to regulate my breathing.

It's fine, Cat. He's not yours, he has no loyalties to you, he can date whoever he wants. It's fine.

Of course, Will has girlfriends. Of course, he's not home on a Friday night. I am such a fricking fool!

So I'm not really surprised when Jay corners me at the store to tell me Will's bringing a girlfriend to Red Rock Cove this year. I knew this day would come. I'm not shocked. I'm not even feeling sorry for myself.

I am livid.

Thank God Lauren called before they left to warn my brother. I'm sure I would have made a complete ass of myself.

I'm furious he would bring her here. This is our place, and now he's going to parade his happiness around in front of my face. Look how well I'm doing without you, Cat. Look how easy you are to replace.

I know everything I'm feeling is unfair. But I still feel it. I still want to hate her. I still want to hate *him*.

Of course! Of course when I figure out I love Will, he decides to be with someone else. Of course, when I decide I maybe want to try this quasi-serious, part-time, long distance relationship thing with him, he's already in a relationship, and a real one with no limiting adjectives. It's so fucking typical I almost want to laugh. You hear that universe? You're fucking typical!

No, I will not be jealous. I will not hate her. I am a rock, cool stone, like granite or something of equal hardness. I will pretend like the little liar I am that this does not affect me in any way.

The Hendersons arrive three days later and I'm fully prepared to plaster on my game face. Will parks his Saab by the Mercedes and I strain to see them from my bedroom window. A willowy brunette slides out of the front seat of the red car, followed by Margot and Andy from the back. Great. They've all been road trip bonding and now I'm odd man out. Seems like a running theme in my disaster of a life.

Jay knocks on my door. He's worried, his face strained when he comes to deliver the bad news. Will and his stupid-ass skanky girlfriend are here.

No. No name calling. Calm. Cool. Under control. My life is a deodorant commercial.

"Hey, they're here. Come say hi," Jay urges and I give him a scowl. I hate that he feels the need to come warn me and that he looks so damn concerned. I can handle this. I'm rock, remember?

"Lauren and I are totally on your side, by the way," he says.

"What, are we gonna rumble later?" I snort and Jay rolls his eyes.

"You know what I mean, Cat. We all know you and Will

have this...thing. I don't understand it and I don't pretend to, but that doesn't mean it isn't there." He fiddles with the knickknacks on my dresser. "I just thought you'd like to know that Lauren and I...we understand, okay?"

Lauren and I, he says it like it defines him, like it's his identity or something.

"Thanks," I mutter, tears filling my eyes. God, I hate crying in front of my brother.

"Hey, Sis. It's fine. Everything will work out the way it's supposed to," Jay says as he sits on my bed beside me.

"You mean, like fate?" I ask, the tears spilling down my cheeks. "Well, fate is an asshole. Besides, I don't even believe in fate. If you want something, you should just go out there and get it."

"Cat..." my brother trails off cautiously and I roll my eyes.

"Oh relax, I'm not going to make a scene," I say and he looks doubtful. "I'll be good, I promise."

"This is just one summer, Cat. He'll be back again next year. And she probably won't," my brother says and I stare at him now. That didn't occur to me at all but he's right. Will has had girlfriends before. He's never brought them here, but maybe he didn't have a choice. Maybe there's a reason she had to come along.

Maybe he loves her.

Maybe she's a distraction.

Maybe she's just pushy as all hell.

God, I hope it's the last one.

Jay and I walk down to the Henderson's unit and Lauren is out the door and in my brother's arms in a heartbeat. She hugs him tight around his middle, her figure tucking into his tall frame, like twin oaks. He whispers something into her ear before giving her a kiss. *Hi, how are you, I missed you, I love you.* It's all conveyed in this one lovely kiss.

Andy and Margot stand in the doorway and I can see the stress on Margot's face. It matches my brother's expression just moments ago. She rushes to give me a hug.

"Don't be mad at him, okay?" she says into my ear and I nod. Of course I don't get to be mad. I've had my chance. I've had dozens of chances and I passed them all up.

Will appears in the door frame, his lips spreading into a sly grin when he sees me and I can't help but smile back. It's like a compulsion now. His hair is really long, almost to his shoulders and he's wearing baggy shorts and a plain white t-shirt. His girlfriend stands beside him, but Will pulls me into a big hug, lifting me off the ground and kissing my cheek.

"I missed you," he whispers into my ear. He smells like soap and cigarettes and I wonder if he's been smoking. I also wonder if he's on something because he's way too giddy giving me a hug and kiss in front of his girlfriend.

"Um, Cat, this is Angela," Will says before she rushes forward and wraps her arms around my neck. What the hell? Welcome to awkwardville, population me. I just stand there with my arms hanging at my side because I don't know why this snuggly bitch is hugging me.

"I've heard so much about you! The infamous Catherine the Great," she says as she pulls away and I finally get a good look at her. Her face is thin and pointy and long, her brown eyes large and dark. She's not overly pretty but she's not ugly either. Her face is just interesting, I guess. Her hair is pulled back in a French braid and she's wearing a black tank top with jean shorts. Typical river clothes. Everything about her is very average.

"Angela goes to school with me. She's pre-med," Will says beside her. He's acting so normal, like this is no big deal and I swear, I'm starting to think I imagined there was something between us. How can this be so easy for him? Oh yeah, because he's the one with a girl on his arm.

"Will tells me you're a photographer?" Angela asks and I shrug.

"Not really, I just mess around," I say and shove my hands in my pockets.

"No, she doesn't. She's really good. Cat, you have to show her your dam pictures," Will says and I bite my lip, suppressing a grin.

"Yeah, my dam pictures are great." I can't hide the grin any longer.

Angela catches on. "Yeah, Cat, I'm sure your dam pictures are some of your best dam work."

Oh Jesus, this is worse than I thought. Will's girlfriend isn't a dumb skank or a pretentious bitch. She's just a girl, like me and she's actually kind of cool. And out of all the things I'm feeling; anger, jealousy, disappointment, sadness, not once do I feel hate. This is bad. This is really, really bad.

"I was going to show Angela the docks," Will says. "We're going to feed the fish."

"Those fish are so gross," I shudder.

"The first time I met Cat, she threw a bag of bread at me," he laughs and I grin. "And then she punched me in the gut."

"You said my eyes were weird!" I defend. "What was I supposed to do?"

"Yeah, well, you love me now, so it's all good," Will says casually and I let my smile falter for an instant, my eyes flashing up to Angela's. But Angela smiles, warm and confident and accepting. I can practically see kindness pulsating around her.

This summer just might kill me.

* * *

For once in my life, I'm glad I have to work in the store. Josie lets me talk all the shit I want. That's what work has become, a megabitch purging session.

"She's just so fucking nice. There must be something wrong with her, no one's really that nice. Maybe she's a crack whore," Josie suggests and I giggle. The snarky bitch in me likes Josie making fun of Angela. Yeah, yeah, it's not gracious behavior on my part, but whatever. I've been gracious all summer.

I was gracious when we barbecued on the Fourth and I had to drive into town to get veggie patties for her because she doesn't eat meat. I was gracious when she couldn't get up on skis and made me keep pulling the boat around because she's ridiculously stubborn and refused to stop trying. I was gracious when she wanted the last IT'S-IT yesterday and I gave it to her, knowing we weren't getting a delivery for two more days. I have been gracious, dammit, and now, I want to be mean. It makes me feel a teensy bit better and I know it's ugly, but Josie doesn't care if I'm ugly. She's on my side no matter what, like Thelma and Louise.

"Maybe she has a sixth toe on her right foot," I say as I glance out the window, noticing a familiar sandy head on the swings outside. It's Will, and he's alone. Where, oh where is his Mother Teresa?

"Hey, I'm taking a break okay?" I barely catch Josie's sarcastic remark about Angela's probable third nipple. Will glances up as I walk down the sidewalk, the heat causing goosebumps on my arms and legs. I wore my hair loose today and I wish I had a band so I could tie it back. God, the sun is so intense, almost as intense as Will's green eyes on me.

"Hey," I say casually and sit on the plastic seat. I've done a really good job of rock impersonating so far.

"Hey," he says and I make the mistake of peeking at him through my hair. He's upset, and immediately my rock wall starts to splinter.

"Where's your posse?" I ask him and he sighs.

"I needed a break. I just wanted to be alone for a second." Will pushes his hair out of his eyes and behind his ears.

"Oh, sorry, I'll go, I just wanted to say hi." I get up and Will grabs my hand and my heart stops.

"No, not you. I needed to be away from them," he says and I stand there, letting him hold my hand. I let the boy that I love who already has a girlfriend hold my hand.

"Don't leave, please?" Will asks and of course, I sit my ass right back down on that swing because refusing Will is just one of those things I can't seem to do.

"So, Angela's nice," I say, trying to make small talk.

"Yeah."

"Your hair's really long." Will nods.

"How's school?" I try.

"It sucks," he says. This is ridiculous. He's acting like a big baby!

"So, how did you get that stick up your ass?" I ask him and his head snaps up. He smiles and lightly bumps his swing into mine.

"I don't have a stick up my ass," he responds. "You have a stick up your ass."

"No I don't. I have been perfectly pleasant," I say proudly and Will chuckles.

"You have. You've been polite and quiet and very nice," Will says, nudging my foot. "And I kinda hate it."

I stare at our feet, his expensive basketball sneakers gently kicking the side of my knockoff Converse and I don't understand. I've done everything in my power to make sure I don't ruin this trip for him, and he hates it?

"How can you act like this doesn't bother you?" he asks and irritation flares.

"What do you want me to do, Will? Storm around here making a spectacle of myself?" I ask him and I'm not even being sarcastic. Does he really expect that of me? Do they all expect that of me? Is that why Lauren called, why my brother suddenly felt the need for a heart to heart, why Margot had to whisper in my ear to play nice?

"That's not what I meant," he mutters and something in his voice makes me deflate.

"It does bother me. But it's just the way it is, you know?" I answer to the ground.

"Yeah, I know," Will says and I look up to see my dad walking into the store. Shit! He's gonna be pissed if he sees me out here with Will when I'm supposed to be working.

"I gotta go," I say in a hurry and stand up. "Hey, I don't have to work tomorrow. We can take my dad's boat out on the water, if you want."

"Yeah, that would be fun. Hey, can we go to Australia?" he asks and I nod. I jog back to the store and sneak in the back door, hoping my dad's not in the stockroom.

Later at dinner, I ask my dad if I can take the boat out and he easily agrees. I think he's glad Will brought a girlfriend. He tells me to watch the prop and use the flag, stuff I already know. He also tells me there's supposed to be a storm rolling in and I'm looking forward to the change in weather. I don't know how much longer I can keep up my rock impersonation.

* * *

So Cat, I was wondering if I could talk to you about Will."

I inhale a jelly belly, a cinnamon one and it's hot and stuck in my throat. I cough, clutching at my chest, the beads of my green bikini smacking against my neck as Angela pounds on my back. I'm going to die on this stupid cove, choking on candy in front of Will's girlfriend.

"Are you okay? Cat? Do you need the Heimlich?" Oh yes, that's exactly what I need. Please save my life, because I'm not pathetic enough already. I gag up the hard candy and spit it out, laughing at my own stupidity.

"Fricking jelly beans," I mutter and Angela smiles softly. "It's a sign I should stop eating sweets, huh?"

"I don't think I could survive without chocolate," Angela says and I nod.

"Sugar is my nemesis. I know it's out there to destroy me, but without it I'm useless," I say, popping another jelly belly in my mouth as Angela laughs.

"Will said you were funny," she says. I don't know what to say, so we sit in silence for a few minutes. Andy and Will took Lauren and Margot out on the WaveRunners, leaving me to entertain Angela. It's surprisingly easy to talk to her, she's friendly and laughs at my jokes. But I do not want to talk to her about Will. I don't want to *think* about her and Will.

"I tried to talk to Margot about this, but she and Lauren said that you know him best," Angela starts out of nowhere and without any distractions, I'm a millisecond away from a heart to heart with my best friend's girlfriend.

"I don't know about that. Maybe Andy? I know he's really close with Andy," I say, trying to deflect the conversation.

"No, this is definitely girl talk," Angela says. She leans back in her chair and grabs her sunblock, slathering the lotion over her chest and arms. Her skin has soaked up the sun, leaving her with a dark tan that looks nice against her black sporty two-piece. She's almost as tan as I am.

"Well, I'm not much of a girl. I mean, I have the anatomy, or whatever, but I grew up with a bunch of boys," I ramble nervously.

"Yeah, Will said that too," Angela laughs and I frown. "He said you think like him."

"I guess he would know," I mutter.

"I also know about your past. You guys kind of had a thing when you were teenagers," she says and I'm sure my face is beet red. Technically, I'm still a teenager. I won't be twenty for another month.

A thing, huh? That's what Will said, we had a thing? I guess there's really no other way to describe it, especially to your new girlfriend.

"This trip is kind of a huge deal in our relationship. Will's really special to me but he's been distant lately. I actually thought he was going to break up with me but then he told me about this trip and I don't know...I just feel like we connect, you know? Like our connection is more than chemical reactions in our brains, like there's this spark between us..." she trails off and I want to kill Margot. She did this on purpose. She sent this poor girl to me to talk about sparks and connections and Will. What the hell does she think this will accomplish?

"I'm not sure what you're asking," I say helplessly.

"I'm getting to it, I promise. Anyway, Will and I get along really well. We're both pre-med, we both like to do outdoorsy things, we both like basketball and the arts, so all in all, I'm pretty satisfied. With that aspect of our relationship." Oh God, I can see where this is going, like it's a lit up billboard on the Las Vegas strip. Sex. She's going to talk about their sex life.

Really universe? Really?

"Um, I don't know if-" I start but Angela's in the zone.

"Will won't have sex with me," she blurts out and then erupts into tears. Oh, holy emotional outburst, what the hell do I say to this? Yeah, me neither?

"I've tried everything, Cat, but every time he has a chance to seal the deal, he diverts. Don't get me wrong, the boy's got skills. Musicians have phenomenal dexterity, you know?" Oh for the love of all that is holy, just shut up. Please, please, please, stop talking. But she doesn't, of course.

"I'm starting to think maybe he's depressed or something. Or maybe it's me? I don't know what to do," Angela wipes her face with her towel and now I'm thinking about his fingers, in my bedroom and that summer when we were seventeen that we spent touching each other while INXS played in the background.

"Have you talked to Will about this?" I try to say in a calm voice. I sound like my mom.

"Yeah, he said he's not ready. You know his reputation. How can he have sex with all those others and not with me? What does that mean, Cat?" Angela pleads and I scratch at an itchy spot on my back. She looks down at her hands. "Do you think maybe you could ask him about it?"

Yes, that is *exactly* what I would like to spend my very tense, limited time with Will talking about. Oh geez, why does she have to be so nice?

"Yeah, I'll try," I mutter and once again, the queen of unsolicited public displays of affection wraps her arms around my neck. I awkwardly pat her back, her skin sticky from the recently applied sunblock before she sits back in her chair, and a hopeful grin takes the place of her tears.

This information is a bit unsettling. If Angela's just a flash in the pan, like those other girls, Will would have no problem sleeping with her. Then again, I pulled this same shit with Scott. Scott's a nice guy, but I didn't want to have sex with him because I knew it wouldn't mean anything.

And just like that I'm anticipating Will's answers just as much as Angela is.

When everyone gets back to the cove, we have lunch and then go for a tube ride. We tie two of the big tubes to the back of the boat and they take turns trying to knock each other off while I drive, sitting on a couple life vests so I can see over the windshield.

"Hey, I want to drive your boat," Will leans over from the seat beside me while we wait for Margot to climb back into her tube. He's wearing his dark sunglasses, his hair falling in his face and his freckled nose and cheeks are tinted pink. I've been avoiding looking at him all summer. I mean, really, why does he have to go shirtless all the time?

"I don't know if you can handle my boat," I say doubtfully and he smirks.

"You can barely see over the windshield! Come on, Cat. Teach me how to drive your boat," he pleads and I want to smack him for being so suggestive.

"Fine," I mutter and he crouches between the seats.

"It's really easy. You push the throttle forward to go, pull it back to stop."

Just then Angela yells *hit it* from one of the tubes, and I push the throttle forward. Will's not ready for the acceleration and he flies back, gripping my knee to steady himself. He quickly removes his hand and mouths an apology that I can't hear as he slides back into his chair.

I snake across the river to create a good sized wake as I pull Angela and Margot on the tubes. Angela has more mass and delivers more of a punch but Margot can sink lower into the tube which helps her stay afloat. Her tube's practically flying at this point, but God help her, Margot is a fighter. She's holding on for dear life and her persistence pays off, because Angela hits the wake and goes flying. Lauren laughs and Andy and Will cheer simply because they love to see anyone eat it. I turn the wheel and pull the boat around to pick her up.

The girls climb into the boat, and we pull in the tubes. I motion to Will to take a seat behind the steering wheel and he grins before pushing my life vest booster seat out of the way.

I show him how to steer and turn, standing beside him with my hand on the back of his chair. Angela sits in the seat next to us and I feel horribly awkward situated in the space between them.

Around late afternoon, the clouds start to hover low and I'm reminded of what my dad said about the storms. Lauren wants to take the WaveRunners out one last time so we jet up the river, Will and Angela on one, Lauren and I take the other, leaving Margot and Andy back at the cove to do God only knows what. The hot sun is covered in clouds, and the humidity of the pending summer storm hangs heavy in the air.

I grip the handlebars and Lauren clutches my vest. We're racing Will and Angela to the next mile marker, the reflective posts stuck in the bank signaling the finish line. I can see Angela's arms wrapped around his waist, her lips pressed into the back of his neck and I grit my teeth. I gun it and peek over my shoulder. Will lowers his head in determination and I smile. I knew he wouldn't back down from a challenge.

I weave in front of him just as a large speed boat races down the opposite side of the river. I wave to the boat, a common courtesy out here on the water but I'm not prepared for the wake. I almost lose control when I hit the frothy wave. The water sprays my face as Lauren screams profanities in my ear.

I steady the WaveRunner and turn around. Will's alone on his watercraft and I can see what I assume to be Angela in the water a good thirty feet behind him. I head over and pull alongside them. Angela starts swimming over to us and Will's trying to start the ignition.

"What happened?" I ask and Will shakes his head.

"We hit that wake and Angela went flying. I must have pulled the kill switch accidentally and now it won't start," he says.

"It's probably flooded." I unhook the switch from my vest.

"Hey, Lauren, can you go pick up Angela?"

"Sure," she says and clips the switch to her vest. I jump in the water and swim over to Will before she heads off towards Angela. I climb onto the back of the WaveRunner, Will's coy grin beaming down at me from under his long wet hair.

"Move over," I say, fighting a smile. I crawl over his leg, trying not to focus on our wet legs sliding against each other, or his hand lightly touching my vest in an attempt to steady the balancing act as we switch places. He hands me the kill switch and I plug in. I turn the key and the engine just turns. No spark.

"Yep, it's flooded. We have to wait for it to dry out. Stand up real quick. I want to check if there's a tow rope in there." Will balances on the back of the WaveRunner and lifts the seat as I stand. Nothing. Shit!

Lauren pulls alongside us. Angela's sitting on the back and she keeps running her finger along the lower lid of her eye.

"Everything okay?" Lauren asks and I shake my head.

"Engine's flooded. We're stuck for at least a half hour or so." I look up at the sky, the clouds darkening while we speak. We're going to need to get off the water soon.

"I need to go back to the marina," Angela says. "I lost a contact when I hit the water."

"O-kay," I say and Angela gives me a pointed glance. Oh crap! The sex talk. She wants me to have the talk out here on the water, with his hair all dripping in his eyes. Is she insane?

"Lauren, can you take me back to the marina?" Angela asks and Lauren gives me an exasperated look.

"We gotta get off the water anyway," I say quickly. "Those clouds are going to dump soon."

"Fine," Lauren grumbles.

"Can you send Jay back for us, just in case I can't get it started and we need a tow? Oh, and maybe give Margot and Andy a heads up," I say and Lauren nods. Angela's hopeful face is the last thing I see before they speed off.

Will and I float silently on the WaveRunner. We sit back to back, our vests bumping together as we rock on the gentle waves and I try to find a discreet way to bring up his sex life.

The words out of my mouth, however, pick a fight. I'm not sure what prompts the outburst. Maybe it's the heavy proton air, or the fact I can't see his face, or the fat rain drops that begin to dot across my legs and arms. Whatever the reason, I lose all communication with my brain filters. *All systems have been disconnected, mayday, mayday. I'm going down.*

"How could you bring her here? To our place? To share our summer? How could you do that to me?" I blurt out. I feel him shift, his body nudging me forward a little.

"What are you talking about?" Will responds.

"You knew this would hurt me and you did it anyway. Why would you do that to me?" I accuse.

"Not everything is about you, you know? God, you're so selfish sometimes. Why couldn't this be about me? Why couldn't this be about me trying to have a vacation with my girlfriend?" he asks, his voice sharp.

"Is that what this is? Because if that's true, I will leave it alone, Will. If it's truly about you trying to have a wonderful vacation with your lovely girlfriend, I will leave it alone. Is that what this really is?" I challenge. I almost don't want his answer. He leans into my back and is quiet for a long time, the sound of the storm thudding against the water the backdrop to his silence.

"I'm not sleeping with her," Will confesses. I guess it's been on his mind too. "I don't want to hurt her."

"You're already hurting her. She thinks it's her fault." Will turns quickly, causing the small watercraft to rock. "She wants me to ask you about it. She thinks you're depressed. Or that you don't find her attractive, I guess."

"It's not her fault. I just...I know, this thing between us isn't going anywhere. She's nice, you know. She's really smart and funny, but I don't want to go there, when I know I don't love her."

"But you sleep with other girls, ones far less desirable," I argue.

"I know. That's the whole point. Those other girls, I'm not myself when I'm with them. I'm drunk or stoned or whatever, it's not me and half the time I don't even remember. But with Angela, God, I don't even know how it happened. One minute she's hanging out sometimes at our dorm, then she's there everyday and she's just really nice, you know. And then she's kissing me and making dates and plans and shit. She bought us tickets to Lollapalooza for my birthday. Then she asked me about summer vacation and I told her about the marina. I think I said something like, you should see the sky out there, it's amazing and she took it as an invitation. And I knew it would hurt you, I did. But you've got that guy, Scott or whatever his name is. We're both with other people, you know." He pulls his leg over the seat, sitting sideways on the bench, his hand picking at the thread on the back of my life vest.

"Scott dumped me. After the houseboat last summer," I tell him. I mirror his position, balancing his weight by pulling my legs over the opposite side of the bench. I'm facing him now, my hip against his thigh, but I can't bring myself to look at his face.

"But Margot said..." Will doesn't finish his sentence and I hear a crack of thunder somewhere over the desert, and the sky opens up.

He pulls his leg across the bench to straddle the seat completely now. He's facing me and there they are, dancing green burning into me and my chest feels like it's going to burst. It's raining hard now and streaming down his face and in his long hair. The water's starting to get choppy and I brace myself against the handlebars.

"I don't like it that you don't call or write me. It's like you forget about me during the year," Will says quietly, his breath on my face, his hand on the back of my vest.

"I don't like it that you get drunk and sleep with skanks," I breathe. "And I did try to call you. Your roommate answered and called me half a dozen girl names when I asked for you so I hung up."

"I don't like it either. I hate myself for it. They're nothing, you know? And I don't mean anything to them either. I don't mean anything to anyone." His rain soaked cheek presses against mine and I close my eyes trying to fight back tears.

"You're wrong," I whisper, my chest heaving because I'm trying to breathe. Before I know what I'm doing, my lips have found his and my tongue forces its way into his mouth and it is the sweetest relief I've ever felt. He's frantic and greedy, sucking on my lip, his fingers clutching the back of my neck and squeezing my thigh. There's another crack of thunder, the electricity humming through the air and the rain falls in sheets now. I can't stop kissing him, his tongue rolling and pulsing with mine. He tastes like sunblock and rain water and a tiny hint of jelly bellies.

His hands are desperate to find my skin but the life vests cause too much space between us. I run my fingers through his long, rain slicked hair and his mouth moves to my neck, his hand running the length of my thigh and the sky alights with flashes of energy.

"We need to get off," I pant and Will snorts, the slip causing my face to burn.

"The water, I mean. We're sitting ducks out here on the water. We need to get to the shore," I clarify and this causes Will to just laugh harder.

"You're such an ass," I roll my eyes and push him away. He grabs my hand, pulling it to his face and kissing my fingers, my palm, my wrist.

"Come to Baltimore with me," Will says softly and I freeze, unsure if I heard him correctly.

"What?" I ask, closing my eyes. The rain is pummeling us, the light wind causing it to fly in sideways.

"It's not like you have anything going on here, come with me to Baltimore," he pleads and I frown.

"I can't just leave, Will. I have a job," I say indignantly. I know what he means, but his words sting, like what I do here means nothing.

"Your dad could hire someone else," Will argues and I shake my head.

"No, he can't. He can't afford to hire anyone right now. I can't do that to him, not right now." Will looks down and I see the emotion invading his beautiful features. Rejection.

"Hey," I say, pushing his hair behind his ear. "I'm not saying no, just not now."

He closes his eyes, his hand clutching mine to his lips again and he nods. Acceptance.

Just then I hear the roar of a boat and I can see my brother standing up at the helm and fighting the choppy water. I wave over to him and he pulls alongside us, throwing me the rope and I tie it off to the front of the WaveRunner when I realize I haven't even tried to start it again. I was distracted.

Will and I climb into the boat and my brother takes us back to the marina. We sit on the back bench, my hip against his calf, his legs stretching a lot farther than they used to. We hold towels up in front of our faces to block the rain and wake water and I can't see him but he uses his toes to pull at the strings of my bikini bottoms. I can't even return the pestering because the tips of my toes barely reach his thigh now. I give him a turtle bite instead, pulling the hair on his leg and he yelps.

It isn't until we pull into the marina, when I see Angela standing on the dock in the rain, her shorts and tank top soaked through, her arms crossed over her chest and her eyes wrought with panic that I realize what I've done. I kissed another girl's boyfriend.

But he was mine first, I try to rationalize.

He's not yours now.

Oh God, I'm going to be sick.

I swing my legs away from Will, and hold the towel to my face as I let the tears spill from my lids. Angela is going to hurt because of this, because of me and she, of all people, does not deserve this. This is wrong, this is so very, very wrong.

I climb onto the bow and jump onto the dock as Jay pulls the boat into the slip. I wrap the rope around the cleat and watch out of the corner of my eye as Will steps off the side of the boat and walks over to her. He keeps looking over at me and I wish he'd stop being so fricking obvious, at least until I can get the hell out of here.

And then, there it is. Confirmation.

She tries to kiss him and he backs away. Then like a dumbass idiot, he glances over at me again. I immediately look down, my face burning red, the rain beating on my back, but I'm far too nosy for my own good. I sneak a look and watch Angela's eyes dart between us, her face changing from worry to fear and then disgust. I catch her eyes searing into mine and I crumble. I can't tell if it's the tears or the rain blurring my vision, but I watch as she lifts her chin. She knows. And she's not going to wait for an explanation.

Without another glance, Angela turns and walks away. She walks away from Will. Something I'll never be able to do. Will and Angela leave the next day in the Saab. He doesn't say goodbye, he sends my present over with Margot, a Chicago Bulls Championship tank top. I don't deserve it, I don't deserve anything. Margot tries to make me feel better but I know in my heart what I am.

"I'm a cheater, Margot. The other woman. I'm disgusting. I should have a big red A sewn onto all my tank tops," I cry into her lap as we sit on my bed. She smoothes her hand through my hair and I like the way my scalp tingles.

"It was just a kiss, Cat. Yeah, it was not exactly ideal, but still, it was just a kiss," she says and I think she's being too easy on me.

"It was like I couldn't even stop myself. That damn storm,

with all the electricity in the air, made me feel all wily. I didn't think, I just acted," I blubber. I sit up wiping the tears from my face, a whole new wave of guilt soaking me through and flooding me out

"You took a risk. It's what people do when they're in love," Margot says.

"But I shouldn't be in love with him! Who knows, maybe in a couple of months, he could have been happy with Angela. She was perfect for him and I ruined that. I'm a monster! I'm a wretched horrible monster!"

"Oh Jesus, now you're just being overdramatic. You're not a monster. Sometimes you just can't fight it anymore."

"Like Heather and Ricky? They couldn't fight it and look at what they did to Josie. I'm like Heather. I'm a slut."

"Yep, Catherine Rossi, virgin slut," Margot laughs and I sock her in the arm. "Ow! Stop it, with the hitting thing!"

"He asked me to go to Maryland and I had to say no. I kissed him and ruined his relationship and then said no to him. Do you know how hard it is to say no to him? It's like we're right back where we started!" I throw my hands in the air.

"Oh, Cat. Sometimes you have to go back so you can move forward."

1992 – THAT TIME WE WENT TO VEGAS

Wayne's World, a film adapted from a sketch on NBC's
Saturday Night Live, is released in theaters.

Michael Jordan and Scottie Pippen are the first NBA players to win
a Championship and an Olympic Gold Medal in the same year.

William J. Clinton is elected the 42nd
President of the United States.

* * *

T ap! Tap! Tap!

I startle out of sleep. I'm alone in my room and I'm panting, my chest and forehead covered in sweat. Weirdest dream ever. I think it was a sex dream but practically everyone I know was there so now I'm just grossed out. I'm still confused when I stumble out of bed and pull the blinds out of the way.

Will grins at me expectantly as I open the window and pop out the screen. I'm disoriented, that dream messing with my mind and I rub my eyes. He climbs in my window and closes it behind him.

"Best pajamas ever," he says and I look down. I haven't done laundry in days and fell asleep in my Chicago Bulls championship tank top and my underwear. I roll my eyes and sit on my bed. There's really no point in being modest. My bikini covers less.

"Did you just get here?" I yawn and he sits across from me on my bed. His hair is still long, and he's wearing a gray t-shirt and baggy cargo shorts. I wonder if he wears river clothes all year long, now.

"Yeah," he nods.

"You're late," I say, pulling the rubber band from my wrist and wrapping my hair back into a ponytail.

"We had to wait for Lauren. She's waiting to hear about this internship thing in Washington D.C.," Will says as his fingers connect the three freckles on my thigh that form an equilateral triangle. Every time he touches me it's warmth and familiarity. It's comfort and care and natural, like turkey on Thanksgiving, or peanut butter and jelly.

"How's school?" I ask and he shrugs.

"I'm just stoked this semester is finally over. I have one more year and then I apply for medical school. I still have to take the MCAT. Four more years, Cat. I have to do this shit for four more years," Will says loudly and I crawl over him to push play on my cassette player. The last thing I need is my dad catching me in my underwear with a boy in my room.

"You don't have to do anything. If you hate it so much, you should do something else." I sit cross legged beside him.

"It's not a choice," he murmurs and I sigh. I understand. I guess he's obligated to medical school like I'm obligated to the marina. He leans against the bed frame, and closes his eyes as Nirvana fills the silence.

"So..." I say after a long while. He opens one eye and looks over at me, the corner of his mouth pulled up in a grin. I'm dying to find out what happened with Angela, but I don't know how to ask. I think Will knows it and is making this hard on purpose.

"I was thinking, we need to go out," Will says mischievously and I raise my eyebrows.

"In case you haven't noticed, we're kind of in the middle of nowhere. Where exactly did you want to go?" I ask.

"Somewhere we can dress up." His fingers play connect the freckles again and I frown.

"I don't know, Will," I say hesitantly. I don't really do dressed up.

"Angela dumped me," he interrupts. "The moment we got in the car last summer. She had me drop her off at the airport in

Vegas." He pauses, waiting for my reaction, but I can't speak.

"So, are you seeing anyone, Cat?"

"No," I whisper as I watch his fingers on my skin. "Are you?"

"Nope," he says quietly and I can't look at his eyes because I'm sure they're doing all kinds of dazzling things. "I haven't been out in months."

"What do you mean by out?" I ask. In my head, when he goes out, he drinks and when he drinks he sleeps with random chicks.

"Out, you know, out," he says and I shake my head.

"No, I don't know. I don't go out. Ever."

"Then we are definitely going out," Will smiles and I'm frustrated.

"Are you still sleeping around?" I blurt out. He chooses his words carefully and my stomach twists the longer he's silent.

"I go out Cat, and sometimes I go out with girls. But I'm not looking for a hook up anymore. I'm kind of over it."

"Then what are you looking for?" I already know the answer. Love. He's looking for someone to love him. Someone in Baltimore. Someone in college. Someone who's not me.

"I don't know. Just looking, I guess," he mutters.

"I don't want you to look." I pout like a five year old.

"What do you expect, Cat? I thought that kiss last year was pretty fucking stellar and then I don't hear from you all year and I'm left thinking I made a mistake, that I broke this nice girl's heart for nothing. Why shouldn't I look? Do I have a reason not to look?" Will asks me desperately and I don't know what to say.

All year long I contemplated contacting Will. I didn't know if he was going to try and salvage that relationship and in the effort to preserve my weary little heart, I didn't call.

He didn't either, for the record. He could have made a move. And he didn't.

"I guess not," I say bitterly and Will throws his hands up in the air.

"You are so fucking stubborn, you know that?" he says

incredulously and now I'm angry. I kick my legs underneath my quilt, kicking him in the process, and he glares at me. He yanks the blanket from my lap and I try to yank it back but he won't let go. A smug grin plays on his lips and I'm shaking with anger now. He's laughing at me.

"Give me my fucking blanket," I growl and he refuses to concede. I crawl onto my knees and attempt to push him off my bed and now he's full on chuckling. "Get out of my room."

"No," he says, his body squirming between me and the white iron railing of my daybed. "Not until you admit it."

"Admit what?" I ask.

"Admit that you don't want me to look at other girls because you like me," he says confidently, his hands behind his head on my pillow, his feet crossed and hanging off the edge of my small bed. His shirt pulls up when he stretches and exposes the small span of skin beneath his belly button. The top of his boxers stick out from under the waistband of his baggy shorts and my whole body flushes with heat. And I hate him for it.

"I really, really don't like you right now," I grumble and he just laughs.

"Yes you do. You just don't like that you have a weakness," Will yawns, his eyes closing. I hate that he knows me so well, I hate that he can read my brain. I especially hate that all I want to do is climb on top of him.

"We're going to Vegas for the Fourth," he says definitively, his eyes still closed and I feel my shoulders slump, my stomach knot and twist.

Vegas? With Will? I guess we'll finally be able to see some damn fireworks.

"And I want to meet your mom."

* * *

So, Will, Cat tells me you play basketball?" My mom takes another bite of her hot fudge sundae, the chocolate dripping onto her chin. Her boyfriend, Paul wipes the smudge from her skin and I almost puke up my lemon meringue pie all over the cafe table. Jay rolls his eyes and sticks his finger down his throat. Lauren smacks at his hand and I try not to laugh.

"Stop making fun of me, Jay, or I'm going to bring up Mr. Blankie." Mr. Blankie was Jay's favorite blanket when he was a kid. He slept with it until he was twelve.

The twinkle in my mom's eye and the smile plastered all over her red lips is all the evidence I need. She's happy, happier than I've ever seen her. She's never introduced us to a guy. I might even be so naïve to suggest she didn't date. But I know better. Everyone dates. Everyone has sex.

Everyone but me.

Anyway, this Paul guy must be pretty special. I think he's living with her. They seem connected, attached at the hip and while it's nice to see her so happy, the constant PDA is grossing me out.

"Sorry, Will, my children are so disrespectful," my mom says.

"Hey! I didn't even say anything!" I respond.

"Yeah, but you were thinking it," she grins.

"I used to play basketball. I had to quit the team this year because I couldn't keep up with practice and classes," Will answers and I look at him perplexed. I didn't know he quit the team.

"Yeah," he answers my unspoken question quietly and I want to talk to him about this but I know now's not the time or place. I check Will's watch and the big, shiny silver face tells me it's almost time to go. We're supposed to meet Margot and Andy at Caesars Palace in ten minutes and traffic on the strip is a nightmare.

Dr. Henderson booked two rooms for the Fourth of July at Caesars as a gift for Will's twenty-first birthday. He made dinner reservations, scoped out clubs and even rented a limousine to cart us around the whole night. The news is both awesome and kind of sucks royally because guess who's not twenty-one yet. Me and only me. Luckily, I was able to persuade

Josie to give me her driver's license. I could maybe pass for twenty-five, if I wear make-up.

I'm a little bit intimidated by how much money the Hendersons actually have. There's no way Jay and I can afford dinner at these restaurants or even pay for our share of the hotel room but Will insists it's all taken care of. When I ask him about it he kind of gets irritated with me.

"Look, my dad likes to buy my love. And I like to let him. It's how he makes up for being gone all the time," he mutters. "Besides, it's for my birthday. Are you going to say no to my birthday, Cat?"

How can I argue with that?

I do, however, have to argue with my dad. After assuring him there will be no coed cohabitation and no drugs, he finally agrees to let me go. It's all a lie, of course. Jay doesn't even need to ask. I shouldn't need his permission anymore either, but something tells me there'd be hell to pay if I just up and left for a night in Vegas.

Then there's my mom. She's just so pushy. She asks lots of questions and I don't want her bringing up the relationship stuff. I keep imagining her asking about our plans for the future and that would be disastrous.

It's not that I haven't thought about my future with Will. I admit it, I've fantasized about marrying him and you know the kids and the house and everything. I've also envisioned him moving on, marrying someone like Angela, and the two of them bring their kids to the river on vacation.

Or worse, he stops showing up all together.

There may be a time when he has to give up the long vacation, when he has to give me up. That's why I'm here right now, suffering through lunch with my mom and her new boyfriend, and introducing her to Will. I might never again have the chance to let my mom know Will, and well, I think it's kind of important for her to know the greatest love of my life, even though he's not really mine at all.

"Time to go?" he asks and I nod. Will pays with a green credit card and my mom gushes.

"Hold on to this one," she whispers in my ear when I kiss her goodbye and I don't know what she likes more, Will or his credit card.

Jay takes side streets, avoiding the main strip and parks in the general parking of the large, extravagant casino. Will leads as we walk into the most beautiful, ornate lobby I've ever seen.

It's enormous and grand and I fumble around in my backpack until I find my camera. I snap pictures of everything, from the glittering chandeliers to the faux marble statues and I'm overwhelmed by the colors and lights. Even the smell is intoxicating, like new carpet and cigarettes and perfume. Here I am, right smack dab in the middle of a perfectly replicated ancient Italy and all it took was an hour-long car ride filled with the *Wayne's World* Soundtrack and four games of Who Would You Do. I could come here every day!

"Hey you guys!" I hear Margot screeching from across the massive lobby. She's followed by a grinning Andy towing a massive pink suitcase.

"We're getting dressed up tonight! I'm talking heels and glitter and sexy dresses. We're going all out, baby!" Margot says and I'm terrified. I didn't bring any heels.

Will checks into the rooms and we haul our bags through the dark, winding casino. The chime of coins is distracting as we weave through the maze of slot machines. Margot squeals when she sees the row of expensive shops and I stare up at the ceiling that looks like a cloudy sky. Will's walking really fast and I grab his arm so I can keep up. He smiles down at me, his eyes alive and vibrant as he throws his arm over my shoulder and kisses the top of my head. It's almost like we're in a different world, like we can forget everything here and just be. It's incredibly liberating.

We finally get to the rooms and I'm twirling. The room is lush and splashed with rich reds, greens and golds. It's so unreal, like my lounge singer fantasy and I wish I had a sequined dress. I'm not sure where to put my stuff so I toss it

191

into the corner. Andy drags the large, rolling suitcase to one of the beds and I'm glad. I don't think I could survive sleeping in the same room as my fornicating brother and his girlfriend.

Will stretches out on the mattress and I sit cross legged in the chair, awkwardly wondering if he's planning on sharing my bed, and if I should shave my legs again. And then I want to smack myself for even thinking about this. What kind of person puts themselves through this torture? Catherine Pricilla Rossi: sexually repressed virgin slut, that's who.

"Oh my God, look at this bathtub!" Margot peeks her head out from inside the bathroom. "You could fit eight people in this thing!"

"This is the hotel where they filmed Rain Man, you know," Andy says as he flops next to Margot's monstrous suitcase. Geez, how much shit could she need for one night in Vegas?

As soon as I see the contents of Margot's suitcase, I start stressing. She piles dozens of dark slinky fabrics onto the bed, shimmering satins and sequined lace with ruffles and stretchy bands and I cringe. It's not that I hate dressing up, I just don't know how to do it. The nicest shirt I have is my white eyelet camisole but there's no way I'm going out with them looking like Gidget when they look like supermodels. Maybe I'll just stay here.

"Cat Rossi, you get that look off your face right now! I can see you making excuses," Margot says as she folds the smallest skirt I've ever seen in my life and I swallow. Will chuckles, throwing open the window shades to display a magnificent view of the strip. We'll totally be able to see the fireworks, even if it's just from the room.

"I didn't bring anything nice, Margot," I say.

"Well, we did. You can borrow whatever you want from us. I always bring at least two back-up outfits, in case I change my mind. What size shoe do you wear?" Margot asks and I look at her tiny feet.

"Not your size," I laugh. "My feet are huge."

Margot shrugs, "What size? I bet Lauren has something you

can wear."

I really don't want to tell everyone my shoe size. It's completely stupid, but my feet are big, like too big for my body. I'm glad Jay's in the other room, because I'm absolutely positive he'd make his trusty, old, "Cat's feet are as big as skis" joke.

"Like an eight and a half," I fudge. I really wear a size nine. And a half. Nine is probably the smallest I could go without losing feeling in my toes.

"Lauren is the same!" she squeals and I try to fake my enthusiasm.

I glance over at Will on the windowsill, a sarcastic smirk on his face and I just know he's got a joke running through his head.

"What?" I ask, my eyes narrowing and he laughs.

"Nothing!" he defends. "I didn't even say anything."

"You didn't need to, I can see it all over your face," I respond.

"Why do you always think I'm trying to make fun of you?"

"Because you are! Come on, what's the joke?"

"No joke," he shrugs. "Just now I know why you're so good on skis."

"Hardy-har-har. What about you, Goofy? Your huge feet didn't seem to help you much," I smirk.

"Yeah, well you know what they say about guys with big feet," Will winks at me.

"They have really big egos?" I ask innocently.

"You're never gonna live that down, you know? Goofy on skis was the funniest thing I've ever seen," Margot says as she pulls a gigantic bottle of tequila from her suitcase and sets it among a half a dozen other bottles of various hard liquors she's already lined up along the counter.

"Geez, Margot! We're only gonna be here one night!" I laugh. Here I thought she was just a clothes horse. More than half her suitcase is filled with booze!

"Yep, one night of gross indulgence and debauchery," Margot announces. She pulls a stack of plastic shot glasses and a little bag of limes from her purse. She doesn't hesitate to pour six shots of tequila, using Andy's pocket knife to slice one of the limes into wedges.

"I forgot the salt," Margot says with a smile. "But I snagged these from the burger place we stopped at on the way here." She pulls out a handful of individualized salt packets and I laugh at Margot's makeshift bar.

"Lauren! Wherefore art thou, sweet Lauren!" Margot pounds on the door joining our rooms. Lauren swings open the door, Jay behind her as they walk into our room, and prop open the door with a trash can.

"Toast!" Margot says as she waves us all over to the counter. Margot hands us each a shot glass, and a single serving salt packet. We each take a lime before she raises her glass into the air.

"To William, you're not only a great brother, but you're a great friend too. Happy Birthday!" she says before she licks the salt from her wrist and empties her shot glass. We all drink and the tequila goes down smooth. Before I can even remove the lime from my mouth, Margot is pouring another round.

"One more, one more, because I forgot something in the toast," Margot argues as we all collectively grumble.

"To old friends," she says, her wide blue eyes twinkling and staring right at me. "To risks and sparks and connections forged. Just because you don't see it, doesn't mean it's not there."

She throws back her second shot and the rest of the group shrugs at her cryptic toast as they down their drinks but I know better. I understand exactly what she's talking about. *Tonight*, she's saying. *Take a risk, tonight.*

I quickly pour the liquid down my throat, forgetting the salt, forgetting the lime and letting the liquor burn. Margot orders a jug of orange juice from room service and makes a big batch of screwdrivers that we take down to the pool in the large sports bottles she brought in her suitcase of sin.

Andy buys a handful of cigars and clove cigarettes, and we spend a couple hours lounging in the hot sun, drinking and smoking and playing Marco Polo in the pool. It's probably not a great idea to play a childish underwater touching game in a public pool whilst intoxicated because now I've been felt up by Will twice and I'm pretty familiar with Margot's left boob. We keep getting louder and Jay and Lauren are sitting way too close. Any moment hotel security is going to escort us off the premises for obscene behavior.

I don't bother with a towel when we walk back to the hotel room, and now I fully understand the term sloppy drunk. The elevator ride is unbearable. Will stands behind me, playing with my bikini ties and threatening to untie my top.

"Knock it off, ass!" I say. When the elevator doors open, Will nudges me into the hall. I stumble forward, my flip flop catching on the lip of the elevator door, and Will's arms wrap around my waist to try to keep me from falling. Margot can hardly stand, she's laughing so hard. I'm using the f-word excessively, trying to break free from Will's grasp and everyone just keeps laughing.

"Cat, stop fighting me! Shit! Why are you constantly fighting me?" Will says. He holds my arms to my body, his bare chest pressed against my back and I don't want to fight him. But I cannot surrender. I can't bring myself to do it. I don't even know why I'm fighting him at this point, all I know is I can't let William Henderson get the best of me.

"Why are you constantly messing with me?" I try to turn my head to look at him and his nose is so close to mine, I can smell his breath. "Vodka breath."

"Vodka breath?" he questions, his tone menacing. "Vodka breath?" Before I know what's happening, he picks me up, and I scream. He hoists my almost bare ass over his shoulder and takes off running down the hall, my stomach bouncing against his back and this situation just went volatile.

"I'm gonna puke all down your back," I struggle to say.

"Do it, I dare you," Will antagonizes and now I'm wishing I could make myself vomit just to teach him a lesson. But in the next few seconds we're in the room and he's throwing me on the bed, my head bouncing on the mattress. He hovers over me, his long hair falling in his face, his lips pursed and I focus on the scatter of freckles across his nose. God damn, I want him to kiss me.

Whoa, I am way too drunk. I need some French fries, and a cold shower. Preferably not at the same time. Will leans in closer just as Margot and Andy stumble through the door, followed by my brother and Lauren.

"I call shower," he says. He winks at me, fucking winks, then grabs his bag and disappears into the bathroom. Andy flicks on the television, turning to the music television channel as Margot collapses onto my bed, her head turning to face me and all she says is one word.

"Spark," she giggles and I give her a push. She laughs and rolls off the bed, opening up her suitcase and I close my eyes, my lids heavy and wanting a rest.

"Cat? Wake up, we're leaving for dinner in forty-five minutes," Will says and I jump up. I must have fallen asleep! Forty-five minutes! I'm still in my fricking swimsuit! I rub my eyes as they adjust and see Lauren putting in her contacts and Margot finishing up her makeup at the vanity. I can hear Andy and Jay in the other room, a thudding drum beat emanating through the wall.

And then there's Will. He's standing by the bed, wearing a faded green t-shirt over a pair of dark jeans with black boots. He looks four inches taller in pants. He's wearing this belt, his shirt haphazardly tucked into the front of his pants, and all I can stare at is this fricking silver belt buckle. His hair is messy, the sandy blond tangles hiding his face and I want to push them away for the injustice. He looks amazing, beyond beautiful. And then he smiles, like he's embarrassed he looks nice and my heart softens at this vulnerability.

I should tell him he looks nice. Because he does. He looks nice. Really, really deliciously nice.

"You look good," I manage to blurt out and Will chuckles, his fingers pushing his hair behind his ears. I fight it, damn it, but I can't help but smile at this boy. Only he's not a boy. He's a man, I guess. Oh my God, when did Will become a man?

"Cat, shower, now!" Margot barks and I don't dispute. I shower off quickly, running a razor over my legs and armpits and wash my hair. I towel off and wrap a ridiculously small towel tight around my chest and peek out the door.

"Margot, I need my bag," I say. She's sitting cross legged on the counter, smudging black liner along her lids.

"Will, get Cat her bag," Margot orders and I throw her a dirty look. She grins as Will carries my bag over to me, that damn smirk on his beautiful face as he shamelessly looks me up and down. He hooks the bag on his finger and I snatch it from him and his smile widens.

"You look good," he says. I roll my eyes and shut the door but I can hear him laughing. Curse him and his blatant flirting!

I put on my underwear and bra and pull my white eyelet tank from my bag. I have no idea what the girls are wearing but there's no way I'm going to stack up in this. I open the door a crack and peek out to see Lauren now stunning in a knee length red spaghetti strap baby-doll dress and a pair of platform sandals that strap around her ankle and I'm sunk.

"Margot! I need help," I ask pitifully and she laughs, motioning to her open suitcase.

"Help yourself," she says and I peek further into the room to find it empty of boys. I quickly dash over to shut the door that joins the two rooms.

"Cat! Are you wearing boy underwear?" Margot asks exasperated and I look down at my Underoos.

"They have She-ra on them," I say indignantly. "She's the princess of power."

Margot rolls her eyes and goes back to her makeup. I wade through the myriad of clothing and feel utterly ridiculous. Margot's clothes are very small and very stylish. Nothing is going to look right on me. My boobs are too big for any of her shirts, all her skirts are way too short and I feel like utter shit.

"I have something you should wear," Lauren says and slips

into the other room. She returns with a turquoise dress, the material flowing over her manicured hand and a pair of silver heels.

"Try this," she says and hands me the soft fabric with a quick smile. I pull the silky material over my head, the top fastening around my neck and I zip up the side. It's a little too big, but it's definitely better than any of the micro-clothing I see in Margot's suitcase. The dress is short but comfortable, with a high waist covered in dozens of tiny pleats.

"Looks good, but you cannot wear Underoos with chiffon," Margot says. "Here, wear these. And take your bra off."

I hold up the ridiculous excuse for underwear Margot gave me, the tags still attached. "Holy mother of rip-offs, thirty dollars for a slingshot? Is this in case we get attacked? Should I put a couple rocks in my purse, just in case?"

"No, smart ass, it's a thong. Just put it on," Margot says.

"I'm not wearing anything that goes up my butt on purpose. I'm already wearing heels. That's enough torture for one night," I say and attempt to slingshot a wadded up sock at Margot.

"Fine!" Margot scowls and hands me a pair of briefs. "Wear these instead, but trust me, some people like it."

"You like having a piece of elastic between your cheeks?" I ask her, sarcastically.

"You get used to it, but that's not what I meant. Some people think they're sexy," she hints again.

"Who thinks they're sexy?"

"I don't know, people! Andy likes them. I bet Will does too," Margot says, her blue eyes are extraordinarily vibrant under the glittery shadows and liner. She slinks into a pale pink sheath, knotting a gold chain belt around her waist and slipping on a pair of gold open-toe pumps. Her wrists are covered in bangles, her short black hair clipped off her face and she looks like she stepped off the pages of Cosmo.

I wait until she's not looking and then slip off my Underoos and put on the damn thong. It's uncomfortable, like I expected, but surprisingly sexy. I'll never tell Margot that, though. I unhook my bra and pull the straps off my arms, yanking the thing out from under the dress and check to make sure it's not totally obvious I'm braless.

Margot helps me with my make-up and smoothes some sticky stuff in my hair. She has me bend over and scrunch my hair up in my hands while she sprays me with something else. I don't really care about my hair, actually. Odds are, I'll end up tying it back anyway.

When she's all finished, she points me to the mirror and says, "Ta-da" and the odd person I see kind of freaks me out a little. My hair looks nice, falling around my bare shoulders in long loose waves. My eyes seem more green than brown and yeah, there's glitter all over my eyelids in soft, subtle golds. My eyelashes are long and black and perfectly separated, my cheeks flushed and a soft golden pink tints my lips. The turquoise of the dress does look nice against my tanned skin and I have to say, if the person in the mirror were anyone else, I'd think she looks pretty. But since it's supposed to be me, I look like a stranger.

I turn around to check out my butt, to make sure you can't tell I'm wearing a piece of elastic up my rear but you can't see anything. Great, now it looks like I'm not wearing any underwear at all. How embarrassing!

We file out of the hotel room, but not before Margot pours us all another shot of tequila. Will holds his arm out to me as we walk down the hallway to the elevator and I take it. I hold on for dear life, because I'm having a little trouble walking in these confounded shoes. He smells so good, I can hardly stop myself from smushing my face right into his thin t-shirt.

"You look amazing," Will breathes into my neck and I sigh, trying to focus on walking. Every so often I skim my hand over my butt to make sure the dress is still there. I don't want to accidentally flash everyone my ass.

Luckily, the restaurant we're eating at is inside the Casino because I'm starving. I order a hamburger and French fries, and Will laughs at me but I don't want anything else. I lay off the drinks because I'm a little hesitant to use Josie's ID, but the others have no problem indulging. Especially, Will.

He orders beer with dinner, then moves on to the hard liquor, ordering a couple Jack and cokes for dessert. He gives me sips and his hand is on my knee, or draped over my shoulder and he's whispering sweet things into my ear and by the time we all load into the Limo, I'm sure he's drunk. He keeps saying, "You only turn twenty-one once, right?"

On the ride to the jazz club, he pops a bottle of champagne and we all have a glass. I'm starting to feel a little tipsy, not drunk or anything, but definitely happy, so when Jay pulls out the weed, I have no reservations about joining in. I share a joint with Will and he does his "I did not inhale" impression and we laugh. Then Andy gives him a cigar and it feels like I'm in a movie. Like, this whole night is a fantasy, and Will is my fantasy boyfriend and I'm wearing a thong and make-up and it's just so unreal.

I don't know if it's the alcohol or the weed or Will's intoxicating cologne, but I let myself believe the fantasy. It's only for one night and Will's right, I don't have to fight him. God, I'm so tired of fighting him. So I cross my legs, and let my skirt ride up high. I touch his chest and his thigh and share his cigar and he laughs and kisses me and it's fun. Probably the most fun I've ever had in all my life.

We get to the club and Will can tell that I'm nervous so he pulls me in close to his body. His touch takes over and it's like a soothing, euphoric, wonder drug or something because when we all hand the big burly bouncer our ID's, I'm completely calm. Will nuzzles my ear and then we're inside the club and I'm being ushered into a booth. The deep, calming rhythms of the bass and saxophone are pulsing in my chest, the enticing plink of the piano vibrating off my skin.

I'm squeezed in between Margot and Will and I'm starting to feel very warm. Will's body is still glued to my side. I can't feel my toes anymore so I slip my feet out of Lauren's shoes and put my lips to Will's ear.

"Remind me not to forget Lauren's shoes," I say and he laughs, his hands cradling my face before he kisses me, a slow, sensual kiss on the mouth and I relish in the fantasy.

A waitress comes to the table and Andy orders something for all of us. I don't even know what it is, but I drink it. It's fruity and good and I could probably drink like eight more but my head is starting to get fuzzy and I have to pee. I grudgingly squeeze my feet into the silver torture devices and nudge Will out of the way so Margot and I can use the restroom. The bartender directs us to a narrow hallway and of course, there's a line. We're waiting and Margot is talking a mile a minute.

"Andy's gonna graduate next year, and then I'm hoping we can get our own place, just the two of us. God, I am so sick of living with my mom," Margot rambles.

"What does Andy want to do?" I ask and Margot laughs.

"He's majoring in accounting," she says and I can't hide my surprise. "He wants to be a CPA. I know, it's hilarious."

Finally, it's our turn to use the restroom and Margot notices I wore the thong. She giggles like a twelve year old and I roll my eyes. We're making our way back to the booth, a charming classical piece being played on the piano when, suddenly, it morphs into a familiar, simple song, the easy melody made complex with chords and scales and the voice crooning over the microphone shocks me right out of my fading buzz.

It's Will. Singing *Twinkle, Twinkle, Little Star.* On stage.

I grab Margot's hand and I drag her over to the booth where my brother and Lauren and Andy are laughing at Will making a fool of himself.

"How did he even get up there?" I ask and my brother just shrugs as Margot slides into the booth next to Andy.

"I don't know. He said he was going to go talk to the piano player because he was really good and then, he's on stage playing fucking Mozart and shit." My brother is totally wasted. "I didn't even know he could play."

"Yeah, since he was little," I mutter.

"Cat, Cat, Kit Cat," Will's voice crackles, the microphone making a high-pitched screech. "Isn't she beautiful, everyone? That's my best friend, Catherine the Great. Cat, remember when you said you wanted to be a lounge singer? Now's your chance!" There's a collective aww from the crowd as dozens of faces turn towards me and I want to die.

"I want to play a song for her. I know the song, the perfect song," he says and I'm watching him on stage, poised behind the large black shiny piano. He leans over to the guitarist, mumbling into his ear and then says something to the rest of the band before the piano sounds. There's an intro, a slow, evenly paced rhythm heavy in bass. And then Will sings and my fantasy implodes around me.

"*Said I remember when we used to sit, On the swings at the marina,*" The audience laughs at his lyric replacement but I can't.

"*Oba-serving those fat and ugly fish, As they eat up all the bread,*" He's staring at me now, his sandy hair a disheveled mess, his nose and cheeks red.

"*Blah, blah, blah, I can't remember the words, La something along the way,*
In this bright future, you can't forget the past, La la something tears I say,
No woman, no cry, no wo-man, no cry,
Said little darlin', don't shed no tears,
*No woman, no cry...*but she will even though she likes to pretend she's a rock.*"

He's singing Bob Marley. His piano work is spot-on, but his singing is awful. And I don't cry. I just stand there watching Will play the piano, a part of him I thought I'd never be able to see, the real Will, completely plastered and playing the piano in a fucking Las Vegas lounge, just like he said he wanted to years ago.

Eventually, Will is escorted off the stage and we are asked, very politely of course, to get the fuck out. Will can barely stand, he is really drunk and I offer to take him back to the hotel. Jay helps us into a cab and I leave the Limo with them.

We finally make it to the room and before I can even turn on a light, I lay Will on the bed, pulling off his shoes and his belt. His eyes are glassy and filmed over and I'm just praying he doesn't puke. He watches me take off his socks and undo his pants. I scoot the jeans off his legs and then he's in his boxers and t-shirt and he's still watching me.

"I love you, Cat," he slurs and my eyes are the size of dinner plates. He's drunk. Good old liquid courage. Or in this case, liquid delusions.

"No you don't," I murmur.

"How do you know what I feel," Will accuses. He tries to sit up, his body swaying on the bed. "You think you know everything, Cat. I do love you. I love when you look at me with those big huge reindeer eyes and I love it when they get all squinty, when I say something you're going to argue with."

I feel the tears welling in my eyes and I pull the rubber band from my wrist, wrapping it around my loose hair.

"I don't have reindeer eyes. That's just make-up." I get a tissue from the bathroom and wipe the glitter from my face. God, I feel like such a fraud.

"I love your big fat braid hanging down your back and how you think you're so tough. I love your hips in that dress and your shoulders. You have really pretty shoulders." He sits on the edge of the bed.

"It's just a dress," I say, and I have to get out of it, the halter around my neck choking me. I unfasten the latch behind my neck, holding the dress across my chest as I search the corner for my backpack in the dark.

Will catches my wrist when I walk past him. He glides his hand along the outside of my arm and up to my shoulder, and my skin peppers with goose bumps. He feels so good. When he touches me it's magic.

I should leave, grab my shit and go into the other room. And I know Will's drunk and that this is a mistake, but I want him. I want the fantasy. And so does Will. At least right now he does.

I release my grip on Lauren's dress, letting the loose chiffon drop to the floor and I stand before him, completely exposed in Margot's stupid thong underwear.

"Oh God, you're just..." Will says in a hushed voice. His hands wrap around my hips, the tips of his fingers pressed into my skin and I sigh at the contact.

He guides his hands up my belly and over my ribs, his palms pressing roughly into my breasts and I gasp as he rolls his thumbs over my nipples. His hands smooth down my back and over my bare ass, his fingers hooked in the elastic of the underwear and he slides them down my legs. His eyes roam every inch of my body, needy, wanting eyes as he guides my hips to straddle his lap, and I can feel him hard beneath me. I rock against him, my hands pulling his shirt over his head and then everything starts moving too fast.

There's a series of loud blasts and pops and Will kisses me, a rough, hungry kiss that consumes me. His fingers push into me and I gasp in shock, not ready for the penetration. The sensation is intense, the stretching of skin, the pulling of the hair there and it's too much, too fast.

I try to slow things down. I run my hands over his chest and I bring his mouth to mine, rolling my tongue with his and sucking at his lip and this feels better. His mouth leaves mine and travels down my neck and he squeezes my breast in his hand, his tongue licking and sucking at the rosy, tightened flesh. I moan loudly against his forehead, my hands pulling through his long hair.

Will stands up, his hands gripping my behind as he lays me on the bed. He hovers over me and I want him inside me. I wiggle my hips against him so that he'll know it's okay, that I surrender to him, that I don't want to fight him anymore. His eyes gaze into mine, his hands push the hair from my face and he kisses my cheeks, my eyelids, my shoulder. Will cradles my head in his hands, his eyes worried and I see it there, pain and sadness and I see him hesitating so I wrap my legs around his waist, holding him to me.

"This is wrong," he says. "It can't be like this. It's not supposed to be like this." He tries to pull away from me and tighten my legs, my arms wrapped around his neck.

"I want this, Will. It's okay, it's fine," I say and he shakes his head.

"No, no, no, this is not okay," his head collapses into my shoulder. "God, I'm such an asshole. I can't believe I almost...I won't Cat, not like this."

Rejection. It fucking hurts.

I unwind my legs and he rolls off of me and I suddenly feel very foolish. I crawl underneath the fluffy comforter and curl up on my side. How could I be so stupid? Will figured it out first, that's all. None of this is real. It can't be.

"I'm not saying no. I'm just saying not now." I hear him say drowsily behind me. I feel his body shift so that he's under the comforter too. His arms wrap around my belly, his chest presses into my back, his lips on the back of my shoulder and my neck.

"Please, Cat, understand. I don't want it to be like this, not with you," he says, his lips pressing into my shoulder a dozen more times. "Please, don't be mad."

"I'm not mad," I say, my body relaxing against his chest and I feel him heavy on my back, his hot breath on my skin and I know he's completely gone, passed out and asleep and I sigh.

I wiggle out from underneath him, and find my backpack. I pull on my soft cotton Underoos and my t-shirt and I instantly feel better, more like myself and less like the girl who almost had drunk sex with Will just minutes ago. I crawl back under the comforter, and squirm my way into his arms, unsure of everything and wishing I would have remained within my granite fortress.

I don't know what time the others get in that night, or morning or whatever. I only know that once again, we missed the fireworks. Will and I were in here, having quasi almost sex during the fireworks show. How ironic is that?

Margot and Andy are asleep in the other bed and I silently creep into the restroom and brush my teeth. I crawl behind the curtain to sit in the windowsill and watch the tiny cars drive along the strip. The people look like ants meandering down the sidewalk.

"Hey." Will's head peeks through the closed curtain, his eyes squinting while he scratches at his stubbly chin. "Coffee?"

"Sure," I murmur. We're going to have to talk about it eventually, I guess. Might as well get it out and over with.

We get dressed and walk down to the coffee shop in the lobby. Will wears dark sunglasses, even though we stay indoors. I can't help but smile at how ridiculous he looks.

"Don't laugh at me," he says, a small grin on his lips as he sips his coffee.

"Hey, you only turn twenty-one once, right? And you definitely had a night to remember," I say and then wish I could shove my foot in my mouth because his face crumbles.

"Cat, I'm so sorry. I was completely wasted and I was out of line. We didn't...did we?" he asks and I deflate. He doesn't even remember, which makes me wonder what else he doesn't remember. Does he remember singing to me? Does he remember that he loves me?

"Nothing happened. Don't worry about it, it's fine," I try to blow it off, my voice terse and tight.

"That's not what I meant, damn it! God, I keep fucking this up." Frustrated, he pushes his hair from his face. "I don't ever want to have that with you, you know, a drunken fuck I can't remember. You deserve so much better."

"So what do you want to have with me?" I ask and Will smiles.

"Coffee? Sundaes? Bowling? Anything, Cat," he murmurs, his eyes dancing across my face.

"You want to go on a date?" I ask him, confused and he shrugs. "I like that. We can start over."

"No, not start over. Start again," Will says, his fingers pushing my hair behind my ear and I smile. I can do that.

Will holds my hand as we walk back to the room to find everyone awake, an odd silence hovering in the air. Margot looks worried, frantic almost as she cleans up her stuff. Andy's tossing the empty liquor bottles into the trash can. He won't look at me.

"What's going on?" I ask and Margot smiles at me nervously.

"Jay, Lauren, she's back," Margot calls, and Jay walks cautiously into the room. I'm starting to panic.

"Cat, can you come here for a sec," Jay says and I pull Will along. I sit on the bed, the one that looks undefiled and Will sits at my side. Lauren and Jay stand linked before me and I feel very small as they exchange odd glances.

"Oh for the love of awkward silences, just spit it out!" I say finally and Jay takes a deep breath.

"Cat, I'm moving to Washington D.C.," Jay says and I freeze.

"What? You're leaving?" I whisper after a long pause, the initial shock turning into anger and I grit my teeth. Will wraps his arm around my shoulders but I barely feel him. All I can feel is this huge fucking knife in my back.

"Lauren got an internship in Washington D.C. She's going to be there for at least the next two years, maybe longer. And I want to be where she is."

"But the marina, Dad and Mom? We need you Jay, Dad needs you. What are we going to do?" I ask him and Lauren won't meet my eyes.

"Dad will be fine," Jay says in a cool voice and I wonder if I'm the last one to know.

"Why are you telling me this now? Does everybody know? Does Dad know you're abandoning us for some part-time girlfriend?" I ask sarcastically. Lauren's sharp eyes glare into mine. I don't care. She can hate me all she wants. I'll hate her right back. She's stealing my brother.

"Nobody knows. Except Margot and Andy, because we needed witnesses," Jay mumbles and I'm confused.

"Witnesses?" I ask, the tears spilling over my cheeks now.

"Lauren isn't my part-time girlfriend, Cat." Jay smiles shyly at Lauren beside him and I already know what he's going to say. It doesn't stop the words from slamming into my chest like a semi-truck.

"She's my wife."

1993 – THAT TIME YOU DIDN'T SHOW

The Fugitive starring Harrison Ford is released in theaters.

Pearl Jam releases their second album, Vs., and in its first week, it outperforms all other entries in the Billboard top ten combined.

Average price of a movie ticket in the US is $4.14.

* * *

"I t still says I'm off by almost a thousand dollars," I complain into the receiver. I pound on the enter button incessantly, but the stupid machine keeps beeping at me.

"Cat, stop pushing buttons. Did you read the directions I left?" my brother asks impatiently. I pull the phone away from my ear and shake it, pretending it's Jay's stupid neck. Of course I read the damn directions!

"Yes," I try to remain calm. "I did everything you said to do and it still won't balance."

"I don't know what to tell you. You're going to have to go through and verify each deposit," he says and I want to ram my head against the wall. And then ram Jay's head against the wall for leaving me to deal with this shit.

"Thanks for nothing, douchebag," I mutter and Jay laughs. He's been exceptionally forgiving of my foul attitude.

"I miss you, Kit Cat," he says and I squeeze my eyes shut, trying not to cry.

"I miss you, too. Are you coming home for the summer?" I ask and I hear Jay sigh.

"I don't know if that's such a good idea." Yeah, I figured.

After we got home from Vegas last summer, Jay quit his job. He told my dad he got married in Vegas and that he was moving to Washington, D.C. in August and, well, shit sort of went flying.

"That's right," my dad had shouted. "Abandon this family, just like your mother!" This was when I began to hyperventilate. It was just the biggest clusterfuck ever. Jay packed his shit and before he left, I begged him to stay.

"Please don't leave me," I said and he cried. My brother fricking cried. I realized this was hard for him too, so I let him go. I let him go with his Lauren.

I was so mad, and hurt, and envious, and disappointed I could hardly stand it.

All the responsibility is now on me. Jay was supposed to help my dad learn how to use the computer. Jay knows stuff about finance and investing and making the customers happy. Jay was supposed to take over the marina so my dad could retire. And now that's all on me. When I tried to explain this to Will he didn't understand.

"If Jay and Lauren can make this long distance thing work, so can we," he said and I shook my head.

"For the next four years? And then what about your residency? Then what are you going to do? Move here? I can't ever leave now. I'm stuck."

"We don't have to know all the answers right now. I thought we were going to take it slow," he said and I felt like a goddamn idiot. Here I was, practically telling him I want to be with him forever and all he wants is to talk on the phone once in a while.

Before Will left, he gave me a phone number to this pager thing that he has. All I have to do is call it, punch in my number and wait for him to call me back. Will says the bulk of the long distance charges will be on his tab. This makes me feel like a complete moocher.

Will also gave me a CD for my birthday, a red cover with clasped hands and the words Pearl Jam in bold across the front. I was confused. I didn't even have a CD player. But he insisted it will play. I thought he was crazy until I noticed he had replaced my tape player with a brand new CD player.

"I do not accept that gift," I said, folding my arms across my chest as he put the CD into the player and skipped to a specific song, a slow, lulling melody accompanied by a throaty, emotive voice.

"Why not? You've never had a problem accepting my gifts before." He tried to pull me to the bed but I pulled back.

"Because I can't give you anything in return."

"Alright fine, I'm loaning you my CD player so you can listen to my favorite song," he smirked and I finally let him pull me to the bed. I rested easily beside him, his arm under my neck, his hand pulling through my hair, his lips on my temple and he quietly sang to me.

Will slept in my bed all night, kissed me goodbye in the morning and then he was gone.

And I was alone.

"How's Steven working out?" After Jay left, guess who my dad hired? Yep, Steven pain-in-my-ass Young.

"Oh, just peachy," I mutter. The truth is, Steven's doing a fine job. He's a hard worker, he's pretty knowledgeable about boats, and he knows this river better than I do; not that I'd tell him that.

"How's Lauren?" I say as I stare at the computer screen.

"She's great, a little stressed, but she's handling it well. She loves her job and she's really happy being right in the middle of the political scene. She was very pleased with how the campaign went." Lauren worked on the Clinton campaign this past election.

"Oh, so she's a democrat now?" I joke.

"She walks the line," Jay laughs. "You should see our apartment. It looks like Captain America exploded."

"So maybe Thanksgiving?" I ask my brother and it's quiet for a long time.

"Yeah, Sis, maybe Thanksgiving," he says. I grit my teeth and clench my eyes, fighting back the tears and the tone that I know will just make him feel worse.

"Okay, I can wait," I say and I hear my brother sigh.

"Check your decimals," he says suddenly. "Sometimes I would put the decimal place in the wrong spot and it would mess everything up."

As soon as I'm off the phone with Jay, Steven barges through the office door, sweaty and stinking up the place, to hand me an invoice. We had some of the docks re-padded and Steven's been overseeing the project.

"Hey, I need a check," he says and I look at the slip of paper.

"Tell them we'll send one out. I'm not paying them until my dad checks their work." I squint at the computer screen, looking for a rogue decimal.

"I told them you'd write a check. Come on Cat, I got these guys to do this for a killer price. You don't want to piss them off, in case you need more work done in the future." He wipes the sweat off his almost bald, knobby head.

"I'm busy and my dad needs to okay the job first, Steven," I say through clenched teeth, scrolling through the entries. Fricking decimal, where are you? Steven leans over my back, his hand on my chair, and he lets his chest lean against my shoulder as he stares at the screen.

"Hey, personal-space-invader, don't you have something to do?"

"You forgot a decimal," he murmurs into my ear, his finger on the screen and my face flushes. The phone rings and before I can answer it, Steven reaches across me and grabs the receiver.

"Red Rock Cove Resort and Marina," he says. I scowl and fix the decimal problem. Enter. Balanced. Finally! I sigh in relief as Steven hands the receiver to me without a word.

"Hello?" I say into the phone.

"Cat?" Will's voice is muffled and distant but it's familiar just the same.

"Hey," I say as Steven messes with some paper clips on my desk. "Knock it off, Steven."

"What?" Will asks and I shoo Steven out of the room. Of course, he refuses to leave.

"Nothing. Steven's an infant," I mutter as he waves the

invoice in front of my face.

"Oh." Long awkward silence. "Is this a bad time?"

My dad walks into the office, and I go mute. Steven shakes his hand and holds up the invoice for him to inspect.

"Um, kinda, yeah," I say quietly, swiveling in my chair so that I'm facing the wall. "The office is full, if you know what I mean."

"Okay." I can barely hear Will's quiet voice.

"What's wrong?" I ask and plug my ear.

"Nothing, I'll talk to you later." Silence. And I feel horrible.

My dad pulls off his hat and sets the invoice on the desk. "We need a check," he says and Steven gloats beside him. I want to punch both of them in the face.

"Don't you think you should at least check out the job?" I argue and my dad's mustache twitches.

"I trust Steven's judgment," he says as he pulls out his cigarettes from his back pocket. He offers one to Steven and the room fills with smoke. It takes me at least twenty minutes to figure out how to print the check, the sawing sound of the machine grating on every nerve. I thrust the check into Steven's hand.

"I'm taking a break," I yell back at my dad. The sun scorches and makes my eyes water after being in the dimly lit office all day. The general store is empty. Snagging an IT'S-IT from the freezer, I walk into the stockroom to find Josie scribbling down quantities on a clipboard.

"These people eat a ridiculous amount of chili," she says and I laugh, licking the chocolate from my fingers and basking in the sweet sugary reprieve. "How are things up in the big house?"

"Miserable. I miss the store and I suck at computers," I say and Josie gives me a tight, apologetic grin.

"You'll get the hang of it."

"Hopefully I won't take down the entire marina in the process."

"Yeah, please don't, because then I'd be out of a job," Josie harps. "How's your photography class?"

"I had to drop it. I kept missing classes and I wanted to get a full refund. Maybe next year." I wad up the plastic wrapping and shove it in the pocket of my jeans as I watch Josie swiftly take inventory.

"So did you talk to lover boy today?" Josie asks, catching me off guard.

"Yeah, I did actually. For a second," I grumble. "We just can't seem to get it together and it's weird. We don't have a lot to talk about. I seriously doubt he wants to hear about the new padding on the docks or how many cans of chili we had to order this month."

"Well, he'll be here in a week and then your life will be complete," she says sarcastically and I give her a glare.

"You think I'm an idiot, don't you?"

"Just be careful, Cat. Don't give your whole heart away. Keep a little for yourself," Josie says, her gray eyes proud and I sigh. Too late, my wise, bitter friend. Too fricking late.

When the Henderson's big, black Mercedes pulls in to park at their unit, I'm eager to see Will's Saab. But I don't. I'm expecting to find him on the swings. But I don't. I'm expecting to see him walk through the door of the store or knock on my bedroom window or even on the bridge feeding the fish. But I don't.

I'm halfway hyperventilating when Steven saunters into the office to see if I have his paycheck ready. I want to puke.

"The Hendersons are here," he says cynically.

"I know." But he isn't. I have to get out of here. I have to go home to the safety of my room so I can fall apart. I jet out the door and run right smack into Margot. Her hands steady my shoulders, her eyebrows creased and worried.

"He's not coming," she says, her eyes filled with pity. Poor, pitiful, pathetic Cat.

"Why not?" I ask bitterly.

"He didn't say. He said he has to stay in Baltimore and figure some school stuff out. We didn't even talk to him on his birthday. Did you?" Margot's eyes look like big blue crystals.

His birthday. Oh my God. Last week, when he called. Oh, no, no, no! He called me on his birthday, and I blew him off. Double fuck shit!

"Oh Margot, I fucked up!" I gasp. "He called last week and I couldn't talk. I didn't even know it was his birthday. It's not something we do, call each other on birthdays."

"No, there's something else going on with him," she mutters. "He's being a complete dick."

"Is it someone else?" I ask, my ears burning but I have to know. Even if it kills me, I have to know.

"I don't know," she says. "I don't think so, but I... I just don't know."

"It's okay. Things change. People do too." I've been waiting for this to happen. Will always leaves and I always knew one day he might not come back.

"I'm sorry, Cat," Margot says and I shake my head.

"It's fine. I knew this wouldn't work. I went against my better judgment and I let-" I stop myself from saying it out loud. If I say it then it's real and I will surely be unable to breathe ever again.

"I am going to kick his stupid ass for this shit." Margot pulls me into a tight hug. My whole body shakes, my stomach twisting, and I feel like Goldie Hawn in *Death Becomes Her*, a big shotgun blast right through the middle of my gut.

* * *

Cat?" I hear a muffled voice outside my bedroom door. Ugh, why won't they leave me alone? "Cat, turn off Smashing Pumpkins and open the door."

It's Margot, and probably Andy. I've been avoiding them all summer. I shut myself in the office when I have to work and go straight home afterward. I don't go on the water, I don't eat ice cream, I don't go to Laughlin for the Fourth. I become a granite statue and refuse to let myself think about him. I hide his pictures, his presents, and his music. I break out my old radio and shove his stupid CD player in my closet.

I don't know what to feel. I want to be angry with him for letting this romance thing come before friendship. Friends do not blow each other off. Friends do not ignore each other's pages. Friends do not keep secrets. I can't believe I let this happen. I did exactly what I told myself not to do and then, like an idiot, I rationalized it. I'm still rationalizing it. I'm still hoping, again, like an idiot, that there's some explanation, that he'll show up, that he'll call. Every day that he doesn't, I feel like a damn fool.

The worst part is that I've lost my friend. My best friend. The greatest friend I've ever known. I don't have that comfort any more, I don't have that soul that knows me best, the one person I've bared everything to, inside and out. He's gone.

Oh God, I miss him.

"Cat, you're not pissing in bottles in there, are you?" Josie's out there too and I scoff. This is ridiculous.

I open the door and find Margot, Andy and Josie looking at me like I'm about to explode or something. I roll my eyes. Yeah, I'm hurting. Yeah, I feel like my insides are being carved out with a spoon, but I'm not going to freak out. I am going to be fine. I am going to be okay. I am going to get Will out of my head.

Because it's obvious I'm out of his.

I don't say a word. I grab my keys from the dresser and walk past them, linking my arm in Margot's and pulling them out the front door.

"Where are we going?" Margot asks as we drudge to the docks, the hot sun soaks into my skin and goosebumps spread over my arms and scalp.

"Andy, have you ever jumped from the cliffs?" I ask him and he chuckles.

"Yeah, once me and Will-" Margot elbows him in the ribs and I swallow. I really, really want to pretend that hearing his name isn't going to bother me, but that's a lie. It rips me up, like I'm outdated newspaper being shredded for kindling. And it pisses me off.

"He can say his name, for fuck's sake!" I spit and Margot looks ashamed and I feel awful. I take a deep breath and try to level with them. "I'm sorry. Okay, yeah, this is hard and I'm in a funk. But I can't stand the poor Cat bullshit. It makes me want to break things."

"Fair enough," Margot says. "No more poor Cat."

"For the record, I have never once thought poor Cat," Josie remarks with a smirk and I laugh for the first time in weeks.

"Wait. Who's at the store?" I ask and Josie grins.

"Steven. I told him he has to clean the bathrooms, too."

"That is the best thing I've heard all year." We walk past the swing set and I close my eyes, forcing myself to ignore the two small children giggling as they fly through the air.

I lead them into the store to find Steven and Josie's little brother, Jake, at the counter. Jake just finished a nine month tour with the army in the Middle East, and looks nothing like the nerdy kid that I made out with once years ago. He's tall, his shoulders are well-defined beneath his tank top and his skin is brown and coppery. His eyes are deep and dark, and his full lips curl over large, white teeth when he sees me.

"Oh my! Well, if it isn't little Kit Cat Rossi," he says in a throaty voice.

"Hey, Jake. How's Saudi Arabia?" I ask as I pull a six pack of Budweiser from the fridge. Margot clears her throat beside me and I roll my eyes and grab a box of wine too.

"Hot," he laughs.

"Really? Hotter than here?" I grab a paper bag from behind the counter and bag up the booze.

"Yeah, but it's not bad. Lots of sand, lots of bugs." He grins and I smile.

"Aw, just like home then," I say sarcastically and he laughs, a loud booming laugh that might be fake. Or nervous.

"Who are your friends?" he asks.

"This is Margot and Andy. They're from California, the Bay Area."

"Ah, Paychecks," Jake nods knowingly and I scowl.

"No, they're my friends," I snap, my snotty attitude making a comeback. Jake's face falls and I feel guilty. Here he's been at war, defending our country and all I can do is make him feel bad. *Nice one, Cat.*

"Hey, do you want to go out on the water with us? We're going to jump from the cliffs. The big ones." Steven thumps on the counter with his fist and I smirk. He's pissed he can't go, which makes me want Jake to come along even more.

"Hell yeah! I haven't jumped from the cliffs in years," Jake beams. He's kind of cute, I decide.

"No, you're not invited," Josie says as she glares at me and I glare right back.

"Cat just invited me!" he says, exasperated.

"Well, you're not coming with us. Go home and see Mom," she tries to push him out the door but he's like a mountain.

"Mom's not even home, she's working," Jake says, pushing her back.

I grab the bag of alcohol and Steven grabs my wrist. "You can't take that. You didn't pay for it."

Rolling my eyes, I try to shrug from his grip but his fingers hold strong around my arm. "I'm serious."

"Let go of me," I growl, my irritation quickly shifting to anger.

"No worries," Jake says and pulls out his wallet. "I got it." Jake throws a couple bills onto the counter and Steven drops my wrist. Jake grabs the bag before we leave the store but not before Steven flips me off, like a thirteen year old.

We climb aboard my father's boat, Jake poised at the bow and waiting to push us out as I start the engine.

"Cat, do not fuck with my brother," Josie whispers in my ear, taking the seat beside me.

"What does that mean?" I snap at her. Wow, Josie *is* a bitch! "I don't fuck with people. People fuck with me. I'm not the fucker,

Josie. If anything, I am the fuck-ee."

"Hey! We goin' or what?" Jake shouts. I nod and pull back on the throttle, steering the boat out of the slip. Jake jumps onto the bow, his dark eyes shining like multicolored river rocks.

I didn't ask my dad if I could use the boat and I don't even care. The hills surrounding the marina burn under the glow of the sinking sun, the sky streaked with red and orange. The dark water glitters like shards of glass. Will's everywhere here.

The sun is gone by the time I steer into Australia. Jake jumps into the water and ties off the anchor and we all wade to shore. I keep marching up the cliff, determined to soften the pounding in my chest and the air tastes like dirt. I have to get up this hill before it gets too dark or I will surely chicken out.

Jake catches up to me, his rough hand on my shoulder sparking my attention. I like the way he feels. It's different; calloused and strong. He smiles sheepishly as he pants from the quick uphill jaunt but I can't return the grin. The muscles in my cheeks fail to cooperate.

"So, Kit Cat, what have you been up to?" he asks and I don't want to tell him. I haven't done one damn thing with my life since I graduated high school four years ago. I've been waiting on a boy.

"Not much, just working at the marina. My brother got married. He's living in D. C. now," I say, steering the conversation away from me.

"That's what Josie said. She said you're taking photography classes and that you're working in the office now. She didn't say if you were seeing anyone," he hints with a sly wink and I snort.

"No, I am definitely not seeing anyone."

"Maybe you could see me sometime," he says boldly and for some reason this makes me laugh. Ah, Jake. He's adorable, like a big floppy puppy. I could go out with him. He might be a good distraction.

"Maybe I could." I say quietly and he beams. We reach the summit and I stand at the edge. We're at the highest cliff, the moon our only lantern, the dark, black water below hauntingly still. There isn't a lick of wind and it's hot, and eerily quiet and I'm wondering if we should just walk back down.

"There's no way in hell I'm jumping," Margot says and Andy gives her a nudge.

"Oh, come on. I'll hold your hand," he says in a low sultry voice and I feel my granite heart split. I remember the time Will held my hand and we jumped together, when he tricked me so he could pinch my leg and I cried. He hurt me and then he kissed me. Oh God, what am I doing here? What am I doing with my life? Why can't I hate him already? If I hate him this won't hurt so much.

"I'll go first," Josie says, her stone gray eyes reflecting the pale of the full moon. Without a second thought, she drops over the edge. She plunges silently into the water and then surfaces, a huge satisfied smile on her face. It's all the encouragement we need.

Margot and Andy go next and then Jake and I follow dead last, the impact sending my shorts right up my rear. I laugh when I surface and we climb onto the boat, popping open cans of beer and drinking wine from paper cups. For the first time in weeks, I don't want to sink. I surface, I smile and I kiss Jake on the mouth while Josie glares at me out of the corner of her eye. She doesn't drink and I'm glad because I am way too drunk to drive the boat back to the marina. She shares her cigarettes with me and I draw the tobacco in and I feel very much like my mom.

Margot, Andy, and I drive into Las Vegas to meet my mom for lunch. My mom immediately loves Margot. Afterward, we walk the strip to see the new casinos they're building and I notice a tattoo place just off the strip. I pull them into the shop and immediately pick one out, a small red and brown spiraling sun, using the money my mom gave me to buy gas to pay for it. I absorb the stinging pain, inhaling sharply through the buzzing of the inked needle digging into the middle of my back. Margot gets a bright blue butterfly right below her belly button, and Andy holds her hand while she winces.

I spend the next few weeks with Jake and Margot and Andy. We swim and ride the WaveRunners up to the dam and I let Jake kiss me and hold my hand. We have bonfires and barbecue out on the cove. We go hiking behind the cliffs and I slip in the mud. Jake picks me up and runs me to the water, his hands moving over my body as he washes the mud from my skin.

It's easy to be happy with Jake, because he does all the work. He plans dates and picks me up. He calls me and brings me dinner when I'm working late at the office. He kisses me and touches me and he'd probably have sex with me. All I have to do is say yes to him.

Jake tells me about the army, about the war. He's killed people, he's almost been killed and here he is, sharing a sundae with me at Baskin Robbins. We sit on the bench outside and we kiss and he's very much a gentleman about it.

"I've always liked you," he says, his fingers on my face and in my hair as he tugs at my lips. Not the same. It's okay, it's good, but it's not the same and it's frustrating. "You're so beautiful, like the sunset."

Jake's mouth moves to my neck, his hands on my lower back and he presses me to his chest. I'm not beautiful, I'm ugly. This whole thing is so ugly, what I'm doing to Jake. I can't be what he deserves. I want to. I'm trying with all my heart, begging myself to like him more.

But it's always there, that stinking persistent what-if.

What if Will comes back? What if he calls? I know I will forgive him. I will accept whatever excuse he offers and I hate myself for it.

I pull away and Jake sighs. His hands leave my body, his eyes fixate on the street. It's the worst possible thing I can think of to do, to allow this sweet boy to comfort me and not give him anything in return.

"I'm sorry," I blubber and I pull my shirt up to hide my face. "I'm going through this thing right now and I just, I can't do this Jake. You're a really nice person. You're too nice for me."

"What are you talking about? I'm not that nice," he tries to pull the t-shirt from my face. "Come on, give me a chance. I'll treat you like shit, I promise." And this makes me laugh and cry even more furiously.

"I really, really want to. You have no idea," I stress. "But I just can't."

"Why not? I thought we were having a good time. Aren't you having a good time?" he says and I hate the way his voice sounds.

"Yeah, I am. You're a really good friend." I wipe the snot from my nose, the tears from my cheeks.

"Friend? Do you kiss all your friends like you kiss me?" he replies sarcastically and his words sting.

"I don't know what's wrong with me," I sob, great big heaving gasps and then I laugh because I'm just now realizing I'm a crier.

"I could tell your heart's not in it. You seem like you're holding back all the time. Or maybe holding on?" Jake pushes my hair behind my ear.

"I'm sorry," I whisper and he kisses my forehead. And it's done.

I don't see Jake around the marina anymore after that and I kind of miss him, but then Josie tells me that he's signed up for another tour and will be flying out at the end of August. It seems like everyone leaves all at once; the Hendersons, Jake, the majority of the motorhomes, all rolling out as the storms roll in.

I'm sitting in the office late one night, finishing some paperwork I should have finished yesterday. Steven leans against my desk, gossiping about some people from school that he saw in town.

"You know her, Trisha Moore, she was in your American Government class," he says. "Remember, she gave Matt Slater a blow job behind the library during the disaster drill sophomore year? I think Jake dated her too."

"Why would I remember that?" I ask him, irritated. He

shrugs.

"Anyway, she married Eric Martin. My brother's fucking her." Steven acts like it's no big deal his brother is sleeping with someone else's wife and I just shake my head.

"Wow, classy. Which brother?"

"Travis. He's working at Safeway now and she always asks him to take her groceries out to her car. Guess she needs help loading her trunk," he winks and I scowl.

"That is really disturbing, you know that right?"

"Hey, who am I to judge?" He fiddles with the stapler on my desk and I snatch it from his hand. "Pearl Jam is playing in November at the Aladdin. I think I'm going to buy tickets. Do you want to go? Do you know Pearl Jam?"

"Yeah, I know them," I mutter and close my eyes. Everything is tainted by memories of him. Vegas, Pearl Jam, even ice cream, it all reminds me of Will and I hate it.

"Well, do you want to go with me?"

"Do you even like Pearl Jam? I thought you listened to rap music, Snoop Doggy Dogg and shit," I ask him as I punch the numbers into the computer.

"I don't know, maybe it's time for a change." Steven stares down at me in my chair.

"He's never going to be with you for good," he says quietly and I freeze. "Come on, you know as well as I do."

We both know exactly who he's talking about. I glare at him, the tears brimming in my eyelids and I force them to not spill over. Not in front of Steven, oh, please not in front of Steven.

"Tell me I'm wrong. Tell me he's coming back to stay or that he'll sweep you away from here and you'll live happily ever after," Steven challenges. "It's what you want, isn't it? It's what you keep waiting around for."

I'm completely still, a single tear slides down my cheek. God, I want to argue with him. I want to prove to him all the ways he's wrong but I don't have one shred of evidence to suggest otherwise.

He stares into my eyes, his face lingering close to mine

and I breathe him in. He smells like weed and beef jerky and cinnamon gum and I feel sick.

What am I waiting around for? I'm still a virgin, for fuck's sake. While I'd never openly admit it, I think I've been saving myself for him. I could have had Scott or Jake and I could have been happy. Shit, I could have Steven. I could have him right now. All I have to do is say yes. All I have to do is let go of the greatest love of my life and the best friend I've ever known. He hasn't called since his birthday, but I've been waiting for him for ten years. I can't waste my life waiting for him anymore.

Just then, like an electric shock straight to my heart, a sound jolts through my entire body and causes my hair to stand on end.

The phone. It's ringing. It's late. It's him. I just know it is.

"You don't have to answer it," Steven murmurs, his hand folding over mine and I just stare at the ringing telephone on the desk, the red light flashing in the dimly lit room.

"Yes I do," I whisper and Steven pulls his touch away. My hand shakes as I pick up the receiver.

1994 – THAT TIME I RAN YOU OVER

Kurt Cobain is found dead in his home in Seattle, WA.

Forrest Gump is released in theaters in July.

The X-Files wraps up its first season on Fox.

* * *

When I think of my parents, the two people who are supposed to teach me how to handle life, I've had two contrasting viewpoints. My dad has always been matter-of-fact. There are no secrets with him. He tells it like it is and sees no point in bullshitting. My dad is a realist. He's honest. He levels with people and they respect him for it.

My mom is the complete opposite. My mom is fantasy. She lives in a pretty, soft world, with silk pajamas and fuzzy comforters. She gets a new car every two years even though she only drives fifteen minutes to work. She has her hair and her nails done and she speaks in clichés. Her advice is always light and fluffy and is never really helpful. Still, she always makes me feel better, even if it's just a fantasy.

I think it's fair to say I've led a sheltered life. I've always been taken care of, and I've always felt loved. I've spent the majority of my time wondering, observing, judging for myself how the world works, why some people are offered opportunities and others have to fight for everything they've got. While none of it is ever equal, it's often the first thing we think when bad shit happens, that it's not fair.

My mom and her boyfriend Paul were killed in a head-on collision coming home from a trip to Los Angeles. I didn't even know she was on vacation. They were speeding and veered into the oncoming traffic lane to pass a slow truck. Paul must have misjudged the distance, or maybe didn't see the other car heading straight for them. My mom died instantly. Paul lived a short while at the hospital but didn't make it through the night. It happens all the time on the long stretch of Highway 15 between Southern California and Las Vegas. Not a year goes by that we don't read about some poor family destroyed by a fatal accident, and we talk about how the traffic will be clogged up for hours.

Well, this year, it's my family that's destroyed.

I was so sure it was Will on the phone that night, so very sure that I didn't even stop to think how it made no sense for him to be calling the office so late. It never dawned on me that it might be the California State Highway Patrol looking for my mother's next of kin.

I was in disbelief. Stunned, really, but mostly I just didn't believe she was gone. I didn't even cry because it didn't seem possible. She's always been gone, you know? I kept thinking she was at the Tropicana and I'd go pick her up on her lunch break. She'd tell me about some drama going on at work and I'd tell her about Josie and Jake and Will and it'd be just like normal.

My brother and Lauren flew in for the week. We don't have any other family. My mom was an only child and my grandparents have been dead for years. We had the service at a little church in Vegas, packed with her friends from the casino and our friends from the marina. I stood with my family: Dad, Jay and Lauren. My dad held onto me the whole time, his arm around my shoulders, his thin frame sturdy and tough next to my soft one. He gripped my arm, holding onto me like he wished he could have held onto her.

A young woman with two small children approached me and introduced herself as Paul's daughter. Her eyes were red from crying and she hugged me tightly and told me she'd heard so much about me and she was sorry for my loss. I didn't know her at all. I didn't really know anything about my mom.

All her friends were strangers to me. She's a stranger to me and it didn't make me sad or wistful or depressed.

It made me furious.

Why does this lady get to cry over my mom? Why does she know my mom and I don't? I couldn't even empathize with this woman. She had lost her father too and maybe that makes me a horribly selfish person but I was so jealous I could hardly breathe.

I questioned everything. Why did my mom have to leave us? Why didn't she take us to live with her, why didn't she demand we spend more time with her? If she really wanted us, she would have done everything within her power to keep us. I began to view my relationship with my mom the same way I look at my photographs, as snapshots in time. That time she let us swim in the Tropicana pool. That time I wore her pajamas. That time she bought me a bikini. That time she met Will. It was all fantasy, only the good, none of the grit, a pretty postcard from a vacation, and not much else. While I missed my mom more than I could bear, I was struck with a profound appreciation of my father. Everything he did was for us. He was tough because he had to be, because he was raising two young children on his own, and trying to run a business. My mom never stepped up to the plate to tackle this responsibility. She was a part-time mom. I loved her, loved every single moment I spent with her, but she never put herself out there for us. She never had to get her hands dirty.

I was very calm through all of this. I kept my cool throughout the investigation, the parade of visitors offering their condolences and the endless amount of cards and flowers. I managed to keep it together until we had to go to her house. Jay and Lauren went with me and we spent the day boxing up her stuff. I had never been inside that house without my mother. We looked at her photo albums and rifled through her drawers. I poked around in her medicine cabinet and went through her makeup. I inhaled every perfume, tried on every lipstick. I pressed her soft silk pajamas to my face and I sobbed until I felt sick, locking myself in the bathroom so my brother and Lauren couldn't see. That didn't stop them from knowing, of course, and my brother broke down the door to get to me. I was so embarrassed, her red lipstick smeared on my face, my eyes swollen and snot pouring from my nose but they didn't say anything. My big brother held me while I muttered "It's not fair" over and over again. "I know Kit Cat, I know" was all he said.

I took her photo albums and her red lipstick and perfume and the silk pajamas and a sapphire ring she always wore and we gave the rest of her stuff to her friends from the casino and to the Goodwill. She didn't have much money but her car was paid for and Jay let me have it since my old VW was on the outs. It's a Beamer. It turns out she was upside-down on her house so Jay decided we should keep the property and rent it out instead of selling it. The property, he called it, like it was nothing to us. It's not home. It's not comfort. It's just a snapshot.

The Hendersons sent a card and a beautiful bouquet of white lilies and I wondered if Will knew my mom was dead. I wondered if maybe he would call or come see me but I got nothing from him.

Lauren and Jay left at the end of the week and everything went straight to hell. I was working in the office because working was at least a distraction, but I couldn't escape the gnawing reality. I was a twenty-two year old virgin, still living with my father and in love with a person that could care less if I existed. Worst of all, I had no aspirations for any of that to change. I had totally forgotten about my own birthday, until I got an envelope in the mail. I quickly tore through the paper to discover a birthday card. I stared at it. It had a drawing of a peanut butter and jelly sandwich on the front and on the inside it said, "Without you I'm just jelly." Written in neat handwriting across the bottom of the card were the words, "Happy Birthday Cat. I miss you. Love your friend, Will." Inside the envelope were two concert tickets to see Pearl Jam in Vegas.

No apology, no explanation, nothing but concert tickets.

I didn't need concert tickets. I needed my friend. I started throwing things. I threw my stapler right through the window. I ripped the concert tickets to shreds. I ran out of the office and looked desperately for something, something to break, something I could hurt, something to take away the horrible gut wrenching cloud of disaster that I couldn't seem to get out from under. I ran home and changed into my white eyelet camisole and the slim black skirt I bought for my mom's funeral. I combed my hair and left it loose and carefully painted my lips red. I coated my lashes with black mascara and sprayed myself with floral perfume. I was done waiting around for him. I was done with the fantasy. Will was just like my mom, a snapshot in time, a friend when it was convenient and I was just done.

I knew exactly where I wanted to go. There's a bar in town where a lot of people I went to school with hang out. Once in a while, they get Paychecks in there. That's what I needed, no strings, no attachments. I wanted to scratch an itch.

In a last minute decision, I pulled my hair up off my shoulders and knotted it at the nape of my neck. Will said I had nice shoulders.

Walking into the bar, I recognized a couple of people. Peter Salazar was bartending that night and I immediately lost my nerve the moment I sat down at the barstool. I had Peter in my class all through grade school. He always stood behind me in line because we had to line up alphabetically and he always pulled my braid. I got in a fist fight with him once on the playground. He looked exactly the same and all of a sudden I was little Kit Cat Rossi again.

"Cat? I never see you in here. You look...great," he stumbled. Peter used to drive a Pontiac Grand Am. "What are you drinking, babe?"

"Whatever," I said and he poured me a drink and I didn't even know what it was but by the time Steven showed up, I was completely wasted and pulling up my shirt to show Peter my tattoo.

I don't even know how it happened. One minute Steven was sitting next to me at the bar and the next we were making out in his bedroom and his hands were up my skirt. I was mean to him, too. I told him that it was nothing more than a one-time thing, that I didn't want to go out with him, that I didn't love him, and that I never would. I told him I didn't want to talk about it ever again and then he told me that he hated me. He called me a stuck-up bitch and said it was just about sex, and he thought he'd won. He never wanted to actually win me, he wanted to beat me. He thought he finally broke me and I laughed at him because I knew the truth. *You didn't break me, he did. I'm using you, idiot. I'm using you to make me feel better, just because I can.*

I didn't even have to take my clothes off and I barely remembered the sex when I woke up beside him. I didn't feel sore or bleed, like Cosmo said I would. I wasn't even sure if it really happened until I saw the condom in the trash and I wanted to vomit. I left before Steven woke up. The sun was just beginning to show itself as I stumbled the two blocks back to my mom's old car.

I fell apart the minute I sat down in the driver's seat because I wanted to drive so far away from there. I wanted to drive to my mom's. I wanted to tell her what happened with Steven and have her spout some trite cliché about how we learn from our mistakes or something, but she was gone and I missed her.

I wanted to drive to Baltimore and punch Will in the face and then kiss him and never let him go. On the way I could stop in Washington, D.C. and hug my brother and let him protect me, like he did when we were kids. I sat there at the intersection thinking of all the places I could go. If I turned left, I could drive away and never look back.

At that moment, the gas light in my mom's car came on, a little ding telling me that I needed to fill up, but it said so much more.

Ding! You don't have any gas money.

Ding! You're not going anywhere.

Ding! You're completely pathetic. And kind of slutty.

Ding! Go home, Cat.

I sighed and wiped my face with the back of my hand before driving the mile of cracked and uneven pavement back to my house.

Every day that month I didn't get my period I wanted to shoot myself. I had never been so happy to bleed in all my life. I swore I would never curse my period again and that next week, I went straight to the clinic in town and got on the pill. I avoided Steven at all costs. He didn't seem to mind. He didn't call, didn't try to talk to me about it. It was like it never happened, and I was more than willing to pretend it hadn't. I didn't tell anyone, not even Josie, but she figured something was up.

"Haven't seen Steven around here much. How'd you get him to leave you alone?" Josie shared her cigarettes with me as we stood on the bridge, the November air blowing in off the water.

"I don't know," I said quickly then occupied my lips by taking a long drag from her cigarette. She's too keen for her own good or, rather, for my good. She narrowed her eyes and pinched my cheeks in her hand and looked me square in the face.

"You fucked him!" she hissed and released my face. I covered my eyes with my forearm, my tears smeared on my skin. I didn't want to hear what she had to say because it was going to be bad and it was all going to be true.

"Oh babe." Josie held me up, and I sank into her side. "God, I hate them, the whole family. They should be castrated."

"It's not his fault. I mean, yeah, he's an asshole, but I used him too. I told him I didn't really want him and then he told me he hated me. I was drunk."

"Damn, Cat. That is some depressing-ass shit."

"I know. Please don't hate me."

"Why would I hate you? You're stupid. You're lost. You made a mistake, but who hasn't? Oh God, my first time was awful! I was at this bonfire out on a cove. There was sand everywhere. It was like wiping with sandpaper. Luckily, it only lasted two minutes." Josie pulled my arm away from my face.

"I hate myself," I muttered and Josie rolled her eyes.

"Look, pity party of one, it's done. There's nothing that can be done. Get over it and move on," Josie said, a fresh cigarette bobbing between her lips. "Besides, it's not your first experiences that should be the best, it's your last."

"Easier said than done. You of all people should know that," I snapped.

"Yeah, I do know. I know all too well where you're going to end up if you continue to make excuses and feel sorry for yourself. Doesn't mean it's not true," she said quietly and I felt awful for snapping.

"I miss my mom. She'd tell me everything is fine. I'm so far from fine right now, and it's so stupid but hearing her say it almost made it true." She handed me the cigarette and I took a long pull, letting the warm burn fill my chest.

"Cat, you're going to be fine. Everything's going to be fine," Josie said into my face. Her eyes were determined stone, and I wasn't the only one she was trying to convince.

Over the next several months I force myself to be fine. I don't complain about work, I submerge myself in taking pictures and fill my top dresser drawer with rolls of undeveloped film. I take smoke breaks with Josie and watch America's Funniest Home Videos with my dad and think of things I can videotape so I can win ten thousand dollars. The cocoon is back and I feel empty and void, but it's better than the hurt.

I almost forget about Will too, but as the summer months approach, I start to thaw. I fight it, but it's like my whole being knows he is supposed to be here soon. I hate this feeling, the anticipation, the dread, the nausea. Oh God, what if he doesn't show?

Shit, what if he does?

It's dusk and I'm hauling my laundry in one of the utility carts down to the Laundromat when the big black Mercedes slowly pulls onto the gravel road in front of me. No Saab. My insides deflate, my heart sinks right into the soles of my feet.

The Mercedes stops and Dr. Henderson rolls down his window.

Margot peeks her head forward from the back seat and shouts a hello. Then the back door opens and Will steps out into the evening heat. His hair is short and looks darker, more brown than blond, and is neat and trimmed around his ears and neck. He stares me down and I wonder if he recognizes me. I mean, of course he knows who I am, but does he see me? Does he see how I have changed? Can he see my thick heart? Can he see my broken spirit?

The black Mercedes disappears down the gravel road and Will's left standing in front of me.

"Cat." His voice wavers. He sounds the same and I soften, which pisses me off. Damn him! God damn his hold on me, God damn my own soul for being so easily swayed by him, God damn his fucking beautiful face.

I ignore him and slam my foot down on the pedal, swerving around him as my wheels spin in the gravel. A cloud of dirt explodes around his feet and he jumps out of the way.

"Cat!" I hear him yelling behind me but I'm determined to get away from him. I don't look back. I drive as fast as the stupid electric cart can go. The gravel crunches beneath my tires, there's dirt in my mouth, and my heart pounds in my chest.

I'm so focused on getting away from him that I'm caught off-guard when he jumps in front of the cart outside the Laundromat. I turn the wheel and slam on the brake and it locks, the back end fishtailing in the loose gravel and knocking him to the ground.

"Will!" I screech and stumble from the cart. I fall to the ground, my hands roaming his face and neck and chest, my eyes frantically searching for damage before I realize he's laughing.

"You fucking ran me over," he gasps and I scoff in disgust. I leave him on the ground but he grabs my arm, his fingers on my skin like a familiar song I've forgotten the words to.

"Whoops," I say sarcastically and yank my hand away. I grab the heavy sack of laundry from the back of the cart and storm into the humid room. Will is right on my heels.

"Cat, look, I know you're pissed at me," he starts and I spin around and throw the bag of laundry at him.

"Don't act like you know how I feel. You don't know anything about me."

"You're not even gonna give me a chance to explain?"

"You had a whole year to explain! And now it's convenient for you, now you wanna talk? Now? I needed you this year. I needed my best friend. And you were gone," I shout, my hands flying through the air.

"I know. I'm not going to argue with you."

"Well, good." I pace the length of the Laundromat, my heart racing. I stop in front of him. "Why not?"

He frowns, his lips soft and sad. "Because you're right. Oh God, Cat, I'm so sorry about your mom."

My chest is heaving as I stand before him, my hands on my hips, my forehead creased. Tears well in my eyes and I try to make sense of his words.

"You know then, they told you," I nod and it's like another stab in the back but I don't let those tears fall. He knew and let me suffer this whole time without him. Prick!

"Not until later, after the funeral, after I sent your birthday card, I promise. I wanted to fly down here right away but I had school and I thought maybe you wouldn't want to see me," he says quietly. "Besides, you have that other guy, Jake, or whatever."

"Jake's in Saudi Arabia," I mutter. "And you completely blew me off last summer, so what's it to you which guys I have?"

"You're right. That's not what this is about."

"What the fuck, Will? After everything that happened with my brother, shit, after Vegas, how could you not show?" It's a guilt trip, but I want answers, dammit!

"I failed a class, okay? Cellular and Molecular Biology of Human Disease," Will shouts back at me, like the name's been festering inside him. "I had to go to summer school. That's why I wasn't here. I had to make that class up, and the summer session was the only time it was offered. I didn't have a choice."

"You could have told me," I argue. "I would have understood."

"I didn't tell anyone. I told my family I was staying home to study for the MCAT and taking an extra course over the summer so I'd have an edge on the competition. Do you know that the MD track at Hopkins on average has over six thousand applicants? Do you know how many they accept? One hundred fifty. Do you know how many of those students fail fucking Biology? As it is, I'm a whole semester behind and my application is due in November but I won't find out if I even get into the program until like April or something, so basically I've lost a whole year."

"Well, that makes two of us," I bite and he narrows his eyes.

"You don't understand. I mean, my dad literally wrote the textbook on this shit. And I can't even pass a fucking class."

"I don't see what the big deal is. So you have to wait a year, who cares?"

"I don't want to wait. I'm tired of waiting," he says and I frown.

"You still should have told me," I say, crossing my arms in front of my chest.

"I know. I've fucked up everything and I'm really, really sorry," he says, drawing out every word.

"You broke my heart, Will." His face crumbles. "It's too late. I can't-"

"Please," he whispers, his hand reaching for mine. I step back and he shifts forward and it feels like dancing. "I was wrong, okay? You win, you're right, whatever you want, please. Just don't say you it's too late. Please?"

"It's not good enough. Your excuse. It's shit," I say, my voice falters and I'm sure he hears it.

"I know I hurt you and I hate myself because of it. Just tell me what I need to do. What do I need to do to fix this?" I find his eyes and they are helpless. Abandoned and pleading circles of green. It's like a fricking slasher flick, seeing that pain in his eyes. I'm Freddy Krueger and he's the dumb boy I'm murdering.

"You pinky promised. You said we'd always be friends, no matter what," he pleads, leaning in. "Please Cat, I need you to be my friend. You can't not be my friend."

"You can't do that, ignore me for so many months and then come back and expect everything to be fine. It's not like everything stops here when you're gone. You can't treat people like that." I look down at that floor so I don't see the tears in his pleading eyes.

"Is it really too late?" he whispers, his face so close to mine and I want to tell him yes. It's too late. I'm hurt, I'm bitter and angry. I don't even know what we could have at this point but all I want to do is hug my friend that I haven't seen in such a long time.

"Fuck it, it doesn't matter," he says and pulls me into him. I cling to his shirt and bury my face in his chest. His lips press into the top of my head and I cry from sheer relief. Everything is shitty but he's here and I let him hold me. It's just a hug but I've never felt such comfort in all my life.

"It's okay, Cat. Everything's going to be fine." And for one second, I almost feel like it's true.

❊ ❊ ❊

And then Andy says, well, is that what you want? A break? And I said, I don't know, maybe, and the next thing I know, I'm packing up my shit to come here and I tell him not to bother," Margot says from her spot next to Josie in the back seat of my mom's Beamer. Her hair is super short, a pixie cut, and it's honey blond, just like Lauren's. Apparently, she's been dying it black all these years. I give up. I don't know what's real anymore. Maybe Jay's right, and we are just part of some fucked up alien experiment.

"Maybe I'm being too demanding, but I'm twenty-four years old. I shouldn't be waiting around for him to decide what he wants. Shit or get off the pot already." Margot has been on a rampage ever since she got here.

"Fuck him!" Josie says. "Boys are so dumb. They think their dick's gonna shrivel up and fall off the moment they commit to somebody."

"Not all men think like that," Will says from the seat beside me and Josie and Margot wear matching scowls. They're bonding over their hate of the male gender.

"Careful. They've combined their forces for evil," I say in a low voice from the driver's seat. "They'll obliterate you."

Will laughs as I drive along the curving two lane highway. A song comes on the radio and I sing along, messing up the lyrics and hoping no one notices.

"Hey Cat, who sings this song?" Will asks me and I look over at him, confused because I'm pretty sure he knows.

"Radiohead," I tell him.

"Can we keep it that way?" He's fighting a smile and I smack at him with the back of my hand.

"They wrote this song about you, you know," I smirk.

"Whatever," Will scoffs, dejected.

"Oh, another valid point from the male," Margot quips sarcastically from the back seat and Will gives her a glare.

The sun begins to sink beneath the hills that shimmer like topaz and the sky ignites. I pull my sunglasses out of the center console and put them on to ease my squinting.

Suddenly, Will rolls down his window and sticks his entire head out just as a foul-smelling gas drifts from the backseat.

"Jesus!" he groans and I roll down my window too, gasping in the fresh air.

"Oh God, it's in my mouth," I gag.

"It was me," Margot says proudly. "And I don't even care. Just one more thing I can't do when I'm with Andy."

"Alright, now you're crossing the line," Josie says and I can't help it, I laugh uncontrollably until tears are streaming down my face. I look over at Will, and he's watching me laugh, his soft eyes creased in the corners and I feel better than I've felt all year.

We're driving into Laughlin for the Fourth of July. They put on a big fireworks show every year, right over the water. I've never seen it, but everyone says it's amazing.

I still haven't told Will about Steven. We've been hanging out this week, he meets me at the office for lunch or he brings me ice cream from the store and we talk. We're friends, and it's comfortable and easy, like slipping into pajamas after a long hard day. But I just haven't found the right time to tell him.

Not that I have to tell him anything. I don't owe him anything.

I exit the highway and drive the street lined with casinos. I pull into the Pioneer parking lot, the casino with the best spot to see the fireworks. It also has fishbowl margaritas, because nothing says God Bless America like a glass the size of your head filled with booze.

I drive around the parking lot, looking for a spot closer to the front, but the place is packed. We end up parking out by the RV's and boats, and my flip flops feel like they're going to melt on the hot blacktop. We carry our folded up camping chairs and Josie and Margot walk ahead, engrossed in their man-hating conversation.

"Nice toes." Will takes my chair and slings it over his shoulder. I look down at the black nail polish.

"Don't look at my toes," I grumble.

"Why, because they look like ET's fingers?" Will says and I scoff.

"They do not look like alien fingers!"

"They do too! Look how long they are!" he laughs and I look down to inspect.

"Whatever," I mutter. I should have worn sneakers.

"What, that's it? No sarcastic comment? No roll of the eyes?" he asks and I shrug.

"I've reached my quota for the year."

"Oh come on, I know you have an eye roll in there somewhere," he grabs my arm and whips me around to face him, his arms pinning mine to my sides, the chairs hanging on his shoulders almost smacking me in the face.

"Let me go, you goon!"

"Nope, not until you roll your eyes at me." I try to wiggle free but his hold is firm and I finally just stop moving.

"Oh come on Cat, look deep into my eyes and give me what I want," Will says in a sultry voice and through sheer instinct alone, I roll my eyes before I can stop myself. His lips curl into a sly grin and there they roll again.

"Nice! A twofer. Must be my lucky day." He winks at me and I fight the urge to roll my eyes yet again.

The place is crammed with people. Families, couples, and groups of teenagers just bursting at the seams with patriotism. A couple of kids run past us, shooting each other with squirt guns and the spray feels heavenly on my ankles.

We wade through the mass of people until we find a spot on the grass beside the River Walk between a large family and a group of tormented teenagers. The teens are covered from head to toe in black, torn stockings and big heavy boots and I'm slightly worried one of them might pass out from heat exhaustion. Josie keeps giving them dirty looks.

"Hey!" Margot shouts as a woman in glittery sunglasses shaped like stars walks past us carrying a gigantic glass filled with red slush. "What is that and why don't I have one?"

"It's a fishbowl margarita," I say and Margot watches the woman intently.

"I want. I need!" she gasps and grabs my hand.

We all drudge through the crowd to join the longest line I've ever seen at the bar inside the casino. Will's standing behind me and he pulls the neckline of my tank down, practically choking me in the process.

"Told you," Margot says.

"Told you what?" I spin around to look at them and he grins shyly.

"She told me about the tattoos. She said you didn't even cry."

"I didn't," I say proudly and whip my head back around.

"It's the exact same color as the cliffs in Australia," he says as he looks down the back of my shirt again and I feel my face blush.

We get through the line and are walking back to the chairs when I hear a grotesque sound behind me.

"Well, look who decided to grace us with his presence. I thought you were too cool for us now, college boy." I try to keep walking but Will turns around. Steven's lips are pulled into a nasty smirk and I fight the urge to run and hide in my car for the rest of the night. He's with his brother Ricky, and Josie's murderous gaze looks like a voodoo hex.

"Steven, good to see you, man." Will, being the more mature of the two, offers his hand. Steven looks at it and then at me before finally smirking to himself.

"She hasn't told you yet," he says and I want to kill him. I'm contemplating how bad prison would really be when Will looks at me confused.

Josie comes to my rescue.

"Hi Ricky," she says and we all turn our heads in complete shock. Ricky looks like he might throw up, like a scared puppy unsure if he's being scolded.

"Josie," he nods. "You look good."

Her eyes narrow. "You still look like a butthole," she says and Margot starts laughing mid-slurp.

"Haven't changed a bit then," Ricky says with a wink and Josie's caught in his stare. Oh what a bag of shit!

Just then, Heather finds us in the crowd. She's holding hands with Claire and I see Josie's face shift when she sees her cousin.

Josie stands there, her huge margarita in her hands while Heather walks right up to her and gives her a hug. A small splash of margarita splatters onto the concrete. Before anyone can say anything else, they're walking away, the little dark-haired girl turning and watching us curiously over her shoulder.

Will's quiet, doesn't even drink his margarita, when we get back to our chairs. The icy slush is turning to lukewarm soup so it's quickly commandeered by Margot and Josie. They're pretty wasted. Margot keeps barking at couples who are making out on the River Walk.

"Oh get a room! That's just indecent," she yells at these two ninth graders holding hands.

"Do you think they're throwing off the earth's magnetic field with all that metal in their faces?" Josie says loudly and a big muscular dude with a spiked collar turns to glare at us. Will's knee bounces up and down in the chair and I can't sit in this mess any longer.

"I need to pee." I stand up and Will instantly stands beside me.

"Me too," he says dryly. I take a few deep breaths and start off towards the bathrooms inside the casino. Will's hand gently slides along the small of my back as he guides me through the crowd. We're not even through the door before he's murmuring in my ear.

"What was Steven talking about, Cat? What haven't you told me?"

I feel like I'm preparing for battle. It's not even that big of a deal. He's slept with lots of girls. I don't owe him anything and he has no right to be angry. Right?

I didn't do anything wrong. Right?

He's not going to see it that way. Even if he should.

Shit, maybe he'll be completely cool about this. He might not even care.

And that would be a whole other world of heartache.

"Cat, what was he talking about," Will persists and I stop in the hallway next to the restrooms where it's not so crowded and sort of quiet.

"Look, I was a mess last year. All this shit had been piling up and then my mom died and you sent those fucking concert tickets. I ripped them up, you know. I was so angry with you."

"Is that it? You ripped up concert tickets?" Will interrupts and I shake my head.

"Just, let me talk for a second, okay?" I take a deep breath. "I went to a bar. I was looking for... sex, I guess. I mean, I didn't consciously make the decision, or maybe I did. I can't remember but all I know is I hated you and I wanted... something."

I swallow. I can't say it, it grosses me out to even think it but Will waits for the words.

"Steven showed up." Will closes his eyes, his fingers squeezing his temples and rubbing deep lines into his forehead. He's a smart guy. I'm sure he's figured it out. "I was already drunk."

"What happened, Cat? What did you do?" Will snarls and his anger pisses me off. He has no right to be upset with me.

"It was just one time. It didn't mean anything. I was just satisfying an itch," I snap at him and his eyes dart up to mine and they are blazing.

"You can't even say it to my face. How can you say it doesn't mean anything when you can't even tell me?" Will asks and he's trying not to yell.

"Fine! I fucked him, okay?" I choke out bitterly and Will startles. "I was drunk and sad about my mom and disappointed because you let me down and I fucked Steven Young."

"Why him? You could have anyone you want, Cat. Why that guy?" He practically whispers it.

"I can't have *anyone I want*. You wouldn't have me, remember? You said no to me. I wanted you and you said no." He pulls at his hair before sliding down the wall to sit on the carpeted floor. A dude with an abnormally huge foam cowboy hat comes out of the men's restroom. He glances between us as he passes us in the hall.

I sigh, and sit down beside him on the floor. I can hear the boom of the fireworks outside, the patriotic music blaring over the loudspeakers. He leans his head against my shoulder.

"I didn't do anything wrong. I can date whoever I want," I say proudly.

"You're right," he says. "I know I have no reason to be mad. Doesn't stop it from hurting."

"I know," I say as I lean my head against his and he traces the lines of my open palm resting on my leg.

"But if I ever see that fucker again, I'm going to rip his head off."

* * *

No, everything's fine. We worked it out," I say over the receiver as I quickly print out a batch of checks.

"Really? You forgave him, just like that?" Jay says and I frown. Yeah, rub it in. Rub it in how I have no balls when it comes to William Henderson.

Just like that, everything's back to normal. Will spends every day with me. He brings his books and studies while I work and my dad sits at his desk and gives us dirty looks. My dad doesn't say anything though, he really can't at this point and I think he knows it. We go see *Forrest Gump* in Boulder City and I cry when the mom dies and Will does too. We listen to music and swim when we get antsy from sitting around all day. Sometimes Margot comes along but lately she's been at the payphone eight times a day calling Andy. She's been a mopey mess the last couple of weeks and joins me sometimes when I take my smoke breaks with Josie. Will never comes along. He doesn't approve.

Josie doesn't approve either. Of Will. She thinks I'm an idiot and that I need to "set boundaries". I don't want to spend my time mad at Will or making him suffer, because that would make me suffer. I want to feel good for a little while and Will makes me feel good.

"Well, it's not like he could help it, he-" I stop myself because I'm sure Will doesn't want everyone to know he failed.

"He what?" Jay asks and I sigh.

"He had to take a class. It was only offered during the summer," I fudge. It's not really a lie.

"He could have called you," Jay says knowingly and I sigh. "He could have called about Mom at least."

"I know that, Jay," I say through clenched teeth and Jay is quiet for a few minutes.

"Look, Kit Cat, I'm just trying to help," he says.

"It would help if you came home. It's almost been a year. Can you come home for my birthday? Please?" I ask quietly.

"I think we can swing that," Jay says and I beam.

"Hey! I've been meaning to ask you. Have you watched that show, X-Files? Cat, it's an entire show based on alien abductions. Freaks me out!" Jay says and Steven walks into the office.

"Jay, hold on," I say and wordlessly hand him his check. He gives me a salute and stalks out the door and a minute later Will walks in, his face red with anger.

"Is there anything you can do to get him fired?" Will asks, motioning out the door to Steven I assume.

"Believe me, I've tried," I mutter.

"What happened?" Jay asks over the phone.

"Nothing-" I say into the receiver. Will leans against my desk, his legs intertwined with mine. He picks up a pad of post-its and a black sharpie. "I haven't seen that show, sounds interesting."

"It is! Dude! It's like these writers are stealing thoughts from my brain." Will scribbles onto one of the post-its and I wrinkle my nose at the chemical marker smell. He sticks the note to my shirt and I pull it from my shoulder.

You me, boat now.

"On the season finale, they found evidence that the government is experimenting with alien DNA," Jay continues and Will's motioning to the door, nodding his head and wiggling his eyebrows and I almost giggle.

"Whoa, that's just like that theory you had in eighth grade," I say and Will scribbles onto another post-it. This time he sticks it to my cheek and I snatch it off my face. There's a picture of two stick figures with big smiles on a pathetic excuse for a boat under a crudely drawn replica of my sun tattoo.

"Are those boobs?" I laugh and Will shrugs and draws

another picture.

"What are you talking about?" Jay asks.

"Nothing, Will's drawing cartoons," I say and he sticks another post-it to my head. This time the stick figure with boobs is swooning over the much larger stick figure with huge biceps, I roll my eyes and crumple the paper into a ball and throw it at him. He swipes at my arm with the sharpie and I quickly use my foot to push him away. He makes a mark on my bare leg instead, a thick black line on my shin.

"Okay Sis, we're going out to dinner. I'll talk to you soon," Jay says and I hang up the phone. Will smiles at me mischievously and I frown, craving retaliation.

"Ass!" I say and rub at the black line but it's no use. His mark is permanent.

"Come on, let's go for a boat ride," he says, capping the marker and setting it back on my desk. He grabs my arm and pulls me from the chair and I don't resist. It's August and Will will be leaving soon.

He twines his fingers with mine as we walk down the sidewalk to the docks, and the sun heats my body. We reach the bridge and Steven's working on the dock. I instantly go rigid. I avoid his eyes when we walk past him. We've almost made it without an altercation when Steven opens his big ugly mouth.

"Aw, how cute, you guys playing house?" Steven sneers. "Hey Cat, give me a call when he splits. I'll be your milkman."

Will drops my hand and spins around, charging towards him and for a split-second I see fear in Steven's face.

"Don't talk to her, don't look at her, you stay the hell away from her!" Will bellows and I'm shocked at his tone. Steven looks amused.

"What bothers you more, Paycheck? The fact that you're playing sloppy seconds, or that no matter how many times you fuck her, I'll always be her first?"

I can't breathe, the statement slaps me in the face. There aren't even words to describe how much I hate Steven right now, but I hate myself even more, because it's true.

"You'll never be anything to her," Will spits and turns to walk away.

"She was tight too," Steven says and I gasp at his vulgarity.

"Motherfucker," Will growls and I watch his fist collide square with Steven's big ugly nose. Steven's head snaps back, his knees buckle and he crumples to the ground. Will shakes out his hand and inspects his knuckles. He opens and closes it as he walks towards me and I look at Steven holding his nose on the ground. He's bleeding and he stumbles to his feet, wiping his face with his shirt before spitting blood from his mouth.

"Are you okay?" Will asks me and I'm stunned.

"Yeah, of course I'm okay. Are you okay? Oh my God, you hit him," I say and he pulls me towards his dad's boat.

"How's your hand?" I ask after we climb into the boat and he goes straight to the ice chest on the back bench. It's still filled with halfway melted ice from their excursion on the water earlier. He shoves his hand in the cold water and sighs.

"It hurts like a bitch," he winces and I laugh.

"Here, let me see it," I say and he bites his lip and shakes his head.

"Come on, you big baby, I'll be gentle, I promise."

He pulls his hand out of the water and I grab a towel and gently dry off his hand. His knuckles are bloodied and bruised, the abrasions pink and peeling and I look up to find his glowing green eyes peering into mine.

"Can you wiggle your fingers?" I ask and the corner of his mouth twitches up into a smirk. "What? I'm trying to be nurturing!"

He laughs and I kiss him full on his lips because I can't believe he punched Steven and while I'm sure it was partly to make himself feel better, it made me feel better too.

"You didn't have to hit him, you know," I say, still holding his injured hand in mine.

"Hey, eventually, somebody was gonna do it," Will shrugs. "I'm kinda glad it got to be me."

"For the record, I could have punched him too, but I was frozen in shock," I say indignantly and Will pushes my hair behind my ear with his good hand.

"I know." Will looks down at his hand. "So, I was thinking. I brought you a present for your birthday. But I really wish I could go back in time and change everything about last summer. So I'm giving you a mulligan instead."

"A mulligan?" I ask, confused.

"Yeah, like in golf when you hit a bad shot and you get to try again. A do over," he explains.

"A do over? I don't understand," I say and he purses his lips.

"I know I let you down and I want to make it up to you. You get one do over of your choice. You want to redo prom, we can go to prom. You want to redo our first kiss, I'll make it happen. You want to redo Vegas, we can do that too," he says quietly, and I blush when I think of that night. "I just want you to be happy, Cat. In every memory you have of me, I want you to look back and be happy."

"I'm happy right now," I say.

"Are you?" he asks, skeptically.

"I'm happier," I admit. "And it gets easier. It gets easier to miss my mom. It gets easier to accept that the marina is my life forever. It gets easier to let down my walls once in a while."

"It gets easier to say goodbye?" he asks.

"No. That'll never be easy," I sigh and he nods in agreement.

"So what happens now?" he asks and I shrug.

"I don't know. You have a lot going on this year so why don't we just meet back here next summer and we'll see where we are," I say. It's the only course that makes sense. "At the very least, we'll be friends."

"And I still owe you a do over," he says and I smile. I kiss his swollen fingers gently and he wraps his arm around my neck, my face presses into his skin and I clench my eyes shut as he squeezes me tight.

"It's a date then."

1995 – THAT TIME YOU DIDN'T GET INTO MEDICAL SCHOOL

*A truck bomb devastates the Oklahoma City
Federal Building killing 168 people.*

The Dow Jones closes above 5,000 for the first time.

*The Smashing Pumpkins release their third album,
Mellon Collie and the Infinite Sadness.*

* * *

"Cat, can you get Dad on the line too? We have some news," my brother says.

"Dad, pick up the phone." I sit at my desk across from him in the cave-like office. It's the beginning of May and already stifling outside. The office is cool though, the windows covered and insulated to keep out the heat.

"Hell-o," my dad says, giving me a questioning glance. I shrug my shoulders.

"So, we're moving back to San Francisco. Lauren has been offered a position in a law firm and she's decided to take it," Jay says. This is great news! At least he'll be in this time zone now and maybe they'll come with the Hendersons this summer.

"Congrats Lauren! How exciting!" I say.

"Thanks. It's a really great position as an Assistant in the District Attorney's office," Lauren adds from the other line.

"That's great hon, I'm real proud of you," my dad remarks and I smile at him across the room. He rolls his eyes and his mustache twitches.

"Why San Francisco?" Dad asks.

"Well, Lauren kind of wants to be closer to her mom and sister. We're going to need their help," my brother hints and I can tell he's smiling. I can hear it in his voice.

"Help with what?" I ask, but I think I know what he's going to say!

"Well, that's the other news. Um, we're going to have a baby. Lauren's pregnant!" Jay says and I scream and bounce in my seat.

"Shit, Jay, are you kidding me?" my dad chokes and I swear he's got tears in his eyes. I've never seen my dad cry before, not even at my mom's funeral and the sight of it causes my heart to swell.

"Nope," Lauren says and she might be crying too. "I'm due in November."

"So when are you guys moving?" I ask. I haven't seen them since my birthday last year. They flew out for a week, just after the Hendersons left.

"Our lease is up at the end of this month and we're planning on heading out as soon as we pack everything up," Lauren says.

"We'll be living with Rachel and Richard for a while, until we find our own place. They have a really big house and it's just the two of them living there. This way we can save money too. I'm not going back to work when Lauren has the baby. I'm going to be a stay at home dad," Jay says, hesitantly. Jay's been working construction in D.C. They have really good benefits.

"That is really cool," I say and he chuckles in relief. I'm sure he's thinking my dad's going to say something about Lauren wearing the pants in the household, but I think it's great. They're doing what works for their family and it might seem weird to my old fashioned dad, but who cares? Jay will be a great father.

"Well, it only makes sense to do it this way. Lauren makes way more cash than I do," Jay says.

"But that's not why he wants to stay home," Lauren interjects.

"Well, it's part of it. Also, daycare is expensive!" Jay says.

"He wants to take care of the baby. My mom's going to help and Margot, when she's not working. Oh, my God! Did you hear? Andy proposed. They're planning a December wedding and everyone's invited," Lauren says.

"I didn't hear," I say quietly. Wow, Margot and Andy are getting married. I'm a little shocked, to be honest. Last I talked to Margot, they were on a break and now they're getting married.

"Yeah, he bought her a ring while she was there last summer and proposed when she got home."

"I'll have to call and congratulate them," I say.

"Okay, kids, I have to get back to work. Good news, Son. Will we see you two this summer?" Dad asks.

"We'll be there for a couple weeks. Lauren can't stay the whole summer because of her new job, but we'll be there for the Fourth at least," Jay says.

I walk to the store to tell Josie the news and get an ice cream, even though the waistband of my jean shorts is cutting into my hips. Ugh, I'm going to have to start buying a size up, I guess. I already had to buy a bigger bra. I don't mind the extra weight, actually because now Josie and I can share clothes. I just hate having to spend the money.

Actually, the money thing has been pretty good. We've been booked since December and my dad took out a loan so he could repave the launch ramp at the end of the season. He also put a ton of money into redoing the electrical hook-ups for RV camping spots and new lighting on the docks. And Dad finally got a new truck. Jay suggested we see if we can get internet service, but this part of the desert is a dead zone. No cable television, no cellular towers, no internet. Not yet, at least.

"My brother's having a baby," I say as I burst into the store.

"Well, thanks for that mental shithole. I'll be burning the image of pregnant Jay from my brain later, in case you can't find me."

"You know what I mean, dorkus," I smile and Josie shrugs.

"I can't say I'm surprised. Lauren is what, twenty-seven, her biological clock is a tick, tick, ticking," Josie says and I frown.

"Twenty-seven's not old. Women can have babies in their forties now, you know," I say.

"Yeah, but after thirty-five you have to get this test done and they stick a needle in your belly button and shit. It's insane, like science fiction."

"What? Why? Why would they do that?" I ask mortified.

"To check for genetic diseases and stuff. As you get older, your little eggs do, too," Josie says and I purse my lips and narrow my eyes, wondering why Josie knows all this stuff about pregnancy.

"Stop looking at me like that. I saw it on Oprah, okay?" she says.

"Why were you watching tips for making babies on Oprah?" I ask her cautiously and she looks at me for a long time, like she's fighting with herself in her head. "Oh my God, what aren't you telling me?"

"I'm kind of seeing someone," Josie says slowly. Her lips curl into a grin and my chin drops. "And we had S-E-X." She spells it like I'm four.

"Are you trying to get pregnant?" I shout, beyond disbelief.

"No, you idiot, I'm not trying to get pregnant. But I might want to get pregnant someday," she shrugs.

"Wait a minute, you had sex? Who is this person that you maybe want to have a baby with someday?" I want to shake her because she's not giving me the information fast enough.

"He works at the bank, in Boulder City. His name is Brett Scott."

I stare at her in shock. When the hell did this happen? And why does he have two first names?

"I went in to cash my check. He was there and he asked me if I needed anything. I told him I needed him to get the fuck away from me and he laughed. He laughed in my face, Cat. I wanted to hit him so bad." A sly smile creeps across her face. She likes him. It might even be love. I mean, shit, she wants to have his maybe baby someday.

"You went out with him? When?" I ask.

"I don't know, a couple weeks ago."

"WEEKS!" I shout. "You've been keeping this a secret for weeks? Who the hell are you?"

"Oh, get bent," Josie grins and I cross my arms in front of my chest. She thinks I'm joking, but this is not a joke. "Are you really mad?"

"Yes, I'm mad. I can't believe you didn't tell me," I say dejected and her face softens.

"I didn't want to make a big deal out of it or anything so I kept it to myself," she says. "Besides, you're the only person I've told now. I haven't even told my mom."

"How many times have you gone out?" I ask her and she shrugs.

"I don't know, like a handful."

"How many is a handful?" I ask her, irritated and she rolls her eyes.

"Fuck, Cat, I don't know, like seven?"

I sigh. Seven! Seven dates with the same guy and then sex. Josie's not seeing someone. Josie has a boyfriend. Lauren and Jay are having a baby, Margot and Andy are getting married, Will's going to medical school, and now Josie's dating a potential baby's daddy. And then there's me, with my drawer of undeveloped film.

"He's frustrating as all hell. He's short and completely bald but no matter how hard I try, it's like I can't insult him. He's not afraid of me and I can't tell if I like it yet. But Jesus, it makes for some pretty electrifying sex." Josie winks at me and I scrunch my face up. Sex is a topic I generally like to avoid and she knows it.

"Okay, that's when I get the hell out," I say and she laughs. I grab an IT'S-IT and walk back to the office. I'm in my chair, ready to bite into the chocolaty goodness when the office phone rings. My dad picks it up and looks over at me.

"Hold on a minute, kid," my dad says and then motions to me to pick up the phone.

"Hello?"

"Cat? It's Will." His voice is muffled and raspy and he sounds like he's been crying.

"What's wrong?" I ask, panicked and he breathes in shaky gasps.

"It's over. I'm done."

"Done with what? What's going on?"

"I didn't get in. They rejected me, Cat."

Will didn't get into the MD program at Johns Hopkins. He had a big fight with his dad about it but I'm not sure why he's so upset. He could apply again next year, or apply somewhere else, but he doesn't want to wait. He's very cryptic on the phone, talking in song lyrics and mentioning his mom and it all really freaks me out. The moment I see the Saab pull onto the gravel road, I'm at their unit before they even park.

"We're getting married!" Margot screeches as she bounds out of the back seat and jumps into my arms. I hug her small frame as a very tired Andy and a disheveled Will slam their doors. God, Will looks horrible, like he's been through the wringer. His hair is messy, tangled on top and curled along his neck, and he has a thick beard hiding his square jaw. He's thin and pale, and I frown at the dark circles under his eyes. He looks broken and all I want to do is put him back together.

"I know, that's awesome. I can't wait until December," I say, my eyes fixated on Will's and he gives me a small smile that I can barely see. He has to shave that thing on his face. I'm not going to go an entire summer without seeing his lips.

"No. We're getting married here. On the Fourth," Margot says and I look at her confused.

"But Lauren said December."

"I know, but you know what? I hate weddings. You know what I hate even more than weddings? Wedding dresses. Wedding Flowers. Wedding Invitations. You put the word wedding in front of something, and it instantly costs a bazillion times more. It's disgusting. So I fired my coordinator and we decided to elope!"

253

"Oh wow, Margot, that is totally unexpected," I say and Will rolls his weary eyes and makes a talking motion with his hand. I bite my lip to stop myself from smiling.

"Since this is the place we fell in love, we want to do it here. We'll get one of those Elvis impersonators to perform the ceremony on the cliffs, and then we'll dive into the water together, like we're diving into life together!" Oh my God, has everyone been watching Oprah?

"Um, that's amazing. But you're not really going to dive, right? Because that's kind of dangerous," I say and Will rubs his temples behind her.

"And we're having hot dogs and hamburgers and beer and wine coolers. Oh! Will you be my wedding photographer?" Margot asks, serious as a heart attack.

"I would love nothing more than to photograph your wedding, Margot." And I mean it. I'm honored.

"Where are your parents?" I ask when Margot finally lets me go.

"They'll be here soon. They had to stop a bunch of times because Lauren has to pee every half hour," Will says before he finally pulls me into a hug, his scratchy chin rubs against my forehead and I don't like how thin he feels. He feels empty, like all his insides have disappeared.

"Come on," I say, pulling him towards the store as Margot and Andy start unloading the car. "You need sugar."

We sit on the swings, and Will slurps his rainbow sherbet Push-Up.

"Ice cream really does make everything seem better. For like two whole minutes, things are perfect," Will says and I grin because that's exactly how I feel.

We swing quietly indulging in the sweet treat and I like the way the sun soaks into the skin of my legs and shoulders. Will sighs. The two minutes of perfection have dissolved and he's back to moping.

"Alright, why the sighs?" I ask.

"You know why," Will retorts. He's irritated and I try not to take it personally.

"Well, do you want to talk about it?"

"Not really," he mumbles. I search for a subject change and I'm about to tell him about Josie's boyfriend when the flood gates open.

"I've completely fucked myself over," he says, his eyes wide as he grips the plastic chain of my swing. "I can't apply again, I'm too humiliated."

"There's nothing you can do? You can't like, go down there and plead your case?"

"What should I say? I'm an idiot and got shit scores on the MCAT? My GPA is crap and I failed a very basic class? Please, put your patient's lives in my very incapable hands," he says sarcastically and again I have to remember that he's not mad at me, he's just mad.

"Can you retake the test? Maybe if you get a better score, you'll have a better chance at getting in next year? Or you can try to get in somewhere else, somewhere not so competitive?" I try.

"I already took the test twice. I sucked at my interview too. They said I lack communication skills. I mean, I am great at communicating. God, Cat, you just don't get it!"

Now I'm pissed. I'm just trying to help and he's acting like an asshole. And his communication skills *are* shit.

"I know, why don't you keep making excuses and blaming everyone else, you big baby? And I'm not the one who rejected you, so stop insulting me," I say fiercely and Will's face crumbles.

"I know," he groans. "I'm sorry. I'm a complete fuck up. I can't do anything right."

"Maybe you needed this to happen, so you can go on to do something that you really love," I offer.

"There is no other option, Cat. I have to become a doctor. You don't know what I'd be walking away from if I fail at this," he says in a low voice.

"Tell me. What would you be giving up? Money? Social

status? A perfect little spot on your daddy's pedestal? I don't understand, Will."

"I don't expect you to."

"Why? Am I'm too stupid to understand, or something?" I snap.

"That's not what I meant," he groans and I feel my insides soften.

God, why can't I control my snotty attitude? Here he is, feeling crappy and I'm just making it worse.

"Look, if I let you touch my boobs, will it make you feel better?" I ask him and his shocked eyes dart up to mine. I know this sounds crazy, and maybe I'm imagining it, but I swear I see it. A flicker. A jolt. A spark.

"It depends. Over or under your bra?" he replies. His grin is mischievous and my whole body flushes when I think of his hands on me.

"Silly boy, you know I'm not wearing a bra," I say as he pulls my swing to face his and slides his knee between mine.

"Yep, I can see that," he quietly hums and I can't breathe.

"I'd kiss you right now, but you have a woodland creature stuck to your face." I can't even say the words before I burst into laughter. He drops his head and pushes me away, my swing swaying in the heat and I can't stop laughing.

❈ ❈ ❈

D on't think I forgot about the mulligan," Will whispers in my ear as we watch a very classy Elvis impersonator deliver Margot and Andy's wedding vows on top of the highest cliff in Australia. The sun is low on the horizon, and my dress is uncomfortable and sticking to my sweaty skin. Man, I wish I could have worn my swimsuit but that would have been tacky. I know because Margot told me so. I know, swimsuits at a wedding are tacky, but Elvis is not. I don't understand it, either.

The last week has been insane, but at least Will's been too

busy to be depressed. We drove into Vegas so Margot and Andy could get a marriage license at the hall of records and we had to commandeer some fresh flowers for a couple of last minute bouquets. We also had to track down an Elvis who would be willing to drive out to Red Rock Cove on the Fourth of July at sunset to perform the ceremony. It's amazing what you can get Elvis to do when you throw a huge wad of cash at him.

A handful of Margot and Andy's friends and family from San Francisco flew into Vegas yesterday, including Margot and Lauren's dad and his life partner. Andy's parents are a trip. They're total hippies. His mom wears flowers in her hair and everything. I guarantee they weren't expecting such extreme temperatures but we used one of Big Jimmy's trucks to drive them out to the cliff so they wouldn't have to hike. Dr. Henderson rented a houseboat, in case anyone needed to use the restroom and he and all the dads set up canopies and lined the beach with tiki torches. My dad loaned them some tables and chairs from the cafe, and is currently down on the cove, lighting up the grill.

Lauren insisted on hiking up the hill, claiming some women run marathons while pregnant. You can't even tell, her belly barely shows a little bump and she looks beautiful standing next to my brother in her deep purple slinky dress. Every so often I see my brother rest his hand on her belly and I capture the gesture on film. It means so many things. *Are you okay, hi there baby, I love you already.*

"I haven't forgotten either," I whisper back to Will as I fill the frame now with the bride and groom.

Margot found this beautiful ivory satin and lace slipdress to wear and her short, honey blond hair is naturally wavy around her face. She's not wearing much makeup, just mascara and lip gloss. I love how easy she stands beside Andy in his linen shorts and pinstriped shirt, both of them barefoot and ready to take the plunge. I watch them from behind my camera lens, frantically snapping shots as the bright blue sky starts to catch fire, the streaks of gold and red and purple offering a spectacular backdrop to their declarations. I get tears in my eyes when I remember how she was so afraid of Andy seeing her without any makeup or with eye crusties. The memories swirl around me and Will lets his hand rest on the small of my back, his cleanly shaven chin sometimes resting on my bare shoulder.

I capture Dr. and Mrs. Henderson, standing linked beside Margot and Andy. Mrs. Henderson dots her eyes with her tissue while Dr. Henderson remains stoic beside her. Margot's dad, Brandon, stands next to them, and Mrs. Henderson holds his hand too.

My camera shifts to Andy's parents enveloping each other in a tight embrace, the two of them crying and mumbling I love yous and I almost giggle. Then I think how my mom won't be there when I get married, if I get married, and I feel my chest ache. *It's okay, Catherine the Great,* I hear her say. *Everything's going to be fine.*

I catch Josie squirming out of Brett's arms and I almost full on laugh. So does he, actually, his dark eyes creased in the corners and his bald head glistening. He's so not her type and totally not what I expected she'd like in a partner, but he doesn't let her go. He holds onto her while she grumbles and I see her succumb. Her shoulders relax as he kisses her cheek and she smiles right as I capture the moment with a click. Then Josie's glaring at me and I snap the shutter again. She rolls her eyes and leans against Brett and my heart feels so happy for her.

"Any idea as to what you want to do over yet?" Will whispers into my ear, his mouth practically on my skin.

This is a trick question. I want to redo everything and nothing at the same time. We've done everything wrong and he's still here with me. He's still my best friend, the greatest love I've ever known. A redo wouldn't change a thing. I'd still love Will, and we'd still be living worlds apart. I don't think that's ever going to change. But he's here now.

"I don't want a do over," I say over my shoulder to him and he leans down so that my mouth is at his ear. "I just want to do."

I press my lips into the soft skin of his cheek and his arms wrap around my waist as Margot and Andy are declared Mr. and Mrs. Harris. Andy dips his bride, giving her an old fashioned swoony kiss. I quickly capture the moment with my camera, and I cry because it's so absolutely perfect. I run up to the front, trying to get every moment on film as Margot hands her bouquet to her sister and kisses her before taking Andy's hand. Her face radiates and she hikes up her skirt and they run together, flinging themselves off the cliff and plunging into the deep glittering blue while we cheer. It's the most beautiful thing I've ever witnessed.

The rest of the party files down the trail and Will watches me intently with a small half smile. I smile back, because I can't help it and bring the camera to snap his portrait. His hair is dark in the fiery sky, there's no hint of the blond without the sun, and the lines of his face are all angles and curves from his pointed lips to his feathery lashes.

"What exactly do you want to do?" he asks as he walks towards me and I snap his picture the whole time. He rolls his eyes and makes a grab for my camera just as I click the shutter.

"Everything," I say confidently. I turn and march down the hill, Will's hand reaching for mine.

The party stretches late into the night. We eat burgers and drink beer and talk about old times and how Andy and Margot met. We laugh about the time we played the Hat Game and when Andy kissed me. Even though it was years ago, I still cringe but also shamelessly take credit for their union. Sinatra and Dino echo off the walls of the cove, pouring from the speakers on the houseboat and we dance in the sand. I'm barefoot and tipsy and feeling high as a kite. I take pictures of everything and everyone and I don't want it to end. Jay and my dad start hauling people back to the marina in the boats. I want to stay out on the water a little while longer and I persuade Jay to ride back with the Hendersons. He leaves my dad's boat for Will and I because Margot and Andy are going to be spending their wedding night on the houseboat.

"That was just perfect," Margot sighs as she rests her head against my shoulder. We're sitting at the tables on the cove. It's still so hot out and I'm itching for a swim.

"I can't believe you kissed Elvis," Will says and Margot and Andy shrug. They both kissed him. I got a picture.

"I can't believe you really put together a wedding in a week," I say and Margot smiles proudly.

"This was the best decision of my life. I think we're going to backpack through Europe for our honeymoon. Shit, with the money we didn't spend on a wedding we could go on a honeymoon every summer for the next five years."

"As long as you stop here first," I say and Margot wraps her arms around my neck and kisses my cheek.

"Of course we will," she says and I can't breathe, she's hugging me so tight.

"It's fucking hot, I'm going swimming," Margot says and strips to her underwear, before running into the water. Andy follows her, kicking off his shorts as he runs, his shirt thrown to the ground.

I look at Will and he shrugs and stands, dropping his khakis to reveal tight shortlike undies and I can't stop staring. He steps out of his loafers and smirks while he unbuttons his shirt and I can see the faint outline of his ribs. God, he's lost like ten pounds. And I'm ten pounds heavier. Oh, the irony.

"Come on, Cat, get naked. Everyone's doing it," he jokes and I blush. It's kind of ridiculous to be self-conscious about my body in front of Will, but I can't help but feel insecure stripping to my undies. My one-size-larger undies, at that.

Geez, it's just Will. Stop being such a baby and take your damn dress off.

I fumble with the zipper in the back and then Will's fingers are there, grazing my skin and pulling the zipper down my back. I let the dress fall and Will's hands caress my sides and, God, he feels so good. He leans in and kisses my shoulder and then my neck and I close my eyes and relish in the sweet tingles erupting throughout my body.

"Last one in the water is a rotten egg," he whispers and then he's gone. I chase him, I almost pass him too but I fall, knocking into him and we crash into the blue shimmering glass. Margot and Andy are sucking face a little ways from us and I don't want to know what's going on below the surface so I swim away from them.

Will follows me, his intense eyes taunting as I swim backwards. He swims a little faster, stalking me like a shark and a surge of playful panic jolts right through me. I turn and try to swim away from him but he grabs my foot and I'm afraid he's going to tickle it. I scream and try to kick him away and he laughs out into the quiet darkness.

He pulls me to him and I let him. I'm breathing heavily when his hands slip over my hips and his arms wrap around my waist.

"I got you," he says and I wrap my arms around his neck, letting my fingers wind into his hair.

"I let you," I smirk and he laughs.

"Do I get to touch your boobs now?" he asks and I snort.

"Maybe. You did shave," I respond and run my hand across his cheek and over his chin.

"Well, I didn't want you to get rabies from any woodland creatures or anything," he says.

"Yeah, because I do not look pretty frothing at the mouth."

"You look pretty always," he says and I feel my ears burn.

He leans in and gently kisses my lips and I think of so long ago when we first kissed here, at this cove, when I told him I hated him and I cried and then he kissed me and it was horrible. I think he's remembering it too because suddenly his grip on me is tight and my body is pressed against his and he's shaking.

"I don't know what to do with my life, Cat," he mumbles into my shoulder. "I've disappointed everyone, I've let them all down. I've let you down and I'm so sorry."

"Will, stop it!" I say fiercely. "Stop beating yourself up over this. You said it yourself, only two hundred out of six thousand applicants get accepted? That's a lot of people that are sitting in your shoes right now."

"It wasn't supposed to happen to me. I had a plan, Cat, and now it's all shot to shit," he mumbles and I sigh.

"Then you make a new plan," I say and Will closes his eyes. I stretch up to kiss his eyelids and I feel his hands move over my back, his lips pressing into my neck.

He's sad and hopeless and I know he might be using me right now to make himself feel better, but I'd rather it be me than some other girl. *This* is my do over. I will let my walls down. I will let him win, I will surrender, and he will get the very best of me.

I reach behind me and unlatch my bra, letting the uncomfortable underwire float away and eliminating the material between us. Will inhales sharply when I press my chest against his, his eyes roaming my face, his arms crossed over my back and gripping my sides. I press my mouth to his and gently pull at his lips, the quiet water lapping at our naked skin.

His tongue glides along mine, his hand slipping across my breast. Oh God, how I've missed his hands on me. He feels like no one else, like nothing else, pure pleasure and tingles and fire and just everything that means anything is right here in my arms. I wrap my legs around his waist and he pulls away.

"Wait," he says and I roll my eyes.

"No, I'm done waiting. We're doing this," I say insistently and he smiles and kisses my nose.

"I don't have anything," he says.

"It's okay, I'm on the pill." I pull his mouth back to mine and then stop. "Wait. You don't have an STD, do you?"

"No, I do not have an STD," he responds exasperated.

"How am I supposed to know? You have a torrid past," I tease but only kind of. "Have you been tested?"

"Actually, yes, I have. When Magic Johnson announced he had HIV, I went and got tested. I haven't had sex since. Have you been tested?" Will asks and I scoff.

"I've only had sex once and they test you for everything when you start birth control."

"How am I supposed to know?" he repeats my words and I frown.

"Well, now you do," I say and he smiles.

"Yep and so do you and now we can enjoy being together and not have to worry," he says as he plays with the elastic waistband of my undies. He pushes them off my hips and I kick them away, letting them sink to the bottom of the river.

"That sounds nice, the enjoying part," I breathe and Will's hands graze over my behind. I'm completely bare now and his hands are everywhere, on my hips, on my stomach, my shoulders, pulling across my chest.

"You're so beautiful, Cat. Every part of you, it's just beautiful," he whispers and I feel his fingers grazing between my legs and I push my lips on his, my tongue in his mouth as his fingers push into me and I whimper. Oh God, it feels so incredible and I'm afraid I'm being too noisy because shit echoes in these canyons so I keep my mouth occupied with his.

I need him, all of him, and I quickly rid him of his underwear. He's hard and smooth, and I run my hands all over him, feeling every part, while he bites and sucks at my lip.

His fingers dig into my hips now and I wrap my legs around his waist again. I can feel him, his hardness between my legs and I writhe and slip against him until he reaches down to better position himself, barely pressing into me and then he stops.

I pull away from his mouth and our eyes connect as his hands weave through my wet hair spiraling down my back. I try to convey everything in this one look, *it's okay, I want you, I love you, please.*

I tighten my thighs and pull him inside me, my eyes rolling back as I let him fill me and I stop breathing for a second. I can feel the slow stretch and it burns but he's mostly warm and quite literally taking my breath away. And then that song from *Top Gun* is in my head and I want to sing out loud but that would be weird so I bite my lip and focus on how amazing Will feels. His head falls to my shoulder, his arms clutching me tighter as we move together. All I can feel is him, all I hear, all I see, all I want to sing now is his name, over and over but I can't because somewhere is this river there are other people and that makes this all just a little bit more exciting.

It isn't long before Will's shaking in my arms. He pants into my neck and I kiss his forehead and then his eyelids and then his lips and he apologizes.

"I'm sorry," he murmurs. "You didn't..."

"No, but I did enjoy myself," I say softly, my hands pulling through his wet hair.

"Most women don't climax from intercourse alone," he says and I laugh. "Well, it's true! Most women need some clitoral stimulation in order to orgasm. Vaginal orgasm is very rare."

"Okay, Doogie Howser," I tease but Will doesn't laugh. "Oh come on, it's okay."

"It usually lasts longer, but I haven't had sex in a long time," Will explains and I can tell he's embarrassed. It's not his fault. I read in Cosmo that a woman should be in charge of her own orgasm, and trust me, my orgasm and I are well acquainted. I'm sure it would happen, if we tried again. When we try again.

"Well, we could practice all summer, if you want."

✳ ✳ ✳

Will mopes around the marina for the rest of the summer. We lounge in the sun on the private beach on my days off and swim when it's unbearably hot. He sneaks into my bedroom at night, just like he did when we were seventeen and it's silly but it's us. Sometimes he wants to cuddle, and he falls asleep wrapped around me. I lay there while he softly snores and think about how hard it's going to be when he leaves this year. There's a tiny part of me that thinks for a second that he might stay. If he's not going to medical school, he could stay here, but I know in my heart that's not going to happen.

Sometimes we make love and it really is just that, love. It's not perfect and sometimes it's downright funny. Like when Will said he'd kiss me, you know, down there, but that my crotch looked like a woodland creature. I think I laughed for an hour. After I got over being ticked off, of course. But then he made up for it.

Sometimes we just talk, whispering conversations under the cover of old familiar songs. We talk about life and the universe and why everything is so confusing. We talk about our moms and most of our discussions have to do with obligations to our family. I sense there's something about his obligations that he's not telling me.

The night before he leaves he sneaks into my room and his eyes are flat and dull. He doesn't say anything, just climbs in my bed when I lift the sheets and I roll on top of him. I straddle his lap as he pushes up my tank top and pulls it over my head. My hair is loose and falls long against my back. Will runs his fingers through it and then trails his hands down my spine. This is how we've made each other feel better all summer and I don't know how I'm going to survive without him this time.

He kisses me, deep and sensual, and he tastes like rainbow sherbet. I'm sad he had an ice cream without me. He pushes my undies off my hips and down my legs and his hands are everywhere. I quickly strip off his shirt, kissing his chest and his neck and his chin, my lips moving haphazardly all over his body because I know I won't be able to feel him tomorrow.

His hands are greedy as they massage into my breasts. He rolls his tongue and moves his lips over the perked flesh and I close my eyes and memorize what it feels like to have his mouth on me. My hands quickly unbutton his pants and I pull them down and then he's inside me and I rock against him. His hands dig into my hips and then slide up my belly and over my breasts and his intense fiery eyes are all over my body. I watch him. I want to see what he feels, I want to see the pleasure on his face and know I put it there. I make him feel this way. Even if it never happens again, I want to see how I make him feel. I want to know that I'm not alone in this, that he feels this too, this connection, the stupid spark. He shows me. And I show him too.

Later, we lie bare together, our legs tangled in the sheets and he draws pictures on my back and I guess what they are. I'm terrible at it and Will surmises it's because I have a limited imagination but I think it's because he's a sucky artist.

"What happens now?" he asks and my chest hurts.

"I don't know," I say and he kisses my back, his fingers tracing the outline of my tattoo.

"I have to drive back to San Francisco tomorrow," he says and he peels a bit of sunburned skin from my shoulder. "I don't even know where I'm going to live. I have to figure out what I'm going to do with my life."

I want so badly to ask him to stay. I want to beg and plead and hold him here forever, but I know I won't. He could end up just like my mom, regretting and resentful and dreaming of everything he gave up.

"I know. You'll figure it out." I turn over so I can look at his beautiful face and I run my fingers through his hair. "It's okay. No obligations, no expectations."

His fingers trail across my cheek and I nuzzle into his bare chest, and he smells like sweat and sunblock and I can taste the salty tears running down my face. What if he can't come back next summer? What will happen when he gets a real job? What will happen when we have to grow up? We can't do this forever. It hurts so incredibly bad that he's going to leave, but it hurts more to know he'll never be anything more than what he is to me right now.

I wake up in the morning and I reach out for him and I feel nothing. My eyes fly open and he's sitting on the edge of my bed, holding a set of books.

"I thought you were gone." I sit up and rub my eyes, quickly removing any crusties that may have deposited overnight. I pull the sheet tight across my chest and push my hair out of my face and I don't want to look at him. It will surely rip my heart out if I have to look at him.

"Not yet." He hands me the books and there's a black and white photo of a mountain of rock on the cover.

"They're photography books. This guy, Ansel Adams, he took pictures of things in nature, like you do. Mostly in California, Yosemite National Park. But I thought these might be interesting to you. You shouldn't give up on your photography. I saw Margot's pictures. They're amazing."

"I didn't even develop those. She took them to Safeway in Boulder City and had them printed," I retort.

"I know. But it's like you see something right before it happens. You never miss those important moments and most people do. I don't know how but you always know when to take the shot."

I run my hands over the paperback books, The Camera, The Negative and The Print.

"Thank you," I whisper and Will gets up to leave.

He leans down and kisses my forehead and then he's gone.

1996 – THAT TIME YOU SAID I LOVE YOU AND MEANT IT

Hootie and the Blowfish wins a Grammy for "Best New Artist."

In 12 months, the number of Internet host computers goes from 1 million to 10 million.

Interest Rates at Year End reach 8.25%.

* * *

L ook, I sent you that invoice three weeks ago and I still haven't received any kind of verification. Well, I realize that, but that doesn't mean you can't fax it over. Not everyone has internet!" my dad argues. I close my eyes and try to take deep breaths but I can't focus on anything but the pounding in my brain. "Fine. That will be fine." My dad slams down the phone exasperated.

"Jesus Christ, there's not one competent person at that company. A bunch of half-wit teenagers running the place." Dad rubs his eyes and smoothes his mustache streaked with gray. He looks tired.

Steven quit on us right after Halloween. He and his new girlfriend moved to Southern California to live with his brother. My dad can't crawl or climb and heavy lifting hurts his back. He's going to have to hire someone. We can afford it. The books haven't been this good in years, but my dad's really particular, and he's stubborn. I think he feels like admitting he needs help is like admitting he's getting old.

Dad's been trying to take care of the maintenance issues and deal with this new launch ramp, but everyday there's some problem. This new ramp is a pain in the ass. We went with a company that looked good on paper, Pillar Concrete, but we've been given nothing but the runaround with these assholes. Now, I feel like an idiot because this is the first big decision I've helped my dad make, without my brother or Steven, and it's a mess.

"I'm going out for a smoke," I say and he looks up at me for a millisecond, his mustache twitching as he rifles through the mound of blueprints, estimates, notes and messages on his desk. I make a mental note to clean it later when he goes home. I walk to the store to meet Josie. It's January and the weather is nice, still cool enough for pants but the sky is sunny and bright. She's already smoking on the sidewalk, her eyes fixated on the dozen or so construction workers pounding the old cracked blacktop that used to be our launch ramp with jackhammers.

"Not a bad view, huh?" she says as she hands me a cigarette from her pack. I look more carefully at the sweaty men in their dirty t-shirts, and a couple of them are really, um, developed.

"Wow, look at his arms," I say, eyeing a particularly fit blond. "They're as big as my thighs."

"I know," Josie sighs. "Brett can barely lift my ass onto the kitchen counter. Last week, we were trying-"

"Et, blah, la, la, rutabaga, rutabaga," I mutter the string of nonsense and plug my ears. Josie grins mischievously but I don't want to hear about her sexcapades. I think her and Brett are going for some kind of world record or something.

We stare and smoke together in silence until one of them looks up and catches us gawking. He's standing by a big blue van, chit chatting with some of the other guys and I want to bark at them to get back to work. We're not paying them to socialize. He smiles slyly and winks and I blush, like I'm fricking fourteen.

"Looks like you have an admirer," Josie laughs and I toss my spent cigarette to the ground.

"Hardly," I roll my eyes. "He thinks I'm checking him out."

"You are," Josie says.

"I am not," I protest and then proceed to check him out. His shoulders are very wide, his face is friendly, and his dark hair is short and neat. He's wearing a tight gray t-shirt and jeans with a silver belt buckle that I've seen before.

"Will has that belt," I murmur and Josie glances at me from the corner of her eye.

Will's in San Francisco figuring out what he wants to do with his life and I haven't heard from him all year. I think he tried to call once, there was a message on the office phone but it was just background noise that sounded like a party or something. I don't know for sure if it was him, but I can't hold it against him because these are the terms that we decided. No expectations, no obligations.

I know Will cares about me, but I'm not unrealistic. This is what I anticipated, but I can't keep waiting around for him. Year after year he expects me to wait and he's never once had to fight for me. And it's disappointing. I neatly wrapped up my love and secured it in a beautiful box inside my heart. It's the only way I can handle this, the only way I'm not hurting. It's the only way I can get unstuck.

Lauren gave birth to a beautiful baby girl with dimples and fuzzy golden hair. Vanessa Jolene Rossi-Bell was born on Thanksgiving, two days after Jay's birthday. He sent us pictures and called us from the hospital when Lauren went into labor. I asked if Will was there and my brother said he wasn't. Then I felt horrible for taking the spotlight away from his good news, so I didn't ask anything else.

"You should go talk to him," Josie urges and I give her a scowl.

Josie thinks Will's a douchebag. That's what she called him. She said he needs to get his head out of his ass, and I'm inclined to agree, but I know it's not all his fault. I know all too well what it's like to feel lost and hopeless.

"I am not going to talk to him," I say. I've been on a couple dates but nothing serious. I went out with Peter from the bar in town. He listens to Hootie and the Blowfish. I could never be with someone who likes Hootie and the Blowfish.

"This is why you'll never get over Will, because you never try to get over him." Her words fester. "What are you afraid of?"

"I'm not afraid," I say with a glare and she snorts.

"Right, and I'm not a chain smoker." She rolls her eyes and I hate the look on her face, like she's got me all figured out.

I'm not afraid.

I'm not, and I'm going to prove it.

I spin on my heel and march right over to the blue van, anger fueling my confidence. I set my gaze on the dark pectoral muscles with the belt buckle who is now enjoying his lunch. He's seated on the inside of the sliding door and I know I shouldn't bother him while he's eating, but I'm determined and angry. I see the man's face change as he notices I'm walking over towards him. In a matter of seconds, he's right in front of my face and has the oddest eyes I've ever seen. They're brown, but more like honey and they catch me off guard the minute they meet mine.

"Hi," I say in a rigid voice and his lips curl into a sly smile again.

"Uh, hi," he says mid bite and, oh my God, I feel like a complete moron.

"What are you eating?" I ask and he looks down at his sandwich.

"Peanut butter and jelly," he smirks.

"Solid choice." What am I doing? *Walk away, Cat, stop humiliating yourself.*

"I initially doubted my decision. But now..." he shrugs and I try not to smile. "Can I help you with something?"

"I doubt it. I'm just trying to prove a point," I say, the willingness to bullshit completely evading me.

"Do you want half my sandwich?" he asks and I can't help it, my lips crack and I grin. He has freckles scattered across his nose and cheeks and they're really cute. In fact, he's really cute and those eyes... they're just the weirdest color.

"No thanks, I've got a licorice in there with my name on it," I say as I motion to the store behind me. "Don't want to spoil my lunch." He chuckles and his laugh is nice.

"I'm Tyler," he says. He holds out his hand and I take it.

"Nice to meet you, Tyler."

"And you're Cat," he says. "You work in the office, right?"

"Yeah," I say hesitantly and he grins sheepishly.

"I'm Tyler Pillar. You know, Pillar Concrete."

"Wait, are you the one who's been dicking me around?" I say and he's taken aback.

"Uh, no, I don't think I've been dicking around." He says the word like he's going to get in trouble for swearing. "We just had a misunderstanding, that's all."

"Weren't you the one who said we wouldn't be having a misunderstanding if we cleaned up our 'clerical issues?'" I air quote.

"Ah, yes, and you're the clerical issue," he says and I squint.

"Okay. I'm gonna go now," I say as I back away from him and his face falls.

"Hey, Cat, come on, let's start over," he says as he gets up.

"No can do, Tyleroni. I'm done with starting over. Time to move on," I say with a terse wave and I turn and walk away.

Tyler Pillar brings me peanut butter and jelly every day for the rest of the month of January, long after the launch ramp is finished, which we magically have no more issues with. He's charming and sweet, and I let him sit with me and share my sandwich. He asks me out on Valentine's day. I have never had a date on Valentine's day.

I try to keep things casual, but by June, Tyler and I have gone out dozens of times and I like him. A lot. He's funny and he lets me win when we play Mancala. He drives in from Laughlin every weekend to see me, and he sleeps over. The first time Tyler stayed over, my dad almost shit a brick. He didn't say anything, thank God, but he did stay at a buddy's house that night. He's gotten used to it, and now they actually get along quite fabulously.

There's really no reason not to like Tyler. He lives close, but not too close. He goes out of his way to kiss my dad's ass, but still holds firm to his convictions. He fishes, he boats, and helps my dad out with things at the marina. I think my dad sees a possibility in Tyler that I've been ignoring. The closer it gets to the end of the month, the more anxious I get. I didn't plan on liking Tyler, not even a little. I didn't plan on going out with him, or kissing him or sleeping with him. It all happened so effortlessly and now I don't know what I'm going to say to Will when he gets here.

If he gets here.

I speak with Jay before they leave San Francisco and he's unsure if Will's coming this year. If he is, he'll be making the drive alone. I'm sure Jay's told him about Tyler and I wonder if that's the reason he's not coming.

I also wonder if he's figured out what he's going to do with his life.

I wonder if he has a girlfriend, what his hair looks like, if he's seen any good movies lately, what new bands he's into.

I miss him.

Things with Tyler are good, the conversation is good, the sex is good, the dates are good, but the truth is, it just doesn't compare with Will and it makes me angry. I don't want to love Will anymore. I don't want to hurt when I think of him because it ruins all the good that he is. It ruins all the things that we've shared and what we've shared is beautiful. It's just not permanent and I can't see a reality where our worlds can be one. I think Will knows this too and that's why he hasn't called.

We're at the drive-in and I decide I'm going to tell Tyler about Will. I have to be honest, because Tyler has to know what he's gotten himself into. He has to know that someone else holds my heart and always will, and I'll let him make the choice if he wants what's left over. It's a shitty deal, and he might walk away, but it's only fair that he knows what to expect.

After the movie, we drive in silence. He parks next to my car outside his apartment and I know I need to tell him now because I'm not going to be coming up to sleep with him tonight. I just want to go home and curl up on my bed and maybe listen to my mixtape.

"So, I have to tell you something," I start and Tyler turns to face me and I take a deep breath. "I have this friend who visits the marina every year. And he might be coming into town for the summer."

Tyler sits there, waiting and unfazed. I'm going to have to spell this out. This is harder than I thought it was going to be. I'm going to look like a total asshole.

That's because you are a total asshole.

"He's my best friend and I care about him a lot. Um, we kind of had a thing," I say and I can't help the smile twitching on my lips because it reminds me of that year Will brought that girlfriend. God, that was like five years ago. It seems like decades.

"What kind of thing? Like, a 'friends with benefits' thing?" Tyler says and it wipes the smile from my face.

"It's hard to explain," I whisper.

"You love him." It's not a question and I nod.

"Then, geez, Cat, what the hell are you doing with me?" And I start to cry. "Right. I'm the rebound guy. God damn it." His hand pulls over his short hair and I can see the frustration in his tense jaw and neck.

"I really like you, more than I expected and this thing with Will is just...I'll always love him but I can't be with him. And I want to be with you, I really do, but I thought you should know what you're dealing with." Tyler's quiet for a long while and I think he's going to tell me to fuck off. I wipe my face and gather my purse and I'm about to get out of the car when he grabs my hand.

"You really want to be with me?" he asks.

"I want to try," I say. He leans over and gives me a slow, lulling kiss.

"I can handle that."

I hope to hell that I can, too.

* * *

My brother and Lauren drive into the marina in a brand new Ford Windstar. It doesn't even have license plates yet. The Hendersons also got a new car, a sleek silver BMW and Margot and Andy are in the back seat. Will's not with them, but this is expected.

I run straight into my brother's arms and I cry into his chest. He lifts me off the ground in a huge bear hug and he laughs.

"And you're already crying," he says and I scrunch my nose at his comment.

"Shut up, I'm never going to meet my niece for the first time again and you are not going to ruin it for me." I give him a shove and he ruffles my hair, like he used to do when we were little. My brother is a dad. This is amazing to me and I haven't even seen the kid yet.

Lauren reaches into the back seat and pulls the baby from her carseat and I instantly see my brother in her chubby, cherub face. Her cheeks are pink and full and her ears are huge and she's flashing me a big drooling, toothy grin. I immediately pull her against my chest and kiss the soft skin of her face. I hold her tight because without my permission, all the ways I could drop her go running through my head. She smells so good. I want to hold her little body forever.

"Hi baby girl," I whisper and give her a raspberry on her cheek. She pinches my face, her little nails digging into my nose and lip and I laugh.

"Ow, chick! That hurts!" She giggles and drools and I laugh at the silly sounds she makes as I balance her on my hip. I play peek-a-boo and mimic her sounds and it feels like we've known each other forever.

"I'm already her favorite," I say. My dad is walking up the gravel road and Jay grabs Vanessa and carries her down to meet him. I watch from a distance as my dad pats him on the back before taking the small hand of the little girl in my brother's arms. Lauren brings her hand to her mouth and I look over at her and there are tears in her eyes. I wrap my arm around my sister and I wish my mom were here.

Lauren, Andy and Margot can only stay a couple weeks because of their work schedules. They'll be leaving after the Fourth, but Jay's planning on keeping Vanessa and staying the rest of the summer. Jay just knows how to take care of a baby, I guess.

It's really strange seeing my friends and family without Will. I'm not devastated like last time, because I was kind of prepared. Still, it hurts. I watch the road from time to time, like any second his car's going to appear on the gravel and everything will be as it should.

God, I miss him. Everything feels off, and I can't relax. I need to talk to him. I feel uneasy, like he's upset with me and his absence is his way of telling me off. And I can't even defend myself because he's not here.

We decide to stay in the marina for the Fourth because Lauren doesn't want to take Vanessa out on the water, even though my dad says that both Jay and I were out on the boat before we could crawl. I invite Tyler, and Josie and Brett come too and we barbecue on the private beach in one of the fire pits.

Tyler is a perfect gentleman, of course, and limits PDA to hand holding and I'm quietly grateful. I told him that this was Will's family and I could see the stress leave his body when I told him Will wasn't here, and it pissed me off. It's killing me that Will's not here.

When it gets dark, Lauren and Jay take the baby back to our house to put her to bed. My dad goes back with them, so Dr. and Mrs. Henderson say goodnight and take off. The rest of us sit around the campfire and talk until the wood has all burned up. All that's left is meandering red and orange lines that slowly burn in the darkness.

"So we bought a house!" Margot announces, her once again dark hair layered and bouncy around her face.

"It's adorable. It's not in the city, but in a little suburb, kinda close to the house Lauren and Jay bought."

"Wow, congratulations!" I say and Margot beams.

"Well, we figured we should do it now, before interest rates get too high," she says.

Oh my God, interest rates? I don't even have a checking account and they're talking about interest rates. I'm an infant.

"Will. He's here," Margot murmurs and I jolt. She gets up from her chair next to Andy and I turn around to see his silhouette heading down the sidewalk by the store. My stomach drops and I feel like I might throw up. Shit, shit, shit!

Tyler's arm snakes around my waist and I'm suffocating. I know what he's trying to do. He's attaching himself to send a very clear message. She's mine. His possessiveness is not endearing. I want to push him away but I know that's the wrong thing to do, so I let his arm weigh on me.

"Will!" Margot calls him over. He's on the sand now by the swings and I see his gait falter. This is going to bother him, like it bothers me to think of him with someone else, but it's just the way it is.

"Hey, kids," he says, cool as a cucumber as he approaches. His eyes are on me, flickering with a soft glow from the dying fire. I can hardly make out the features of his face, but I can see his eyes, his long lashes interrupting their glare. I don't care, I have to hug him.

It's okay to hug your friends, even in front of your boyfriend.

Not friends you sleep with.

Slept with. Whatever.

I detach from Tyler's heavy arm.

Will's surprised when I approach him. His cool façade falters for a moment. He smiles sadly, but then it's gone and a cynical grin replaces it. I hug him nonetheless. I know he's disappointed, but I want him to know that I stand by my pinky promise. Best friends, no matter what.

"Glad you could make it," I say and he snorts. No one says a word and I hate this feeling so much, like we're dancing on shards of glass and with one wrong move, we're slicing open an artery and bleeding out. Will's eyes shift to Tyler on the sand and he stands, a whole head shorter than Will and I see a cocky grin. Will's eating this up and it makes me grind my teeth.

"You're new," Will says and I swallow.

"Tyler Pillar," he says and holds out his hand and Will stares at his rough, calloused hand.

"I'm Willy," he says and accepts the handshake. It's my turn to snort.

"Nice to meet you, Willy," Tyler says and I cringe.

"No one calls him Willy," I interrupt and they both turn to glare at me. "Well, except evil vampire witch monsters." Tyler looks confused but Will's lips twitch into an almost smile, and I'll take it.

"So, what deep, philosophical topic are we discussing tonight? Time travel?" Will says as he settles to the ground and I exhale with relief. I sit down next to him and Tyler hesitates before seating himself at my side, his arm around my waist again and I let him leave it there.

"Interest rates," I mutter, and the conversation resumes. Will glances out of the corner of his eye, his eyes drifting to Tyler's arm and back up to my face and I'm itching to explain. I try to convey it all in this one silent look: *I'm sorry, I need to explain, I missed you.*

Will looks away and my stomach knots. At least he came. That must mean something. If he really hated me, he would have just stayed away.

Or, he would have showed up at the last minute and acted like an ass in front of my boyfriend.

I sigh, my eyes fixated on the smoldering embers in the fire pit. Once I explain, he'll understand.

Be real Cat, what's there to understand? You moved on and you hurt him.

He hurt me, too.

God, who am I kidding? It's not a competition, and neither

of us ever win.

* * *

The next month is the most awkward month of my life. Tyler drives into the marina every weekend and he sleeps over and we have sex and it feels empty. I have to fake it because Tyler's a hard worker and won't give up until he thinks I'm good. That's what he asks me, "You good?" and I nod and it's done. I'm a fraud.

Lauren, Andy and Margot leave shortly after the Fourth of July. Will sticks around but I don't know why. I see him outside on the docks, feeding the fish or taking off on the boat all alone. He keeps his distance and I'm irritated because of all the times he brought various people to our place, I never once treated him poorly for it. At the very least I maintained our friendship, even when it killed me. I always put Will, my best friend, first, because I promised him that I would. No matter what.

Josie's living vicariously in what she perceives to be sweet vindication. "Give him a taste of his own medicine," she says, but everything's different now. We're getting too old for this game.

I play with my niece and help Jay change her diapers and feed her and put her to sleep. My heart pulses when I think of how she's going to leave in a few weeks. I want to go with them. I've thought about it, packing my shit and moving with Jay to San Francisco. I would do it if it weren't for the fact that my dad needs me here now more than ever.

It's not just my dad anymore. Josie's like my sister, and the thought of not seeing her every day sends me into a panic. Even Brett has gotten under my skin.

Then, there's Tyler. I don't know if I could give up the certainty of what I have with him for a possibility of what I could have with Will. Tyler is a sure thing. He's a good second choice, maybe the best second choice I'm ever going to get.

Will is just confusing. I know close to nothing about Will's life in San Francisco. What if I don't fit in there? What if I move there and everything falls apart? I used to think that Will would be my friend no matter what but now he won't speak to me.

I'm on the dock, having a smoke with Josie when I see him on the swings. He's watching me and I've had enough. This isn't fair, the way he can just disregard our friendship because his ego is bruised. He's acting like a spoiled brat. I'm going to talk to him, get it all out, and I can't think of a better time than right now.

I toss my spent cigarette to the ground and Josie shakes her head as I march over to the swings. He watches me the whole time and he can tell I'm coming over to fight with him. He's gearing up for it, his face changing from sad to slate when I grab the chains of his swing and look him square in the eye, our noses bumping as his swing sways.

"You pinky promised," is all I say. I walk away and he follows me. I head into the Laundromat because it's the only place I can think of that's secluded enough for a raging argument. And believe me, I plan on yelling.

"What do you mean by that?" he snipes and I turn around and slam the door shut once he's inside.

"You know what I mean. You pinky promised. You said we'd be friends no matter what. You are such a hypocrite," I yell, poking him in the chest and he's furious.

"I'm a hypocrite. Oh Christ, Cat!" Will paces in the small room. "You...you have no idea what this is like for me, you have no clue. To see you with that guy. He's...he's short and his hands were all over you-"

"He's not that short," I interrupt and Will glares at me.

"Do you love him?" he asks me and I'm momentarily stunned.

"I don't think so." Will stares into my eyes and I think my response has him confused.

It has me confused, too, because up until this moment my

answer would have been a definite no. I don't love Tyler. However, the consideration and loyalty I'm harboring for Tyler right now, has me thinking maybe I do. I know I love Will; that will never change. But maybe I love Tyler too? Is it possible to love two people at the same time?

"Then what are you doing with him?" Will lips sneer and I stammer.

"I'm trying to finally have a real relationship. My life doesn't stop when you leave. I'm tired of waiting for you to maybe show up or to maybe want me. I can't do it anymore."

"Bullshit! It's all bullshit, Cat." His voice booms through the small room, amplified against the metal casings of the machines. "You're with him because he's here, because he's easy and safe. You're with him because you're scared."

"I'm not scared," I say through clenched teeth, my eyes blurred, my skin prickling at his words.

"I know what you're doing. I used to do it, too. I searched frantically for someone who could take you off my mind."

"You're just mad because I'm not sitting around waiting anymore. Things change, people change." I can barely get the words out. All my reasons seem ridiculous now.

"Nothing ever changes, Cat! Every year I come here, I hope it will change. Every year I think I won't want you, that I'll be able to leave you alone, and every year it's still there, this unbearable ache that I can't get rid of. Persistent, gnawing, and gouging out the inside of my chest. It never changes. It's been thirteen years. And nothing's changed."

His face is very close to mine, and I can feel the frustration vibrating in the room.

"You break me, year after year and still, I come back to you. I spend every fucking day, ten months, three hundred days, waiting for the summer. It's all I live for. It's all I worry about. How can I get back to you. And every year, you push me away. And you pull me back in. You keep me at a distance, even when you let me get close. Every year, I want to give up. And every year, I can't." His voice is soft now and my head swims with his declarations.

"You didn't call me. You had sex with me and then you ignored me for months, Will. We've been through this before. If you wanted to get to me so bad, you should have found a way," I spit back.

"I was a little freaked out when I left here last summer. I've had sex, but I've never had love," he says. "I didn't know how to deal with all the things I was feeling. I shut down. And you moved on." It's an accusation.

"We don't make sense. All we ever do is hurt each other," I mumble as the tears stream down my cheeks. I break him? This whole time I thought it was so easy for him to leave me behind but he's been hurting, just like me.

"I love you, Cat." He grabs my shoulders and I watch the words leave his full lips, his tongue dancing around his teeth.

"I've loved you since I first saw you on that dock, with your bread and your braid and your big snotty attitude. I know we're not the same, but together we balance. Can't you see how well we balance? You've always said no obligations, no expectations but I want to be obligated to you. I want you to expect me to call and then get all shitty pissed when I forget. I want to make it up to you by bringing you ice cream and then I want to make love to you until you forget anything wrong I've ever done and just love how much I love you." I inhale as he drags his thumb across my cheek, his fingers pushing my hair away from my face. Tears fall and his face is blurry. All I see is green and it's so quiet now, like a vacuum in space. I almost don't want to interrupt it with breathing. He loves me. Will wants to be obligated to me.

"I love you, too," I whisper, and the room wakes up.

I hear the hum of washing machines around me, the buzz of the light, the soft whisper of Will breathing. His hands still pull through my hair and over my face, and then over my shoulders and back to my arms.

"But what are you going to do, Will? Give up school and move to some Podunk shit town to run a marina and be with a river girl?" I pull away. Will was right, nothing changes. It doesn't make a bit of difference if we love each other. He can't move here, we both know it. And I can't leave.

"All you've ever had to do was ask and I would have given it all up, everything." He's pleading with me.

"I would never ask you to give up everything. It's what my dad did to my mom and she left us. You'd resent me. Maybe not at first, but later, when we're old and you think of what your life could have been. I...I could never be responsible for ruining your life."

"Why do you think that would ruin my life? You think you're at such a disadvantage here, when, truthfully, you've never tried to be anything other than 'just a river girl.' Don't even take that the wrong way because I know what you're thinking." He catches my eye and I look away. Damn him for knowing my brain. "If you don't like the way it is, fucking change it. Stop bitching about your life and start living it, Cat! You could do so much, you could fucking publish a whole goddamn book with all the pictures you've taken, but you never will. You're afraid. You're afraid to leave, you're afraid to live, you're afraid to love. You're afraid to love me. Shit, you're afraid to love yourself."

I can't even retort because everything he says is true. I am afraid. I'm afraid to try because if I try and fail then there really is no hope for me. What if I try to be with Will and it doesn't work out, and I lose him forever? I keep him at a distance not because I'm afraid to love him, but because I'm afraid that it won't be enough. I've seen too many failed relationships to know love isn't enough.

"You could have left with me. We could have gotten in my car and I would have driven you anywhere you wanted to go but you'll never leave here."

"My dad..."

"Is an excuse. He'd be fine. He'd hire someone else."

"It's not reality Will. When you're here, you're on vacation. It's a fantasy. You don't have to worry about work or school or...laundry. We have ice cream and boat rides and naps on the cove. What we have, it isn't real..."

"Cat, you're the only real thing I have. Why don't you understand that?"

"I can't-" I choke out.

"I know. And I know what's going to happen. I'm going to leave and you're going to marry this guy and have his babies, and take care of the marina and your dad and Josie and everyone else. And it'll be a second-choice life. Won't it? Because I know your first choice. I know it includes me and Vegas and I play the piano and you wear a sequined dress and you sing. You sing, Cat, and it's the most beautiful thing I've ever heard."

I'm sobbing. My heart is wrenched open and it's bleeding. Gushing. And it's just pain, so much pain I wonder if I'll ever breathe again.

"And you know what shits me? You know what really makes me pathetic? When it happens, on the day you get married or when you have your first kid, I'll still be here. I'll still be your best friend, no matter what." He kisses my forehead and I grapple onto him. I hug him so tight, I'm afraid I might be hurting him. He pulls away, his hands fold over my arms and he wrenches free from my hold.

"Will, please? I just need time to figure this out," I murmur and he shakes his head and kisses my cheek.

"We've had time." He lets his lips graze against my skin, he inhales once and then he's out the door. I'm yelling for him but it's like I'm underwater. My voice isn't loud enough, my legs can't move fast enough. It's not enough. I stand at the swings and watch the tail lights of his old Saab disappear down the uneven road.

How many times are we going to do this? It can't continue, this tidal force of push and pull, the constant pummeling of monumental rock until all that's left is tiny grains of what we used to be. I'm confused and trembling and all I can see right now is Will and I in a church only he's not the one I'm binding myself to and I feel sick to my stomach.

I stumble home, a hysterical mess of a human being. My dad is seated on the couch, watching Seinfeld and he's laughing but he immediately jumps up when I burst through the door.

"Cat, what's wrong?" he asks me and my lower lip trembles when I try to speak.

"Dad," I sob and I'm in his arms in an instant. "I don't know what to do."

"It's okay, honey. Everything's gonna be fine," he shushes me and I breathe him in great heaping lung-fulls, all cigarettes and beer. And I know he's right, everything will be fine eventually. It just really, really sucks now.

"How did you do it? When Mom left, and never came back. How did you get over losing her?" I ask him and his hold tightens.

"I didn't. I'll never get over losing her," he says and I frown. This is the answer I expected. I want him to have some secret, some dumb saying that will make it all better. But my dad's a straight shooter. He tells it like it is, even when it hurts.

"Everything's so messed up. I don't know what I'm doing with my life. I'm scared this is all there is," I mumble into my dad's t-shirt.

"That's my fault," my dad says and I look up at him, confused. "This marina, it's all I've got. It's all I have to give you. I grew up here, same as you Kit Cat. I know what it feels like to be obligated to something you don't want."

"It's not that I don't want it. I just want other things too. I want experiences outside of our marina. I want to fail at things and succeed too and I want to feel proud of myself. I don't know, it sounds like a lot to want and it's selfish. But I feel like I'm a stranger, like I don't know me."

"Well, then there's only one thing to do," my dad says and he pulls away and sits back down on the couch. "You're fired."

"What?" I ask him, unsure if I heard him correctly.

"You're fired." His eyes don't sway from the television.

"But what about the bookkeeping? Who...what are you going to do?" I ask him dumbfounded.

"I'll hire someone. Maybe move Josie up to the books. She's good at math and logic and stuff. I've seen some of those puzzle books she obliterates while she's supposed to be working," he winks at me.

"You can't fire me," I argue. "I know what you're trying to do and I'm not going to let you. You need help."

"Like hell I can't! I can do whatever I want. And you're fired. It's about time you learned about the real world and how good you've had it here. Now you give me a hug before I change my mind, missy."

I throw myself into my father's arms and I cry while he chuckles. I whisper into his shoulder and he kisses my forehead and his mustache tickles my skin.

"Thank you."

1997 – THAT TIME YOUR DAD GOT DIVORCED

Batman and Robin is released in theaters June 20th.

Scientists in Scotland reveal the first successful cloning of an adult mammal, a sheep named Dolly.

The Foo Fighters release their second album, The Colour and the Shape.

* * *

S hoot at a variety of focal lengths," I read aloud from my textbook on the roof of the general store. I need a sunset photo for the photography class I'm taking at UNLV. Brett helped me fill out the application for a student loan. He said to think of it as an investment. It's so much easier to keep up with classes now that I don't have to worry about work.

My dad put Josie in the office and she's a whiz on the computer. He hired Brett's sister to work in the store and although he still needs help around the marina, he won't hire me back.

After Will left last summer, I threw myself into, well, myself. I wanted to chase him, drive to San Francisco and find him, but I knew if I did that I'd be trading one crutch for another. I wanted to find out what I was capable of on my own, without the marina, without Will, without my excuses and fears.

Okay, so driving to Las Vegas a couple days a week isn't exactly fearless, I know this. But it's a start.

I'm not sure if any of the Hendersons are coming to the river this year. Lauren has to work, but my brother might bring

Vanessa closer to my birthday. Margot and Andy are going to Jamaica for their anniversary and Jay said things haven't been too great between Dr. and Mrs. Henderson. She left him and now they're talking divorce.

I haven't heard from Will, but I asked my brother about him. He's gone back to school at San Francisco State and is working at the university. They have dinner once a month with him and his new girlfriend, Heidi. It's true, he will always be my first choice, but sometimes you don't get your first choice. Sometimes, being happy with your second choice isn't so bad.

I am happy, too. Tyler is a really great person and fits well in my life. I love him, and when he asked me to marry him last week, I only suffocated a little bit. I haven't given him an answer yet.

Well, actually, I told him he was insane, but he was really sweet about it. He said he doesn't care if we ever get married, that he'll take whatever part of me I'm willing to give, but I know Tyler wants a family soon. I've always been a bit late to the self-discovery party. I might want that stuff too someday. Just not today.

I adjust to a quicker shutter speed and decide to use the wide angle to get a landscape shot. The river bends like ribbon through the gentle rolling hills. There's a few cottony clouds dotting the sky and I adjust the focus to get a clean, crisp shot. The sky starts to change, prismatic iridescence dashing across the wide blue and I keep shooting.

The sun is sinking quickly and the fading color reflects off the dozens of motorhome windshields parked in the campground. The flashes of light are blinding and I bring my lens to capture the wide frame…and I stop.

A sleek silver BMW curves along the gravel path and parks at the Henderson's unit. Will gets out of the passenger seat, followed by Dr. Henderson from the driver's side. It's just the two of them.

I zoom in on him in the fading light like a total weirdo. I want to see how he's changed, really see him, before he sees me and it becomes awkward. But it's dusk and I can't see anything now.

The sun is gone.

I sigh and toss my things into my tote bag and inch my way towards the ladder I set against the side of the building. My sweaty hands are slippery on the railing, the metal hot from being outside and I have to wait until it cools before I can climb down.

I'm sitting on a towel on the edge of the roof when I see Will traipsing down the sidewalk to our swings. I put my fingers in my mouth and whistle loud and clear and he looks up and I wave. He startles before changing direction and stops at the base of the ladder.

"What the hell are you doing up there?" he asks as he looks up at me and I can see the soft bulbs of the marina lanterns flickering in his green. He looks the same, like a boy I once knew and I can't help but smile at my old friend.

"Didn't you hear? I'm a superhero now. I sit up here and wait for superhero stuff to happen. They're going to summon me with a huge spotlight any moment. It's a pretty cool gig." I shrug and his lips curl up into a grin.

"Do you need a sidekick?" he asks.

"You want to be my superhero sidekick?"

"Depends. Who's your favorite Batman?" he grins and I scoff.

"Oh my God, like it's even a contest. Michael Keaton, for sure."

"That's my girl." He starts to climb the ladder. "Shit! That's hot!"

"I know. That's why I'm still up here." He shrugs out of his plaid overshirt and uses it to guard his hands against the heated aluminum as he climbs the ladder and sits beside me. Will's body is cool from the miles of recent air conditioning and I let my arm rest against his.

"So, really, what are you doing up here?" he asks and I motion to my tote.

"I was working on something, for school," I say and he nods, his lips pursed in contemplation.

"Jay said you were taking classes. Photography?"

"Yeah, amongst other things. Turns out I'm not so bad at this photography thing." Will stares at me.

"No shit, Sherlock! I told you that, like eons ago," he says and I shrug.

"Apparently, I have a thick skull. And I might just be a little bit stubborn," I concede and Will laughs, the loudest I've ever heard him laugh before.

"So you're still with that guy, Taylor, or Tyrone or whatever?" he asks with a teasing grin and I roll my eyes.

"His name's Tyler. And yeah, I'm still with him." I settle into his side and he leans his head against mine.

"Do you love him?" he asks quietly and I nod.

"Yeah, I do."

"Then, I guess I love him too," Will murmurs and I feel my chest expand, my eyes fill with silent tears that don't spill.

"I missed you," I say and I feel him shift. The moon is low now and reflects off the glassy water. There's not even a hint of a breeze out here, and the heat still swells around us even though the sun is gone.

"Yeah, I missed you too."

"I thought you weren't coming back," I say and he sighs.

"I wasn't. I didn't want to come, but my dad gave me a huge ass guilt trip. Rachel left him. She wants a divorce."

"I'm glad you're here. And I'm glad you don't hate me anymore," I say and he pulls away, his eyes intent on my face.

"Cat, I have never hated you. I've been disappointed and frustrated and jealous but I've never hated you," he says with sharp conviction.

"Well, I've hated you. Lots of times," I exaggerate the words and he laughs because he knows it's only a little bit true.

"I'm sorry I hurt you," I say after his laughter has quieted.

"I'm sorry I hurt you," he repeats my words and pushes my hair behind my ear and I'm embarrassed by how sweaty I am.

"So we're even then," I joke and he chuckles.

"Yeah, we're even."

* * *

Y ou should come along," I say and Tyler sighs over the phone.

"I can't, I have to be at a site early in the morning. Can't you wait until next weekend?"

"There's going to be all kinds of smoke in the air after the fireworks. I think it'll add an interesting element to my sunrise photo. It can't wait," I explain. Again. He's worried. I guess I wouldn't like the idea of Tyler camping out on a cove with his... Will equivalent. Will's never been my boyfriend, but he's never been just my friend, either. He's just my Will. There really is no other way to explain it.

"I have to get this shot. Will's dad will be there. It's not a big deal, I promise." I feel like a child asking for permission.

"I know, I trust you. I just...call me as soon as you get back into the marina though. So I know you're safe." Tyler's voice is full of doubt. Right, because it's my safety he's worried about.

My dad follows Dr. Henderson's boat out to Home Cove and I can see Will sitting on the back bench all by himself. He's pissed at his dad. He begged me to come along, said he couldn't stand the thought of spending all night on the water with his dad alone.

"Please," he pleaded. "You don't want that man's murder on your conscience, do you?"

"I guess not," I shrugged. "Besides, you're far too pretty for prison."

"Like I'd go to prison. I've seen every episode of Law and Order. I'm pretty sure I could get away with murder." He's such a cocky little shit.

Josie and Brett sit on the bench in the back of my dad's boat and she keeps giving me these looks. She's wary of this whole situation, and I've just about had it with her lack of confidence.

Like I can't spend one night with Will without jumping his bones? It's completely insulting.

Will wants to go for a hike before it gets too hot. My new water shoes cut into the back of my heels and sweat saturates my tank. I'm tempted to discard the fabric but then I think of Josie's disapproving glances and I frown. Will doesn't give a shit about disapproving glances and he sheds his shirt as soon as we start the climb. A baseball cap hides his hair and he tucks his shirt into the back of his shorts. I walk behind him, watching his Vans scatter dirt. The muscles of his back flex and tiny trails of perspiration slide over the freckled skin as he marches forward. I'm glad I let him lead.

We reach the summit and are met with blinding brightness. The sun reflects off the shale and granite, thousands of rocks set in the hard earth like cobblestone. Will bends down to inspect a shiny, black stone. It's sharp and oddly split at curved angles.

"Volcanic glass," he says. "Obsidian. See how the fissure is concave? That's because the molten rock cooled so quickly, the crystals were unable to organize. So now, when it breaks, it breaks at the bonds that are the weakest."

I run my fingers along the ridges of the black rock settled in Will's palm, the unorganized bonds having succumbed to the pressure of the intense heat. It's sharp like a knife and splintered, a curved fraction of what it used to be. It's oddly shaped, unique in its imperfection and completely one of a kind. I like this rock.

"Can I have it?" I ask and he puts it in one of his large cargo pockets, my eyes glancing at the lithe muscles of his chest and stomach and I quickly look away.

"Sure. I'll hold on to it for you. It also doubles as a weapon." He grins and pushes up his hat to wipe the sweat from his forehead, smudging dirt on his skin. So fricking cute. People with boyfriends are allowed to think other people who have girlfriends are cute, I've decided.

We keep walking and my blistered heels are killing me, the

dirt grinding into the wounds but I force myself to ignore it. Will pockets half a dozen more rocks and shells before we find what we're looking for. This hilltop is covered in stones that visitors have arranged into patterns. Over time, as it storms, the rocks become trapped in the claylike mud and frozen in their arrangements. Initials, names, messages, swear words, forever immortalized in the dry cracked earth.

"D & K, 1978. Peace. Bite me. 4:20," Will says as he reads some of the messages.

"Fucking potheads," he laughs and I'm searching. Ages ago, Jay and I arranged our initials but I'm having a hard time finding them. I remember I used a red rock, but it's been years and they all look the same.

"I can't find mine," I frown and Will chuckles.

"So make a new one," he says and starts collecting his own free rocks. I do the same, searching out a vacant spot and Will follows me. I form my initials CPR and the year, '97 beneath them and step back to observe. Will's initials are beside mine, but not too close. It reminds me of that shell Will gave me the very first summer he was here, when we formed our connection, the very strongest of bonds that all the pressures in the world have yet to break. We've called it friendship. We've called it love. It doesn't matter what shape it takes, it's always there. Even when we can't see it.

"Your initials are CPR," Will snorts.

"You're like fourteen years late to that one," I say, my hands on my hips. The glare of the sun makes me squint. We start heading back down the trail and I give him a shove. "Yours are WAH, like a baby."

"Whatever, Cat the Brat."

"Will the Pill."

"Catman," he counters.

"Free Willy," I offer and he laughs.

"Catherine the Great," he says and I roll my eyes. He smiles softly and continues ahead of me down the hill.

Shit, I think he was being nice. Now I look like an ass for

293

dismissing him. I *am* a brat.

We gently jog back down the hill and I'm burning up, ready for a swim. Josie gives me one of her looks when she sees Will has abandoned his shirt. I stick my tongue at her. It's not my fault Will isn't wearing a shirt.

I remove my shorts and shirt and slather on sunblock, smoothing the lotion over my chest and stomach and the tops of my legs. I throw the tube at Josie and she fumbles to catch it.

"Josie, can you get my back," I ask sweetly and she glares at me but I don't care. I'm sick of her dirty looks.

"What is your problem?" I ask her in a hushed voice as she splatters a big dollop of sunblock right in the middle of my back.

"You're going to fall in love with him again," she says and I roll my eyes. "You have a boyfriend."

"Look, Captain Morality, I think I can handle myself just fine, okay? What kind of person do you think I am?" I whisper, her hands sloppily push the lotion around.

"Just be careful. You don't want to give him the wrong idea."

"Who? Will?" She looks at me with raised eyebrows.

"We're friends. And stop giving me dirty looks or I'm going to punch you," I say and I can hardly get the words out before laughing. She shoves me and I head out into the water.

After lunch, we go for a boat ride and my dad pulls us on skis. Will wants to try the single ski this year and actually gets up a couple times. He's wobbly, but by the third try he's signaling for my dad to go faster. Josie gives it a run, then Brett, too. I ask my dad if he wants me to pull him and he declines.

"Naw," he says. "I don't need to spend a whole day feeling like my arms are going to fall off." And I laugh because that's exactly what my arms are going to feel like tonight.

After our ski ride, I'm exhausted. I lay across the bench in the back of the boat, under the shade of the canopy, and rest my head on a wadded up towel that smells like my mom. The sway of the boat soothes me to sleep and I feel like I could nap for days.

When I wake up, I'm groggy and my sweaty skin sticks to the vinyl of the seat. Will's stretched out on his back on the floor of the boat, his arm over his face. I watch the breath enter and leave his body, the hollow span of his stomach stretching to welcome the oxygen and then sinking to reveal the contours of muscle and bone. The honey hair on his chest glints gold in the sneaky streaks of sunlight, and he's beautiful. I don't know how long I lay there watching him but I don't remember blinking. I want to stay here forever, floating and barely aware, watching my favorite friend breathe.

Eventually he stirs and I close my eyes and pretend to be asleep. I hear him groan as he shifts. The boat sways and his hand grazes my cheek, pushing my hair off my neck. I force my face to stay frozen even though little shivery impulses are melting down my spine and over my scalp. He crawls over my legs onto the back of the boat and then I hear a splash and he's in the water.

I stay where I am, thinking about Will and his breathing. I haven't thought about Tyler once today, not since this morning. I feel guilty. Maybe Josie's right. Maybe I do need to be careful and keep my distance. I decide that I cannot watch Will breathe again.

After dinner, Brett, Josie and my dad are ready to head home and I start to feel odd about my decision to stay with Will and his dad. I remind myself that I'd be out here alone anyway and I feel more confident.

My dad kisses my cheek before I pull up the anchor. Josie gives me one last wary look while Brett shakes hands with Will and Dr. Henderson and then the boat is gone, the loud engine fading behind the hills as it veers out of the inlet.

Dr. Henderson zips himself up in his tent, and Will and I sit around a small fire, enjoying an easy silence until we hear a deep throaty snore from the tent. My eyes flash up to his and I snort with laughter. Will laughs too and shakes his head before fixating his eyes back on the fire.

"So, Jay said you have a girlfriend?" I ask and Will gives a shrug.

"Yeah, Heidi. She's a court runner at Lauren's office," he says and I lean forward in my seat to pick up a stick and start to dig.

"How did you meet her?" Curiosity makes the words fall from my lips.

"She belongs to Lauren's book club," he says and I stab at the earth. "She was at Lauren and Jay's Halloween party."

"They have Halloween parties?" I ask quietly.

"Well, this was the first one but they want to make it a yearly thing. Vanessa was a ladybug," he says and my eyes glaze over. He knows more about my brother's life than I do.

"I miss them," I say and Will looks into the fire.

"They miss you. We all do. You should come visit, you can even bring Travis or Trent, whatever his name is," Will teases and I scrunch up my face.

"He asked me to marry him," I say carefully.

"What did you say?" he asks after heavy silence. I stare at him across the flames and I can feel his gaze right in the pit of my stomach.

"Nothing yet. I'm still weighing my options," I sigh.

"You don't want to marry him," Will says confidently and I scowl.

"How do you know what I want?"

"Come on, Cat! Weighing your options? What, are you buying a dishwasher or choosing to spend the rest of your life with your greatest love?"

I can't look at him because Tyler is not the greatest love of my life. Not by far.

"I just want to make sure I'm doing the right thing," I defend. "Blindly leaping into marriage is idiotic."

"When you want it, you won't give a shit about options. You won't even care about looking like an idiot. You won't need to make a decision, Cat. You'll just know." He silently leans back into his chair and the air is dead around us.

"How do you know all this?" I challenge him.

"I just do," he says and I'm not convinced.

"That's bullshit," I retort. "Weighing options is a good thing. It's good to think things through."

"Have you thought about how if you marry him, your name will be Cat Pillar? Thank God no one calls you Catty anymore," he laughs and I roll my eyes. It's true, this is the most unfortunate thing about Tyler but Josie already brought this up.

"I don't have to change my last name, he could change his," I reply indignant. "Or I could start being Catherine."

"Sounds like you're good, then," he says.

"I am. I am good," I say with a quick nod. "I'm afraid I'm going to fall asleep and not be able to wake up in time for the sunrise, though."

"I have an alarm on my watch," Will says and I stare at him. Of course he does.

"Alright, set it for like four," I say and stand up. He fiddles with the buttons before taking the watch off his wrist and handing it to me.

I unzip my tent and strip to my suit, because it's far too hot to sleep in clothes. I hear Will snuff out the fire and then he's stumbling around in his tent too. I lay directly in the middle of my air mattress, my legs and arms spread out like a starfish. It's the only way I'm not stifling. I close my eyes but Dr. Henderson starts snoring again and I can't help but laugh.

"Shut up," Will says from his tent. Dr. Henderson snores again and I hear the squeaky slip of polyester and vinyl. Then Will's outline is at the door of my tent.

"Move over," he says and I sit up, startled. "I can't sleep in there with him."

"Well, you can't sleep in here," I say but he steps inside the tent anyway.

"Yes I can, it's my tent."

"Fine, but you can't touch me," I say. I scoot over and he crawls onto the bouncy air mattress. He settles and I close my eyes and I'm just falling asleep when his leg nudges against mine.

"Stop touching me. It's too hot," I gripe. Will chuckles and I pinch at his leg with my toes.

"Ow! Did you just pinch me with your ET toes?" He jerks his leg away.

"I can sleep on the boat." I'm struggling to get up when he grabs my wrist.

"I'll stop touching you. Sorry, just go to sleep," he says and I sigh and lay back down. I feel him shift and turn a few more times, but he doesn't touch me again.

A persistent beeping wakes me up and I turn my head to find Will's face turned towards mine, his eyelashes feathered across his cheekbones, his pink nose freckled, and his pointy lips slightly parted. I want to wake him, but instead I fight my way off the confounded mattress and search for my tank-top and shorts. It's pitch black outside so I grab my flashlight and my camera bag and grudgingly shove my feet into my new, blister giving shoes.

I'm halfway up the hill when I remember there could be mountain lions out here, and I start to get a little paranoid. I hear sounds I'm sure are nothing but visualize a huge paw clawing my face.

There's a rustling when I turn the corner, then a flapping of wings before soft downy feathers graze the top of my head and I scream bloody murder. Will calls my name, and my heart beats in my throat. I'm panting as I slump to the ground. And then I laugh. Hysterically. When Will reaches me, the beam from his flashlight dancing around the bend, I have tears streaming down my cheeks.

"What happened?" he says as he tries to help me up. He thinks I'm injured or something, I'm sure.

"An owl tried to decapitate me," I gasp and I let him pull me to stand.

"Why didn't you wake me up?" He shakes me, his voice harsh, and the brat rises within me.

"I'm fine. I just overreacted, not a big deal." I match his tone and dust myself off. He's still panting from the jaunt up the hill.

"Jesus, Cat...don't ever do that again!" He grips my shoulders and then pulls me into his chest, my face pressed against his sticky skin. He smells like sunblock and vinyl from the air mattress and I don't even mind his sweat on my cheek.

"It's okay," I murmur against his skin, and he releases me too soon. I blame my no touching rule. He looks uncomfortable and motions for me to walk ahead of him.

We reach the top in silence and cross the broad span of dust and rock until I find a silhouette that makes me stop dead in my tracks. The sky is beginning to lighten and there's burnt sulphur in the air, the low haze dusting the tops of the hills.

I quickly pull my camera from my bag and adjust the aperture and shutter speed. I set it to manual focus, and look through the lens and I can feel Will behind me, our bond tugging at every element in my body. I want to lean into him to brace my unsteady hands, but I don't. The camera clicks and his breath is in my ear. I snap my photos in the same rhythm as his chest grazing my back with every inhale.

I feel the sun before I see it, the sky burns in pastels and then primaries and the earth smolders around us. My skin absorbs the heat, the tiny hairs on my arms and neck vibrate as the energy seeps into my cells. The air is still, the heat coating the land in waves and, all the while, Will breathes and I capture. My feet root into the earth and my skin melts with the fiery sky. The universe is sending me a message.

Confirmation. Reassurance. Balance. I'm right where I'm supposed to be.

We don't speak, yet there's comfort in the quiet. We weave down the trail together, alone in our thoughts, the afterglow of the transfer of energy radiating between us. I go for a swim when we return. The sun has yet to flood over the hills surrounding the cove and it's eerie disrupting the still, gray water. I'm drowsy and drained, yet my muscles surge with life. My heart thumps madly against my ribs as I kick and propel myself forward and I wait. I wait for the sun to pour in.

* * *

Since I don't have to work, I have time to spend with Will during the week. Tyler drives in on the weekends and we take boat rides with Josie and Brett once in a while, and Will and Tyler actually seem to get along.

Being with Will is easy again. We sit out on the cove and he writes in his old leather bound notebook I haven't seen in ages. I read my photography books and when we feel like talking, we do. Then we disappear back into our solitary activities and I'm at ease just knowing he's close.

It's the beginning of August and I want to get a picture of the high rock walls by the dam. Will suggests we take the kayak. It's a long trek but I'm on river time and I crave the exercise.

Our paddles dip into the deep water in long languid strokes. Will's behind me and every once in a while he splashes me with his paddle, a quick spray of relief fragmenting the heat's hold on my skin.

He talks about school and his dissertation, something to do with cellular biology and the only words I understand are DNA and gene amplification. He wants to teach at the University now and is really excited about what he's working on.

I feed off his enthusiasm. I tell him about my classes and how my photography teacher loves me. He chuckles and ruffles my hair, and I'm almost embarrassed discussing my classes in comparison to his work load.

"Don't be ridiculous," he says. "There's no way I could pass your classes. I have good study skills and a knack for memorizing shit. You have a gift. You could be famous. Like that chick who photographs all the rock stars."

"Annie Leibovitz?" I ask as I turn around and Will taps me on the nose.

"Yeah, her. You could do so many cool things, fly all over the world taking pictures. You could work for National Geographic or Cosmo, you have tons of options." Will rests the paddle across his lap.

"I kind of made you something," I say and my ears burn. It's not a big deal, really. I had stacks and stacks of river pictures, our summers chronicled in black and white that I finally developed.

"You made me something?" he asks with his coy grin and I roll my eyes.

"Well, it didn't start out being for you, but the more I worked on it, the more I thought you should have it, since it's your fault I have aspirations and shit," I say, my voice laced with sarcasm as he nudges me in the back. "I'm serious. If you hadn't verbally attacked me last year, I wouldn't be doing any of this."

"Verbally attacked you? I declared my love. I bared my soul, for Christ's sake. I was fucking poetic," he declares.

"Yeah, you were kind of poetic." I reach over the side of the kayak into the water and splash the back of my neck. The water feels heavenly.

"I meant every word," he says quietly and goosebumps dance across my skin. "I'll always love you. I don't think it'll ever go away."

"Will..." I say and he tugs on my braid.

"Oh, relax. I'm not going to try to steal you away from Mr. T," he snorts and I can't help it, I smile too.

"So what happened with your dad and Rachel?" I ask and I realize this is probably the first time I've called her that. She's always been Mrs. Henderson to me.

"She got tired of being alone all the time. She said she didn't marry him so she could grow old by herself and she moved out. She wants a divorce."

"Wow, that's gotta be rough on your dad," I say.

"Fuck my dad!" Will growls and I'm startled. "He always does this. He screws everything up and then thinks he can buy his way out of it. This trip's supposed to make up for the fact that he's been ignoring me for the last twenty years. It's so typical of him, to think he deserves a second chance- shit a third, fourth, fifth chance. How many chances do I give him before I cut my losses?"

"But he's your dad. And he's trying. He's the only family you have," I say gently as I skim the surface of the water with my paddle.

"That's not true. Margot and Andy and Lauren and even Jay, they care more about me than he does. And you, you understand me better than anyone ever will. You saw me before anyone. You're my family. Not him." I feel my heart swell at his words and I know he speaks the truth. I know because I feel it, too.

"I know he's hurt you-"

"Hurt doesn't even begin to describe it. All I wanted was to be good enough for him and I'm finally at a place where I feel comfortable with my life, and now, he wants to make amends. When I've already done all the hard work? It's too late, it's done."

"It's never too late, Will. Not for the ones you love," I say over my shoulder. "Do you honestly think your father's goal in life was to ruin you?"

"Of course not, but he can't look past himself to care about anyone else."

"Maybe. Or maybe he can't look past the past, to care about anything," I say and Will is silent behind me. "What he did was wrong, okay? I'm not arguing that. Maybe losing your mom destroyed him too. Maybe keeping you at a distance was his way of protecting himself."

"But I was just a kid. I didn't know...I didn't understand. I still don't understand," Will says quietly.

"I know. He handled it horribly, but he's trying to do the right thing now. I think you should talk to him about it. What have you got to lose?"

"My dignity," he mutters and I chuckle.

"Naw, you lost that a long time ago." There's a cool spray on my back as he splashes me with his paddle.

After that trip, I see less of Will. He goes fishing with his dad.

They drive into Vegas. They go for boat rides and hikes and Will seems really content.

Before Will leaves, I bring him his present. I've never given Will a present and I'm nervous. I wrapped it up, like it's special or something and now I want to rip off all the wrapping and toss the damn book at him.

It's my old portfolio, the one he gave me when I turned eighteen, only now it's filled with memories of our summers on the river.

"God, look how skinny I was! And my hair is like a rat's nest. A big blond rat's nest," he laughs. His finger traces my face in the print. "We were such dorks."

"Why did you guys let me wear my hair pulled back so tight?" I scrunch up my nose.

There are pages and pages of our time on the river. I remember all of it like it was yesterday, the snapshots reminding me of every opportunity, every fear, every misunderstanding I could have avoided if I just would have had the guts.

"Oh my God, the houseboat. That was a crazy trip. I was so disappointed in you. I really wanted to see you punch Andy for hitting on you," Will says with a grin.

"I didn't know he was hitting on me!" I defend as he turns the page. The next pictures are of Vegas and we laugh at how we got kicked out of that bar. Then there's Margot's wedding and Will looks miserable. After Margot's wedding the pages are blank and he looks at me questioning.

"Those are for future summers," I say and he smiles as he goes back through the photos again, his eyes taking in every moment, every line and shadow. His lips keep quirking into remembering grins.

"I'm going to try to publish it," I say, a little embarrassed. "Brett knows an agent who's going to help me. They think they can market it for tourism, really play up the shots of the scenery and stuff. You'll have to sign a waiver, because your picture's in there a bunch. Is that okay?"

"Of course. Holy shit, Cat, you're really doing this! I mean, I always knew you could do it. I'm glad you know now too." His eyes softly hold mine before he sets the book down and gets up to grab an envelope from his backpack on the counter.

"This is for last year too, so don't even bitch about the price." He sits down beside me as I tear through the paper and inside is a voucher for an airline ticket. I'm speechless.

"You can use it to go anywhere. I thought you might want to come visit your brother," he shrugs and I can't stop the tears from streaming down my cheeks. I throw my arms around his neck, ignoring my own stupid rule, and press my lips to his cheek.

"I love you," I say firmly and I kiss him again, this time closer to his ear.

Will leaves the next morning and I watch the silver BMW kick up dust as it slowly drives away down the uneven road. I'm trying to find some kind of solace in my wide variety of depressing literature, when I hear the phone in the kitchen ring.

"Cat!" my dad yells through the house and I grudgingly stalk out of the room. It's probably my brother, calling with another delay in visiting. Or it's Tyler and I'm just not in the mood to be nice. He holds the phone out for me and I snatch it out of his hand, my foul mood ruling my decisions today.

"Hello?"

"Did you know you can't get cell phone service for five whole miles surrounding the marina?" The phone crackles and hums but I know this voice.

"Will? What...You have a cell phone? Why are you calling me?" I ask, feeling like a moron.

"I forgot to ask you something."

"Okay?"

"Nirvana or Foo Fighters?" he asks after a heartbeat, like it's the most important question in the world.

"What?"

"Which band is better, Nirvana or Foo Fighters?" He's

serious.

"You can't compare them." I slide down the wall to sit on the floor beneath the phone. I pull my knees into my chest and I pick at the scarred skin of my heel.

"That's a bullshit answer. On pure, raw, musical talent, which one is better?" His voice sounds close, like he's just in the other room.

"I'm gonna have to go with Foo Fighters," I say and I hear him groan.

"What? Who are you?" I knew he wouldn't like my response.

"Dave Grohl is a better front man. There. I've said it. Let the flogging commence." My braid is digging into my back so I pull the rope of hair over my shoulder.

"Dude! I can't believe you said Foo Fighters," Will says but it sounds like he's smiling.

"So what, you don't want to be my friend anymore?" I ask.

"I'm not gonna lie, your dismissal of the driving force that is Nirvana is highly disappointing," he says.

"You can't pick Nirvana just because they were the first. That's like saying David Lee Roth is a better frontman than Sammy Hagar just because he was first," I argue.

"Okay, you might be a little right," he says.

"Of course I'm right. I'm always right." There's a long pause and I think he's going to hang up when the silence is interrupted.

"Top five rock bands of the eighties," he says into the receiver and I get comfortable in my spot on the floor. "Go!"

1998 – THAT TIME MY DAD
SOLD THE MARINA

*Two Stanford students, Larry Page and Sergey Brin, launch
a new search engine running on Linux called Google.*

*Record high global temperatures are recorded
by NASA and the CRU.*

*Michael Jordan wins his sixth NBA championship and sixth Finals
MVP award in six full basketball seasons, an unprecedented feat.*

✳ ✳ ✳

Butterscotch sun pours in through my apartment window, and I grumble. I just woke up and I'm already sweaty. I turn over, my face sticking to the plastic wrapping of my midnight fruit roll-up and I feel a sharp, hard object under my arm. I pull the cellophane from my cheek while searching for the evil disturber of sleep. It's the phone. And it's still on.

"Hello?" I ask on the off chance someone's on the line.

"Cat?" His voice is groggy and I'm perplexed.

"Did we just phone sleep together?" I ask and I hear Will laugh.

I sold some of my photographs to a magazine, Arizona Boating and Watersports, last month. It's a pretty small publication and I don't make that much money, but the very first thing I bought with my commission was a cordless phone.

"Don't tell your boyfriend," he teases and I frown.

I told Tyler I didn't want to marry him. I told him I wanted to live on my own, and I moved into a tiny apartment closer to campus. I asked him to hold off on the marriage talk until I was done with school.

He agreed and then we had a month of awkwardness because he didn't really mean it when he said he'd take whatever part of me I was willing to give. We fought and he said I never really loved him. I told him I'd never marry him because he's a selfish asshole and I cried because it wasn't true in the slightest. I apologized. And then it was done.

"We broke up," I say quickly and he's silent. I can't even hear him breathing.

"What happened?" His voice is gravel.

"I told him I didn't want to get married."

"You don't want to get married ever, or don't want to get married now?" The words are quick off his lips.

"I don't know, I just don't want to get married. That's how I feel today."

"Okay, fair enough," he says quietly. "Are you sad?"

"I am sad. He's a nice person and he loved me and I hurt him," I ramble and my chest feels empty. "But you were right. I don't want to marry him."

"I'm sorry you're upset, Cat. I wish I was there to buy you ice cream or something," Will says and I sigh.

"Me too. Thanks for letting me talk about it," I say, because I really am glad we're at this place now, where we say what we mean and we mean what we say.

It's been brought to my attention, on more than one occasion, that I'm a thought hoarder. I keep all my thoughts in my head and then expect people to understand how I feel. I don't know why it's so hard to find the words, but it's something I'm working on. It's easier on the phone, when I don't have to see Will to tell him how I feel. It works. Better than I thought it would.

"My dad's looking for a partner. He can't run the marina on his own anymore so he's going to sell off a portion of it. He's had offers, but he's picky," I say after a moment.

"He's selling the marina?" Will asks.

"No, he's looking for help. He's old. He can't do it all anymore, but this is all he's ever known. This is his livelihood and he can't just let it go, you know?"

"What do you think about this?"

"I kind of hate it. I hate someone squirming in on our place, you know? And these people that he's been meeting with, they don't know anything about the river. They don't know what they're getting themselves into. They're suits, nothing more."

"What if the suit was someone you knew? Like my dad?" Will asks and I frown.

"My dad wants to retire. He needs a partner, someone who's not only financially invested, but someone who's here to help him."

"I wish it could be me," Will says and I sigh.

"I know. Me too."

"So when are you coming to visit your brother?" Will asks.

"I'm flying up in two weeks." I get out of bed and wrap my hair in a rubber band. I wanted my dad to come too but he refused. January isn't really a busy month at the marina, but I think he wants me to go by myself.

"It's going to be cold, you know."

"I know. I'm going shopping with Josie tomorrow. What do I need to get? Like hats and mittens and things? Is it so cold that I'll need long underwear? I've always wanted to wear long underwear," I say.

"Yes, the kind with the flap in the butt, you'll definitely need those," Will says and I don't know if he's serious. "And maybe some of those knee high fuzzy boots and a catsuit. A really tight one. It helps retain body heat."

"Are you messing with me?" I ask.

"Depends. What are your thoughts on catsuits?"

"You're so gross," I smile and I bet he's smiling too. My phone beeps.

"My phone's about to die. I'll call you later," I say as I run my fingers over the small white shell bearing our names on my dresser.

"Okay." He hangs on the line. "Oh, and Cat,"

"Yeah?" I'm reluctant to let him go.

"Good morning," he says and I'm warm.

"See you in two weeks, Will."

My dad picks me up and takes me to the airport, and I feel like I'm going to throw up. I've never been on an airplane. I've never even been in an airport and I'm freaking out that I might miss my flight or, you know, crash land in Death Valley. My dad walks me to the terminal, through the metal detectors and he stands with me at the gate. I clutch my ticket in one hand, my tote bag slung over my shoulder, and we wait until my boarding group is called.

I'm tense the whole flight. My hands grip the armrests and the lady I'm sitting next to is irritated I'm monopolizing them but I don't care. My stomach drops, my ears pop and then I'm in San Francisco.

Opaque clouds hover around the tall buildings. It's cold, and the wind blows straight through the threads of my new sweater. Jay and Vanessa pick me up in the minivan. Jay gives me a big hug and Vanessa looks at me warily from her carseat. My teeth chatter as I climb into the front seat.

"Holy frozen appendages," I mutter and Jay laughs. He wears a beanie and a heavy fleece coat. I don't think I brought enough clothes. It gets cold in the desert sometimes, but not like this.

"Vanessa, honey, this is your Aunt Cat," Jay says to his daughter in the back seat and I can't believe how she's grown. Her hair curls around her ears and her eyes are big blue sparkling marbles. She has a face like an angel and long eyelashes and I think she might be the most beautiful child I've ever seen.

"Hi Vanessa," I say with a big smile and she hides her face.

"It's okay, she's just being shy," Jay explains.

"She doesn't know me," I say. I mirror her shy stare, peeking around the side of the seat. She lets a small smile slip and my heart sings. We play peek-a-boo and by the time Jay parks in the driveway, she's saying my name and telling me about her doggie, Muller.

"Mulder, the dog's name is Mulder," Jay says and I laugh. "We have one named Scully too."

Jay's house is lovely. It's tiny but two-stories, with white siding and green trim. There's a set of steps leading to a small porch, and the door opens to the top level of the house. The inside is all wooden floors and the walls are soft browns and reds. It smells sweet and tart, like apple pie. Jay gives me a tour and his dogs lick my hands before he puts Vanessa down for a nap. He makes a pot of coffee and we sit in the living room. We talk about my classes, about San Francisco, about politics and this global warming thing everyone's so worried about. It's comfortable, curled up on my brother's couch with a big, fuzzy sweater and a cup of hot coffee.

Jay explains that Vanessa has a play date with these two other kids and I think this is hilarious. Jay and these two neighborhood moms take turns watching the kids once a week so they can have some free time. Jay usually goes swimming at the gym or grocery shopping. It's hard to imagine my brother grocery shopping but he says he does what he can so Lauren doesn't have to and I've never been so proud of my brother.

Vanessa and the two little girls, Charlotte and Maggie, play with blocks on the floor of the living room while *Sesame Street* plays on the television. Jay sits on the floor with them, my big huge brother stacking pink and purple blocks and humming along with a song about the letter c. I think I've officially entered an alternate universe. Maybe we flew through a wormhole on the way here or something.

"What?" Jay asks and I shake my head and smile.

"Nothing, Big Bird. Except that you're adorable," I tease. He rolls his eyes and throws a block at me. I dodge the throw but Vanessa copies and Jay scolds her.

"If I'm Big Bird, that makes you Oscar the Grouch, you know?" Jay says and I shrug.

"That's cool, Oscar's badass." Jay tosses another block. This time I catch it and he's surprised, just as the phone rings. Jay gets up to answer and Vanessa comes over and hands me a block.

"Block," she says clear as day.

"Thank you, Miss V," I say and she crawls into my lap. Her curly hair tickles my nose and I breathe her in.

"It's for you," Jay says and hands me the cordless phone. It must be my dad. I forgot to call him and he's going to give me a guilt trip.

"Hello?" I ask.

"Cat! Are you here?" It's Will and it's a bad connection. He might be driving or something.

"Will? I can barely hear you," I say and plug my ear.

"I have class till late. Stay up for me?" he asks.

"Of course," I say and he laughs.

"Okay, good. I can't wait to see you." And then he's gone. I hang up and feel the heat burn in my cheeks as I look at the phone in my hands.

"Quit molesting my phone," Jay says and I toss it aside. "Look at you, all twitterpated and shit."

"Shit!" Vanessa shouts and Jay grabs her.

"No! That's yucky," he says. "Yucky word."

"Shit!" Vanessa shouts again and then giggles. Charlotte copies and soon there's three foul mouthed toddlers running circles around the room just as Lauren is walking in the front door. She's wearing a long beige wool coat and a black pants suit with heels. She looks very much like a lawyer, the shift drastic from the swimsuit and shorts I usually see her in.

"Momma!" Vanessa shouts and wraps around her mother's legs. Lauren bends down to scoop her up. They share a cuddle and a kiss. Then Lauren is hugging me and she smells like flowers.

"Hey Cat! You made it!" Lauren holds Vanessa on her hip and they look very similar, same blue eyes, same porcelain skin. "Margot's on her way over. She'll be here in like ten minutes."

Margot and Andy drive up in an old clunky hunk of metal. I expected something small and sporty, like a Porsche or something but leave it to them to surprise me. Andy calls it the

"Cuda" and says it's a classic and all I can think of is that Heart song that's now stuck in my head.

We go out to dinner at a hidden Italian restaurant on a tiny cobblestone road that's decorated with twinkling lights. Lauren loans me a heavy coat because night time in San Francisco is far colder than the day. We have wine with dinner and we catch up on all the stuff we've missed in the time apart. I haven't seen Margot in forever and I miss her. I miss her so much I want to fold this moment up and put it in my pocket.

San Francisco seethes with life. The sky darkens early, the rising streets buzz and the solid wall of buildings soar. The air smells like the ocean and I fill my lungs. I feel refreshed, the cool air in my lungs almost hurts but I breathe it in. I like the way it feels to breathe here.

It's just before ten when Will gently raps on the door. I'm already in my pajamas, lounging on my makeshift bed on the couch and watching Buffy. I open the door and Will pulls me into a tight hug on the porch. He's wearing a thick wool coat and a beanie and I freeze in only my pajamas. Will's hands are clutching the back of my pajamas and he kisses my forehead, and I shiver.

"Oh shit! I'm sorry!" Will says as he pushes me inside and shuts the door behind him. He pulls the beanie from his head and smoothes his hair. I plop back down on the couch, a blanket pulled around my legs while he takes off his coat. He sits down next to me on the couch, and his smile never falters.

"Nice jammies," he says and ruffles my hair and I push his hand out of the way.

"Shut up. This is my one chance to wear warm pajamas and I'm going all out," I respond and his knee rests against my thigh.

"Do they have a flap in the butt?" he asks.

"Of course. I don't mess around," I smirk and Will pulls at the side of my bottoms.

"Let me see the flap. Show me your butt," Will says and my ears are on fire.

"I will not show you my butt or any rumored flap," I say indignantly. "I'm going to tell your girlfriend you said that."

"Oh really?" Will says and yeah, I'm fishing. Pathetically.

"Am I going to get to meet her?" I ask and his smile can't be contained. He sees right through me.

"I don't think that will be possible. Seeing as how I am no longer in possession of said girlfriend." Fluttering in my chest and tingles on my scalp and I feel bold.

"So, you're alone then?" I ask and his gaze burns.

"Nope, I'm here with you." Will leans into the couch, his hip against mine and I ease into the closeness. "What are you watching?"

"Buffy," I answer and he rolls his eyes. "What? She's protecting the world against the dark evils of the supernatural. What could be more important than that?"

"Isn't NYPD Blue on right now?" Will tries to swipe at the remote control but I get to it first.

"If I'm going to watch blood and guts, it's going to be fake vampire blood and guts," I say. He makes a swipe at the controller again and it's odd to see him act so juvenile in his button-up shirt and Dockers.

"Stop it, Will! You cannot have the control."

"Oh, I know. I realized that a long time ago," he chuckles. For a minute I think he's done trying but when I least expect it, he grabs my wrist and snags the controller and I scoff.

"Though, let it be known, Cat. I'm not a quitter."

Over the next week, I fit myself into their busy schedules. Lauren leaves early and gets home just before dark and I spend the day with Jay and Vanessa. We go to the Golden Gate Park and the zoo and the aquarium and I snap pictures of everything. I photograph Vanessa the most, desperate to capture every beautiful or sassy or funny moment.

Did you know they make IT'S-IT in San Francisco? I didn't but Will takes me on a tour of the facility and I'm in heaven. We have drinks at jazz bars and coffee in bookstores and they feel like dates. We eat in a different country every night and I try oysters for the first time. Spoiler Alert: they're gross. We go to a big farmer's market in Union Square, and we hold hands and talk, and he kisses my forehead when we say goodnight.

I feel it, that ever present spark. We're different now, our relationship is different, no longer a sparked flame but more like a smolder. Hot coals smothered under earth and I feel like all we need to do is brush that dirt aside.

I stay over at Will's apartment. He puts on *Forrest Gump,* I think it's his favorite movie, and I curl up into his side while he plays with my hair. I fall asleep and he lays me in his bed. When I wake up, he's asleep on the couch and I'm disappointed.

"You didn't have to sleep on the couch, you know," I say when he's finally awake. I make coffee in his kitchen in my sweatpants and he watches me from the couch. His hair is a tangled mess, his face red and creased from sleeping and he stares at me dazed.

"I didn't want to assume anything. I thought you might want space," he rubs his eyes and scratches his chin and I bring him coffee. I sit cross legged next to him on the couch, and his eyes hold mine as he sips.

Fitting into Will's life here is surprisingly easy. I know his life isn't like this all the time, but being in Will's apartment feels natural, like I've been here all along.

"I don't want space, Will. I kinda just want you," I say confidently and I sip my coffee, my eyes on him the whole time.

"You've kinda always had me," he responds, his coffee cup paused at his lips.

"Just kinda?" I tease and he smirks.

"Barely. Like by the skin of your teeth."

"That's a horrible saying. Makes me sound like Hannibal Lecter." I'm rambling because I'm nervous.

It's just Will, you idiot.

But he's kind of everything.

I lean over and gently kiss his lips, and it feels familiar but new. Different. It's a possibility. It's hesitant and hopeful and I know he's not expecting it.

It's a first kiss.

Again.

He runs his fingers down my spine and I enjoy the tingles. I kiss him again, deeper this time. I pull his lip into my mouth and his tongue moves with mine. It's a good thing I'm still holding my coffee. Because nothing says you're moving too fast like a cup of scalding hot coffee in your lap.

Moving too fast? It's been fifteen years since William Henderson first snapped my bathing suit strap.

Still, I feel as clueless about how to handle this situation as I did when I was eleven. Will pulls away and his eyes shine, his lips curled into a cocky grin and he doesn't even need to say a word. I know what he's thinking.

See how well we fit, I told you we could do this, you love me.

And I do. I really, truly do.

The next day, Will takes me to Baker Beach and I walk in the sand. It's different from the sand at the river. Most of the coves at the river are hard, packed earth, or covered in rocks. This sand is soft and cold and I take my shoes off. I know my toes will freeze but I have to put my feet in the water. We look at shells and rocks and I inhale the salty air and fill the pockets of my borrowed white down coat.

Will finds a spiraling shell and we stand together and study the arc. He tells me how it's all math, how there's an equation to explain the curves but all I see is the fact the circle just keeps getting bigger and bigger and further away from the center.

That's what my life feels like, the outer edge of a curve and too far from the heart. I want to get back there, to the heart. I think I know the way now.

The night before I leave, Will stays with me at my brother's house. I feel vacant and sad as we watch some alien movie that my brother rented from Blockbuster. Will wasn't planning on sleeping over but since it's well into the early hours of the morning, he decided to stay and ride along to the airport.

"So did you have fun this week? Did you like the city?" Will asks. He passes me a bag of gummi worms, and I dig through the bag, searching for the red and white ones because they're my favorite. "Stop it! You can't pick out the good ones."

I roll my eyes and pass the bag back to him. We lay on our stomachs on a nest of blankets we've created on the floor.

"I love San Francisco. I love the steep streets, the sounds, the people. I even love that guy who scared me half to death jumping out of the bushes," I say.

"Like, you love it so much, you'll come back?"

"Yeah, definitely. I'm definitely coming back." And he gives me a cocky smile.

"I knew you'd love it here. You should have listened to me years ago. Think of all the San Francisco you've been missing."

God, think of all the life I've been missing, all because I was afraid. Was being the operative word there. I'm not afraid anymore.

"Do you still love me?" I blurt out the words and I don't know what I'm doing. Okay, maybe I'm a little afraid. "I mean, do you think that maybe we could try again? I feel like maybe we connected at the wrong time and...everything's different now and I'm different and...Like, if we would have met yesterday, would you still like me?"

Will lays his head flat on his crossed arms and looks at me with his glowing green eyes and he's thinking. I'm afraid of what is running around in his head, but I need to hear it. So I wait.

"I've known all these different versions of you. I've known you snotty and stubborn and naïve and scared. I've known you bold and sexy and hopeful and funny. And now, here you are, a conglomeration of all the girls I've loved, all the girls I've lived for but it's always just been you, Cat. And you've always just been everything to me." My hair stands on end as he speaks, his voice quiet, his face inches from mine.

"You didn't really answer the question," I whisper.

"Yes, Catherine the Great," he says with a smile. "Yes, I would still like you. I'd annoy the shit out of you until you noticed me. And, well, once you spent any decent amount of time with me, you'd be smitten."

"Oh really," I roll over onto my side to face him and prop my head up with my arm.

"Yep," he says and pushes my hair from my face. "And you'd roll your eyes half a dozen times but I'd keep saying cheesy stuff just to see you do it. I'd find any excuse to touch you, and I'd definitely try to kiss you. You would let me, too. Because you'd feel it. That little hum that's always buzzing when we're together, like neon lights. Do you ever feel it? Like static?"

"A spark," I whisper and Will nods.

"We match, like complimentary colors. Red and green. I don't know why it works, but it just does. You're the peanut butter to my jelly, the eggs to my bacon, the cheese to my macaroni," he says and I shove him a little and roll my eyes. He catches my hand and pulls me close.

"Do me a favor, Cat?" I nuzzle into his neck, pressing my lips into his skin. "Don't go on any more dates, okay?"

"Are you asking me to go steady?" I tease and I feel all the tingles.

"Yes, I am," he says.

"Are you going to give me your pin? Do you want me to be your girl?" I say and Will smirks.

"You've always been my girl, you just didn't know it yet."

"I will neither confirm or deny that claim," I say indignantly.

"Cat, will you be my obligation?" He's teasing but I know what he means.

"Pinkie promise?" I offer quietly and his face is serious now.

"Deal," he whispers, his fingers twist in my pajamas as his mouth closes over mine. His hands roam and I arch into him, desperate to get closer. He grasps frantically at where the hem of my shirt should be before pulling away. "What the hell are you wearing?"

"It's a onesie," I blurt out laughing and he grabs at the flannel fabric, looking for an entry point.

"How do you get it off?" he growls and I giggle as I set to work unbuttoning the tiny buttons down the front. "Are you kidding me? Why would you buy this? What if you have to go to the bathroom?"

"I'm assuming that's why there's a flap in the butt," I snark but this just makes him more frantic. His fingers make quick progress, and I gasp when he pops a few buttons. He pushes the flannel off my shoulders and down my arms, his hands wrapping around my waist and slipping down over my behind.

He pushes the pajamas down my legs and I kick them off. He's seen me naked before and it shouldn't be such a big deal, but everything feels new. His lips kiss everywhere they can reach, and I'm trying not to pant too loudly because this house is full of people.

Everything is different now, but everything's the same. He rolls on top of me and I unbutton his pants. He clumsily kicks them off and hastily strips off his shirt, and I giggle until his hands start to explore. I suck in a breath, his fingers caressing and grasping and pulling and pushing and nothing feels like Will.

"Fuck," I pant and I think profanity turns Will on because now his eyes are blazing into mine.

"Shhh," he breathes against my mouth and then moves to get the remote. I grin because his naked, dimpled butt is adorable. He turns up the volume and grabs the blanket off the couch before crawling on top of me with a smirk. I think Will likes being on top of me naked. My hands wrap around him and the green disappears and all I see are feathered lashes.

"What do you feel?" I whisper, my lips at his ear.

"I feel my heart beating in my chest, like I can't breathe," he murmurs against my neck. He positions himself against me and I make room for him between my legs.

"I feel nervous, but excited. I'm scared that it'll be different." He kisses my lips, neck and breasts, and my hands run across his perfect little behind. "I feel like I'm right where I'm supposed to be." He holds my face in his hands, his thumb grazing my cheek as he pushes inside me, and I arch into him and hold my breath.

"I feel love," he whispers and tears fill my eyes.

"I feel it too," I murmur before his lips consume mine. When Will moves inside me, it's so much more than tingles. It's sublime comfort, like chocolate cake made from scratch or the smell of the earth right after it storms. His fingers trail across my lips and I kiss each one of them.

Our movements become more hurried and I can hardly feel my body anymore, just sensitive sparks in my thighs and belly. Bliss floods over me when I unravel beneath him. I feel the tears spill onto my cheeks, and my head spins. Soon Will's shaking in my arms and I'm grasping onto him for dear life, and I can't let go.

"Cat? What's wrong?" he whispers. I shake my head, damn tears pouring from my face, and I feel like an idiot.

"Nothing's wrong. It's just, you're right. We're so right together. This, the way you make me feel, it's just beautiful. You're beautiful. I don't tell you enough, how much I love you, how much I've always loved you and I'm sorry. It's just not me, you know? To be so verbal with how I feel. But it's there, every minute of every day, I feel it."

"Silly girl, I know exactly who you are," he says, and kisses my nose and my cheek and my neck until the morning sun is streaming in through the window. I don't get a lick of sleep but I don't care. Today I have to pack my bag and leave him.

* * *

C at! We need to leave now or we're going to be late." I check my hair in the mirror once more and wipe a smudge of mascara from under my eye. I don't know why I even need to go to this thing, it's not like I was involved in this decision.

My dad found a buyer for the marina. He actually found a couple buyers and had to decide which offer he wanted to accept. He and Brett, who's handling the appraisal and this commercial Real Estate agent, Carmen Flores, make the decision together and I'm completely left out of it. It's highly irritating.

My cat, Ansel, weaves around my legs. I bend down to scratch his head and he purrs in appreciation. My dad has to sign the papers here in Vegas and he wants me to go with him, so I can meet this investor. He's waiting in the living room of my small apartment and I give him a scowl as I fasten my sandals.

"This is what you wanted, right? To be free of the marina?" He's messing with me because I'm so bent out of shape.

"What does this Carmen chick even know?" I say. "And what kind of name is Carmen? It reminds me of Baywatch. Nothing but boobs on a beach. I have no respect for that name."

"Cat, stop being mean," my dad says and his mustache twitches. "It's not cute."

"I'm not trying to be cute, Dad. I just hope you're making the right decision," I say. "Does this person even know anything about the river? Does he- wait, is it a he?" Just then the phone rings and I run to answer it.

"Hi, is Bennie there?" The low voice says over the receiver and I recognize him immediately.

"Bennie?" I ask, confused.

"Yeah, B-B-B-Bennie and the Jets," Will sings.

"Oh my God, you are such a dork," I laugh.

"It's not my fault you don't appreciate the classics," he says, sounding far away.

"Where are you?" I ask.

"I'm driving into the city," he says. "Are you getting ready to go sign the papers?"

"Yeah, my dad's giving me the stink-eye right now. He doesn't want to be late."

"Are you okay?" he asks quietly and I sigh.

"Yeah, I guess. In case you haven't noticed, I'm not partial to change." Will laughs and my dad motions to the door. "I'll call you when we get home."

"Good luck."

"Let's hope I don't offend anyone," I say and Will laughs again.

"I love you," he says and my cheeks twitch. It always gives me goosebumps when he says this.

"I love you too," I say and he's gone.

My dad drives his truck and we listen to oldies on the radio. He's quiet and thinking and I know this is melancholy for him. This is his life's work, everything he's ever known and he has to give a part of it up. I feel like shit. I have been nothing but sullen through this whole process and he's been suffering too. No wonder he's kept all the details to himself. He doesn't want to hear me bitching about it.

I look over at him and he looks at me apprehensively. I smile with the hope of offering him some relief. He smiles back and squeezes my shoulder and we drive the rest of the way in silence. It's not far from my apartment.

We park at the small brown building and my heart is beating in my throat. Brett is waiting by the door and I can see little Miss Baywatch in her starched suit next to him.

"Wait," I say and he looks over at me. "Don't do this. I'll help you. I can move back home, work at the marina and still go to school. We can hire people if we need to. You don't have to do this."

My dad takes a deep breath and he smiles. "Cat, it's done. Now, come on, let's go meet my new partner."

"He better not be wearing a suit," I say and my dad chuckles. Dad shakes hands with Brett and Carmen and I do too, because I'm trying to not be offensive. Carmen is all plastic smiles. She leads us into a large room with an oval table and we sit in padded rolling chairs.

He's late. Whoever this partner is, he's late and I'm already judging him.

The door opens and the first thing I see is green. His tie is green, a sharp contrast to his gray suit and striped collared shirt. I grit my teeth as my eyes follow the familiar lines of his square jaw and pointed lips and freckled nose. And there they are, feathered lashes and glowing green circles.

Motherfucker.

He's wary as enters the room with the two other suits he's brought with him, and I glare at him. I feel like I've been punched in the gut. How is this even possible?

"Carmen, it's good to see you again," Will says, shaking plastic lady's hand, and my mouth drops open. He gives Brett a friendly hand shake and then he shakes my dad's hand and his face is calm but intense.

"Cat," he says quietly. I want to throw a fit, right there in that room, but that would make me look like an idiot so I clench my jaw and remain silent. Carmen lays out the paperwork and Will's lawyers hover over it and all the while his eyes are on me. I fold my arms over my chest and cross my legs, but I can't stop my knee from bouncing. I just talked to him thirty minutes ago, and he lied to me.

The suits move around me in slow motion, joking and making small talk, and still he just stares. He signs and then it's done. And I bolt.

"Cat!" he calls after me. He clutches my arm and I shake him off until I can get outside.

"I can't believe you!" I shove him in the chest. "Liar!"

"I never lied. I omitted, there's a difference," he says, cautiously.

"You said you were driving into the city!" I yell, waving my arms.

"I was. I just didn't say which city," he says and he's smug. He's proud of that one.

"Whatever, Clinton," I say sarcastically. "Fraud, then. Manipulator. Defiler of truth."

"Oh come on, I wanted it to be a surprise. I thought it would be kinda romantic," he shrugs and his hands are in his pockets. I sigh, my anger dissipating slightly at his words.

"You could have told me. We're supposed to be a team, you know, united for world domination. Partners, and shit. Partners don't keep secrets. Partners don't lie to each other about major life changes and decisions. I feel like an idiot, Will!" The anger is back, my mind spinning as my dad walks out the door, followed by Brett and I glare at my father. This is his fault too. Both of them are liars. They should go to a liar convention or something, have matching liar t-shirts made.

"You!" I point at my father and he rolls his eyes.

"Stop being so overdramatic," my dad says as he gets into his truck. I can't believe I'm being dismissed like this.

"Look, I'll explain everything," Will says and he kisses my cheek and I soften.

"That suit is ridiculous," I say bitterly. He chuckles and walks over to his Saab parked next to my dad's truck and unlocks the door. I take a closer look and I can see it's filled to the roof with his stuff, piles and piles of polo shirts and boxes of books and again, my mouth gapes open.

"Will?" I ask and I'm flabbergasted. He winks at me and I'm furious.

"Let's talk about this when we get home." He slides into the driver's seat and with a soft click of the car door, he's pulling out of the parking spot. I hope Will remembers how to get to my apartment. He was just here in March and he didn't mention anything about buying the marina.

I jump into my dad's truck and he smiles over at me. I shake my head and narrow my eyes, and he laughs.

"It's not funny, Dad," I say and tears fill my eyes. I'm not exactly sure why. Will owns half the marina, and his car is filled with his stuff. He's moving here, for good. He didn't even tell me. It's everything I've ever wanted and I didn't even get to plan for it. I just feel left out, I guess.

"How could you do this?"

"He loves you and he wants to take care of you. He had the best offer," my dad smirks and I can't stop the tears from spilling onto my cheeks.

"That's not what I meant," I whisper, wiping at my face and my dad chuckles.

"I know," his mustache twitches.

He drives to my apartment, and the whole way there my mind is racing. Will's standing outside his parked car in front of my building, still wearing his dark sunglasses and the stupid suit. God damn, it looks good. His hair is neat around his ears and neck and his hands are shoved in his pockets. I hope he's sweating bullets.

My dad parks beside him and looks over at me, expectantly. He's not coming in. He's going to drop me off and high-tail it out of here. What a chicken shit!

"Fine, but we're so not done here." I get out of the truck and slam the door shut. I take a deep breath and turn around to face Will as my dad's truck roars down the street.

Will grins at me, the corner of his lips pulled up into a triumphant smirk and I try my damnedest not to smile back. I mean it, I am fighting the muscles in my cheeks with all my heart. But my heart is a traitor. It surrenders. My lips twitch and Will sees it. He laughs and pulls me against his chest and I wrap my arms around his waist.

"I missed you," he whispers into my ear and he kisses my lips. It's soft and hesitant, like he's testing the waters to make sure I'm not going to bite his head off.

"I'm still mad at you," I scowl but it's half-hearted. I lead him to my apartment and he follows behind. His hand grazes my hip as we walk the stairs, and I let myself smile fully because he can't see my face.

"I know." His hand rests on my back as I unlock the door. Ansel rubs against my legs when I walk into the kitchen. Will closes the door behind him and I throw my keys on the counter. I pull the rubber band from my wrist and wrap my hair into a bun before turning to face him.

He takes off his sunglasses and shrugs out of his suit jacket and I frown.

"Lose the tie too," I say and his fingers pull the knot loose, but he doesn't take it off.

"Make me," he smirks and I roll my eyes and walk into my bedroom, pulling my stupid dress over my head. I dig through my drawer, looking for my shorts and Will is standing in the doorway.

"It's my mom's money," he says quietly. I face him and he moves into the room. "She set up this trust fund before she died but there was a stipulation. I had to finish school. I had to go all the way, Ph.D., M.D. it didn't matter as long as I finished. I finished, Cat."

"Wait, what?" I ask him, thoroughly confused. "I don't understand. Why didn't you tell me?"

"I don't know. I didn't want you to think I was just some spoiled trust fund. You always saw more in me. I didn't want to mess that up. But I needed that money, so I could make sure you were taken care of. No matter what."

"How long have you known about this? Like forever or..."

"No. When I failed that class. My dad told me about the money then. He thought I might need the incentive, as if his constant pressure wasn't incentive enough."

"And that's why you were so upset about not getting into medical school? Because you wanted to take care of me?" I ask and he sits on my bed.

"You've kind of been my purpose for everything." He picks at the threads of my quilt and I collapse onto the bed, my knees feeling like jello.

"After you told me about your dad needing a partner, I called him. I asked him to wait until I was done with school and I would have the money. I could pay cash and I would take care of you. I wasn't trying to trick you, or lie to you or anything deceitful, I promise. I wanted everything to be perfect, so you wouldn't have any way to say no to this. I'm staying, whether you like it or not."

"So you spent all that time and money, put in a massive amount of effort to finish school, so you could give it all up and stay here?" I murmur and he shakes his head.

"Doesn't matter, I want to be with you. I don't care where it is, as long as we're together." He traces the three freckles on my thigh that form an equilateral triangle and I let my hands fall from their crossed position.

Ansel jumps onto the bed and stretches out between us and Will rubs his head and along his ears. I scratch his neck and his purring makes the whole bed vibrate. I look up, into Will's green and our fingers find each other. He took a risk, made a sacrifice so he could get what he wants... and he wants me.

"Where do you think you're going to live?" I tease, because it's obvious he's going to live with me. Right?

"Oh, yeah, that. I bought my dad's unit, at the marina. I can live there," he smirks and I give him a light shove. He laughs and grabs my wrist and I let him pull me into his chest. Ansel whines and acts annoyed as he jumps to the floor.

"See, even Ansel thinks you're an ass," I say and climb onto his lap. His hands clutch my hips and I quickly free the stupid tie from his neck, the silky green material falling to the floor.

"He's just jealous another man's going to be sleeping in your bed from now on," he murmurs against my neck, his lips moving over my skin.

"I still haven't forgiven you," I mutter and my eyes close because his lips can be very persuasive. "I wish you would have told me."

"I wish I would have done a lot of things," he says, and his hands slide along my thighs and over my hips as my fingers thread through his hair. "I wish I would have told you how much I love you every day. I wish I would have made you mine that first summer."

His arms wrap around my waist, his fingers pressing into my sides and there isn't an ounce of space between us. The buttons of his stiff shirt press circles into my skin and he sighs against my neck. I let my cheek rest on his and I breathe. He smells like cologne and aftershave and laundry detergent. He's still tingles and sparks, like the warm sun prickling my skin after being inside all day, or the first whisper of a cool breeze off the water. He's relief. He's comfort. He's home.

"But then we wouldn't have much of a love story, now would we?"

1999 – THAT TIME WE SAW FIREWORKS

*President Bill Clinton is acquitted by the Senate
concluding his impeachment trial.*

*Star Wars Episode 1 - The Phantom Menace
is released in theaters May 19th.*

*Computer programmers scramble to rectify the
Y2K glitch, which many thought would severely
disrupt the world's financial institutions.*

❉ ❉ ❉

When I was a kid, I thought love would hit in an instant. It was in all the movies. All it takes is a look, a touch, a sappy ballad, and you know. This is the person I'm going to spend the rest of my life with. Apparently, sometimes it takes fifteen years of emotional turmoil and confusion. It was all worth it, though, every minute. Because now I'm here.

For the first time ever, I'm driving from Arizona to San Francisco. Well, I'm not driving, Will is. I'm napping mostly. I rub my eyes and stretch my arms over my head and wiggle my socked feet on the dashboard of Will's new car. It's a sedan, a family car.

"Where are we?" I ask and dig through my bag on the floor. I swiped a pack of red vines from the store before we left the marina.

"Almost to Bakersfield," Will says. We're driving through California and stopping in Yosemite. It makes the drive twice as long but we don't really have a schedule. When we want to stop, we stop. When we're tired, we sleep, and I photograph everything.

I got a job with a magazine in San Francisco. It's nothing big, but I'm able to finish school at SFU and work on my portfolio. I start the Monday after New Year's.

I didn't tell Will I was looking for a job in San Francisco. We lived in Vegas during the school year and moved back to the marina during the summer and it was effortless how Will fit into my life there, but I couldn't shake this nagging guilt. Will sacrificed so much for me. When I asked him about it, he tried to make me feel better.

"Do you miss San Francisco?" I asked him as we climbed into bed.

"I do. But it's nothing compared to living without you. It's like a paper cut, it stings, it gets irritated once in a while, but it's nothing. Don't even need a bandaid."

"What do you miss the most?" He took a deep breath, like he didn't want the discussion so I propped up on my elbow expectantly.

"I don't know, there's no one thing. But it doesn't matter. I like where I am." His persuasive hands pulled at me and I almost forgot to be stubborn.

"Paper cuts hurt like a bitch, you know," I persisted and again, he sighed. "And they take forever to stop bleeding."

"This is exactly why I didn't tell you I was moving here." I took the hint and kissed him instead of arguing, basking in the sacrifice he made and partaking in all its glory.

But as I laid there, wrapped in weighted arms and legs, the guilt wouldn't go away. I hadn't sacrificed shit. I know I'm not responsible for Will's choices, but the whole point is that he had to make the choice without me

Is that how Will sees me, unwilling to compromise? Why did he think the only way for us to be together was for him to move here? In all honesty, I was a little excited at the prospect of living in California. I love the marina but I was ready for a change. I could have moved to San Francisco and it wouldn't have even felt like a sacrifice

I had my own selfish reasons too. I missed my brother and

I wanted Vanessa to know me. A photographer captures life, and there's so much life I haven't seen. I want to experience the world before I have other priorities, like kids.

Yep, I want to have Will's maybe babies.

A few days after Christmas, we said good-bye to my dad and Josie and I cried and cried. I got to California and wiped the tears from my face. Dad will be flying up to San Francisco soon. He's going to bring Ansel. I gaze out the window at the rows and rows of naked fruit trees as the new Third Eye Blind CD plays in the background. Will insisted his new car had a CD player.

"You were dreaming," he says and I snort.

"I had a dream we got abducted by aliens but they sent us back because you wouldn't stop talking about the Bulls."

"You did not," he laughs.

"I did. They kept saying Michael Jordan wouldn't be anything without Scottie Pippen and you were irate. You kept trying to punch them," I laugh and cross my legs.

"That is ridiculous! I could totally take on some stupid aliens. In case you haven't noticed, I'm kind of a badass," he smirks and I roll my eyes. I lean down to grab my camera from my bag. Rolling down the window, I start snapping pictures.

"I can stop, you know," Will says but I shake my head.

"No, I like the moving shots. They look fast."

"Fast?" he asks with a chuckle.

"Yeah, like life, you know. It moves fast, like everything is a blur but there are these moments of noticeable brilliance. Like you can't see the grass or the dirt or the rocks. But you can see the twisted trees and the uninterrupted sky. The sky always seems to stand still," I try to explain and I'm rambling but I don't care. Will gets it.

"Uninterrupted Sky, cool band name!" he says and then winks at me. Oh my God, he's a nerd. And he's all mine.

We pull into a gas station and I get an iced tea and a box of Mike and Ike's. Will tops off the tank while I go to the restroom. I'm flushing the toilet when I get a call from Margot. Will got me a cell phone for my birthday. I have specialized ringtones for everyone. Margot's is Pat Benatar.

"Where are you guys? Did you get to Yosemite?" she asks and I wash my hands.

"No, I think we're in Fresno?"

"Okay." She pauses. "Did Will give you a present yet?"

"No! Why would Will give me a present? Do you know what it is? What is it?" I say, and then change my mind. "No, wait, don't tell me. Just give me a hint."

"A hint? Oh Christ, hold on, let me think of one," she says and I wait patiently. "Oh, I know. You'll have a whole new *image* after he gives it to you." I frown. Image. Like a makeover or something?

"I need more," I say and Margot laughs.

"Um, I think Will will *capture* the moment excellently." Jesus, this could be anything. Capture is the word of importance. Maybe it has something to do with photography.

"One more," I say.

"Ugh, no. I've already said too much," Margot says and I shamelessly beg.

"Come on, Margot, one more!"

"Alright, your *dad* may have had a *hand* in it." I can practically hear her smiling like an idiot over the receiver. My dad?

"Margot, what did Will buy?" I ask, petrified, because the clues are all coming together in my head and I think I might throw up.

"It'll leave a lasting *impression*," Margot squeaks out before she hangs up, and I stare at my phone, completely stunned.

Image, like a bridal image.

Capture, like till death do us part.

My dad's hand.

Lasting impression, like forever.

Oh God. Will bought me an engagement ring. He's going to propose. Shit, what am I going to say?

I mean, I think it's pretty much a given that we will be

together, you know, for good. But now that I know it's coming, I'm going to be anxious as all hell. I know I want to say yes, but I can't control my stupid mouth sometimes.

What if I don't say yes with enough enthusiasm?

What if my tone is all wrong?

Shit! What if I hesitate? Will told me once that when I know, I won't hesitate or worry about looking like an idiot, but he was so incredibly wrong.

I know with every fiber of my being that I want to be with Will forever. But I won't be able to breathe until it happens. He'll probably do it in Yosemite, under a waterfall or something. And he has no idea that I know, which is great, because it gives me a chance to prepare, and he still gets to surprise me. Win, win.

We stop to sleep at a Marriott before driving into Yosemite and we order room service. When our dinner arrives, I start to dig into my hot fudge sundae first and then stop.

What if the ring is in the sundae? What if I swallow it and then have to spend the evening in the emergency room chowing down laxatives so I can shit out my engagement ring? That would be a great tale for our grandchildren.

Shit, grandchildren.

Oh Jesus, this is it. This is for the rest of my life.

My heart is pounding and I offer him a bite first, just to see if he hesitates. He squints his eyes and tilts his head to the side. So I carefully put the spoon in my mouth, and I probably look ridiculous trying to feel around the cold cream with my tongue. Will grins and relaxes back on the bed with his burger. I eat the whole sundae and feel sick, and I do not find a ring.

The next morning we drive into Yosemite and it's freezing. There's snow on the ground, and I press my face to the glass as we drive into the park. I gape when Half Dome comes into view. We check into the big lodge, the Ahwahnee, and I bundle up in my new beanie and scarf.

"Got enough layers there?" Will teases.

"Us river folk aren't used to such extreme temperatures," I

say as I wrap another scarf around my face but I stop. What if he's going to do it now? I don't want this ugly scarf hiding my face. I guess I shouldn't wear gloves either, so he can put the ring on my finger. I toss them aside and hastily put on lip gloss instead. I grab my camera and the rocks tower above us.

"Oh wow!" I breathe and focus my old camera. "It's just so massive here."

"Do you want to hike Half Dome? It's only like 10 miles," Will says and I hope to God this is not his proposal plan. Apparently, my face answers for me because Will laughs. "I'm kidding! But we can get a good view from Mirror Lake."

"It's all granite, you know? An entire mountain made of rock," Will says as we head out on the path.

"I can relate," I joke and he squeezes my hand.

"Did you forget your gloves? We can go back and get them. We're not that far." He starts to turn back and I shake my head, my face flooding with heat.

"No, I'm fine," I answer quickly and he's unsure. "It's easier to operate my camera without them." And he's convinced. I'm an idiot.

The place is pretty much deserted because it's off-season and eerily quiet. It feels like Will and I have the whole park to ourselves and I take pictures of everything. My hands are fricking freezing. Everytime he pulls something from his pocket, Chapstick, a tissue, gum, I almost hyperventilate. I keep thinking of the most ridiculous scenarios where he will pop the question but he doesn't.

We don't get to San Francisco until late the next day and Jay and Lauren are waiting up for us. We sit in the living room and chat because we're kind of keyed up from the drive.

"Vanessa's going to stay with Mom and we have reservations tomorrow at Scoma's. Then we're going to a party at Andy's friend's place. It's near the new park and we'll be able to see the fireworks," Lauren says and then looks perplexed. "Is that okay? Would you guys rather just veg with Dick Clark?"

"I want to go out," I blurt out immediately. Will's going to propose on New Years. That's got to be it. "I mean, it's a new millennium. I am not missing the fricking fireworks."

"So Josie and Brett move in okay?" Jay asks and I nod. Josie and Brett are going to run the marina during the offseason. They moved into one of the units by Dad. He took the news surprisingly well. It might have something to do with the fact that Josie's mom also moved into one of the units.

"We have Christmas presents for everyone!" I say.

"And we have to go see my dad tomorrow," Will reminds me. I think Dr. Hend-, I mean Richard, is excited we're moving back. He called Will every day last week to see if we needed anything.

The next morning, I play with Vanessa and catch up with my family. Margo pops in after breakfast to fill us in on all the gossip. Andy passed the CPA and got a promotion. She's looking into buying a coffee franchise. Richard stops by after lunch and he has a folder of real estate properties he wants us to look at and Will gets antsy. I know Will feels like his dad is still trying to control things, but I think he's just trying, any way he can.

We drink champagne at dinner and our table has a view of the water. I order a cheeseburger and gelato and Will makes fun of me because we're in the finest seafood restaurant in San Francisco on the eve of the millennium. But I know what I want.

After dinner, we ride the streetcar to the party. I'm introduced to a million people I'll never remember and Will reconnects with old friends. He's mingling with Andy and his buddy Drew and a few other people who I don't know. He drinks his beer and laughs loudly, and he glows.

Will always glows. It's swagger and braggy and sometimes it's a show, but damn if it doesn't make me confident too. He's like the sun, freely offering his energy and making everyone around him radiate.

We put on our coats and I grab my camera bag and move outside to the rooftop patio as midnight approaches. It's a little early still, but I want to get a good spot.

"They're setting the fireworks off from a boat. We should be able to see them over the water," Will says as we stand at the ledge, and I squirm under his arm.

"Oh good! I want some fireworks pictures for my portfolio," I say before craning my neck to kiss his jaw. Will checks his watch and whispers into my ear.

"So, I got you something. It's a gift, so you can't complain about the price." My heart is pounding in my throat. Oh my God, this is really happening. *This is not a drill. I repeat, this is not a drill.*

"Okay?" I can barely say the word and Will holds a small box in front of me for me to take and my fingers shake. What if I drop it off the roof? It's closed, the lid heavily hinged and I carefully crack it open with a creak. I stare. I hesitate. I tilt my head and narrow my eyes because I don't know what I'm looking at.

"It's a memory card," Will says as he pulls the black plastic rectangle from the box. "It's for your other present." He reaches in my camera bag and I deflate. I thought I was getting a ring, dammit. Will pulls out another box, a much larger one and I quickly unwrap it to find a camera. It's a Nikon, and it's digital.

"I don't understand," I tell Will and he takes the box from my fingers.

"It's a digital camera," he explains and I don't have the heart to tell him that's not what I don't understand. I know I was freaking out about this whole ring business, but now that I'm not getting one, I'm kind of devastated. We don't have much time, you know? Not if I want to have kids without any science-fiction experiments involving needles. I thought this was it. I thought it was time.

"It's awesome," I face him while he puts the card into the slot and snaps it into place.

"It's all charged up and everything," he says as he looks through the lens and snaps my picture. I roll my eyes and he laughs and keeps taking my picture. There's hardly even a click, just a beep to let us know a picture has been taken, and I find it hard to smile in any of them.

"And see, you can view the pictures right after taking them so you can delete the ones you hate and keep the ones you like," he says, scrolling through the pictures. "Oh, now that's a keeper."

He hands me the camera and I look at the little screen. Filling the picture is a black box with a ring, a square diamond, surrounded by dozens of tiny stones on a thin band. I squint, confused and I'm thinking this picture must come stock with the camera. You know, like when you buy a picture frame. When I look up at Will, he kneels before me and in his hand is an open box, holding a ring, the very same square diamond, surrounded by tiny stones on a thin band.

And it all makes sense.

I look at his face and he winks at me. He winks!

I'm completely shocked, my body frozen and I don't know what to do. I can't breathe and I can't believe Will tricked me. He probably told Margot to call me. He is such an ass!

So I do what I always do when Will acts like an ass. I punch him in the gut. I don't hit him hard because it's difficult to get a proper swing, but it's enough to get my point across and he laughs.

"You knew I've been waiting for this, didn't you?" I say and he's still kneeling on the ground, his hands clutching my pants and he's laughing so hard he can hardly speak.

"So, is that a no?" he chokes out and the tears, they roll. This is exactly what I thought would happen. Will trying to make a fool of me and my snotty attitude rearing its ugly head. So completely typical. And kind of completely perfect. For us, anyway.

"No," I say and smack him with the back of my hand.

"Wait, no yes, or no no?" he says as he stands and wipes the tears from my cheeks. He holds the ring in front of me again. He raises his eyebrows, his lips part and I bring my finger to trace the stone. "I didn't know what you would like since you never ever wear jewelry. Margot and Lauren helped a little," he rambles, and I grin. I kiss his lips and then his nose and his cheeks and his eyelids. His arms wrap around my back, and he lets me adore him.

"So is that a yes?" he murmurs.

"Yes to what?" I tease, because he hasn't really asked me yet. He grins, his lips press into my neck, and then his mouth is at my ear.

"Will you wear this ring, Catherine the Great? Will you be my favorite for always? My friend, my love, my obligation?" I close my eyes as the tears slip from my lids. His lips quiver against my skin, his heart beating with mine, and his whispered words are like the splashed sky at sunset.

"My wife?" I nod, my cheek rubbing against his before the words are even out of his mouth. His hand is on mine and there's metal and stone slipping along my finger.

And then it's done.

"One minute." His breath tickles and a little shiver goes through me. The patio has filled, our family pushing through the crowd to reach us.

"I'm waiting for something to go wrong," I say to him and he laughs. The city erupts with cheers and whistling. They're counting down now, their voices ringing out in unison.

Ten, nine, eight...

I lean back against Will's chest, and feel him breathe.

Seven, six, five...

He winds his arms around my waist and our hands unite, his finger fiddling with the band of gold on my finger.

Four, three, two...

The sky ignites. There are pops and booms and cheers and singing and I kiss Will. His nose is cold but his mouth is warm and I'm desperate for the heat. I clutch the back of his neck and I can't get enough as the dark sky fills with color. He pulls his fingers through my hair and then places a light kiss on my lips, then on my nose, and then my lips again.

"You're missing the show," he says quietly and I grin.

"Totally worth it."

I relax back into his chest and pick up my new camera. It's pretty fancy but I capture the explosions of color, focusing on the way the light reflects off the water.

"You have no idea how many times I imagined this exact moment." Will's lips move against my neck as he speaks and I snap my eyes to his.

"I think I have an idea," I say and it only sounds a little bit snotty.

It all started with a snap, a shove, a snotty attitude that was meant to push him away but pulled him right in.

When a cocky, smart-ass kid with glowing green eyes and white blond hair had the audacity to snap the strap of my bathing suit, it changed my life forever. We've had nearly two decades of multilayered rock, cutting and sharp in places but rolling and soft in others. We've had fiery heat and choppy water. We've had heavy air and tall red cliffs. And like the earth that succumbs to the persistent stream, we've carved a monumental canyon. We balance, a delicate bend of give and take and, together, we flow.

We'll be heading back there in June, of course. To the river, to our place.

For the summer.

ACKNOWLEDGEMENT

Everything I know about the river, I learned from my best friend Jason DeBord and his family, Del, Kathie, and Matt. Thank you for taking me on your trips and sharing your love of the river with me. Those experiences helped shape who I am, and I'm beyond grateful to have you as my second family. Jason, you first put this idea in my head during one of our four hour drives to Cottonwood Cove twenty years ago. I always knew someone would write a book about us Paychecks one day.

My grandma Bobbi Harrell is the best writer I know. I'm so lucky to come from a brood of artists, and that art was valued and encouraged. To my family and friends, who support me even when I'm living out my ADHD fantasies, I hope you know I'm always thinking about you, even when I forget to call you back. To my darling teenagers, who will never admit their mom wrote this book and my sweet baby girl, who reminds me everyday to have a healthy work/life balance, you three are the very best of me.

A psychic once told me the love of my life's name would start with an "M". Meridith Daniel and Marisa Bauson, I'm positive she was talking about you two. Thank you for your time, your patience, your smarts, and your encouragement. Sorelle Orson, you light up my life. Thank you for your insight and unique perspective.

I literally wouldn't have done this without my husband's constant nagging and persistent heckling. Ian Henderson

Harte, you are my greatest love, and I just can't believe how much you believe in me.

Most importantly, to all the pop and rock icons of the 80's and 90's, you provided the soundtrack to my life, and it has been the best mixtape ever.

ABOUT THE AUTHOR

Camille Harte

Raised in an Italian restaurant in Southern California, Camille wanted to be a lot of things when she grew up. Geologist, pastry baker, lead actress in a community stage play of Anne of Green Gables. The ADHD is strong with this one. A self-professed nerd, she's always loved writing and telling the frustratingly flawed story of a completely typical hero.

Camille is a lover of nature, math, and puns. She has an uncanny ability to memorize song lyrics and thinks the 90's were the best decade for music. Mom to 3 incredible humans, she lives with her super awesome husband, their kids, and several pets in Riverside, CA. Vacationing with her best friend of 30 years and his family at Cottonwood Cove inspired her to write her first novel, For the Summer.

Made in United States
Orlando, FL
19 July 2022

19962590R00207